PRAISE
THE NEIGHBO

* * *

"[A] warm and welcoming new contemporary. . . . The book breathes easily and pulls you right into its world. Especially recommended for anyone who ships Janine and Gregory from *Abbott Elementary*." —*The New York Times Book Review*

"Warm, witty, and deeply romantic. Kristina Forest is a fantastic storyteller, with an eagle eye for detail and a knack for crafting lovable characters. It's impossible not to smile while reading this book!"

—Rachel Lynn Solomon, *New York Times* bestselling author of *Business or Pleasure*

"*The Neighbor Favor* is the type of charming, feel-good story that reminds me why I love romance. I dare anyone to try reading Lily and Nick's adorably awkward encounters without smiling. Impossible."

—Farrah Rochon, *New York Times* bestselling author of *The Hookup Plan*

"I'm swooning for *The Neighbor Favor*, and not because I'm stuck on a too-hot subway car: because of the heat between Lily and Nick. You'll swoon too for this joyful story and these bookish lovers as they find their way."

—Amanda Elliot, author of *Best Served Hot*

"This literary love story is full of delightful surprises, with resonant characters whose perfectly paced professional struggles underline deeply real questions of family and daring to dream. *The Neighbor Favor* is the perfect celebration of falling in love on and off the page."

—Emily Wibberley and Austin Siegemund-Broka,
authors of *The Breakup Tour*

"I fell head over heels in love with Lily and Nick. *The Neighbor Favor* is sweet, swoony, and full of heart. I didn't want it to end!"

—Lynn Painter, *New York Times*
bestselling author of *Happily Never After*

"Anchored by two endearing leads and a touching plot filled with a wonderful cast of side characters, Kristina Forest's signature style absolutely shines in this one. *The Neighbor Favor* is as comforting as it is lovely—an admirable example of everything a heartwarming romance can be."

—Claire Kann, author of *The Romantic Agenda*

"In a world of swipe right for love, this electric debut crackles with old-fashioned chemistry. Forest writes with so much heart. Nick and Lily absolutely simmer together and make you feel like 'high fantasy' could be right next door!"

—Nikki Payne, author of *Sex, Lies and Sensibility*

"Forest expertly balances this perfectly matched duo's emotional connection with their physical chemistry, making them easy to cheer on. This is a winner."

—*Publishers Weekly* (starred review)

"This swoony, contemporary romance with fully realized characters will have readers hooked from the first page, and the protagonists, who are Black, have deep, relatable backstories."

—*Library Journal* (starred review)

"Book-loving romantics will be charmed." —*Kirkus Reviews*

Berkley Titles by Kristina Forest

The Neighbor Favor
The Partner Plot

The
Partner
Plot

Kristina Forest

BERKLEY ROMANCE
New York

BERKLEY ROMANCE
Published by Berkley
An imprint of Penguin Random House LLC
penguinrandomhouse.com

Library of Congress Cataloging-in-Publication Data

Names: Forest, Kristina, author.
Title: The partner plot / Kristina Forest.
Description: First edition. | New York: Berkley Romance, 2024.
Identifiers: LCCN 2023035712 (print) | LCCN 2023035713 (ebook) |
ISBN 9780593546451 (paperback) | ISBN 9780593546468 (ebook)
Subjects: LCGFT: Romance fiction. | Novels.
Classification: LCC PS3606.O74747 P37 2024 (print) | LCC PS3606.O74747
(ebook) | DDC 813/.6—dc23/eng/20230825
LC record available at https://lccn.loc.gov/2023035712
LC ebook record available at https://lccn.loc.gov/2023035713

First Edition: February 2024

Printed in the United States of America
1st Printing

For Jason

The
Partner
Plot

PROLOGUE

Eleven and a half years ago

FOR VIOLET GREENE, THERE WAS A DISTINCT MOMENT when her life stopped feeling like monotonous days on a calendar and suddenly began in earnest. A moment that changed everything.

It happened at sixteen years old, when she laid her eyes on Xavier Wright.

It was the first day of her junior year, fourth-period PE. Because the PE teachers didn't even attempt to teach on the first day of school, the students were left to their own devices. Violet was sitting on the bleachers with some of the other girls on the dance team, and while the rest of the squad talked about upcoming routines and new uniforms, Violet stared off into space, replaying the argument she'd had with her mother earlier that morning. The night before, Violet had been caught sneaking through the back door after midnight, even though her parents had told her she couldn't party before the first day of school. They'd grounded her, and this morning, as she entered the kitchen, her mother, Dahlia,

thought Violet was purposely adding insult to injury with
her chosen ensemble: a sleeveless cropped cable-knit sweater,
skinny jeans with rips in the knees and the beat-up leather
oxfords she'd thrifted over the summer. To leave one's home
in ripped and/or cropped clothing was a big no in Dahlia's
book, and she couldn't understand why Violet would willingly dress in such a fashion. She'd ordered Violet to go back
to her room and change.

But to Violet, clothes were a form of expression. She often spent hours curating her closet and poring over fashion magazines. In her daydreams, she imagined what her
future life would be like once she escaped Willow Ridge,
New Jersey, her small, stifling hometown where no one and
nothing changed. Violet couldn't wait to escape to New
York City or Los Angeles, maybe even to Paris or Milan.
Any city that was immersed in the fashion world. Cities
filled with creatives and individuals who would embrace
Violet exactly as she was and wouldn't wish she were more
academically accomplished like her older sister, Iris, or of a
sweeter nature like her younger sister, Lily. The plight of
the middle child was that you were never enough one way
or another.

In the end, Violet had refused to change her clothes.
Steam blew out of Dahlia's ears at Violet's defiance, while
her father, Benjamin, looked on, rubbing his temples with a
sigh. Because Violet hadn't changed her outfit, more days
were added to her grounding sentence. The prolonged argument with her mother caused Violet and Lily, who was a
sophomore, to be late to school. The school secretary, Mrs.

Franklin, had written Lily's late slip with a forgiving smile, but she'd given Violet a stern look.

"You're already off to a rocky start this year, Ms. Greene," she said. "Let's not make a habit of tardiness." Then she paused, eyeing Violet's outfit and her bright green polymer-clay drop earrings. "Those are quite the attention grabber."

"Thank you," Violet said, smiling sweetly, even though she knew she hadn't been paid a compliment.

Violet was aware that the majority of the adults in her life had their opinions about her. She was too distracted. Too defiant. Just *too much* in general. She knew that she'd never be able to truly thrive in a town like Willow Ridge. The minute she graduated, she'd be on the first train out of there. She'd become a celebrity stylist and attend couture shows around the world. She'd feel the high-fashion fabric between her fingertips and finally hold her dreams in the palms of her hands.

That was what she was thinking about when Bianca, her friend and fellow dance team captain, nudged her.

"Have you seen the new boy?" Bianca asked.

Violet snapped out of her daydream and turned to Bianca, whose attention was fixed on the other end of the gymnasium.

"What new boy?" Violet asked, following Bianca's line of sight.

Then she saw him. He was tall and slim with light brown skin. He wore a bright red polo and matching red-and-black Jordans. He aimlessly dribbled a basketball as he stood among a group of boys underneath the basketball hoop. He held their attention, gesturing with his hands while he spoke and laughing with his whole body. Alive. New.

Violet sat up straighter.

"He's Raheem's cousin," Bianca continued. Raheem was Bianca's on-again, off-again boyfriend of two years. "His name's Xavier. I told you about him, didn't I?"

"Maybe," Violet said, still staring. She'd given up on boys her own age after too many disappointments. They were immature and only wanted to know what she looked like naked. This new boy—Xavier—was cute. Cuter than most of the boys in her year. And it seemed like he'd actually made an effort with his outfit, rather than rolling out of bed and throwing on sweats. But chances were, he wasn't much different than the rest. "Where'd he transfer from?"

"Philly," Bianca answered. "He's really good at basketball. At least that's what Raheem told me."

Violet watched as Xavier smoothly passed the basketball from palm to palm as he spoke. The motion mesmerized her.

"It sucks that he had to leave Philly and move here," she said.

Then, as if he knew she was talking about him, Xavier glanced over and caught Violet staring. His full lips curled into a smile and butterfly wings immediately fluttered in her stomach. She cleared her throat and began searching through her bag for lip gloss or gum. Anything to make herself look busy and like she hadn't just been gawking. Gawking was something that Violet Greene did *not* do.

"He's coming over here," Bianca suddenly said.

Down on the bleachers below them, Shalia McNair, another junior and quite possibly the biggest gossip in Willow Ridge, quickly whispered to their group, "I heard that Xavier made all-state basketball at his old school. They say colleges are already scouting him, *and* he doesn't have a girlfriend. I saw him at Wendy's the other day and he said what's up to me. I think he likes me."

Bianca rolled her eyes. "You think everyone likes you."

Shalia huffed and tossed her braids over her shoulder, but she didn't disagree.

All the while, Violet kept her head down, pretending to be engrossed in her effort to find her lip gloss. She heard Xavier's footsteps grow closer as he climbed the bleachers. Then the other girls fell quiet as his sneakers appeared right in Violet's line of sight. His shadow loomed over her. She slowly applied her lip gloss and took her time as she screwed the cap closed and dropped the gloss back inside her purse. Finally, she looked up into Xavier's face. He was smiling at her, displaying a deep dimple in his right cheek. The persistent, fluttering butterfly wings threatened to undo her composure, but she tamped them down and schooled her features. Cool as a cucumber.

"What's up?" Xavier said. His voice was smooth like velvet. He held out his hand. "I'm Xavier."

Violet gingerly placed her hand in his, and his long fingers curled around her much shorter ones. Her pulse pounded in her ears. "Violet."

"Pretty name," he said. "I thought I'd come over and introduce myself since you were staring at me and everything."

Violet sucked in a breath and pulled her hand from his grasp. "I was *not* staring at you."

He tilted his head and smirked. "Then what would you call it?"

She frowned at him and pursed her lips. Her only defense.

"I was staring at you too, though," he continued. "I couldn't help it. You're the prettiest girl at this school."

That sent the girls sitting around Violet into a frenzy of whispers.

Secretly, Xavier's compliment warmed her, but she refused to be so easily won.

"You're going to have to do better than that," she said.

"Don't worry, I will." He sat down beside her and goose bumps spread across her skin as their arms brushed. He smelled like fresh laundry. "I'm new here."

"I see that."

He smirked again. "What do I need to know about Willow Ridge?"

"Isn't Raheem your cousin? He should have already told you."

"So you've been talking about me?" He leaned past Violet and glanced at Bianca, who looked away, hiding her grin.

"Not really," Violet said. "It's a small school. Whenever there's a new person, we find out your business real quick."

"Well, they don't know *all* my business."

She quirked an eyebrow. "What else is there to know?"

"That you and I are gonna chill on Friday night."

Violet stilled. Beside her, Bianca made an *oop* sound.

She knew Violet's stance on dating high school boys all too well: Violet no longer bothered giving them the time of day. A hush fell over the dance team girls, and they watched Violet, poised to hear her response.

"Can I have your number?" Xavier asked, pulling out his BlackBerry, which had a cracked screen. "I promise I'll show you a good time."

Violet remained silent, eyeing Xavier as he patiently held his phone out to her. He was smiling again, like he knew it was just a matter of time before she gave in.

He was cocky. Too self-assured.

He was a breath of fresh air. Exactly what Violet craved.

She took his phone and entered her number.

LIKE VIOLET SAID, pretty soon, the whole school knew everything there was to know about Xavier Wright. He was newly transplanted from West Philadelphia, where he'd lived as an only child with both parents until irreconcilable differences—otherwise known as his father's infidelity—led to his parents' divorce, and because neither parent wanted the burden of paying the mortgage alone, along with city and state taxes, they sold their house. Xavier's dad moved down south to Savannah, while Xavier moved with his mom to Willow Ridge to be closer to her sister and Xavier's cousin Raheem.

Willow Ridge was one of the first Black municipalities established north of the Mason-Dixon Line. It had a reputation for being a tight-knit community filled with Black people from all walks of life. Thanks to the local transportation center, Willow Ridge was also a commuter town with a train that could take you to New York City in an hour. Xavier's mother, Tricia, who'd grown up in Philly and who'd never had a backyard, was elated with their Cape Cod–style house and their new lot in life.

But in Xavier's opinion, the suburbs were where people went to die a slow death. He missed the convenience of the SEPTA and corner stores. And where the hell could he get a decent cheesesteak around here? Willow Ridge was the kind of town he saw on television. People mowed their lawns on Saturday mornings and neighbors beeped their horns and waved when they passed you on the street. It was nice to have a slightly bigger bedroom and it was cool to see his cousin Raheem every day, but where was the excitement? Xavier missed his old life. Moving halfway through his high school career was ass. But he reminded himself that it didn't really matter, because college was going to open new doors for him. He'd been scouted by college basketball programs since he was a freshman. He'd been playing basketball since he was five years old. He was tall and agile. Those factors helped, of course, but Xavier also studied the game like nobody's business. He ate, slept and breathed basketball.

Xavier's reputation in the tristate area preceded him. Mr. Rodney, the coach at Willow Ridge High, was so excited for Xavier to join the team, he came by Xavier's house to personally welcome him and his mom to the neighborhood. His new teammates seemed cool, and so far, everyone in Willow Ridge had been more than kind. Xavier just couldn't help that he felt so *bored*.

Then he'd noticed Violet staring at him across the gym. She was petite with brown skin and curly hair. In one word: beautiful. Once they'd caught eyes, Xavier's reaction had been so visceral, so intrigued, he'd felt like lightning had struck him right in the chest. Violet had looked away stubbornly, like she hadn't meant to stare and was mad at herself for doing so. Xavier smiled instantly. Finally, some excitement.

"Who's she?" he asked, nudging his new teammate, Leonard Davis. He nodded toward Violet.

"That's Violet Greene," Leonard said. "Don't waste your time, though. I guarantee she won't give you any play."

Xavier decided he'd just have to see for himself.

THE FOLLOWING FRIDAY, Violet gave Xavier specific instructions to meet her on the sidewalk in front of her neighbor's house. Violet and her family lived in the Oak View development, where people had mini mansions, much different from Xavier's more modest neighborhood on the other side of town. At exactly 9:32 p.m., Violet opened her bedroom window and saw that Xavier was waiting for her. She meticulously yet quickly climbed down the sturdy sycamore tree in her side yard, like she'd done it a million times before, because she had.

She landed with a soft thud and jogged toward Xavier, still wearing her green-and-yellow dance team uniform from the football game earlier that night. She would have chosen something else for a first date, but she'd needed to sneak out while her parents were still busy watching television in the den after dinner.

"Are you a fugitive?" Xavier asked once she reached him.

"I'm grounded."

"Why?"

"For sneaking out."

He raised an eyebrow. She shrugged. "Where are we going?" she asked.

"I thought we'd hit up Martin Wilson's party."

"Oh," she said. Martin Wilson was the football captain, and even though the team had lost tonight—they were always losing—he was throwing a party anyway. "I thought you promised that you'd show me a good time."

"I will," Xavier said, total confidence.

They arrived at Martin's house a few streets over, and Violet quickly realized that Xavier was the kind of magnetic person who made friends wherever he went. As soon as they walked through the door, people were calling out to him, rushing forward to dap him up. In Willow Ridge, everyone knew everyone, and it was exciting to become friends with somebody who hadn't gone to the same daycare as you. But somehow, Xavier had gone from being the new kid to being one of the town's most popular boys in about five seconds flat. Violet herself was pretty popular, but that was because of her status as a Greene. Her parents, who owned a florist shop and nursery, were staples in the community, and Violet and her sisters had been involved in almost every club since they were toddlers. She was amazed to see the effect Xavier had on her classmates so quickly.

She and Xavier played a round of beer pong against Raheem and Bianca, which was fun, but nothing special. Violet had played beer pong and flip cup and quarters plenty of times. After the way Xavier had approached her during PE, Violet had expected a little more from him. She was beginning to think she might be wasting her time. Maybe he wasn't so different from other high school boys after all. Then, as if he could read her mind, he leaned down to her.

"My neighbor has a pool," he whispered.

She turned and looked at him. "Okay?"

"A nice one. Heated. He's probably asleep by now. He usually dozes off a little after nine thirty."

"What are you suggesting?"

"Do you like to swim?" he asked.

"Sure."

"Wanna go?"

She thought this over. "Will we get in trouble?"

He smirked, arching his brows. "Asks the girl who just broke out of her own house."

"Fine," she said, answering the challenge she heard in his voice. "Let's do it."

Xavier's neighbor, Mr. Bishop, had drifted off to sleep by the time they snuck into his backyard. While Xavier flung his T-shirt and jeans onto the deck chair and cannonballed from the diving board, wearing only his boxers, Violet carefully slipped out of her dance team uniform, leaving on her bra and underwear, and eased into the pool. There would be no cannonballing for her tonight. Not after how long it took to slick her curls into submission for the standard high pony she was required to wear for each game.

She swam toward Xavier, and he met her halfway. They

treaded water and grinned at each other, high on adrenaline, casting quick glances at Mr. Bishop's kitchen window
to make sure the light was still off.

"None of my neighbors in Philly had pools," Xavier said,
adjusting himself so that he was floating on his back. He
stared up at the night sky. "Sometimes I like how quiet it is
here, but other times I just feel . . ."

"Bored?" she supplied. "Stalled? Like you're going to lose
your mind?"

He smiled at her. "Like I'm not meant for this kind of
life," he said. "I'm going to the NBA. I know a lot of people
say that, like it's a pipe dream, but I really am. I want to play
in the Olympics. All that. I'm gonna travel the world."

"*Me too.*" She gripped his arm in excitement. His skin
was warm, and she felt an instant jolt travel through her
body. "I'm gonna be a celebrity wardrobe stylist. Like June
Ambrose."

"I have no idea who she is, but that's dope," he said. "I
noticed that you always come to school looking fresh."

He eyed her plain black bra, causing her to blush. "You're
not too bad yourself," she said.

He grinned. "That's a big compliment coming from you,
Ms. Future Celebrity Stylist. Maybe you can dress me for
the ESPYs one day."

"You won't be able to afford me," she said, grinning too.

She gazed at him, eyes alight in wonder. Here was the
first person she'd met who also wanted to get away and see
the world. Even with all of her smarts, Violet's older sister,
Iris, had only gone to college forty minutes away, in Prince-

ton, when she could have gone anywhere. Violet didn't want that for herself, and apparently neither did Xavier.

"Damn," he said. "So you're trying to say that I'm gonna be broke?"

She shrugged. "You said it, not me."

He splashed her then, and Violet sucked in a surprised breath and splashed him back. She laughed as she swam away from him, and he was right on her, reaching for her ankle when Mr. Bishop's kitchen light suddenly cut on and they saw his short silhouette in the window.

"Hey," he called. "Who's out there? Get out of my yard before I call the cops!"

Violet and Xavier scrambled out of the pool, grabbed their clothes and ran, hopping over the fence. Once they were safely hidden behind the toolshed in Xavier's backyard, they finally turned to each other and burst into laughter. Violet's heart was pounding, not just from getting caught by Mr. Bishop, but because she realized that Xavier looked even more beautiful when he was laughing. She felt electrified from the tips of her toes to the top of her head.

"I think I like you, Xavier," she said quietly.

His mouth curved into a soft smile. "I think I like you too, Violet."

She leaned back against the cool metal of the toolshed and Xavier stepped forward and gently cradled her cheeks in his palms.

"I brought you to Martin's party because I wanted everyone to see me with you," he whispered.

Then he pressed his lips to hers, and as Violet kissed him

back, she reasoned that being stuck in Willow Ridge might not be so bad if Xavier was stuck there with her.

And so began their journey of first love.

In Xavier, Violet found what she hadn't been able to find in anyone else. A kindred spirit, an understanding. A mutual support of each other's desires and dreams. A feeling of being wholly accepted.

They loved each other fiercely and wholeheartedly, which meant they had big breakups and even bigger makeups. Usually their breakups were brought on by a silly argument due to unnecessary jealousy, lack of communication and/or raging hormones. Like if Xavier didn't call Violet before he fell asleep after basketball practice, or if Violet didn't come to one of his games with his number painted on her cheek, they took those moments as personal affronts. They'd argue in the middle of the cafeteria, and Violet would storm away, calling Xavier some variation of a fuckboy asshole who didn't care about her feelings, and Xavier, offended, would chase after her and they'd argue some more. Days, sometimes weeks later, missing each other would outweigh whatever reason they'd been upset, and they'd sneak out to the parking lot during lunch and hook up in the back seat of Violet's car, groping at each other and apologizing for overreacting.

The first time they had sex happened after they snuck off to a hotel room one abnormally hot day in late April during spring break. While the rest of their friends were on their way to the beach or at the movies or the mall, Violet and Xavier whispered promises to each other in the dark, saying that they'd always be there for each other, no matter what.

Before senior prom, they'd been broken up for three weeks and two days because Xavier had laughed when Violet said they needed to have a meeting to discuss prom aesthetics. Clearly, as a soon-to-be fashion major, aesthetics were of the utmost importance to Violet, and she and her date had to be on point. She didn't like that Xavier thought she was being silly. She'd called him inconsiderate. He'd told her she was taking this prom shit too seriously. She'd hung up on him, and he'd ignored her call when she'd later tried to call him back. Violet then asked Leonard Davis to be her prom date instead, and in turn, Xavier asked Shalia McNair.

So it was ironic when Violet and Xavier were crowned prom king and queen anyway.

On prom night, Violet's classmates cheered for her as she sashayed across the dance floor wearing a satin black vintage Alaïa gown with a scoop back that had cost almost half the money she'd saved while working weekends at Charlotte Russe. Their teacher Mr. Rodney placed the plastic tiara on her head, careful not to ruin her skillfully crafted updo, and as Violet grinned and looked around at her classmates, who'd chosen her as their prom queen, she mused that maybe high school wasn't so bad after all. Why was she in such a rush to leave it behind?

"Ready to dance?" Xavier asked.

He beamed at Violet and held out his hand as the DJ cued up Drake's "Hold On, We're Going Home." His prom-king crown was tilted to the side, and he'd ditched his suit jacket and loosened his tie. His light brown cheeks were flushed from all the dancing he'd done that night, because per usual he'd been the center of attention. And he was giving Violet his signature smile. A smile that said he was handsome and he knew it.

Violet frowned at him and uttered, "Ugh."

Xavier's smile only grew bigger. He wiggled the fingers of his outstretched hand. "Come on, you gonna leave all our classmates hanging? They want to see their king and queen dance."

Violet cast a glance at said classmates, who indeed were watching them eagerly. And for good reason. Violet and Xavier had provided much steam to the rumor mill over the last year and a half. They were even voted Cutest Couple for the senior superlatives.

"*Fine*," she said, rolling her eyes.

Xavier laughed, and she looped her arms around his neck. He was so much taller than her, she had to crane her neck slightly to look at his face. His hands went to her waist and they swayed to the music. She had ignored him in every possible way since their most recent fight, but that didn't stop her body from responding to his with muscle memory now. Her stomach did a little flip when he tightened his hold on her waist, and as Drake crooned over the speakers, Xavier leaned down and whispered, "So what's up with you and corny-ass Leonard?"

Violet jerked back and glared at the wisecrack he'd made about her prom date. "Why do you always have to be such a hater?" she hissed. "Leonard isn't corny. Do you see me making any comments about how your date, Shalia, is wearing the tackiest dress in the entire ballroom? It looks like she bought her dress at Party City."

Xavier smirked. "But *I* look good, though, right?"

She rolled her eyes again. "You're insufferable."

"You love me."

Violet frowned. He raised an eyebrow, daring her to deny it.

She didn't.

"You love me more," she said.

"You got me there." One of his hands inched around and settled gently at the small of her back, bringing her closer. "I'm sorry, you know. I've been trying to tell you, but someone's been ignoring my calls and texts."

"Mm-hmm," Violet mumbled.

He leaned down again, and his lips were at her ear when he softly said, "You look beautiful tonight, Vi. Really. I wish we would have come here together."

She pulled away slightly to look at his face. He was watching her, alert and earnest. The tiny wrinkle between his eyebrows surfaced, and that only happened when he was being particularly sincere. The ice around her heart began to melt.

"So do I," she finally said. More quietly, she added, "I'm sorry too."

Xavier smiled and gazed at her. "I love you like Mr. Bishop loves his pool."

Violet laughed. This was a game they played. "I love you like Mrs. Franklin loves writing late passes."

"I love *you* like LeBron loves Spalding."

"And *I* love *you* like the House of Chanel loves pearls."

"Damn, for real?" He whistled and placed a hand over his heart. "That's deep, Vi."

Then he kissed her, completely thawing her heart, which now beat rapidly in her chest. Poor Leonard and Shalia, who were somewhere on the dance floor, thinking they might have had a chance with either of those two tonight. But Leonard and Shalia were the last thing on Violet's mind. Instead, she was thinking about how later that fall, she'd be at the Fashion Institute of Design and Merchandising in Los Angeles, and Xavier would be attending the University of Kentucky on a basketball scholarship. They'd be in different time zones, thousands of miles apart. And they'd spent the last few weeks fighting again. What a waste of precious time.

The song finally ended, and Violet reluctantly dropped her arms from around Xavier's neck. He quickly caught one of her hands and pulled it up to his mouth, planting a kiss against her knuckles.

"Are you going to Post Prom?" he asked.

Post Prom was being held at the Skate Zone not too far from their high school. There would be an indoor ice rink, an arcade and free pizza until three a.m. It was the school's way of making sure that everyone stayed safe after prom.

Violet took one look at Xavier's mischievous expression.

"Not if you aren't," she answered.

"I was hoping you'd say that." He reached down and linked his fingers through hers.

"We never got our tattoos, you know," she whispered.

It was something they'd mentioned before, late one night while lying side by side in Violet's bed. Tattoos dedicated to each other so that they'd be tied forever, no matter what.

"You wanna get them tonight?" Xavier asked.

Violet nodded. She didn't know how they'd pull it off, though. While Xavier was already eighteen, her eighteenth birthday wasn't until October. She'd need parental consent for a tattoo, and her parents hated tattoos. And furthermore, she didn't know of any parlors in their area that were open this late at night.

"Okay, bet," he said, leading her off the dance floor.

"Where will we go?"

"I know a guy who knows a guy."

Violet didn't ask for clarification. Xavier made friends wherever he went. She didn't doubt that he knew someone who would give two teenagers tattoos at midnight.

Half an hour later, they were at a tattoo parlor in Jersey City, owned by the cousin of one of Xavier's friends from basketball camp. Violet got a small *X* on her left hip, and Xavier got a violet flower on the inside of his right bicep.

Afterward, they went to Violet's house. She entered through the front door because she knew her parents would be watching television in the den and they'd want to hear about prom. Iris was home from college, and as a junior, Lily had opted to skip prom, so both of her sisters were already upstairs in their rooms. And Violet was grateful, because while her parents asked a few simple questions about the food and music, she knew her sisters would have wanted to have a more in-depth discussion about prom, and Violet didn't have time for that. Because when she made it up to her room, Xavier had already climbed the sycamore tree and was waiting outside her window. She let him inside and they wasted no time getting undressed and climbing into her bed.

Later, they lay in a tangle of sheets, their legs intertwined, breathing softly. At this point, Xavier had stayed over dozens of times without her parents knowing. They were pros at being quiet in her bedroom.

He let out a sigh and turned onto his side, propping himself up on his elbow to stare down at her.

"I can't believe it's all ending," he said.

Violet smirked at his wistful expression. "You mean high school?"

"Yeah," he said. "And this. Seeing you every day."

She found his hand under the sheets and squeezed it. She thought of the moment that Xavier had told her he loved her for the first time a year ago. They'd been lying side by side in her bed just like this, and he'd whispered the words. She remembered the husky yet nervous tone of his voice. And she remembered his brilliant smile when she'd said she loved him too.

"We're onto bigger and better things," she said, attempting to hide the sadness she felt at their inevitable separation. "You're going to be an NBA first-round draft pick in a few years."

"True. I'm gonna be a millionaire."

"Not if you spend all your money on cars and jewelry."

Xavier blinked at her. "Wowww. So you're saying I'm irresponsible?"

"You're the one who spent almost all the money you saved mowing lawns last summer on two gold chains from the Piercing Pagoda."

"Those were quality investments. I'm gonna have those chains for life. But what about you and your expensive Aaliyah prom dress? Are you even gonna wear it again? How responsible was *that* purchase?"

"It's an *Alaïa*, thank you very much," she hissed.

He smiled, gazing at her furious expression. "I'm gonna marry you one day."

Violet shook her head, fighting off the elation she felt. "We'd drive each other nuts."

"Some people would call that love, baby."

She snorted and rolled her eyes. "You are so cheesy."

"Your cheesy future husband," he corrected.

"My life is going to be chaotic because of all the celebrities I'll be working with," she said. "And you'll be a superstar basketball player. You'll never be home. *I'll* never be home. We'll be thinking the worst of each other. Our futures don't align."

"Nah, I don't believe that," he said, taking her hand in his again. "I'm not saying it will be easy, but we'll be able to overcome whatever life throws at us. Because that's what love is. I love you and you love me. I think it's pretty simple, actually. I know we're young and everything, but there's no one else I want to do life with, Vi."

She bit her lip, holding back tears at his words. His

confidence was infectious, effectively melting away her worries.

"Me neither," she said softly. Plus, the thought of Xavier marrying someone else made her blood boil.

"So you'll marry me?" he asked. "When the time is right?"

She nodded and gently looped her arms around his neck, pulling him back down to her. "Yes," she whispered.

IN THE MORNING, Xavier slipped out of Violet's window and climbed down the tree. She leaned out of the window and watched him go. She wiped her eyes, tearing up. They still had a couple of months left until college, but it was already the end of an era.

"Don't forget our plan!" Xavier called from the sidewalk, clearly not caring if he woke her parents or sisters.

"I won't!" she called back, just as loudly.

Then Violet's mom opened her window and looked down at Xavier. She gasped, then turned to see Violet leaning out of her window wearing only a camisole and underwear.

"Violet, close your window!" Dahlia shouted. "And, Xavier Wright, you'd better go home right now!"

"Sorry, Mrs. Greene!" Xavier said. "I was just . . . um . . . seeing if Violet wanted to get breakfast!"

"Don't bother lying, young man! I'm going to call your mother, regardless!"

Since they were already in trouble, Violet didn't see the point in playing innocent anymore. She leaned out the window again and blew Xavier a kiss. "I love you!"

"I love you too!" He mimed catching the kiss and placing it in his shirt's front pocket.

Violet laughed, and Xavier smiled up at her before he climbed into his car and beeped the horn as he drove away.

He was the love of her life. Nothing was going to keep them apart.

She was young and naive enough to believe that was true.

1

VALENTINE'S DAY WAS NOTHING BUT A CAPITALIST SCAM, and the world would be a much better place if everyone accepted this simple truth about this senseless holiday.

At least that was Violet's new philosophy.

She'd never thought of herself as a love cynic or someone who crapped on things that most of the population enjoyed for the sake of being difficult or edgy, but Valentine's Day could kick rocks this year. It might be a pessimistic outlook to hate the day of love, but Violet figured she deserved to revel in her animosity, considering that five months ago, just two weeks shy of her wedding day, she'd discovered that her charming, successful and seemingly dedicated husband-to-be had been sleeping with someone else.

Now it was the middle of January and she was standing in line at a Walgreens in Las Vegas, surrounded by Valentine's Day balloons and teddy bears and silly cards with weird romantic puns, like *Thanks for bacon my Valentine's Day eggs-traordinary!* She imagined each of the fluffy pink teddy bears laughing at her and her silly attempt at a love life, which had so easily gone up in flames. It was all a huge joke. *Love* was a joke. At least the romantic variety.

But she wasn't at Walgreens to shoot the stink eye at innocent teddy bears. She needed vitamins and snacks to cure her fatigue because she had a tendency to get so caught up in work, she forgot to eat. Between her consistent twelve- and sometimes fourteen-hour workdays and her crumbling personal life, she was grateful that fatigue seemed to be the worst of her symptoms and that her stress wasn't creating bigger problems, like a stomach ulcer or something.

"Did you have any trouble finding what you needed?" the cashier asked when it was finally Violet's turn to be rung up.

Violet placed a bag of salt-and-vinegar chips and a box of Goobers on the counter next to the bottle of multivitamins. She kept her Dior sunglasses perched carefully on the bridge of her nose as she shook her head. The cashier, a youngish guy with shaggy blond hair and a thin mustache, looked her up and down in a slightly suggestive manner. Violet sighed and rolled her eyes behind her glasses. Men had been objectifying her since she'd sprouted boobs in the ninth grade, so while his behavior was exhausting, it wasn't new. This guy was really reaching, though, because you could hardly see anything about her figure underneath her black oversize Off-White T-shirt and matching joggers.

"Nope," she said.

Then, as he was bagging up her items, Violet spotted something behind his head.

"Wait." She pointed at the latest edition of *Cosmopolitan*. "Can I have that too?"

He scanned the magazine and started to slip it into the bag, but Violet reached to take it from him. "I'm going to read it now. Thank you."

She hustled out of the store toward the black Mercedes-Benz SUV that was waiting for her in the parking lot. Her eyes were glued to the photo of *Cosmo*'s January cover star, Meela Baybee, the up-and-coming alternative R and B singer whom everyone was obsessed with lately. Meela's silver hair was cut into an asymmetrical bob, and she was wearing her signature biker-shorts-and-nipple-pasties combo—a look that Violet had created specifically for her. Violet flipped to the interview, quickly skimming over the uninteresting sections about Meela's upcoming album, and when she reached the inevitable question about who Meela was dating, Violet narrowed her eyes.

> **Cosmo:** There's been a lot of talk about your
> relationship with your manager, Eddy Coltrane.
> Can you speak to that?
>   Meela coyly takes a sip from her drink and laughs.
> **Meela:** We're together. I'm happy. That's all I'm
> going to say.

Eddy Coltrane, Meela's manager turned boyfriend, was otherwise known as Violet's ex-fiancé.

Otherwise known as the world's biggest asshole.

An unfaithful asshole who'd called and texted Violet so

many times after she broke things off, she'd had no choice but to block him.

She'd met Eddy at a Halloween party the year before last in LA. She'd heard of him in the way that people working in the entertainment industry always vaguely hear of one another. Eddy was a talent manager for some of the most popular up-and-coming musicians, and Violet had happened to work with some of his clients on various music video shoots, where she'd gotten her start. At that fated party, Violet had been dressed as Cruella de Vil, with a faux-Dalmatian-print coat and elbow-length red satin gloves. Eddy hadn't been wearing a costume at all, just a white button-up and black slacks. He'd bumped into Violet by the bar and bought her a drink in apology.

He was older than her, in his late thirties, and right away he was very clear about his desire to meet someone and settle down. Up until that point, Violet had been solely focused on her career. She had fun with guys here and there, but she never let them get too close. Her career was flourishing, and she felt like she was ready for her personal life to finally flourish too.

They'd only been dating three months when he proposed. He'd flown out to Italy while she was at Milan Fashion Week and he'd whisked her away to Venice. While riding in a boat through the Grand Canal, he'd kneeled down and popped the question. Violet had said yes because she cared about Eddy. They might not have had a love that was overwhelming or all-consuming, but it was steady. *He* was steady. With Eddy, there would be no surprise breakups or intense heartache that lasted for years. She'd been through that once and didn't care to experience it again.

Eddy understood her busy lifestyle. Often, he was even busier. He'd felt like the smart choice. The safe choice. So it was ironic that while Violet had been celebrating her bachelorette party in Miami, TMZ posted a video of Meela and Eddy kissing on the beach in Jamaica. Even worse was that, at the time, Violet was Meela's stylist and had introduced them.

"Damn, girl, I thought somebody went and kidnapped you inside that store."

Violet snapped her head up, and her best friend, Karina, aka Karamel Kitty, the number one rap artist in the country and Violet's biggest client, was leaning out the SUV window, beckoning Violet forward. The glittery polish on her long stiletto nails shimmered in the sunlight.

"We've got things to do, mama!" Karina said. "Hurry that cute ass up."

"I'm coming, I'm coming." Violet grinned and tossed the magazine in the trash before sliding into the back seat beside Karina. She handed her the box of Goobers.

"Oooh, you know I love these." Karina squealed and wrapped her arm around Violet, hugging her closely. The hair of Karina's jet-black waist-length wig brushed against Violet's leg. Karina opened the box of chocolate-covered peanuts, shook a handful into her palm, then placed the box in her highlighter yellow Telfar bag. "Thanks, boo."

"You're welcome," Violet said, eating a handful of chips before chewing two vitamins and taking a swig of water.

"I'm pretty sure you're the only person in the world who still eats those."

"All the more candy for me." Karina eyed Violet, who was rolling her shoulders and stretching her neck from side to side. "You good?"

"I'm fine. Just tired, but what else is new?" She shrugged, and Karina leaned her head on Violet's shoulder.

"We've been through worse. At least it's not as bad as that night in Québec, right?"

Violet snort-laughed. *At least it's not as bad as that night in Québec* was one of their mottos. Two years ago, when Violet had dressed Karina for a festival performance in Québec, they'd gotten stuck in the hotel elevator for three hours. They'd gone into the elevator as a stylist and client who got along pretty well and had a decent rapport, and they'd left the elevator with a new bond. That was what happened when you decided to pass the time by sharing your worst fears and deepest, darkest secrets. Karina ended up missing her scheduled performance that night, but it would forever go down in history as the day that Violet gained a new best friend.

Karina's driver peeled out of the parking lot, and Karina reached past her bodyguard in the passenger seat to turn up the radio. They were playing her hit single, "Bad Bitch Antics." Vegas was showing Karina love because she had an appearance that night at the opening of the brand-new Luxe Grande casino.

But they'd only be in Vegas for less than twenty-four hours. Tomorrow, Karina would fly to Atlanta to film episodes as a guest judge on *Up Next*, a new hip-hop competition reality show, and Violet would be on the first flight back to New York for an interview with *Look Magazine*, as she was currently under consideration to be included in their "30 Under 30 in Style" issue.

After years of hustling, Violet had amassed a small but impressive client roster. In addition to working with Karina, she worked with Gigi Harrison, who was mostly known for action flicks and had just starred in a superhero movie. She also worked with Destiny Diaz, a former Nickelodeon star who was making a big splash as the lead in a gritty teen drama, and Violet's most recent client was Angel, a pop R and B singer who was turning into a bona fide sex symbol. She had a fitting scheduled with him in LA next week for the Grammys. Then she'd fly back to New York again to begin the marathon that was fashion month, which would start with New York Fashion Week, then take her to London, Milan and Paris.

Afterward, she'd return to LA for a fitting with Karina for the world premiere of her visual album, *The Kat House*. It was Karina's sophomore effort, and the album was about women's empowerment. In the accompanying visuals, Karina led a rogue group of women around the world, liberating cities of evil, ain't-shit men. In each scene, Karina and her backup dancers donned custom and vintage catsuits. The team had filmed the visuals in November and December of last year. Violet had acted as head stylist for the entire project. At only twenty-eight years old, she was one of the youngest stylists to ever achieve such an accomplishment. The hype surrounding the visual album, which was set to release in March, was one of the main reasons Violet was being considered for *Look Magazine*'s deeply coveted and exclusive "30 Under 30" list.

If the *Look Magazine* team deemed her impressive enough during her interview and ultimately decided to include her on the list, it would be a huge deal for Violet's career. *Look* was read mostly by industry insiders: fashion people, of course, but also managers and publicists of major stars who wanted to keep an eye on stylists who could help improve their clients' images. If Violet was featured on the "30 Under 30" list, she'd be put directly on the radar of some of the biggest power players in the industry.

Violet's younger sister, Lily, always said that Violet's life moved at lightning speed. She wasn't wrong. Violet's job required her to be on the go constantly. She missed birthdays and holidays. She missed a normal sleep schedule. More often than not, she was running on empty. But she was living the life she'd always dreamed of. That was what she reminded herself whenever she felt moments of emptiness creeping in.

BACK AT THE hotel, controlled chaos ensued—the norm for Violet's line of work. Thankfully, because of her vitamins and snacks, her energy was beginning to return. Music blasted as Karina talked to fans on her Instagram Live while getting her hair and makeup done. Violet and her assistant, Alex, were on the other side of the suite surveying Karina's many dress options for the night. They stood in front of a rack of gowns that they'd selected after a fitting earlier that month. Karina was voluptuous, with big boobs and shapely hips, and she loved showing off her figure. She'd been that way since she was a college student in Pennsylvania who uploaded her rap freestyles to YouTube. Violet was often invited to the showrooms of top high-fashion designers who specifically wanted Karina to be seen donning their clothes.

Violet pulled two dresses off the rack: a floor-length Versace leopard-print gown with a thigh-high slit and a rose gold LaQuan Smith corset minidress. Alex snapped a few photographs for Violet's archives. Alex was soft-spoken, and a hard worker. With her pixie cut and serious personality, she reminded Violet of her older sister, Iris. She'd met Alex at a FIDM career fair and had hired her as soon as she graduated last spring. Sometimes, Violet felt like she'd lose her head from her shoulders if Alex wasn't there to help her.

After Alex took more photos, then uploaded them to her laptop, Violet brought the dresses over to Karina once she ended her Instagram Live.

"Okay, so what are we feeling tonight?" Violet shouted over the music. She held up the dresses side by side. The plan was for Karina to walk the red carpet with the other celebrities who were invited to the casino's opening, and later she'd have a section at the club inside the casino. "I was thinking the Versace for the red carpet and the LaQuan Smith for the club."

Karina handed her cell phone to her assistant, Edwin, and turned toward Violet to view the dresses.

"Feel free to weigh in," Violet said to Brian, Karina's hairstylist, and Melody, her makeup artist.

"It's giving jungle queen," Brian said, pointing at the

Versace dress. He took a moment to dab a little gold shimmer from one of Melody's makeup brushes onto his dark brown cheeks.

"What?" Violet scowled at him. "Do not come for my taste, Brian! This dress is bomb."

"It can be cute and jungle queen at the same time."

Violet huffed and looked at Melody. "Mel, what do you think?"

Melody kept her eyes on her makeup brushes and pulled her silky black hair into a ponytail at the nape of her neck. "Don't drag me into this. I like both. Karina will look good regardless."

"I know that's right," Karina said. "I'm always on the best-dressed lists at the end of the night, okay? Vi, Versace for the red carpet and LaQuan Smith for the club is perfect. Brian's just salty because somebody on my Live said he looked like a bootleg John Boyega."

Violet snorted and looked at Brian. "Oh my God, you do kind of look like him! Why have I never noticed this?"

"But he doesn't have a sexy British accent, sadly," Melody said.

"And none of the *Star Wars* fame," Alex added, coming over to take the dresses from Violet to hang them up again.

"Or money," Edwin noted.

"And he's not as tall," Violet said.

"Okay, keep it up," Brian said, "and after I'm done with Karina's hair, I won't be doing freebie touch-ups for any of you." He shot a pointed look at Violet specifically.

She blew him a kiss. "Then I won't help with your outfit. Have fun at the club sweating in your velour tracksuit."

"We do not need you sweating in VIP, Brian," Karina said, swiveling back toward Melody, who began painting Karina's lips in a deep fuchsia shade that popped against her brown complexion.

Brian gave Karina the finger and stuck his tongue out at Violet, and she laughed. Their crew was like a little family. Given how often they traveled together, Violet spent more time with them than she did with her own sisters.

After laying out Karina's shoes and jewelry and helping her get dressed, Violet went to her own room to change. She often joined Karina on the red carpet and followed her discreetly to make sure her dresses weren't dragging or twisting, because she needed to look good for photographs. At the end of the night, Violet posted those photos to her social media and added them to her portfolio.

As Violet slid on her own dress, a black Valentino halter with intricate cutouts on her hips, her phone vibrated nonstop. There were emails from her agent, Jill, about fashion week shows, and a series of texts from Angel, who treated Violet like a big sister and was more interested in asking her for dating advice than about what he should wear on the red carpet. Violet slipped her phone into her clutch, promising herself that she'd reply to everyone during the flight to New York the following morning. She just had to get through tonight first.

Brian came to her room and quickly swooped her curls into a chic topknot. Then she helped put together his outfit, and they met the rest of the team at the elevator bank.

"Okay, whole team looking good," Karina said, angling her phone to record a video as they crowded together in the elevator, along with the hotel's security. Karina's bodyguard pressed the button for the lobby and down they went.

Alex, who hated being on camera, ducked behind Violet to avoid being seen by Karina's millions of followers. She paused and pointed at the visible skin on Violet's left hip.

"I don't think I've ever seen that tattoo," she said. "What's the *X* for?"

Violet glanced down, seeing that her small tattoo was in plain view thanks to the design of her dress. Sometimes she forgot the tattoo was there. And other times, when she was in the shower or putting on lotion before bed, she stared at the *X* for a while and wondered whether or not the boy, now a man, whom she'd gotten this tattoo for still had the image of a violet on his inner bicep. And if so, she wondered if he'd considered getting it removed. She thought about removing the *X* sometimes, but she could never bring herself to actually go through with it.

Everyone thought that Violet's breakup with Eddy had been devastating. And it had been to a certain degree. Mostly because Hollywood was a small town and Eddy had played Violet for a woman who used to be her client, and that was embarrassing. So much so that Violet had even thrown herself an anti-wedding party on their wedding day in order to save face.

But the truth was that what had happened with Eddy didn't scratch the surface of how she knew heartbreak could *really* feel. Like your chest was caving in and half of you was missing. She knew what it was like to be in love where nothing else mattered and your life seemed utterly pointless without that other person. She'd felt that way for someone once, and he wasn't Eddy.

Violet hadn't seen or spoken to Xavier in almost a decade. And that was for the best, given how their relationship had ended.

"It's just this thing I did in high school," she finally answered, adjusting her dress to cover the tattoo as much as possible.

Then the elevator doors opened and the paparazzi in the hotel lobby descended, shouting for Karamel Kitty. The bulbs of their cameras flashed, snapping Violet out of her melancholy trip down high school memory lane.

She didn't have time to think about lost love or old ghosts.

She reached down to grab the train of Karina's dress.

The show must go on.

2

"THE THING IS, XAVIER, I'M REALLY LOOKING FOR SOME-one to build a team with me. Someone who will stick around and won't only be invested in *their* growth, but the growth of Riley's program in general. That's what I need from an assistant coach."

Xavier was sitting on the edge of the tub in his Las Vegas hotel room, nodding eagerly as he FaceTimed with Tim Vogel, the head coach of Riley University's men's basketball team. On the other side of the door, he could hear his cousin Raheem outside on the balcony, talking loudly on the phone with his fiancée, Bianca, and he hoped Coach Vogel couldn't overhear him.

"I understand that, sir, I do," Xavier said. "I'm ready and willing to do what it takes to help Riley grow."

Xavier had been talking with Coach Vogel since late last year, when he'd found out that one of the assistant coaches was leaving their post at Riley, the local state college in New Jersey. Xavier had earned his bachelor's at Riley and had played on the Division III basketball team after his short-lived stint at the University of Kentucky. Tim Vogel had been Xavier's coach. An assistant coach position at the college level could finally put Xavier on a new career path, like he'd been hoping. A move to get him back on track.

"I understand that you're eager, son, and I appreciate that," Coach Vogel said, taking a sip of what Xavier assumed was a nightcap. It was almost eleven thirty p.m. in New Jersey. "You're just so young. You're not married. You live alone. You could pick up and decide to move at any time. And, look, there's nothing wrong with that, but it means in the near future, I'd most likely have to start the assistant coach search all over again. I need someone who has a little more stability and who would be willing to make a long-term commitment. I'm not going to get that kind of promise from a bachelor such as yourself." He laughed, then added, "No offense, but I can't trust ya!"

"No offense taken," Xavier said, sighing.

Per usual, Tim had made a joke that only he found funny. But how could Xavier argue with Tim's assessment? Xavier *was* a bachelor. He was unmarried. Unencumbered. Unattached. All the "uns." But he needed this new job. He was a high school English teacher who coached JV and varsity basketball on the side, and he loved working with his students, but he couldn't deny that he felt unfulfilled. If only things had gone the way he'd originally planned years ago. Right now, he would be a professional basketball player in his prime. And he wouldn't be unmarried.

"Listen, you should be enjoying your birthday trip," Tim said. "We'll talk when you get back, all right? Happy birthday."

"Thanks," Xavier said. But because Tim Vogel was the hardest person to follow up with, Xavier needed to act fast and get their next call on the books.

"Wait—" he started, but Tim had already hung up.

Xavier rubbed his temples. He had to figure out a way to prove to Tim that he was serious about the assistant coach position. He just didn't know how to go about doing so.

He stood up and stared at his reflection in the mirror, wondering if he actually looked like someone who was celebrating his twenty-ninth birthday. From an objective point of view, he still appeared young. His skin was smooth and clear. He didn't have any gray hair yet. There were no bags underneath his eyes and he looked pretty fit.

He just *felt* ancient.

He grabbed his bottle of collagen supplements off the counter and downed two pills with water because his joints were beginning to bother him again. Not to mention the occasional minor discomfort he felt in his right lower calf. He guessed that was what happened when you spent every evening after work demonstrating basketball drills for a team of teenagers. Truthfully, Xavier would have been more than happy to spend his birthday weekend at home in Willow Ridge, maybe having dinner at Raheem and Bianca's house, where he could fall asleep in front of the television. Then when he woke up, he'd go back to his apartment and think about how to get the boys' varsity basketball team to the playoffs.

But fate had intervened in unfortunate ways during the faculty holiday party when he'd won a raffle for a free hotel room at the new Luxe Grande casino in Las Vegas. He'd tried to give away the winning ticket, but the rest of the teachers had made him feel so bad about not wanting to take advantage of the trip.

The hotel room itself was dope, though. There were two extremely comfortable-looking queen-size beds, a Jacuzzi tub, a spacious balcony and a fifty-inch flat-screen television mounted on the wall. Xavier wanted to throw on one of the soft, cozy robes and order room service. He wanted to drift off to sleep to the lulling background noise of a Netflix docu-series. Eight, maybe nine years ago, celebrating a birthday in Vegas with a free hotel room would have been a dream come true. He would have partied so hard and gotten so plastered, he'd have been hungover for a week. But here he was instead, twenty-nine and tired.

He wondered when he'd turned into such a square.

He walked out into the room just as Raheem stepped back inside, closing the balcony door behind him.

"Ayyy, okay. I see you, cuzzo," Raheem said. "Fit looking fresh as hell, my guy."

Xavier turned to his reflection again. His curly hair was cut into a fade. He was wearing a plain white T-shirt underneath a cream-colored cardigan with black jeans and a pair of black suede Chelsea boots. Even though he'd opted to wear his contacts tonight instead of his glasses, he still looked exactly like who he was: a homebody attempting to let loose in Vegas. Raheem, on the other hand, thought he was in a music video. His hair was freshly cornrowed, and he wore gold wire-framed glasses, which were definitely not prescription, gold grills on his bottom teeth, two gold chains around his neck, a buttoned tan blazer with no shirt underneath and matching slacks. Raheem made decent money as an auto mechanic. So much so that Xavier had invited him to speak to his class for his annual informal career day next month. But Raheem wasn't always smart about the ways he spent said money. Hence his discussion minutes ago with Bianca, who was convinced that Raheem was going to gamble away their one-year-old son's daycare tuition. The minute they'd landed, Xavier had received a text from Bianca, asking him to keep an eye on Raheem. It was hilarious that Xavier was seen as the more responsible one now, when back in high school, all the trouble that he and Raheem had gotten into had often been Xavier's idea.

"Thanks," Xavier said, responding to Raheem's compliment. He gave himself one more once-over in the mirror and walked across the room to the minibar, where Raheem was mixing two cups of Hennessey and Coke. "You look fresh too. Everything good with Bianca?"

"Yeah, she's all right." Raheem handed a cup to Xavier and they went to stand outside on the balcony. They looked out onto the bright lights of Vegas glittering below them. Raheem turned around so that his back was to the nightlife backdrop and snapped several selfies. "I might look good enough to eat, but I'm really just out here for decoration. It's all about you, cuz. Tonight, you're gonna meet a fine-ass woman, and whatever happens from there is up to you and her."

Xavier snorted and took a sip of his drink. It burned in a smooth, familiar way. "Nah, I'm good."

Raheem sighed. "You don't know what I had to do to get out of work this weekend and offer my wingman services."

He clapped Xavier on the shoulder. "Don't let my sacrifice be in vain."

Xavier laughed and shook his head, taking another sip of his drink.

This was also why he'd been pressured into going to Vegas. Everyone from Raheem and Bianca to Xavier's mom, Tricia, to his nosy but well-meaning coworkers wanted Xavier to get back out there and put a real effort into dating. They assumed he was reluctant to get serious with someone because he was still stuck on his ex-girlfriend, Michelle, who'd dumped him over a year ago. But his seven-month-long relationship with Michelle wasn't what inhibited him from dating. It was just that he found dating to be so *exhausting*. And whenever he met someone new, he failed to feel that spark, like lightning in a bottle, and he was beginning to give up hope that it would ever happen. He hadn't felt that way for someone in a long time, not even Michelle, truth be told. They'd been coworkers who'd dated out of a lack of other options in Willow Ridge. When Michelle broke up with Xavier and bought a one-way ticket to South America to go backpacking, Xavier hadn't been surprised.

Lightning had struck him once, though, over a decade ago. There'd been a beautiful girl with a fiery spirit for whom he would have done anything. He had the tattoo on his inner bicep to prove it. But he'd let her go because that had been the best thing for her, regardless of how he wished things could have gone differently. Now she was busy living her best life, and he was . . . in Vegas, reluctantly celebrating his birthday in a hotel room he wouldn't be able to afford under normal circumstances.

"Let's just have some fun tonight," he said to Raheem, wanting to change the subject. "Shots?"

Raheem beamed. "Oh, hell yes."

HOURS AND MANY shots later, Xavier dragged Raheem away from the blackjack table so that he wouldn't return to Jersey penniless.

"Just a few more minutes, cuzzo," Raheem said, tripping over his shoelace. "I'm gonna hit. Just wait."

Xavier threw his arm around his cousin's shoulders and laughed. His laugh sounded extra to his own ears. He was beginning to feel like his old self—the one who would walk into a party and turn everything up. Despite his early apathy for Vegas, he now wanted to keep the night going, and they couldn't do that if Raheem lost all his money.

"Let's go to the club." Xavier glanced at his phone. It was almost ten p.m. "I wanna go back to the room and change first, though. I'm not feeling this fit anymore."

Raheem, who was a lot less sober than Xavier, attempted to nod seriously. "Yeah, I'm not trying to hit up the club with Mr. Rogers. Ditch the sweater."

Xavier burst out laughing. "Man, fuck you."

"What?" Raheem said, laughing too as they left the casino section of the hotel and walked back toward the lobby. "Karamel Kitty might be at the club tonight. I don't need you embarrassing me."

At the mention of Karamel Kitty, Xavier momentarily froze.

"Karamel Kitty is in Vegas tonight?" he asked.

"Yuppp." Raheem said. "She's probably gonna have her own section and everything."

If Karamel Kitty was here, then . . . No, that didn't mean Violet was here too.

His high school sweetheart.

He knew that she was Karamel Kitty's stylist because everyone in town knew the Greenes. Every time he turned around, one of his coworkers was giving him an update on a new accomplishment from Violet or one of her sisters, and of course there was social media. Xavier had an Instagram, but he had yet to post a picture. He didn't like social media—too many people sharing their thoughts and lives at once—but he did check Violet's account, @viewsofviolet, every now and then. She posted pictures of herself and her clients, each photo more chic and impressive than the one before.

It had been almost nine years since he'd last seen her. But he thought of her often, more than he'd ever admit to anyone. He wondered what their lives might have been like if they'd stayed together. But then he would hear an update on her life or check her Instagram, and he'd be reminded that she was thriving. If she'd stayed with him, he would have held her back. He would have hated himself for doing that to her, and eventually she would have grown to resent him.

Despite their severed connection, and the painful months and years he'd somehow managed to survive after their breakup, he was comforted to know that she was doing well. At least one of them had successfully followed their dreams.

"Yo, who is *that*?"

Xavier ran into Raheem's back because he'd stopped walking. Xavier turned his head in the direction that Raheem was looking.

A woman with chestnut brown skin was standing at the front desk in the lobby, wearing a skintight black dress. Her hair was styled in a complicated-looking updo, and Xavier had a flashback to his senior prom. His heart began to pound in his chest. Even all these years later, with the distance and separation, he'd know her anywhere. His senses had always had a way of reacting to her before his thoughts had a chance to catch up.

She glanced to her left, and Xavier got a view of her profile. A confirmation.

Violet.

3

VIOLET DIDN'T LIKE TO THINK ABOUT THE DAY THAT
Xavier had broken up with her. The memory was under
strict lockdown behind a dead-bolted door.

It had been her sophomore year of college, the first day
of winter break. That morning, her dad had picked her up
from the airport, and before even bothering to unpack, she'd
gone to see Xavier. They'd since learned that long distance
wasn't necessarily their forte. For one thing, there was the
three-hour time difference between Los Angeles and Kentucky, and on top of that, they were both so busy. Violet had
hit the ground running as soon as her freshman year began. Unlike her fellow classmates, who'd scored internships
and connections through nepotism, Violet took a job working nights and weekends at the Forever 21 on Olympic Bou-
levard. She began assisting the visual manager and his team,
who dressed the mannequins and redesigned the store's
layout each season. The visual manager had become so impressed with Violet, he put her in touch with his old roommate, who happened to be a fashion editor at *Teen Vogue*'s

LA office, which resulted in Violet landing her first internship. Things only got busier from there. The summer after her freshman year, she'd interned at *Elle* in New York City, and she'd spent the fall of her sophomore year back in LA, interning at *Flaunt*.

Xavier's schedule was packed around the clock with classes and basketball. Violet knew that he'd had a tough time adjusting to life in Kentucky, and during basketball season his freshman year, he'd spent more time on the bench than on the court, which frustrated him, since he'd been the star player for most of his life. She'd received this information anecdotally during their intermittent FaceTimes between classes and games and internship shifts. The only upside to their new way of communication was that they no longer had time to bicker like in high school.

Then, sophomore year, shortly before winter break, Xavier tore his Achilles tendon at practice and returned home to Willow Ridge to recuperate after surgery. Suddenly, Violet couldn't get a hold of him. He didn't answer her calls and he barely responded to her texts. This was the same boy who used to send her a good-morning text every day like clockwork. She had a feeling that something was wrong, but she hoped the reason that he wasn't answering her calls or texts was because he was so high on painkillers, he couldn't differentiate his cell phone from his foot. That would be the only acceptable explanation for why he'd gone off the grid.

But with the exception of being on crutches, when Xavier answered the door, wearing a Kentucky blue sweatshirt, he looked perfectly fine and alert.

"I've been calling you," Violet said, struggling to tamp down her agitation. He was injured after all. Plus, his mom, Tricia, loved her, and Violet didn't want to be overheard chewing Xavier out. She lowered her voice. "Are you ignoring me?"

Instead of inviting her inside, Xavier maneuvered onto the porch on his crutches. He closed the door behind him, and Violet took a step back to give him more space. Something about the guarded look on his face gave her pause.

"What's wrong?" she asked.

"Violet, I . . ." He looked out onto the street behind her. She continued to stare at him, wondering why he wouldn't meet her eye.

"What is it?" she asked, growing increasingly wary.

"I . . . I think we should break up."

She was stunned into silence. Her brain moved in slow motion, struggling to catch up. Xavier wanted to break up. He was breaking up with her.

"Wh-what?" she stammered, blinking. "But why?"

"It's different now. Everything is . . ." He lifted his hands, like she was supposed to find further information in the air around them. "Different."

How vague. How *confusing*.

From his tone, she knew that this wasn't like one of their high school fights when a breakup would be followed by a makeup. He'd spoken with finality.

"I don't understand." Her voice cracked. "What's different? The way that you feel about me?"

He looked down at his cast, still refusing to meet her eye.

"You were right before when you said our futures wouldn't

align," he said, not really answering her question. "I think we'd be better off going our separate ways."

His words were so out of left field, she didn't know what to think. All she knew was that she didn't want to lose him. Desperately, she grabbed one of his hands.

"I know we've been busy and it's been hard," she said. "But I love you and you love me. Didn't you say that was all that mattered? That things were simple?"

When he finally did look up at her, his eyes were red, brimming with tears. She was so confused. If *he* was breaking up with *her*, why did he look so heartbroken?

"Why are you doing this?" she whispered.

"I'm sorry, Violet," he said, so softly, she had to lean forward to hear him. Using his free arm, he hugged her close with a fierce strength and quickly kissed her temple before backing away and repeating, "I'm sorry."

Then he went back inside, as she stood on the porch in the cold, abandoned.

She'd gone home and yanked the photographs of the two of them off her bedroom wall, pulled them out of the picture frames on her dresser. Photos of them at prom, at the beach, on the bleachers at school, Violet leaning her head against his shoulder. Looking at the pictures made her heart feel like it was on fire. She wanted to burn the photos, but she couldn't bring herself to do it. Instead, she stored them in a shoebox, deep underneath her bed, never to be seen again.

For the duration of winter break, she could barely bring herself to get out of bed. If she wasn't crying, she lay there with puffy eyes, staring at the ceiling and wishing she could think about anything other than Xavier. Food tasted plain and flavorless. Her usual holiday activities lost meaning. No ice skating with her sisters. No assembling poinsettia bouquets with her parents. What was the point? How could she be happy without Xavier? Her misery grew through her like a thick vine, encasing her, weighing her down. She kept waiting for him to call or text, to show up at her front door and say that he was wrong, that he'd made a mistake. But the calls and texts never came, and the doorbell never rang.

On New Year's Eve, her misery took a sharp turn toward anger. Who the hell did Xavier think he was to leave her this way? After everything they'd been through? No, he wouldn't get the last say. She tore out of the house, donning the plaid Christmas pajamas she'd worn for the past week, and sped in her car toward Xavier's house. She was going to curse him out, tell him that his life was going to absolutely suck without her, and then she'd force her way inside and stab holes in all of his precious basketballs. Then *he'd* be the miserable one!

But when she pulled up in front of Xavier's house and saw his empty driveway, she remembered that he'd planned to spend New Year's Eve with his dad in Georgia. He wasn't even home. The fight went out of her then. She leaned her head against her steering wheel and sobbed. Eventually, she pulled herself together and drove back home. The days afterward passed slowly, excruciatingly so. But soon it was time for her to return to LA, where fashion and her classes welcomed her with open arms, serving as the best distraction.

The pain from her breakup with Xavier had almost ended her. For a long time, it felt as though someone had died.

The loss of Xavier's presence in her life had been so soul crushing, she'd feared she'd never be the same. But eventually, the tears stopped and the pain dulled. She landed more internships, made new friends. She graduated and dove headfirst into her career. She learned to build a life around her grief, until it gradually became a small speck in her larger makeup.

She'd trained herself not to think about Xavier, and after nine years, she'd gotten pretty good at it. So as she stood in the hotel lobby and heard a vaguely familiar voice from her past shout "Ayo, Violet!," alarm bells immediately sounded in her head.

Violet turned and quickly scanned the clusters of people moving through the lobby. She'd lost her room key at dinner and was waiting to receive a new card while Karina and the rest of their group got ready for the club. She didn't spot a familiar face in the crowd. Maybe she'd been imagining things. Alex pointing out Violet's tattoo must have put her on edge. She turned back toward the desk, and the person shouted her name again. This time, Violet spun around and found herself looking directly at Raheem Anderson from high school.

He was walking right toward her, smiling huge and waving. The ceiling lights reflected off his flashy gold chains and grills. Violet was so dumbfounded to run into Raheem here, of all places, she could only stare and blink. The last time she saw him, she'd been seventeen years old, smoking a bowl with him and Xavier in his basement. She kept in touch with his fiancée, Bianca, here and there, so she knew that they were the parents of an absolutely adorable one-year-old, Raheem Jr. But she hadn't spoken to Raheem directly in a very long time. She'd deactivated her Facebook a while back and had no interest whatsoever in reviving it. And other than Bianca, she didn't follow anyone from high school on Instagram.

"What's up, girl?" Raheem reached Violet and enveloped her in a tight hug. As a teenager, he'd been short and scrawny, the kicker for their football team, who'd rather run in the opposite direction than be tackled. Now, he was still short, but he'd gotten stockier, like he worked out. He lifted Violet with ease through the sheer strength of his hug before setting her back down. "How you been?"

"Good." She was still blinking, still baffled. She placed her hands on his shoulders and leaned away slightly, getting a better look at him. His eyelids were droopy, and she inhaled a faint whiff of alcohol on his breath. "Wh-what are you doing here?"

"Partying, of course! What else? You know how I get down."

"Ha." She didn't know how he got down. Not anymore.

"Your room key, miss."

Startled, Violet turned to the front desk associate who was holding out her replacement key card. She thanked him and slipped the card in her clutch before turning back to Raheem.

"Well, it was good to see you . . ." She began to edge away, glancing down at her vibrating phone. There was a text from Edwin on behalf of Karina, asking if Violet was having an issue getting another room key. Alex had also texted and asked where Violet had packed the extra roll of boob tape for Karina's outfit change.

She needed to get back to her team. Plus, suddenly seeing Raheem in this unexpected way stirred up a lot of memories that she'd rather keep buried deep in the crevices of her mind, where they belonged.

"Wait, one second," Raheem said, holding out an arm to still her. He glanced back and stood on tiptoe, waving his hand and beckoning someone else over.

Somehow, without having concrete proof, she knew who Raheem was calling out to. Because who else would it be? The blood drained from Violet's face. Her throat grew dry, and she swallowed thickly. She took another step back, ready to escape.

"Actually," she croaked. "I can't—"

"X!" Raheem shouted, his hand placed lightly on her elbow. "Come here, cuzzo!"

She squeezed her eyes closed. Her insides were screaming at her to make a run for it.

I'm not ready for this! I was supposed to be cool, calm and collected when I saw him again! Not exhausted and running on three hours of sleep! He was supposed to look at me and immediately regret the day he broke my heart!

She forced herself to take a deep breath and open her eyes. Then the air whooshed right out of her. Standing a head taller than everyone around him and striding in her direction was the former love of her life.

Xavier Wright.

He and Violet locked eyes and the room tilted off-center.

She blinked rapidly and cleared her throat, silently scolding her heart for its erratic beating. But her heartbeat only defied her more as Xavier drew closer. She took in his strong build and alert gaze. His shiny, perfect curls atop his fresh haircut. His smooth, acne-free skin. Oh, fuck, he was still gorgeous. Why?! Why hadn't he developed a receding hairline? Why didn't he have a struggle-bus beard that refused to connect? That was what he deserved!

And he was smiling at her. *Smiling.* Like he was overjoyed to see her. Like he hadn't shattered her poor, fragile, young heart into a million little pieces.

"Violet," Xavier said, coming to a stop right in front of her. He sounded dazed, somewhat breathless. "Hey."

Then he was hugging her. He wrapped his arms around her, enfolding her against his body. He was still so much taller than her. Her face was adjacent to his chest. Her pulse thundered, and she commanded herself to breathe deeply and stay cool. God, he smelled good. Minty and clean. For a moment, she was so overwhelmed, she didn't know what to do, how to respond. Stilted, she lifted her arms and brought them around to rest at his upper back. The awkwardness and shock she felt at his presence momentarily melted into familiarity. It was so natural to hug him. Like nine years hadn't gone by since they'd last spoken, standing on his front porch on the first day of winter break.

Their hug was both never-ending and brief. Xavier's arms fell away and he stepped back, putting a polite amount of distance between them. Violet cleared her throat again and let her eyes roam his face, noticing the differences between then and now. For one, there was his full goatee and the deeper laugh lines around his mouth. He'd put on more weight, and it looked good on him. His cheeks were fuller, his build slightly huskier. He was no longer the wiry beanpole from high school. But some things remained the same, like the beauty mark above his left eyebrow and the scar on his chin from when he'd fallen during a game.

In today's day and age, it was easy to keep tabs on someone without actually ever talking to them, but as far as Violet could tell, Xavier had zero social media presence. Through her parents, she knew that he still lived in Willow Ridge and that he was teaching at the high school.

"He's so handsome and kind," Dahlia had once mentioned during one of Violet's visits home last year. Dahlia had run into Xavier at the supermarket and he'd helped her carry a case of water to her car. Then she'd went on and on about what a difference he was making with the high school students, like she hadn't called him a menace to Violet's education when they'd been high school students themselves. For some reason, Dahlia had also felt the need to mention that Xavier was single.

At the time, Violet had feigned nonchalance and tried her best to ignore the prick in her chest. But now that she and Xavier were face-to-face, she had proof that her mom had been telling the truth. He *was* still handsome.

She stared at him, fumbling for something to say.

What do you have to be nervous for? You are that *girl. Act like it.*

"It's nice to see you," she said. Her voice took on a cool level of indifference. Her easy smile required a mountain of effort. "What brings you to Vegas?"

"I won a raffle for a free room at the hotel." His voice was deeper. Another change. He smiled a little and shrugged. "Celebrating my birthday."

"Oh, right," she said, as if she'd forgotten that his birthday had passed just a few days ago on January twelfth. "Happy belated."

"Thank you." He was staring at her so intently, her cheeks were beginning to burn under his gaze. "I'm guessing you're here for work? With Karamel Kitty?"

Ah. He might not have been on social media, but someone had apparently been keeping tabs.

"Yes." She nodded, even though that was unnecessary because she'd just said yes. "About to go to the club, actually."

"Oh shit, us too!" Raheem said.

"Oh, really?" Violet glanced over her shoulder, hoping to see Alex or Edwin. Even Karina's surly bodyguard would do right now. Anyone to pull her away and put an end to this encounter. "Cool."

"You look beautiful, Vi," Xavier blurted.

Her gaze snapped back to him. Hearing him say her nickname so softly threatened her mask of composure. She watched his Adam's apple bob as he swallowed, his jaw working as his eyes quickly swept over her. She saw the moment that he noticed the X on her hip. He paused, and his eyes widened for a millisecond. Embarrassed, she adjusted her dress once again to cover the exposed skin. Apologies to Valentino Garavani, but she was going to burn this dress the first chance she got. She could only imagine how she looked right now. Walking around in a dress that showed off the tattoo that was dedicated to him!

Yet she was dying to know if he still had his tattoo as well. Pride kept her from asking.

"Thank you," she finally said, looking away again.

"This is a beautiful thing." Raheem put his arms around Violet and Xavier and pulled them into a group hug. "The old crew back together again like old times. We're just missing B."

Violet looked across at Xavier, who stared back at her. The corner of his mouth lifted into an awkward smile. God, this was so weird.

Suddenly, the lobby grew louder, and people pulled out their phones, angling them toward the elevator. Fans began shouting for Karamel Kitty.

"That's my cue," Violet said, disentangling herself from the group hug. She glanced at Xavier, struggling to come to terms with the fact that he was really in front of her, flesh and blood. "It was, um, nice to—"

"Wait, Violet, you gotta introduce me to Karamel Kitty," Raheem said, clasping her hand in his. "Please, she's my favorite rapper. Bianca's too. We love her!"

"You don't have to do that," Xavier said, removing Raheem's grasp from Violet's hand. He smiled at her again, and her silly, traitorous heartbeat went on the fritz. "But if you're ever back in Willow Ridge, maybe we—"

"No, I need to meet her!" Raheem begged. "When will I ever get this chance again?"

Violet shot Raheem an annoyed look. What had Xavier been about to say? If she were back in Willow Ridge, maybe what? More importantly, why did she care?!

The shouts from the crowd grew louder. Violet turned,

and Karina and crew were walking in her direction, flanked by her bodyguard and the additional hotel security. Karina waved and blew kisses to her fans. When she spotted Violet, she threw her arms up like, *Girl, where the hell have you been?*

"Sorry," Violet said, once Karina plus entourage reached them. "These are old friends from high school, Raheem and Xavier."

Karina raised an eyebrow, and Violet nodded once. Confirming that, yes, this was *that* Xavier. Karina knew all about Violet's harrowing bout with first love thanks to that fateful day they'd spent trapped inside the elevator in Québec.

"How y'all doing?" Karina asked. Raheem's open-mouthed stare could have caught flies as he shook Karina's hand. Xavier shook Karina's hand as well, but Violet felt his eyes on her the entire time.

"Okay, we really need to get going," Edwin said, coming forward.

"Oh, which club y'all going to?" Raheem asked.

"The one in the hotel," Karina answered. She smirked, like Raheem amused her.

"Same as us! We should go together."

Raheem suggested this so easily, as if he and Karina, a Grammy-nominated rapper, had been friends for years and didn't just meet two seconds ago. Beside him, Xavier grimaced.

Violet and Karina exchanged another glance. Karina furrowed her brows, her way of asking if Violet cared whether or not Xavier and Raheem joined them. Violet would prefer it they did *not* join them. But she didn't want to make this situation more awkward by telling them no, especially because Raheem looked so *excited*.

After she and Xavier had officially ended things all those years ago and Raheem had no real reason to keep in contact with Violet, he'd continued to reach out every once in a while to see how she was doing. Before she'd changed her number to one with a New York area code.

In answer, Violet subtly lifted her shoulder and shrugged. Karina blinked once. *You sure?* Violet cleared her throat. *Yep.*

"Yeah, you can come," Karina said. She gestured to Edwin. "Can you add their names to the list, boo?"

Edwin quickly took down Xavier's and Raheem's information, and Violet finally had a chance to break away. She went over to Alex and asked if she'd found the boob tape for Karina, then she asked if the rest of the dresses were ready to be shipped back to her Manhattan studio space in the morning. And all the while, she pretended like she couldn't feel Xavier watching her.

At the club, she'd make sure to put a fair amount of distance between them. She didn't have to make a big deal out of this. He'd popped her cherry and had been the object of her hormone-crazed teenage affections. So what? It was old news.

After tonight, she'd never have to see Xavier again.

4

AS VIOLET SAT ACROSS FROM XAVIER IN VIP, SHE TRIED her hardest to pretend he wasn't there at all. Karina and Raheem were passing a bottle of Rémy back and forth and shouting to the crowd below, while Karina's bodyguard kept his eyes trained on Raheem like he was ready to tackle him at any moment. Melody and Brian were sharing a plate of chicken wings, and beside Violet, Edwin and Alex looked like they were comparing schedules on their phones.

Unwarranted, Violet's gaze found its way across the table to Xavier. He sat with his arms spread out on either side of him. His cardigan looked out of place in their current setting, but she begrudgingly admitted that he wore it well. He turned suddenly and caught her staring. She quickly glanced away and pulled out her phone. She needed to text an update to the sister group chat, stat.

Hey, she texted Iris and Lily, are either of you awake?

Iris spent her days as the head of partnerships at a makeup company, commuting to the city from her house in Willow Ridge, where she lived with her four-year-old daughter, Calla.

And Lily, a children's book editor, lived in Brooklyn. Neither was a night owl, and it was after one a.m. on the East Coast, so Violet expected her text to fall into the void. Thankfully, she received an immediate response.

Iris: I'm awake. Stuck watching Flip or Flop on HGTV. Do you think I should redecorate Calla's bedroom?

Violet: Does Calla want her room redecorated?

Iris: She hasn't said anything about it.

Violet: Then no. Anyway, you will not believe who is in VIP with me right now

Lily: I'm up too! Crash editing. Please tell me you're in VIP with Beyoncé

Violet: If only I could be so lucky

Iris: Hmm. Let me guess, another famous person?

Violet: Not famous

Lily: Why don't you ever hang out with Beyoncé?

Violet: Lily, focus!

Iris: I hate guessing games.

Lily: Is it Michael B. Jordan?

Violet: I just said they're not famous!

Iris: Why don't you just tell us? We clearly don't know.

Violet: Jesus. It's Xavier.

For several long seconds, neither sister texted back.

Violet: Hello???

Iris: As in Xavier Wright?

Lily: Your ex-boyfriend???

Violet: Yes, that Xavier! He's here in Vegas with Raheem

Lily: Oh wow. What are the odds??

Iris: That has to be so awkward.

Violet: Awkward doesn't even begin to cover it!

"So, I'm an old friend from high school?"

Violet startled at the deep voice in her ear. She turned to find Xavier sitting right beside her. Within the last few minutes, Edwin and Alex had left VIP and Xavier had taken their place on the couch, and Violet hadn't noticed because she'd been so preoccupied with texting her sisters.

She blinked at him and his sudden closeness. "What?"

"You told Karamel Kitty that I was an 'old friend' from high school." He put "old friend" in air quotes. "Is that what we are to each other now?"

She raised an eyebrow. His expression was curious, no hint of teasing.

"Well, we were friends too." She paused, assessing him. "Weren't we?"

He nodded. "Best friends."

He *had* been her best friend. And then one day in the blink of an eye, that was no longer the case.

"Yeah, well, you had a lot of friends in high school." She pointed at Raheem, who was letting Karina pour cognac into his mouth straight from the bottle. "Like that one over there. Looks like he's having the time of his life."

Xavier laughed. She cataloged his husky chuckle as another difference between then and now. "He won't be able to shut up about tonight once we're back home."

Violet smiled a little, unsure of what to say next. She didn't want to invest too much energy in this conversation or in Xavier, period. As curious as she was about him, she didn't think he deserved her attention. A delicate silence stretched between them.

"Do you—" he said.

"So—" she said.

Xavier laughed again. "Go ahead."

Violet shook her head. "No, you first."

"Do you do this often?" he asked, gesturing at their surroundings. The DJ shouting over the music, the roaring crowd on the dance floor below them. Karina being larger than life, twerking like it was a sport.

"Sometimes," she answered. "It depends."

"On what?"

"My client. My energy levels."

"Huh," he said, and she wondered what he really thought about her lifestyle. Was it too chaotic for him? Years ago, he would have been soaking it all up just like Raheem. That was another difference. Adult Xavier seemed calmer. "What were you going to ask me?"

She didn't remember what she'd been about to ask. The questions she really wanted answers to were not allowed to pass her lips. Questions like, How did he break her heart so easily and never look back? Did it take him years to get over her too? Did he spend his early to mid-twenties avoiding serious commitment because he was terrified someone else would break his heart the same way?

"My mom told me you're teaching at the high school now," she said. "I was going to ask what that's like."

"It's not bad." He shrugged and leaned back on the couch. She noticed his large wingspan as he spread his arms out on either side of him again. "I teach sophomore English. Definitely not what I saw myself doing with my life. That's for sure. But it could be worse." He smiled, boyish and self-deprecating. "Why are you looking at me like that?"

"I'm just . . . surprised," she said. When her parents had

first told her that Xavier was teaching, she'd assumed he taught PE. He'd been so active in high school, and sitting in class made him antsy. She'd pictured him with a whistle around his neck, wearing Willow Ridge High's green and yellow school colors. She didn't expect him to be teaching English. She thought of their long-suffering junior-year teacher, Mr. Rodney, who they'd all jokingly said looked like Morgan Freeman, and who'd tried his best to get their class excited about *1984* and *Macbeth*. Whenever they'd read the play aloud, Xavier always requested to be Macbeth, and he'd read in a deep, gravelly voice that made everyone laugh, even a slightly exasperated Mr. Rodney. "I bet Mr. Rodney loves having you as a colleague now. If he still works there, that is."

"Oh yeah, he's still there," Xavier said. "Mr. Rodney is a lifer, the type of teacher who won't quit until you have to wheel them out on a stretcher. He showed me the ropes when I first started. Every Thursday we get Taco Bell for lunch and eat together in the teachers' lounge. Sometimes it's the highlight of my week. Teaching is rewarding but hella stressful."

"I'll bet."

"Mr. Rodney still coaches boys' basketball, and I'm the assistant coach now, actually," he said, and she heard the hint of pride in his voice. "We've been undefeated this season. We might even have a championship on our hands. It'll be the first time Willow Ridge has won since we were seniors."

"Wow, that's awesome." She wanted to ask what had happened to *his* basketball dreams. After his injury, she knew that he hadn't gone back to Kentucky and instead finished his degree at the local state college, Riley University. But she didn't know if that was a sensitive topic.

"Thanks," he said.

He smiled at her, and as her eyes drifted down to his mouth, she noted another similarity: he still had nice lips. She cleared her throat and looked away. Melody and Brian were now up dancing with Raheem and Karina, which meant Violet and Xavier were the only two left sitting.

Xavier leaned forward and poured himself another shot of Rémy. He held the bottle out to Violet. "Do you want some?"

She didn't really feel like drinking. It was almost eleven p.m., and she was exhausted. Then again, one of the reasons she was so exhausted was because she was overthinking everything about her current interaction with Xavier. She wouldn't be able to get through the rest of this night completely sober.

"Sure." She held out her tumbler and watched as Xavier slowly poured her a shot. They knocked glasses and downed the cognac. Violet winced, and Xavier coughed. She felt herself grin. "Remember when we drank a whole bottle of my dad's peach schnapps after junior homecoming like it was nothing? Now we can't take one shot without damn near choking."

Xavier laughed. "There was also that time we drove to Wildwood and you drank half a handle of Jose Cuervo and tried to run into the ocean with the seagulls. Luckily I was there to save you."

"You know that is *not* what happened," she said, rolling

her eyes. "A seagull stole my bag of chips and I chased after it."

"But I was still there to save you."

"If lifting me over your shoulder caveman-style while the seagull got away with my salt-and-vinegar chips counts as saving me, then sure."

"Salt and vinegar." Xavier shuddered. "I forgot how much you loved those."

"Still do," she said proudly. "The best flavor there is." He started to speak, and she held up her hand, stopping him. "Don't say honey barbecue is better. I'm not up for an argument."

Xavier placed a hand over his chest, feigning shock. "Violet Greene refusing to argue? I never thought I'd see the day."

She narrowed her eyes at him, and he smiled slowly, as if he knew exactly what he was doing. Goading her. Just like old times.

It was both exciting and alarming.

He was still smiling as he shifted a little closer to her, and as if she was being pulled by an invisible string, Violet moved closer as well. His eyes lowered, searching her face, briefly landing on her mouth. Her pulse quickened, and— Wait, what the hell was happening?

Violet stood suddenly. If they were going to be stuck together, they needed to be as preoccupied as possible. No more sitting and talking alone. She poured herself another shot and swallowed it in a quick gulp.

She wasn't going to see Xavier again after tonight, so there was no reason to regret what she said next.

"Wanna dance?" she asked.

Xavier raised an eyebrow. "Up here?"

"No." She pointed to the dance floor. "Down there."

He threw back another shot too. Apparently, she wasn't the only one who needed a little liquid courage. "Let's do it."

5

XAVIER FOLLOWED VIOLET ONTO THE DANCE FLOOR, HIS gaze glued to the back of her as she expertly snaked her way through the dense, pulsing crowd. The base vibrated through the sticky club floor and people pressed against Xavier from either side. But his attention was trained on Violet. His eyes traveled from the elegant slope of her neck to her small waist and generous hips. She was stunning. She'd only grown even more beautiful in the last decade. She glanced over her shoulder to make sure that he was still behind her, and when she caught him obviously checking her out, she quirked an eyebrow and turned back around, continuing her journey through the throng of bodies.

He wanted to touch her somehow, place his hand on the small of her back or gently brush the curve of her elbow. Anything to feel closer to her, even if it was just a facade. She still had that signature Violet air. A slight aloofness. Slightly uninterested. Slightly unattainable. It had been the reason she'd caught his eye all those years ago across the gymnasium. When he'd approached her that day, he had no way of knowing she'd become the most important person in his life. The person he'd never be able to forget.

In the years since their breakup, he'd often imagined what he might do or say if he ever ran into Violet again. He'd explain why he broke up with her the way he did. That after his injury and his lackluster year and a half spent in Kentucky, he'd realized that maybe he didn't have what it took to go professional after all. Meanwhile, Violet was soaring, just like she'd planned. He couldn't keep up. He was holding her back. He wasn't good enough for her. He was a failure, and in the long run, she would be happier if he let her go. The logic of an insecure nineteen-year-old. He'd tell her how sorry he was and that breaking her heart broke him.

He didn't know if Violet ever forgave him in this imagined conversation. His daydreams never dared go that far.

Once they were smack-dab in the middle of the dance floor, Violet finally stopped and spun around to face Xavier. She began nodding and moving her hips along to the music. Xavier nodded too. The DJ was playing another Karamel Kitty song. Violet rapped the lyrics bar for bar, not missing a single word. She looked so *cool*. Without even trying, she had always been the coolest girl in the room. She was what his students would refer to as "goals."

"My students would be impressed by you," he said. When he spoke, his words felt slow and delayed on his tongue. He was a lot tipsier than he'd realized.

"What?" Violet shouted over the music, leaning forward to hear him better.

His gaze fell to her full lips and he cleared his throat. "I said my students would be impressed by you!"

"Me?" She tilted her head. "Really? Why?"

"Because you're you."

He inwardly grimaced at his honesty. *Reel it in, X, damn.*

Violet's eyes swept over him, curious and assessing. He wondered what she thought of him now. Was she disappointed in him? His life was a far cry from the dreams he used to whisper to her in the middle of the night while they lay side by side in her bed.

Violet put her hands in the air with the rest of the crowd as she continued to dance. Her cheeks were flushed, her forehead and neckline slightly damp with sweat.

The DJ suddenly switched the song to "No Hands," and everyone, including Xavier and Violet, shouted, "Ayyy."

This song had played at almost every house party during their senior year of high school. It was as if they'd passed through a time machine as they moved closer to each other, laughing and rapping along to the music, lulled by the booming base and nostalgia. By the time the DJ switched to another song, Xavier and Violet were sweaty and breathless. She was grinning at him, and the corners of Xavier's mouth curved upward in response. The coolness that had cloaked her since earlier tonight was finally beginning to lift, and he felt intense relief.

She pointed to the bar. "Buy me another drink?"

"You don't even have to ask. You know I got you."

She rolled her eyes but laughed. At the bar, Xavier opened a tab and ordered two glasses of Rémy and Coke. He was burning a hole through his wallet and he'd chastise himself in the morning, but he could go back to living on a budget tomorrow. Tonight, he wanted to keep Violet happy. After everything, the very least he owed her was a top-shelf cocktail.

The bartender returned with their drinks, and Xavier and Violet crowded close together to avoid bumping into the people around them. He was enveloped by her floral perfume, and when their arms brushed, tingles spread across his skin.

"You smell nice," he said, taking a swig of his drink. He was grateful for the way the alcohol continued to loosen him up so that he wasn't a blubbering mess in her presence, unsure of the right thing to say.

Violet looked over at him with a smirk. "I know."

He chuckled and shook his head. "Damn, that's how you accept compliments nowadays?"

"Was it a compliment or was it just a fact?" She pivoted so that she was facing him head-on. His gaze landed on her full lips again, painted a deep plum shade. He watched intently as her smirk morphed into an alluring smile.

"Both," he said, easily entranced.

"Then I guess I should say thank you." She was still smiling at him as she shrugged and took a long sip of her drink. "You smell nice too."

He laughed. "You're just saying that because I gave you a compliment first."

"No, I mean it," she argued, laughing too. "You smell minty."

"Minty?"

"Mm-hmm." She finished her drink and set it on the bar. "Fresh."

"I'll take fresh." He downed the rest of his cocktail as well, beginning to feel warm in his cardigan. "Thank you."

"You're welcome."

Violet waved down the bartender for another round. As they waited for their drinks, Violet placed her hands flat on the bar top, and Xavier looked down at her bare left ring finger. Last spring, when he'd checked her Instagram, he'd noticed the sparkling diamond on her left hand in one of her photos as she posed beside a brown-skinned bald dude who was wearing a clean-ass suit. Xavier had felt an intense pressure in his chest, like his heart was literally being squeezed. But he had no reason to be surprised. Of course Violet was engaged. Of course someone had scooped her up. Of course her fiancé was a well-to-do person who could afford to buy her a huge rock.

But then a few months later, in another photo, the ring was noticeably absent, along with the fiancé. She'd deleted all evidence of their relationship from her page. In place of a wedding, she'd thrown a lavish breakup party where everyone wore black. He only knew about it because Bianca had gone.

"You can ask me, you know," she said, as the bartender placed their drinks in front of them and they reached for their glasses. This time, the liquor no longer burned when Xavier took a sip. It went down easy.

He glanced up at Violet. She was watching him. "Ask you what?"

"You can ask about my lack of an engagement ring. I'm sure you've heard about it."

"Oh." He wanted to know more, but he had no right to that information. "I mean, it's your business."

"Yeah, my business that was printed in TMZ." She sipped her drink again and cleared her throat. "Two weeks before our wedding, my ex-fiancé cheated on me with Meela Baybee." She set down her glass. "Before I started working with Meela, she wore neon bodycon dresses with Air Forces to her shows. *Air Forces.* She opened a show for Karina once, and I offered to be her stylist because I saw that she needed help. Then I introduced her to Eddy because she needed a new manager. I was trying to be kind. Look where that got me."

"Damn, that's fucked up," Xavier said, frowning. He wracked his mind for a mental image of the singer she'd mentioned, but he came up empty. Even if he was completely sober, he was unsure if he'd be able to place her. "But I'm sorry, Meela who?"

"Oh, I love you for saying that." Violet cackled, throwing her head back. Her movements became looser as she took another gulp of her drink. Then she abruptly froze when she realized Xavier was gaping at her. "I mean, you not knowing who Meela Baybee is makes me feel better. I don't, like, love you. I mean, I—" She stared down at her glass and forced a laugh. "Jesus, what's in this drink?"

Xavier tried to pretend that the quickening of his heartbeat had nothing to do with hearing Violet say that she loved him, even in an unserious context.

"What's he like?" he asked, because, fuck it, he was curious. "Your ex."

"Eddy is . . ." She trailed off, shrugging. "Eddy is a 'we' guy."

"A 'we' guy?"

She nodded. "From the beginning, it was we. *We* are going to get dinner Friday night at the new spot he's heard about on the West Side. *We* are going to Cardi B's birthday party in the Hamptons. *We* are going to spend Christmas in the Maldives."

Xavier whistled. "The Maldives?"

"He could be unnecessarily lavish," she said, sighing.

"Damn," Xavier mumbled under his breath. He'd never be able to afford a vacation like that.

"Yeah, it was a whirlwind," she said. "We'd only been dating three months when he proposed. It sounds stupid now, but I thought we'd be happy. We looked good together on paper." She pursed her lips. "But it was all for show. He just liked having me in his pocket and on his arm. I don't think he actually cared about me that much as a person. He even had the nerve to be shocked when I called off the wedding. Now I guess he's with Meela. Good riddance to both of them."

"He's a clown," Xavier said, feeling pissed on Violet's behalf. "Fuck 'em."

"Yeah . . . well, he wouldn't be the first guy to break my heart." She slid him a cool glance.

Shit. He deserved that. It had been a long time coming.

"I'm sorry," he said, turning to face her completely. "Breaking up with you the way that I did without warning . . . it was so wrong. It's one of my biggest regrets. I was young and stupid. I'm so sorry."

He wanted to continue, to tell her the full truth behind his ill-conceived decision to end their relationship, but as he looked at her, so glamorous and accomplished, he couldn't bring himself to admit the rest. How he'd felt unworthy of her love or invested time. He didn't need to tell her that he'd thought about that moment on his porch for years afterward, and that the memory still materialized in his thoughts at the most unexpected times. She'd moved on. Her life seemed great. She didn't want to hear any sad old shit from him. Plus, his thoughts were too hazy. The last place they should have this conversation was in the middle of a loud-ass club when neither of them was fully sober.

She stared at him, and her tight expression softened somewhat. "I've waited years to hear you apologize to me. And now . . ."

"And now?" he prompted, his gaze searching.

She blinked, then snorted. "And now I think I'm too drunk to have this conversation."

Xavier laughed. "If it makes you feel any better, karma did come to get her revenge. My most recent ex broke up with me through text to say that she was not only leaving me but also leaving the country."

"Really?" Violet's eyes widened comically. "*Damn.*"

"Yep."

"My mom did mention that you were single again. She said your ex was a guidance counselor who quit her job to hike through, um . . ." She squinted, trying to regain her train of thought as she swirled her drink in her hand. "The rain forest!"

"That's basically what happened."

Xavier thought of that morning over a year ago when he'd woken up to Michelle's text. By the time he'd read it, she'd already been on her way to the airport to begin her carefree lifestyle backpacking through Chile. Their breakup had hurt, but ultimately Xavier had been relieved. He cared about Michelle, but no matter how hard he'd tried, something had never felt quite right between them. He'd loved her, but it was more like the love you have for a friend instead of a soulmate. In fact, he and Michelle had remained friends. Every now and then, she emailed pictures of her travels. They weren't really in each other's lives anymore, but they weren't on bad terms.

"Wait," he said. His brain was working overtime to function through the cognac fog. "That's the second time you mentioned your mom told you something about me."

"She's randomly updated me on your life once or twice," Violet said. She took one look at Xavier's expression and rolled her eyes. "Stop smiling like that. It's not like you're the topic of conversation every time we speak."

He didn't stop smiling. "It's cool. My mom asks about you every now and then too. She's in Key West right now with her boyfriend. He has a house there, so that's where she stays during winter."

"Okay, Tricia's got herself a little time-share boo," Violet said, and Xavier laughed. "How's your dad?"

"He's good. Still in Savannah. We talk every few weeks or so."

After his parents' divorce and his dad's move down south, Xavier's relationship with his dad had been rocky. There was the physical distance between them and the fact that his dad's infidelity had broken up their family. Xavier had been mad at his dad for a long time. But he realized the resentment was eating away at him, and he no longer wanted to hold on to that energy. He decided to forgive his dad, and through him he'd learned a valuable lesson: never waste a woman's time.

Xavier finished the last of his drink, and Violet finished hers as well. He pointed to her empty glass.

"Another?"

She nodded. "Yes, please."

"Well, since you said please," he joked, signaling to the bartender.

"You know, it's funny that you and my mom are such big fans of each other now, when she always acted like she wanted to have you arrested back when we were dating," Violet said.

Xavier smiled, and their new drinks landed in front of them. They both took slow sips. "I always knew I'd win her over eventually."

Violet shook her head, smile still in place. "My mom was so upset about the Eddy stuff. She never really liked him. None of my family did, actually. They thought he was too smarmy. Lily was the only one who was nice to him, but she likes everyone."

Xavier remembered how kind and welcoming her younger sister, Lily, had always been, while Iris had always been a little harder to get to know.

"How is Lily?" he asked. "And Iris? I was really sorry to

hear about her husband's car accident a couple years ago, by the way."

"Yeah. Terry's death was pretty hard on everyone," Violet said. "It was the hardest for Iris, obviously."

Everyone in Willow Ridge knew Iris's story. How she'd graduated from Princeton with top honors and then went to business school at NYU, where she'd met her husband, Terry, and when they'd discovered that she was pregnant, they'd left the city and moved back to Willow Ridge to live in the same subdivision as Violet's parents. Iris gave birth to a baby girl, who was just shy of a year old when Terry died. Xavier hadn't known Terry very well, but he'd easily immersed himself in their close community and shown up to every fundraiser and event with a smile on his face, ready to help. He was a good dude.

Violet fell quiet for a moment, using her straw to move around the ice in her drink. "Everyone's doing okay, though," she said. "Iris is busy with work and being a supermom. Lily's in New York, editing children's books. She has this writer boyfriend that she's obsessed with. They're so cute it makes me want to barf."

"Wow. Good for Lily."

"Maybe. Some people get lucky. But in my opinion, love is for suckers. I'm done with that shit. I'm focused on me and my money. That's it."

"I hear you," he said, thinking of how he was choosing to put his energy into landing the assistant coach position at Riley. "I just want to get further in my career."

"Cheers to that!" She lifted her glass, and Xavier did the same.

They knocked their glasses together and laughed when some of their drinks spilled onto the floor.

"Remember when we thought we'd get married?" she said, still laughing. "God, we were so naive."

He stopped laughing then. They'd been naive, yes. But he'd meant every word he'd said to her that night.

"Oh! This is my song!" Violet squealed, unaware of how her words affected him. "Come on!"

She dragged him back on the dance floor and intertwined her fingers with his as they were absorbed by the crowd again. His heartbeat quickened. Being together with her like this felt so natural. He didn't know if he should be relieved or worried.

They'd only been on the dance floor for a few minutes before one of her friends (Brian maybe?) pushed forward toward them, calling to Violet.

"Karina's ready to go to the next spot," he yelled over the music. "I'm tired as hell so I'm going back to my room. You staying or going?"

"Oh, um. I think . . . I'll stay a little longer," Violet said. She turned to Xavier. "Unless you want to leave too."

His answer was automatic: "I'll stay."

Brian glanced between the two of them and smirked. "Okay. Have fun and stay safe. Don't forget the car is taking us to the airport at six a.m." He pecked Violet on the cheek and disappeared through the crowd.

Xavier pulled out his phone and sent a quick text to Raheem. Staying out with Violet.

Raheem replied immediately. Oh shit!! You want that old thing back!

Xavier ignored his cousin's response and returned his phone to his front pocket. When he looked at Violet again, she was smiling at him. He felt airless.

"You sure you can hang, Mr. Teacher?" she asked, raising an eyebrow. A seductive challenge.

"Absolutely."

"Okay then." She turned so that her back was to him and she began to slowly wind her hips to the beat. He placed his hands on her waist, pulling her closer. He leaned down to her and when his lips gently brushed against the back of her neck, Violet didn't move away. He inhaled the flowery, intoxicating scent of her perfume.

. . . And that was the last thing he remembered.

6

AN INCESSANT VIBRATION WOKE VIOLET IN THE MORNING.
She cracked one eye open and winced at the sunlight peeking through the blinds. Her mouth was dry, like something
had died on her tongue overnight, and her temples were
throbbing, a punishment for drinking too much. Her body
felt unnaturally heated, and it took her a delayed moment
to realize that an arm was draped across her midriff. The
arm was attached to a body that was spooning her from
behind. All hard angles pressed against her softness. Startled, she struggled to sit up. Pain zinged across her forehead
at the sudden movement. She looked down to see Xavier
lying beside her, snoring softly. Naked. His body was so
beautifully sculpted with his strong arms and defined chest,
she was momentarily too dazed to react. Then she felt the
cool air against her bare breasts and she realized that she
was naked too.

"*Oh my God,*" she hissed, grabbing the comforter to cover
herself.

Her eyes darted around the room. Her dress was draped
across the chair near the bed, and her heels were lying on

the floor at least a yard apart, like she'd thrown them off while hastily undressing. What the hell happened last night? She rubbed a hand over her face, and that was when she noticed the most damning things of all.

Two shiny gold rings on her left ring finger: a small white diamond set against a yellow-gold band, atop a matching plain gold band.

Suddenly, memories from last night flooded her brain. Laughing with Xavier at the club. Grinding against him on the dance floor, his hands on her waist, her ass on his crotch. His lips lingering at her neck. More drinks. More grinding. Oh God. Making out with him on the dance floor! And later, mentioning their marriage plan and teasing him, saying that she'd never get married now because she was too much for any man. She remembered the self-assured look on Xavier's face as he'd accepted her challenge, saying he'd marry her that night. The moments after were a blur, but she could vaguely recall stripping off her clothes and straddling him on the bed.

"Oh my God. No no no no no." Violet scrambled out of the bed, tripped over the tangle of sheets, and fell into a heap on the floor . . . where she discovered a used condom in the trash bin. She put her head in her hands and felt the cool plastic of the rings against her forehead.

Stupefied, she stared at the rings. The fake princess-cut diamond and gold bands were garishly shiny. Maybe they'd only joked about getting married and hadn't actually gone through with it. Yeah, that made more sense! There was no way this could be real. The ring had a rhinestone diamond, for fuck's sake!

Her phone vibrated on the bedside table and Violet quickly reached up and grabbed it because she didn't want the noise to wake Xavier. She wasn't ready to face him yet. Not until she felt like she had a hold of herself and this situation. She silenced her alarm and—oh crap, it was 5:50 in the morning! She was supposed to be in the lobby with everyone else, waiting for the car that would take them to the airport. Her phone vibrated again with a text from Alex saying that everyone was downstairs waiting for her. With rapid-fire speed, Violet texted back to say that she was on her way. She grabbed the side of the bed and heaved herself upright. Then she sucked in a gasp when she saw a photograph of her and Xavier on the bedside table.

They were kissing inside a wedding chapel. Xavier's hands were clasped on either side of Violet's face, and her arms were wrapped around his torso, squeezing him close. They looked nothing like a typical newlywed couple, with Violet in her sexy black gown and Xavier wearing a cardigan and jeans. They looked like two horny, drunk people who'd made a terrible mistake.

"Oh my Godddddddddd," she groaned. Her heart was beating out of control. Was she about to have a panic attack?

"Wh-what?" Xavier mumbled, stirring awake. He rolled onto his back and rubbed his eyes, blinking at Violet. Slowly, he sat up in bed and looked around the room. His brows furrowed in confusion, and Violet froze, staring at him and his smooth, muscular chest. His tight abs. Her stomach filled with butterflies.

Xavier's gaze returned to her and she saw the heat in his stare as he openly appraised her equally naked body. She suddenly felt warm all over as they viewed each other, so exposed. Then she came to her senses and hustled across the room, shrugging on a pair of underwear and her Off-White sweats combo from yesterday. She turned to face him again. She didn't even know where to begin.

"Hey," he said, scratching the back of his neck. He smiled hesitantly. "Last night must have been wild. I don't remember anything." He paused and took in Violet's silence. He frowned. "Are you okay?"

"Xavier . . ." Maybe it would be best to show him rather than tell him.

She walked to the bedside table and picked up the wedding chapel photograph and handed it to Xavier. His face scrunched up as he tried to make sense of what he was looking at. He glanced back and forth between Violet and the photo, and his eyes grew wider as the seconds ticked by.

"Shit," he whispered, dragging a hand over his face. And in that moment, they both realized he wore a gold band on his left ring finger too. He stared at his own hand in shock. "*Fuck*, I kinda remember getting an Uber to the chapel after we left the club. Shit, shit, shit."

"So this is real?" Violet squeaked. "We really got married?"

"I—I think so." More quietly, he mumbled, "Fuck. What the fuck."

He glanced at Violet's left hand, and she tugged the rings off her finger and slipped them into her pocket.

"I don't even know where we got these," she muttered.

Xavier reached down and grabbed his wallet off the ground. He sifted through the contents and pulled out a tiny piece of paper. Then he let out a relieved sigh.

"You'll find your answer here," he said, holding out the piece of paper for Violet.

She stepped forward gingerly and took the paper from him. It was a receipt from the Ye Olde Vegas Chapel. He'd been charged one hundred and forty-nine dollars plus tax for the Pretend Package: a fake wedding service performed by a pretend officiant, which included a minister's fee, a photograph and a set of rings.

"Oh," she murmured, overcome with relief. They weren't actually married. Thank God.

They fell silent, staring at each other. The familiar comradery that they'd worked hard to revive last night was no longer present. Now they were estranged again. Estranged... and fake spouses?

"Crisis averted, I guess," Violet said. Her gaze dropped to Xavier's chest again and heat crept up her neck as she glanced away.

"Yeah," he said quietly. "That would have been wild, right?"

Before she could answer, her phone vibrated again, this time with a call from Alex. Violet snapped back to the more important matter at hand. She had to fly to New York. She had a potentially career-catapulting interview with *Look Magazine* in a matter of hours. *That* was what needed her attention. Not the consequences of her drunken hookup with her ex-boyfriend.

"I'm so sorry, but I have to go," she said to Xavier, as she dashed around the room, grabbing her suitcase and stuffing her feet into her sneakers. "I have to catch a flight to New York, like, right now." She zipped her Valentino gown into a garment bag and placed her heels in her suitcase. Then she rushed to the bathroom and brushed her teeth, haphazardly wiping makeup remover across her eyes and lips. Her one saving grace was that Brian's updo from last night had stayed intact.

She hurried out of the bathroom, and Xavier was still sitting up, watching her.

"Do you need help?" he asked, climbing out of bed.

He bent over and reached for his boxers, and Violet caught a quick glimpse of his body in its full glory. An electric jolt shot through her and settled right between her legs. She wished she could remember their sex from last night. Had it been good? She'd been sprung off him in high school. But they were adults now, with more experience. Surely it had been even better?

Her eyes were drawn to the tattoo of a violet on the inside of his right bicep. It was the first time since their reunion that she'd gotten a glimpse of the simple purple flower, the thin green stem and leaves. Her chest tightened as sudden relief washed over her. After everything, he still had his tattoo as well. She hated that it mattered to her.

Xavier cleared his throat as he buttoned his jeans and she realized she'd been staring. Her gaze flew back up to his face, and for a second, she swore that she caught him grinning at her.

"I don't need any help, thanks." She shoved on her sunglasses and hustled to the door. "Checkout isn't until eleven, so you can sleep in if you want. Or not. Your choice. It was, um, interesting seeing you again. Have a great life."

Xavier made a reply, but she couldn't hear what he said

because she was too busy rushing out of the room like a wild woman. Running from Xavier. Running from her embarrassment. What in the world had possessed her to hook up with him like that? She needed to put her own damn self in time-out. She also needed to do an alcohol detox, apparently.

Once she reached the lobby, her team let out a collective sigh of relief.

"Oh, thank God," Alex said, rushing forward with a water bottle. "I thought you might need this."

"*Thank you.* I'm so sorry for running late, everyone."

She unscrewed the cap and chugged half the bottle.

"Okay, camel," Brian said, snorting. Violet shot him a look.

"Somebody had fun last night," Karina whispered, looping her arm through Violet's as they walked out to the SUV that would take them to the airport.

While Violet and Alex were flying to New York, Karina and the rest of the team were headed to Atlanta. Violet and Karina sat side by side in the back row of the SUV, and while everyone else quickly fell asleep, Violet was wide awake. She had a hangover, and on top of that, she had to ruminate on her ridiculous, drunken decisions. How could she have behaved that way last night with *Xavier*, of all people? She was furious with herself. After the way he broke her heart, she shouldn't have allowed him to have such easy access to her. It only proved that nine years later, she was still weak where he was concerned.

"Girl," Karina said quietly, softly nudging Violet. "Are you gonna tell me what happened with you and your high school boo last night or nah?"

Violet winced. "Or nah?"

"You better tell me." Karina playfully smacked Violet's shoulder, but her laughter stopped when she noticed the stricken look on Violet's face. "Vi, what happened?"

In a hushed whisper, Violet told Karina everything. At least the parts that she remembered. And she told her about her interaction with Xavier moments before she met everyone in the lobby. When she finished speaking, Karina's jaw was on the floor.

"Damn," she hissed. "I thought you were out last night finally getting some D, but you were in the process of becoming somebody's whole-ass wife."

"*Shhh.*" Violet covered Karina's mouth with her hand and Karina pushed her away, laughing. "It was fake. Nobody can ever know, so don't say anything."

"Hmm." Karina tilted her head and gave Violet a long, appraising stare. Then she shrugged and swiveled forward.

"What?" Violet said. "What is that 'hmm' supposed to mean?"

"I don't know. I'm just wondering what it says about you and ol' boy that in your most vulnerable, inebriated states, y'all decided to have a pretend wedding when y'all could have done literally anything else. That's pretty significant, don't you think?"

"*No,*" Violet said. "It's not significant. It's foolish."

Karina shrugged again. "I'm not about to argue with you, Miss Bride."

Violet glared at her and Karina laughed, hugging Violet sideways. "It's all good. Like you said, it wasn't real. You know how I do. No need to stress over somebody who isn't cutting a check."

"Yeah, no need to stress," Violet mumbled.

Karina nodded and snuggled down in her seat, promptly falling asleep. That was what Violet needed to be doing. Sleeping. Mentally preparing for her *Look Magazine* interview. She didn't need to overanalyze Karina's words, because Karina didn't know what she was talking about. There was no reason to read any deeper into Violet and Xavier's actions. They'd spent their entire relationship challenging each other to do silly, ill-conceived things. Like sneaking into pools and getting tattoos. Last night's fake wedding was proof that as adults, they somehow still felt the need to needle each other into making big mistakes.

But unlike her tattoo, this mistake was one she could forget about.

7

HOURS LATER, VIOLET LEANED BACK AGAINST THE FLOOR-to-ceiling windows in her downtown Manhattan studio and surveyed her workspace, hoping it looked organized and accomplished. Olivia Hutch, the *Look Magazine* journalist, would arrive soon, and she was one of the most prominent fashion journalists in the business. She'd been covering fashion since Violet's time at FIDM, and for the past five years, she'd worked as a senior editor for *Look Magazine*, profiling noteworthy stylists, like Law Roach before his retirement and Jason Bolden. Violet's portfolio had been impressive enough to land her on the long list for the "30 Under 30 in Style" feature, but Olivia Hutch was essentially the final boss. There was a rumor that she'd once barred a stylist from making the list because she'd found their workspace to be too cluttered. Luckily, that wasn't a particular problem that Violet had to worry about.

Before her, racks of clothing stretched from wall to wall, concealing a large wooden table in the center of the room that was dedicated to shoes and jewelry. She began renting this studio two years ago when her client roster allowed her to afford her own space instead of sharing a studio in Williamsburg with two other stylists. Her studio, with its classic white walls and ample sunshine, was her happy place. A symbol of her accomplishments. But it was also the same place where she'd spent dozens of sleepless nights, fought off tension headaches and chewed on Kind bars in between fittings because she didn't have time to eat a full meal. In her early twenties, she'd thrived in hustle culture. Now, although she hated to admit it, she sometimes felt like she was hanging on by a thread.

Violet turned and gazed off in the direction of her Union Square apartment building about fifteen blocks away. For the interview, she'd chosen a black Celine blazer with matte gold buttons, which she paired with a black turtleneck, a plain pair of black slim-fit Tommy Hilfiger jeans and classic suede Manolo Blahnik pointed-toe pumps. On her face she wore nude lipstick and enough concealer to hopefully hide the bags underneath her eyes. She was still hungover, and she'd only managed to get exactly one hour of sleep on the flight from Vegas because she'd been too preoccupied with thoughts about her night with Xavier and how she'd become his pretend wife.

The chances of her seeing Xavier again in the future were low. In the years since their breakup, they'd thankfully never run into each other whenever she was back home in Willow Ridge. That was why it was so odd that she'd seen him in Vegas of all places. She thought back to how he'd apologized last night for breaking up with her so abruptly. He'd said something about being young and stupid. But the why of it didn't matter anymore. She'd loved him without caution or inhibition, and their breakup had taught her a big lesson: to never love someone like that again.

She forced herself to shake the thoughts of Xavier away. She had to keep her head in the game and mentally prepare for this interview because it was too important to screw up. If she was chosen for the feature, and the right client representative read her interview, Violet might have the chance to work with more A-list stars and dress them for the Venice Film Festival or the Academy Awards, aka her dream events. If she wanted her career to keep progressing, she had to say the right things today. She had to be perfect.

Alex appeared at the door and knocked softly. "Olivia Hutch from *Look Magazine* is here."

"Thanks, Alex," Violet said, steadying herself with a deep breath. "Please show her in. And you can take the rest of the day off, okay? It's been a long week."

"Don't forget to eat something," Alex reminded her as she grabbed her purse. Violet nodded, promising she'd get some lunch after the interview ended.

As Alex was leaving, Olivia Hutch walked into Violet's studio, smiling warmly. She wore a simple tan trench coat, a loose white button-up, blue jeans and all-white sneakers. Her blond hair was pulled back into a neat bun at the nape of her neck.

Violet greeted Olivia and ushered her toward the empty seat on the other side of her desk. They sat down, and Violet crossed her legs at the knee and pushed away her ball of nerves. She was ready. She was awesome.

"Of the people I've spoken to for this feature, I've been most excited to speak with you, Violet," Olivia said.

Violet blinked. "Really?" Did that mean she was a shoo-in?

Olivia nodded, pulled out her leather-bound journal and placed her phone on Violet's desk. Violet eyed the recording app and returned her gaze to Olivia's face.

"Your work with Karamel Kitty is so impressive," Olivia said. "I mean, she's obviously a stunning woman, but with her wardrobe, you've managed to strike the same wonderful balance of the classic yet playful sexiness in her music."

"Thank you so much," Violet said. She couldn't help but grin at the praise. "Karina is really a dream to work with. She's always down to experiment and collaborate on mood boards, and she's so confident and embraces her curves. Regardless of what she's wearing, I think that confidence shines through."

"You were the head stylist for her upcoming visual album, *The Kat House*," Olivia said. "Can you tell us anything about what we can expect to see her wearing?"

"Lots of big cat prints," Violet said, laughing. "But seriously, this is Karina's sophomore album, and the songs on *The Kat House* are about women loving themselves and being bosses, not caring what other people think about them. The album title is a play on Karina's stage name, but cats also have an air of superiority that we wanted to capture in the wardrobe. Vintage couture animal print was heavily incorporated. I started my career as a stylist assistant on music videos, so it was nice to return to that medium."

"I can't wait to see it," Olivia said, nodding. "So, basic but mandatory question: When did you realize that you loved fashion?"

Violet thought back to the days when she'd come home

from middle school, toss her backpack full of homework across the room and lie out on her bed to read the latest issues of *Vogue* and *Elle*.

"The clothes that you wear tell people who you are," she said. "That's something I think I've always known. I come from a small town where everyone dressed the same because they were following whatever trend was popular, and that uniformity bothered me. Fashion gives us the chance to be unique, to be individuals. Other people had sports or clubs. I expressed myself through what I wore."

"This has been a lifelong interest for you, then? What did your parents think about your fashion dreams? Having a career in fashion is more practical now, but ten years ago I'm sure they might have had questions."

Violet smirked, picturing her straitlaced parents, who'd met at Brown, gotten married shortly after graduation and later opened their own florist and nursery in Willow Ridge. She remembered how she'd argued with her mother almost every morning before school because Dahlia had disagreed with Violet's outfit choices.

"I think they assumed my obsession with fashion was just that, an obsession. A hobby," Violet said. "They thought I'd go to college for business or something more practical like my older sister. They didn't love the idea of me going to FIDM, but once I landed internships at fashion magazines, I think they were better able to wrap their heads around what I was trying to do because at least they knew I could get a job after I graduated. I don't regret disappointing them in the beginning, because I really found my people in college, you know? I remember during my internship at *Elle*, I was asked to clean a couture dress, and I thought it was the coolest thing ever. I had the chance to examine the beading and seams of a Carolina Herrera gown. How many twenty-year-olds have the chance to do that? And later when I told the other interns about it, they were so excited for me. I enjoyed being around other people who loved fashion the same way."

Olivia nodded. "I definitely empathize with you there. I might not win a Pulitzer for fashion journalism, but that doesn't make it any less important. It's hard to explain that to other people."

"Exactly! Whenever I try to talk about my work with my family, their eyes glaze over. My dad once said I played dress-up for a living. He wasn't trying to be mean, but he made my career seem so trivial. But I can talk to *you* for fifteen minutes about shoes or finding the perfect black clutch and you won't think I'm an airhead. We'll both walk away from that conversation feeling understood and validated."

Olivia smiled. "Your passion is very clear. Your clients must realize that too." She glanced down at her notes. "Angel, who is making waves on the R and B charts, said that he never really put much thought into coordinating outfits until he started working with you. And Destiny Diaz said you have the best style instincts."

"That was kind of them," Violet said, making a mental note to text Angel and Destiny to thank them. "I'm lucky to work with some really great people."

"Meela Baybee was also a client of yours, correct?"

Violet stiffened. Despite her history with Meela, Violet reminded herself that this was a perfectly reasonable question to ask. "Yes," she said. "I used to work with her as well."

"I remember seeing photos of her on the red carpet at last year's Soul Train Awards and wondering who her stylist was. I'd never heard of her before that."

Violet recalled the metallic blue Pyer Moss suit Meela had worn that night. It had been a fight to get Meela into that outfit because she'd wanted to wear a terry cloth sweat suit and pointed-toe pumps. On a red carpet. Violet had elevated Meela's style, but the journey hadn't been easy. "It was a nice look for her."

"It was," Olivia agreed. "When I was doing research about you and your clients for our interview, I noticed that Meela is now dating her manager, who I just discovered is your ex-fiancé, Eddy Coltrane." Olivia tilted her head to the side and gave Violet a searching look. "That must be ... complicated."

Violet's palms began to sweat. This was not good territory.

"I try not to pay attention to the love lives of my previous clients," she said carefully.

"Of course," Olivia said. "I just found it to be so shocking. Meela also didn't provide a quote when we reached out to her team, which surprised me since you completely changed her look."

"She has a new album coming out," Violet said, keeping her tone neutral, her smile amiable. "I'm sure she's busy."

"But it must be strange, right?" Olivia pressed. "I don't think I've ever heard of a stylist's relationship being disrupted by one of their clients."

The interview, which had been going so well, was getting derailed. What if Olivia took this interview back to the *Look* team and they ultimately deemed Violet's old drama with Meela too messy for her to make the final cut for the feature? Or worse, if she did make the final cut, and Olivia included the conversation surrounding Meela and Eddy. Violet imagined how many people in the industry might read this once-in-a-lifetime profile and assume that her personal life got in the way of her work. After the embarrassment of Eddy cheating on her so publicly, the mention of his infidelity, and therefore the deterioration of her work relationship with Meela, was the last thing Violet needed.

Desperately, she realized she had to do something, anything, to save this. The future trajectory of her career could depend on it.

"I'm happy for Eddy and Meela, and I wish them the best," she blurted, wrestling her mouth into an easy smile. "I just got married myself, actually."

Olivia's eyes widened. "You did? Oh my goodness, congratulations! Who's the lucky person?"

"He's my high school sweetheart," Violet said. The lie burned on her tongue. "We recently reconnected and realized that the love was still there. It happened so quickly, but we're very happy." Olivia glanced at Violet's bare left hand, and Violet quickly added, "The ring is getting resized."

"Amazing. Is your husband also in the industry?"

"No, God no." Violet laughed, throwing her head back. She was the picture of marital bliss. "He teaches high school English and coaches basketball. He's very involved with his students and the community. Our lifestyles are different, but we balance each other out."

Jesus. Where had *that* come from? Clearly, Xavier was still top of mind.

"I love a good happy ending," Olivia said, beaming. "It goes to show that career women don't have to sacrifice everything. We can have it all too."

"Absolutely." Violet nodded. Her smile was frozen in place.

"Well, that feels like a perfect note to end on, don't you think?" Olivia said. "It was so nice to meet you, Violet. I can't wait to see Karamel Kitty's looks on the red carpet for her press tour. Good luck with everything."

"Thanks, Olivia. It was wonderful to meet you too."

Violet showed Olivia out, slithered back to her desk and slumped down in her chair. She let out a deep breath and absently gazed out the window onto the busy street below. She hoped she'd done a good job. She hoped she'd make the list. Her little white lie had managed to salvage the interview, so that was a relief. And really there was no reason to worry about what Xavier might think. She'd used details from his personal life, but she hadn't mentioned him by name. She could have been talking about anyone. Well, technically, he was her only high school sweetheart, but the chances of him reading an article in *Look Magazine* were very low.

Better yet, the chances of anyone in her personal life reading the article were low. *Look* was a niche publication targeted toward the fashion industry, not the average consumer. It was mostly only available on newsstands in New York and LA. She hadn't told her sisters about the interview because she hadn't wanted to jinx herself. If she was ultimately included on the list, and Olivia kept in the part about Violet's husband, Violet would tell her family that she made the list, but she wouldn't send them the article link or show them a physical copy of the magazine. Her sisters might be able to handle the husband lie, but she'd rather avoid telling them about it if she could. And under no circumstances was she going to tell her parents. She could already picture her mother's distressed expression. If someone in the industry asked about Violet's mystery husband, she could simply say they were separated and getting divorced. If people in fashion and Hollywood understood anything, it was a short marriage.

The interview had drained the last bit of Violet's energy. She wanted to go home and crawl into bed. She should take the rest of the day off, like she'd allowed Alex. But there was too much to do. She wanted to go to the Dior showroom to look at new shoes for Angel. She needed to return clothes from a recent fitting with Gigi Harrison. But she had to eat something first.

She shoved her arms into her black-and-white houndstooth pea coat, dragged herself outside and walked down the street toward Sweetgreen, wobbling in her Manolos. She was *exhausted*—she needed more strength for this walk. Pulling her coat tighter around her as her breath clouded in front of her face, she felt dehydrated and delirious, like she was walking on autopilot, still hungover. It was a good thing Sweetgreen was only three blocks away. Otherwise, she wasn't sure if she'd actually make it without needing a break.

Her increasing delirium explained why she crossed the street without looking both ways. A loud horn woke her from her disoriented state and she turned to her right and saw a yellow taxi speeding right toward her. She gasped and started to run, then tripped in her heels, painfully twisting her ankle as she fell in the middle of the street.

The taxi was coming right toward her. She held her hands over her head and waited for her life to flash before her eyes. The sad part was that she was too exhausted to even conjure her life's greatest memories.

Instead of flattening her, the taxi came to a screeching halt. The driver jumped out, ran up to Violet and shouted, "What the hell is wrong with you? Why would you walk out into traffic like that? Are you nuts?"

Violet reached down to touch her throbbing ankle and winced. She blinked up at the angry taxi driver. "Can you take me to the hospital, please?"

"IT'S A STRESS fracture," Violet said. "I won't need surgery."

She was lying in a hospital bed, wearing one of those ghastly yet extremely comfortable hospital gowns. Her right ankle was freshly wrapped in a plaster cast, and the pain she felt was less intense thanks to the painkillers the nurse had provided.

Alex sat beside Violet and held up Violet's phone while she spoke on FaceTime with her agent, Jill.

"So what does that mean for you in terms of recovery?" Jill asked, sweeping her blunt dark brown bangs out of her face.

"It's going to take about six weeks to heal." Violet's lip trembled as she delivered the most damning update. "The doctor said I should try to stay off the ankle as much as possible. He advised skipping fashion month."

"Oh, Violet, I know fashion month is important, but honestly, it's low priority right now," Jill said in her perpetual no-nonsense manner. "Thank God something worse didn't happen to you. That cab could have run you over."

"But I'm supposed to be in LA next week to fit Angel for the Grammys," Violet said, ignoring Jill's logical response.

"Alex can handle the fitting in person and you can video in," Jill said. "Better yet, Alex can attend New York Fashion Week in your place. Can't you, Alex?"

Alex nodded. Then she turned to Violet and gave a reassuring smile. "I can handle it."

"I know you can," Violet said, sighing. "It's a good idea."

She wasn't worried about Alex in the slightest. She was worried about *herself*. What was she going to do for six weeks, isolated in her 750-square-foot apartment while the rest of the world moved on without her? She didn't even want to think about the fashion shows she'd miss or not being able to assist her clients on red carpets.

"What about the *Kat House* premiere?" Jill asked. "That's in March, so you should be cleared to attend, right?"

Violet nodded, then frowned thinking about the dull, sensible heels she'd probably have to wear.

"It should be a seamless pivot," Jill said. "The only thing you need to worry about is focusing on getting some rest. I've got to head to a meeting, but I'll call you tomorrow to check in. I'm glad the interview went well, but now I need you to take care of yourself, okay? I mean it."

"I hear you," Violet said. Jill had been Violet's agent since her early days of styling music videos for independent artists based in the city. Jill knew all too well how Violet threw herself into work.

After the call ended, Violet stared blankly at the cast on her foot. If she weren't so tired, she might have cried over this sudden turn of events. Instead, she just sighed and closed her eyes.

"*Fuck*," she whispered.

"I'm sorry, Violet," Alex said. "I know how terrible this must feel, but I promise I won't let you down."

Violet opened her eyes and absorbed Alex's earnest expression. She reached out and patted her hand. "It's fine," she said. "This is going to be a great opportunity for you, and I have complete trust that you'll be able to carry on our work. I hired you for a reason."

Alex smiled and nodded. Then she stood. "I guess I should probably go now. Do you need anything?"

Violet shook her head. "I'm all right. Thank you for coming."

"Of course," Alex said. She gave Violet a hug before she left.

For a few brief moments, Violet was left alone with the sounds of beeping noises and nurses walking past her room in their swishy scrubs. She closed her eyes again. Maybe she could simply sleep until the hospital discharged her.

"Knock, knock."

Violet's eyes snapped open and she saw her sisters, Iris and Lily, standing in the doorway.

Lily rushed over to her. She was wearing a dark green bubble coat with a chunky yellow scarf wrapped around her neck. Her hair was pulled back in her go-to topknot bun. She gathered Violet up in a bear hug. "I'm so glad you're okay."

"How did you know I was here?" Violet asked as Lily squeezed the life out of her.

"Alex called us." Lily perched on the side of Violet's bed and gingerly held Violet's hand. "How are you feeling?"

"Like my ankle is broken," Violet said. Lily's brown cheeks were flushed from the cold. The new publishing house where she worked editing children's fantasy novels wasn't too far away in Soho. Her old office was located up in Midtown, and it was a good thing that Lily had escaped that toxic environment with her horrible boss. She seemed to be much happier overall nowadays. She'd celebrated her twenty-seventh birthday a couple of weeks ago, but Violet had missed her party because she'd been in London with Karina for work. "You really didn't have to leave your job to come here."

"Of course I did," Lily said. "What are you even talking about?"

Violet glanced over at Iris, who was peering at the X-ray images of Violet's ankle on the table beside Violet's bed. Iris was bundled up in a black knee-length North Face coat, and her short pixie cut was concealed under a black knit hat. She tapped her finger against her chin, like she could understand everything she saw on the X-ray images. Iris was thirty years old and the smartest person Violet knew. She'd graduated first in her class in both undergrad and business school and her mind constantly seemed to brim with information most people didn't care to learn. Violet wouldn't be surprised if Iris somehow knew how to read the notes on her X-rays.

Iris walked closer to the bed and examined Violet's cast. "What's the verdict?"

"Fractured, no surgery," Violet said. "Sadly, the cast is covering the sister tattoo."

On Lily's eighteenth birthday, the three of them had gotten tattoos on their feet for their namesake flowers. Violet had purposely chosen a very different design than Xavier's violet. Her own tattoo was smaller, daintier.

"Did they put you on bed rest?" Iris asked.

"Why do they use the term 'bed rest'? Do I also need to relocate to the seaside in order to recover?"

Iris frowned. "Please answer the question, Vi. How long will it take your ankle to heal?"

"Six weeks," Violet answered, sighing.

"Well," Iris said, sitting down on Violet's other side. "I can't say that this break isn't needed."

Violet balked. "What?"

"Oh, come on, Vi. You've been running around like a chicken with its head cut off for years. You need to take some time for yourself."

"Says the woman who goes into the office on Saturdays."

"You know I stopped doing that last year," Iris said, narrowing her eyes. "And anyway, it's different."

"How so?"

"Because my office is in one location. I'm not flying around the world."

"I don't *always* fly around the world. I mostly commute between here and LA."

"And you think a six-hour plane ride is a normal commute?"

"Y'all, please," Lily said, motioning with her hands for them to lower their voices. "We're in a *hospital*. Other patients are trying to rest."

More quietly, Iris said, "You're obviously going to stay with me while you recover."

Violet scoffed. "Um, hello, I have my own apartment."

Iris folded her arms across her chest. "I've done the research. Only about a quarter of subway stations in the city have elevators or ramps to make them fully accessible, which is ridiculous. You'll end up losing a fortune on Ubers and cabs every day. Not to mention that your cast would get filthy if you found a way to navigate the subway steps."

"And Nick said that the main elevators in your building won't be renovated until the beginning of next month," Lily added. "Everyone in the building has to share the service elevator. Imagine how long you'll have to wait every day since you can't take the stairs."

Lily's boyfriend, Nick, lived down the hall from Violet, and he and Lily had met last year while Lily had been temporarily staying on Violet's couch. Now Lily lived in her own studio apartment in Brooklyn. Violet adored Nick and she enjoyed being his neighbor, but right now she hated that he'd given Lily insider information to use against her.

"I feel like they're always doing construction in your building," Iris said, frowning. "Why don't you find a new apartment?"

"Because I like my apartment," Violet said stubbornly. She'd gotten a deal on her rent through the housing lottery and she wasn't going to give it up.

"Don't make this harder on yourself," Iris said. "I have a guest bedroom on the first floor, and you'll be there by yourself most of the day while I'm at work and Calla's at preschool. It's a better alternative than staying with Mom and Dad."

Violet grimaced. Her sisters had presented very valid points. It would be tough for her to get around the city given her injury, and staying at Iris's house would be the more ideal option over staying with her parents. Violet and her mom were currently at odds because of the anti-wedding party Violet had thrown last summer in lieu of an actual wedding. The venue and caterers had already been paid. Violet didn't want to waste money, and why would she let Eddy cheat and win? She'd asked her guests to show up and wear all black. She'd worn a black Vivienne Westwood ball gown. Karina had performed, and it was basically a fuck-cheaters party. Violet had masked her pain by dancing and getting drunk with her friends. It was a bittersweet day, but cathartic. Dahlia had found the whole shindig to be tactless and embarrassing. She and Violet had argued afterward, and because Violet refused to agree with her mother's opinions about the party, they'd never reached a resolution. The tension between them had lessened, but it was still there, brimming underneath their every interaction. This wasn't new to Violet, though. She'd more or less been at odds with Dahlia to some degree her entire life.

At least by staying at Iris's house she'd get some peace. And she'd be able to go back to her apartment in a few weeks once the elevators were fixed and she got her cast removed. This decision sucked, though, because it meant that Violet would have to spend an extended amount of time in Willow Ridge, a place that made her feel suffocated.

First her ankle. Now her freedom.

"Whatever," she finally huffed. It wasn't like she'd have much work to do anyway if she was missing fashion month. "Fine."

"Well, that was only slightly painless," Lily said, opening her purse. She pulled out a granola bar and offered it to Violet. "Are you hungry?"

"*Starving.*" Violet took the granola bar and savagely ripped it open. Lily and Iris laughed as Violet practically inhaled half the granola bar.

"So how was Vegas?" Iris asked. "You never told us about what happened after you saw Xavier."

Violet choked on a piece of granola and let out a harsh cough. "Oh. Um."

"Did you hook up with him?" Iris asked, squinting. Lily's eyes widened as she waited for Violet's response.

Violet swallowed and cleared her throat. "Maybe."

"See, I told you!" Lily held out her hand and Iris sighed, slapping a five-dollar bill into Lily's palm.

Violet's mouth dropped open. "You bet on whether or not I had sex with Xavier?!"

"Not exactly," Lily said. "I told Iris that I thought something went down between the two of you because I know how much you cared about each other in high school, and the way you broke up was so . . . Well, anyway. I just had a feeling. And Iris disagreed with me."

"I remembered how you didn't even want us to say his name before," Iris said. "But I was wrong. Obviously."

"You weren't wrong," Violet said. "It was a onetime thing."

"So you're not going to see him while you're staying with Iris?" Lily sounded slightly disappointed.

"No. Of course not."

Lily frowned, and Iris shrugged. Violet was grateful when they dropped the subject and moved on to discuss how they'd help Violet pack for her stay with Iris. Violet definitely wasn't going to tell them about her and Xavier's little fake marriage ceremony. They'd read into it too deeply, just like Karina had.

Violet wondered if Xavier had kept the chapel photograph. Hopefully, he'd made the smart choice and thrown it in the trash. That way there would be no real evidence of what they'd done.

No one else ever needed to know.

XAVIER HUSTLED ACROSS THE PARKING LOT TOWARD THE doors of Willow Ridge High School, holding his travel mug in one hand and his cell phone in the other. It was a Monday morning, also known as Tricia's favorite time to FaceTime him.

"It looks so cold there," his mom said, squinting at the screen. Her light brown skin was tanned from the Florida sun, and her tight curls were pulled back away from her face. "Did it snow last night?"

"Four inches." Xavier bundled his scarf tighter around his neck and adjusted his black-framed glasses. "It's twenty-three degrees today."

"Mmm." Tricia shook her head. While Xavier wore layer upon layer like he was planning a trek through the Himalayas, Tricia was sitting in a rocking chair on her boyfriend's front porch, wearing a sundress and drinking an iced latte. She'd met Harry three years ago through an online dating app, and because she worked remotely as a customer service supervisor for a home goods company, for the past couple of years, she'd spent the months of January through March in Key West with Harry.

Xavier missed Tricia during this time, of course. He liked being able to randomly drop in on his mom and spend time with her, and her home-cooked meals were definitely a plus. But being with Harry made Tricia happy, and that was what mattered to Xavier.

"You stay warm up there, okay?" Tricia advised. "January is always my least favorite month."

Xavier smirked as his breath clouded in front of his face. "Yeah, I know."

January tended to be rough for Xavier too. The holidays were long gone. The air was frigid. The sky looked dreary, and waiting for springtime in New Jersey felt endless. But this marking period, Xavier and his students were reading some of his favorite books. *If Beale Street Could Talk*, *Lord of the Flies* and *Their Eyes Were Watching God*. And there was basketball season, which kept him going. The boys varsity team had won another game this past Saturday, continuing their undefeated streak.

"Have you heard from Tim Vogel yet?" Tricia asked.

"Nah, but hopefully soon." Xavier hadn't spoken to Riley's head basketball coach since his birthday weekend, two weeks ago. He was hoping to get Tim on the phone again soon. If not, he'd just have to bug the school secretary, Mrs. Franklin, who was Tim Vogel's aunt.

Xavier was almost at the school doors now, and his hand was beginning to freeze from holding his phone.

"Ma, I'll call you later, after work, okay?" Xavier said. "I'm heading inside. Tell Harry I said hi."

"Okay, baby. Have a good day." Tricia was beaming at Xavier as she hung up. She was so proud of his career as a teacher. Teaching brought him joy. But at the same time, he wanted more. He wanted the assistant coach position at Riley.

Between chasing after Tim Vogel, basketball season and teaching, Xavier clearly had a lot on his plate. But he couldn't stop thinking about Violet. It had been two weeks since she'd run out of the Vegas hotel room before he'd even had a chance to ask for her number. Seeing her again had felt good in that distracting, feverish way like when they'd been teenagers. At first, he'd remembered very little about their drunken escapade. But as the days passed, bits and pieces of that night rose to the forefront of his mind. The two of them grinding on the dance floor, groping each other in the back seat of an Uber, stumbling into the chapel for their pretend wedding ceremony. He also recalled her straddling him in the early morning hours, and how soft her breasts had felt in the palms of his hands.

He'd thought about different ways to get in touch with her. He could message her via his seldom-used Instagram account. He could ask Bianca for her number because he knew they kept in touch. But then Bianca would ask him a bunch of questions that he didn't want to answer. The fact of the matter was that if Violet wanted Xavier to have access to her, she would have made it so. He just needed to let go of her and the night they'd spent together. They'd returned to their separate corners of the universe, and that was probably for the best, because in what world would he and Violet make sense? She spent time with celebrities, jet-setting around the world, and he was a teacher in his New Jersey hometown. He needed to figure out what to do with that picture of them kissing sloppily in the chapel. It was still folded up in the top drawer of his dresser, right beside his fake wedding ring.

He entered the school and turned in the direction of the teachers' lounge to place his lunch in the fridge. He passed the athletic achievements display in the main hallway, which housed the state championship trophy that the boys varsity basketball team had won during his senior year. Beside the trophy there was a plaque with Xavier's senior yearbook photo and basketball stats, stating that he was the second-highest scorer in Willow Ridge High School history. He hated looking at the display because he came face-to-face with his headstrong, cocky eighteen-year-old self. The one who'd left this small town to attend one of the best basket-ball colleges in the country and then gave up at the first sign of adversity. The display case only reminded Xavier of the ways his life had gone in a completely unplanned direction.

He never thought he'd become a teacher. After graduat-ing from Riley with a sports and fitness administration de-gree, he couldn't find a job to save his life. Desperate for income, he got certified to substitute teach and took a job substituting at the high school. About three months in, Mr. Rodney went on leave for hip surgery, and Xavier had devel-oped a good rapport with the students, so he was hired as the interim sophomore English teacher. There, he unex-pectedly discovered a love for literature, a love he definitely didn't have when he'd been a student himself. When Mr.

Rodney came back and another teacher retired, Xavier took the steps to get his teaching certificate, and he was hired full-time. Then he saw that Mr. Rodney needed help coaching the basketball team, so he got certified to become the assistant coach too. His life had just sort of fallen into place this way. One day, he looked up and wondered how he'd veered so far off his path. He didn't want to teach in his hometown for the rest of his life. While he'd be sad to leave his students and the other high school staff behind, he knew that there had to be more out there for him.

He was deep in thought when he opened the door to the teachers' lounge and nearly jumped out of his skin when his colleagues shouted, "SURPRISE!"

"Wh-what?" Xavier blinked as he was guided toward the rickety long table where he was presented with a cake that said *Congratulations on Your Marriage!*

Xavier's fellow teachers descended, hugging him and talking over one another as they congratulated him. Bewildered, he disentangled himself from their embrace.

"What the hell are you talking about?" he asked.

"Language!" Mrs. Franklin chided. She'd been the school secretary when Xavier had been a student, and over a decade later, she was still there, writing tardy slips and defending her title as the woman in Willow Ridge who knew everything about everyone. She even sent out a monthly newsletter that was supposed to be about school activities but often included details from people's personal lives, like weddings, new babies and if someone was putting their house up for sale. Her brown skin had more wrinkles now and her short dark brown hair was beginning to turn gray, but otherwise, not much about Mrs. Franklin had changed. She pulled out a magazine and flipped it open to an image of Violet wearing all black, leaning against a window. She brought the magazine closer to Xavier and pointed at a block of text.

"You know how I like to keep up with all of our previous students. When I saw Violet post on her Instagram about being featured in a major fashion magazine, I drove all over trying to find a copy. I ended up finding one at a newsstand in Jersey City. And look, she says right here that the two of you got married recently." Mrs. Franklin wrapped her arms around Xavier and squeezed him as tight as her fragile limbs would allow. "Oh, I'm so happy for you, sweetheart. I always had a feeling that you and the Greene girl would end up together. You used to be attached at the hip!"

Xavier grabbed the magazine and quickly skimmed over the article. Mrs. Franklin had to be mistaken. There was no way Violet would falsely claim Xavier as her husband. Nothing about that made sense. But then he reached the end of the profile and read Violet's words for himself.

Greene has also managed to find balance in her personal life. As our interview is wrapping up, she reveals that she is newly married to her high school sweetheart.

"We recently reconnected and realized that the love was still there," Greene says, sporting a secret smile.

After I express my congratulations and excitement for her, she continues to gush.

"It all happened so quickly, but we're very happy."

Despite what some may know about her previous relationship to a successful talent manager, Greene's new husband isn't involved in the entertainment industry whatsoever. She tells me that he teaches high school English and coaches basketball.

"Our lifestyles are different, but we balance each other out."

What a sweet happily ever after for the fashion world.

Xavier stared at the page, dumbfounded.

What . . . the fuck?

"You'll have to bring Violet in for a visit," Mr. Rodney said, nudging Xavier's other shoulder. Last fall, Mr. Rodney had celebrated his forty-fifth teaching anniversary. He was divorced, with two adult children who lived out of state, so teaching at Willow Ridge High was his whole life. He was in his late sixties, and Xavier didn't expect him to retire anytime soon. "You two sure do know how to keep a secret. She doesn't even mention you by name. Just last Thursday at lunch you told me you weren't seeing anyone!"

"What does your mom think?" asked Nadia Morales, who taught AP Spanish.

"I . . . I," Xavier stammered, glancing back and forth between the magazine and his coworkers' smiling faces.

Luckily, the bell rang, signaling that it was time for faculty to head to their respective posts. Xavier extricated himself from the lounge and hurried to his classroom. What was happening? Violet knew that their wedding had been fake, so why would she tell a major magazine that he was her husband?! Why didn't she give him a heads-up beforehand?

And why had his pulse accelerated at the thought of her claiming him as such?

How many other people had read that article? Probably not very many. He hadn't even heard of that magazine until Mrs. Franklin showed it to him just now. Maybe this whole situation could stay contained in the teachers' lounge until he had a chance to speak to Violet himself.

IN TYPICAL WILLOW Ridge fashion, by fourth period, the whole school knew about Xavier's alleged new wife.

"The conch is used when one of the boys wants to speak his mind," Xavier said to his class of sophomores. "When a person holds the conch, the rest of the group has to listen to him. Yet the conch breaks very easily after Piggy is killed while holding it. What do you think the conch is supposed to symbolize?"

Xavier looked around at his silent students. Usually by this point, they were a little more animated, knowing that they'd have lunch soon.

Xavier sighed and leaned against the whiteboard. "Anyone? We've been reading *Lord of the Flies* for weeks now. I know somebody has an answer." He looked at Cherise Fisher, in the front row, who was usually the first person to shoot her hand in the air, but today she stared at Xavier with a flat expression. "Cherise? Any ideas?"

Cherise shrugged. "I don't know, Mr. Wright. But I do have a different question."

"Okay," Xavier said, grateful to begin some sort of discussion. "Go ahead."

"Why didn't you tell us that you know Karamel Kitty?"

"Or that you married her best friend," added Jerrica Brown, sitting behind Cherise. She held up her phone and showed the rest of the class an Instagram post of Violet and Karamel Kitty laughing and hugging each other. "Like, I thought we were cool. You said we were your favorite class."

"Yeah, after Ms. Gibson left you high and dry last year, we were all there for you," said Dante Jones, seated in the back by the class bookshelf. "But we had to find out about your wife from the other teachers gossiping. That's foul, Mr. Wright. Very foul."

Suddenly, his class catapulted into an agitated uproar, wanting to know why their favorite teacher would hold out on them this way. Xavier dragged a hand over his face. Violet's confusing interview was throwing his whole day upside down.

"The *conch* symbolizes free speech and democracy," he said, raising his voice above their chatter and refusing to answer their questions. "When the conch breaks, it represents the fragility of democracy and how it only survives if it's protected by all participants."

In the middle row, Jeffrey Colson raised his hand.

Xavier pointed at him. "Yes, Jeffrey?"

"Can you introduce us to Karamel Kitty? Actually, Face-Time her real quick. We won't tell."

Xavier sighed again. *"Piggy's death—"*

He was interrupted by the sound of the bell. The students immediately stood and began gathering their books and backpacks, stuffing away their old copies of *Lord of the Flies*.

"Remember to read the next two chapters for homework," Xavier advised, even though he'd already lost their attention.

"See you tonight at practice, Mr. Wright!" Dante called, slapping the top of the doorway on his way out.

Xavier plopped down at his desk. He had to find a way to get in contact with Violet, fast, before this situation blew up even more. He retrieved his phone from his messenger bag and sent a text to Bianca.

Yo B, can you give me Violet's number?

He watched a response bubble materialize then disappear.

"Mr. Wright?"

Xavier glanced up, and Cherise and Jerrica were lingering in front of his desk.

"Yes?" he said, looking at his brightest students, who'd decided to incite a minor mutiny just minutes ago.

"Is it true that your wife was your high school sweetheart?" Cherise asked.

Xavier gave her a look. "I'm not discussing that. You're going to be late for lunch."

"She's pretty," Jerrica said, pulling up Violet's Instagram page again. She showed Xavier a picture of Violet standing on a busy Los Angeles street with palm trees on either side of her. She wore a cool-looking black leather jacket and she was smiling widely as her curls blew in the wind. "Good for you, Mr. Wright. Maybe she'll help you with your wardrobe."

"You know you're not supposed to use your phone during school hours." Then Xavier glanced down at his white polo and tan khakis. "Wait, what's wrong with my wardrobe?"

The girls exchanged a look and laughed. "No offense, Mr. Wright," Jerrica said. "But you kinda look like a park ranger today."

Xavier sucked in a breath. "A park ranger? Just so you know, I was voted Best Dressed my senior year, right along with Violet."

This only made the girls laugh harder. "Yeah, okay, Mr. Wright," Cherise said.

Xavier sighed for the third time in twenty minutes. "I'll see you tomorrow, all right?" He began ushering them out of the classroom. "Don't forget to do the reading."

On his way to the teachers' lounge, his phone vibrated again. He expected to see a reply from Bianca, but instead he'd received a text from Tim Vogel.

My aunt just told me about your marriage.
Congratulations! I guess I was wrong about you
being a bachelor. I'd love to meet your new wife.
Dinner soon?

Now, *that* was interesting. After weeks of radio silence, Tim suddenly wanted to get dinner?

But Xavier couldn't reply to Tim's text because he didn't want to breathe more life into this strange lie.

As the day went on, he received more offers of congratulations from his coworkers. His students continued to be baffled as to why he would hide such an important life event from them.

He was walking into the locker room after school when Bianca finally texted him back.

Violet probably wouldn't want me to give you her number.

Xavier let out a frustrated breath.

I need to talk to her, he responded. She told a magazine that we're married.

I did hear that lol

Xavier frowned. So the rumor had spread beyond the school walls. I don't think it's funny.

Look, Bianca replied, I'm not giving out her number. But I can tell you that she's been staying at Iris's house. Do with that what you will.

Violet had been in Willow Ridge this whole time and he didn't even know?

He poked his head in the locker room office to tell Mr. Rodney that he had an emergency and needed to skip practice. He jogged outside to his car and headed straight for Iris's house.

9

AS VIOLET LAY SPREAD OUT ON THE COUCH IN IRIS'S DEN with her ankle elevated on a pillow, watching *The Real Housewives of Potomac*, she struggled to see the silver lining in her situation. Having a fractured ankle during one of the most important fashion seasons of the year did not provide many upsides. At least she was healing at the average rate, according to her podiatrist. It was true that recently, she'd felt like she was reaching her limit with her workload, but now that it had been taken away from her so unexpectedly, she missed the hustle and bustle of her life, the constant change in scenery. The excitement of seeing new clothes in a showroom or on a runway. The way her clients' faces would light up when they witnessed themselves wearing a new outfit that spoke to them. Fashion month brought Violet back to life. It was inspiration, rejuvenation. Instead, she'd have to settle for getting updates from Alex and watching the action from Iris's couch.

In the past two weeks, the most excitement Violet experienced was when Calla's babysitter dropped her off after preschool.

"All done," Calla said now, motioning for Violet to look at the newly completed art on her cast. Because it was wintertime, she had to wear a toe cover to conceal the exposed part of her foot. Without it, her toes would likely freeze and fall off.

Like Iris, Calla could be pretty somber, so instead of smiling and awaiting praise like most other kids, she stared at Violet gravely. "Do you like it?"

Violet sat up and tilted her head. The drawing looked like a stick figure man with no eyes and large ears. An odd choice, but she wouldn't question a budding artist.

"I love it," she declared. "He's very handsome."

"He?" Calla said, furrowing her little eyebrows. She nervously pulled on the hem of her light blue knit dress. "It's a flower."

"Oh, yes, of course. It's beautiful. You're better than Leonardo da Vinci."

Calla squinted. "Who?"

"Someone that you shouldn't confuse with Leonardo DiCaprio."

"*Who?*"

Now Violet felt ancient. "No one. I really like the flower. Thank you."

"You're welcome." Calla finally allowed herself a shy smile. "I'm going to draw a butterfly now."

"Go for it."

Violet leaned back, reassuming her comfortable position on the couch. She was wearing her favorite Everlane French terry sweat suit, and a bag of Cheetos fit in the space between her hip and the couch cushion, serving as her early evening snack. Iris was in the kitchen, cooking eggplant Parmesan for dinner, and Lily was there too, chopping ingredients for a salad. Violet could barely boil ramen noodles, so they'd banned her from helping.

Her phone vibrated on the couch beside her, and she glanced down to see that Dahlia was calling. She silenced her phone and told herself she'd call her mom back later. Since Violet's injury, Dahlia felt the need to voice her opinions, per usual. She had ideas about what doctors Violet should be seeing and which exercises she should be doing. She was upset that Violet had opted to stay with Iris instead of staying at her childhood home. It was too much. Violet couldn't think straight with her mom hovering over her like that. Plus, she was feeling so crappy about having to miss out on fashion month. It cast a sour glow over her mood. She didn't feel like talking to anyone. It wasn't personal. She'd screened Bianca's call ten minutes ago too.

The doorbell rang, and Lily called out, "I'll get it!"

Violet returned her attention to the television as she heard the sound of Lily speaking to whoever had rung the doorbell. Violet popped a Cheeto in her mouth and snuggled deeper into the couch.

"Um, Vi?"

Violet glanced up to see Lily standing in the den's entryway with a strange look on her face.

"Yeah?" Violet asked. "Is someone at the door selling solar panels—"

The words caught in her throat as Xavier Wright appeared behind Lily.

The gears in Violet's brain screeched to a halt; then they turned slowly as she tried to piece together why Xavier had suddenly materialized in her sister's living room. She stared at him, unblinking.

"What are you doing here?" she asked hoarsely.

Xavier was frowning at her. "What happened to your foot?" he said, walking over toward the couch. Calla took one look at this new stranger and gave him a wide berth, opting to sit on the love seat across the room. Xavier's frown grew more intense as he crouched down and examined Violet's cast.

"It's my ankle, not my foot," she said. "And I fell."

He looked up at her. "Where?"

"In the city."

"Damn," he said, gingerly touching the white plaster. "How long ago?"

"Two weeks." She pushed his hand away. "Xavier, *what* are you doing here? And why are you wearing glasses?"

For some reason, this was the most shocking detail Violet was able to compute. Xavier was wearing a pair of thick, black, square-framed glasses. He looked like a hot librarian. No, a hot *teacher*.

"My eyesight is shit now," he said, standing. He crossed his arms over his chest and frowned at her. "Why did you say that we were married?"

From her spot in the entryway, Lily gasped. When Violet and Xavier looked at her, she covered her mouth with both hands.

Violet returned her attention to Xavier, who stared at her in outright frustration. She knew that the *Look Magazine* interview went on newsstands that morning. A few days after the interview, Jill had received confirmation that Violet had made the official cut for the "30 Under 30 in Style" list. Violet's elation made her momentarily forget about the literal and metaphorical ache that she'd felt over her injury. She'd bought herself a bottle of champagne to celebrate. She'd read the profile as soon as it went up online two days ago, and she'd been able to confirm that Olivia Hutch had indeed included that little tidbit about Violet being married. Violet had been slightly amused at how Olivia had made Violet's imaginary husband sound like such a wonderful guy. Mostly, though, Violet was pleased that the write-up was so positive. Her agency had posted a link to the interview on their website, which would help with visibility. But aside from discussing the interview with Jill and Alex, who thought Violet's fake-husband Hail Mary was pretty clever, and quickly posting about it on her Instagram, Violet hadn't talked about the interview with anyone else yet. Not even her sisters. There was no way that Xavier somehow knew about the profile. *Look Magazine* was so far off his radar. He had to be talking about something else.

"Your interview in that fashion magazine," he clarified.

Okay. Now it was time to panic.

"How did you even know about it?" she asked, totally deflecting.

"Mrs. Franklin read it and she told everyone."

"Mrs. Franklin . . . the school secretary?" she said, confused. "How did *she* know?"

Xavier jerked his shoulders in a shrug. "She follows you on social media or something. She always knows what you're up to."

This was only more confusing. "But Mrs. Franklin hated me!"

"She didn't hate you—anyway, that's beside the point, Violet. Why did you say it?"

"Um." Violet gulped. "So. I can explain."

"I hope so," he said, raising an eyebrow, waiting.

At that moment, Iris walked into the den, wiping her hands on her black apron. She stood beside Lily, and Calla joined her mom on the other side of the room, still eyeing Xavier with curiosity.

"Xavier Wright," Iris said calmly, assessing him, "why are you in my home?"

"I'm sorry to barge in on you like this," Xavier said. "But Violet owes me a very serious explanation for something that she said in an interview."

Iris tilted her head and glanced back and forth between Violet and Xavier. Violet would prefer not to have this conversation in front of her sisters because it would just lead to more questions later, but oh well.

"That interview was really important for my career," she said, looking at Xavier. "And the person who interviewed me brought up how my ex-fiancé is dating my old client, and I freaked out. I thought mentioning that situation would create bad press, so as a diversion, I lied and said I was happily married. I'm sorry. Never in a million years did I think you would somehow find out about what I said. But it wasn't even a total lie! We *did* get married, technically."

Lily gasped again.

"You did *what*?" Iris demanded.

Violet glanced at her sisters sharply, then turned back to Xavier.

"No, technically we did not get married," Xavier countered. "The ceremony wasn't real."

This time when Lily gasped, Iris gasped too.

Violet spun to face her sisters. "You're not helping!"

"Sorry, sorry," Lily whispered, eyes wide. "We're just gonna . . ." She nodded toward the hallway and motioned for Iris and Calla to leave the room with her. Iris shot one last confused look over her shoulder before they disappeared down the hall.

"I didn't mention your name, though," Violet said to Xavier. "You can tell people I was talking about someone else."

He shook his head, exasperated. "You think they'd believe me? You didn't have to say my name. *I* was your high school sweetheart. *I'm* an English teacher who coaches basketball. Who else could you have been talking about? Everyone here knows that it was me."

Everyone? Violet glanced at her phone. Suddenly, the multiple missed calls from her mom and Bianca made sense.

The doorbell rang again. Violet's stomach dropped.

Oh no.

She scrambled to sit up straighter, brushing Cheetos crumbs off her lap. She only had about five seconds to collect herself before her parents walked into the living room. Dahlia, petite like her daughters, was sporting a fresh blowout, and she and Benjamin were wearing their matching Greenehouse Florist and Nursery sweatshirts. Lily, who must have answered the door, mouthed *sorry* to Violet before scurrying off down the hall again. Dread brewed in Violet's gut as she looked at her parents.

"Good, you're both here," Dahlia said, her tone clipped. "Do you want to know what I just heard at the hair salon?" She pointed at Xavier. "In fact, I heard it from one of your students' parents, the mother of a young lady named Cherise Fisher. Mrs. Fisher told me that the two of you are *married*, and that Violet announced it to the world in a magazine before telling her own family. I, of course, did not believe Mrs. Fisher. Because my daughter would never fail to tell me something so important. But then Mrs. Fisher pulled up the magazine interview on her phone and showed me the proof, and I read it with my own two eyes. Now, what do the two of you have to say about that?"

Crickets.

Violet and Xavier stood there, still as scarecrows. Suddenly, Violet felt like they were teenagers again, caught in the act of sneaking in or sneaking out, enduring another lecture from her parents. Violet turned to Xavier and he angled his head, raising an eyebrow. This was Violet's mess. She had to clean it up.

Violet gulped. "Well—"

"And, Violet, you didn't even tell us about this magazine feature," Dahlia said, not giving Violet a chance to properly explain. "Why would you keep something like that from us? Don't you think we would want to know if you were being recognized in a major publication?"

Violet bit her lip. She honestly didn't think that her parents would have cared. To them, it would simply be another frivolous fashion thing for her frivolous fashion job. "Mom—"

"Can you imagine how foolish I looked to the ladies at the salon, not knowing that my own daughter got married?" Dahlia continued. "Really, Violet. First you got engaged to Eddy, even though your father and I told you we didn't think it was a good idea. Then there was that messy business last summer with the anti-wedding soiree you insisted on throwing. How could you let us find out about you and Xavier this way? Don't you know people talk in this town? Many people know us, and Xavier too, because of his position at the high school, and they might feel slighted that they weren't invited to a wedding ceremony. These things might not matter to you because you don't live here anymore, but there are larger ramifications from your actions. Your father and I have a public-facing business to run. Think of your family."

Dahlia's eyes began to well up. Benjamin, a tall and supportive man of few words, and the more laid-back of the two, silently rubbed Dahlia's back and gave Violet a reproving look. That was when she realized that while her parents were angry, they were also hurt. And despite their many differences and disagreements, the last thing Violet wanted was to hurt her parents in any way.

"I'm sorry," she said quietly. She genuinely hadn't expected that anyone in Willow Ridge, least of all Mrs. Franklin, would find out about her interview and that it would get back to her parents. She thought she'd be able to collect this accolade and progress even higher in her career and that her little white lie would be easily forgotten.

But her parents would only become more upset once she revealed the messy truth behind her lie. Then all of Willow Ridge would know that she'd lied, and that she'd dragged Xavier into it too. She'd further sink her parents in the pit of town gossip, and *she* would be the cause of their embarrassment.

In that moment, she felt small. Smaller than small. She was no longer the woman who'd moved away and made a name for herself through sheer determination. Once again, she was the unruly daughter who couldn't be good like her sisters. She was the screwup, the black sheep of the Greene family.

"We wanted it to be a surprise," Xavier suddenly said.

Violet blinked and turned to him. Dahlia and Benjamin looked at Xavier as well.

"Excuse us for a moment," Xavier said. Then he bent down and gestured for Violet to put her arms around his neck so that he could lift her off the couch. With his lips at her ear, he said, "Let's talk somewhere private."

"Why?" she whispered back.

"Just go with it."

Bemused, she held on to him and he hoisted her up onto her feet. This close, she was hit with the scent of his minty cologne again, and she pretended not to notice the toned muscle of his biceps as he helped position her crutches underneath her arms. Her parents watched them as they slowly maneuvered out of the living room and down the hall into Iris's guest bedroom.

Violet placed her crutches against the wall and eased

down onto the foot of the bed. Xavier closed the door behind them.

"Looked like you needed a minute," he said. "I remember how flustered you used to get around them."

"Oh." She glanced down. "Thanks."

When she looked up at him again, his expression was thoughtful. He moved to sit next to her, and her gaze drifted from his brown eyes behind his glasses to his nose to his thick goatee; then she paused at his full lips.

Slowly, Xavier said, "Saying that we're married might actually be a blessing in disguise."

Violet jerked to attention. "What? How?"

"You lied to save your career," he said. "And I'm just realizing I could use this lie in the same way."

She frowned at him. "What do you mean?"

"An assistant coach position is opening up with the men's basketball team at Riley University. I've been trying to get the head coach to consider me for the job, but he kept saying that he couldn't trust me to stick around and commit to the program long term. Until today, when he found out that I had a wife. I think he assumes this means I'm more stable and not a restless bachelor."

"That's silly. You can be married and restless."

"I know," he said, shrugging. "I guess he's just old-school. But he said he wanted to meet you and have dinner with us. This is the same person who couldn't be bothered to call me back a few days ago. Saying you're my wife might help me get this job. And think about how it can benefit you. It'll keep your reputation intact with your fashion people *and* with your parents and the rest of Willow Ridge."

"Xavier, that is nuts," she said, laughing at the sheer absurdity. "We can't tell people we're married! We barely know each other anymore. I mean, the whole thing would just be crazy."

But what she didn't admit was that his logic appealed to her, which was concerning. Because if the past was a proper indicator, whenever she and Xavier concocted a plan, things turned disastrous.

"I do know you," he said, giving her a direct look. "I might not know how you take your coffee or all the names of the designers you work with. But if I've learned anything from teaching high school, it's that we're our most natural, raw selves as teenagers, and over time we either expand on those aspects of our personalities or we fight to cover them up. There's a lot we need to catch up on, but I know you, and you know me too."

Violet's heart picked up its pace. She wished that his words didn't have such an effect on her. Xavier had willingly forfeited the right to know her years ago, and piecing herself back together after he'd dumped her had been such an excruciating process. She didn't want to be knowable to him.

But she had to do *something*. She personally did not care about the small-minded politics or social rules of Willow Ridge. People could say whatever they wanted about her. But her parents were the only florists and plant nursery owners in town. She imagined how people would whisper to one another as they came into her parents' shop. What would people think if they knew that Dahlia and Benjamin's daughter had lied about being married to Xavier, who'd become so important to the community? Violet didn't want to bring more shame to her family or create more drama for herself. And because she was injured and off the scene, she didn't have to worry about explaining her new husband to anyone in the industry like she'd originally thought. What if temporarily pretending to be Xavier's wife *was* the easy way out?

"I don't drink coffee," she finally said. Then, "There has to be a time limit on this lie."

Xavier's lips spread into a smile. She resisted the fluttering sensation in her stomach.

"How long are you planning to stay in Willow Ridge?" he asked.

"Another four weeks. Until my ankle heals."

"Okay, I feel like I can probably convince Coach Vogel that I'm serious about the job at Riley by then."

"But how would we explain our inevitable separation? Wouldn't that just cause more of a scandal around here?" She bit her lip. "Maybe we should keep the lie going for a little longer after I leave, just for believability's sake."

"Yeah, maybe a month or so more," he said. "And we don't have to worry about trying to see each other or keep up appearances then. Eventually we can say that the different lifestyles and schedules were too much and we decided to divorce but stay friends. I think people would understand that explanation more than they would understand the truth."

She nodded. She couldn't believe that she was agreeing to this.

Then a worrisome realization hit her.

"If we're married, people—especially my parents—are going to wonder why I'm staying with Iris and not with you," she said.

"Damn, good point." He rubbed a hand over his face. "I have a pullout couch in the living room."

She frowned. "Is it comfortable?"

"Not really. It's like ten years old. You'll probably hate it."

"But what about my ankle?"

"I guess we can prop it up on some books while you sleep," he said, shrugging.

Violet sucked in a breath, ready to tell him that was a terrible solution, but he held up his hands in surrender, smiling. "I'm playing. I'll take the couch. You can sleep in my bed."

Violet imagined Xavier lying naked in bed like he'd been that morning in Vegas. Her cheeks warmed, and she cleared her throat.

"Maybe we can switch who gets which bed when," she said, because that was only fair. It was *his* place. And this was all Violet's fault at the end of the day. Damn Olivia Hutch and her probing journalism.

"Should we stick with the married-in-Vegas story?" she asked. "At least that is partially true."

"Sounds reasonable enough," he said. "Do you still have the rings?"

She winced, thinking of the tacky, shiny rings that were still sitting at the bottom of her purse. "Yes, I have them, and I'm only going to wear them when absolutely necessary because they look like they might start chipping at any second. People are going to think you're cheap."

He laughed. "I have no choice but to be cheap, so they wouldn't be wrong."

The sound of his velvety laugh caused her to smile, unwarranted. She made herself refocus on the task at hand.

"Do you have your ring?" she asked, and he nodded.

Later, maybe she'd unpack why neither of them had tossed their rings in the trash, but for now, they had to prepare themselves to face her parents.

"We'll call this off in the near future when the time is right," she said. "Agreed?"

"Agreed." He held out his hand for a shake.

Violet placed her hand in his and she felt the rough calluses on his palm. Xavier had always been so graceful with his hands. Dribbling the ball. Shooting the ball. Touching her.

She pulled her hand away and didn't look at him as she sucked in a deep breath and pushed the air slowly out of her lungs.

"Okay," she said. "Let's go back in there."

Dahlia and Benjamin were sitting on the couch when Violet and Xavier returned to the den. Violet had no idea where her sisters and niece had disappeared to, but they'd smartly chosen to steer clear. Xavier wrapped his arm around Violet's waist and she jumped in surprise. Then she leaned against him, reminding herself that they needed to look natural.

"Mom, Dad, I'm really sorry that you found out about

our marriage in a magazine," she said. "Everything happened so quickly, we weren't sure how to tell you. The truth is that Xavier and I reconnected very recently. We took a trip to Las Vegas a couple weeks ago and decided to get married. We wanted to do something small, just the two of us. I knew you might not like that, so I was afraid to tell you. We wanted to surprise you with the news at the right time."

Dahlia tutted. "Of course I don't like it! After almost ten years, you get back together with Xavier and you decided to get married just like that without talking to us first? Xavier, we might see you around town sometimes, but you haven't really been around the family in years. You didn't ask us for our permission to marry Violet."

"Mom, really?" Violet said. "We don't need *permission* to get married. This isn't the eighteenth century—"

"I care about your daughter very much," Xavier said, discreetly nudging Violet's side to quiet her. "You're right that I should have spent more time with your family before we decided to make such a big life decision. Your opinion is important to me, and I apologize."

Benjamin nodded, sternly eyeing Xavier. Dahlia huffed and crossed her arms but didn't further push the issue.

Amazing. It would appear that Xavier still had the ability to smoothly appease those around him, including her parents.

"If you're married, then why are you staying at Iris's house instead of with your husband?" Dahlia asked.

Violet and Xavier exchanged a quick, knowing glance.

"I was getting work done in my apartment," Xavier rushed

to say. "My shower was . . . malfunctioning. But they finally fixed it this morning."

"That's why he's here, actually," Violet said. "He's picking me up."

"Right," Xavier said. "Exactly."

Dahlia and Benjamin stared at them. "What about your apartment in the city?" Dahlia asked. "Are you moving back to Willow Ridge permanently?"

"No!" Violet said. Then, "Um, I mean, no, not yet. We're still deciding where we want to live."

Violet and Xavier held their breath, waiting to see if her parents would buy their story.

"I don't approve of your decision to get married in Las Vegas without telling us," Dahlia said. "And I definitely don't approve of this decision to get married so quickly. But there's nothing to be done about it now. The very least you can do is let us throw you a dinner."

"That's not really necessary, Mom," Violet said, and she noticed Benjamin shoot her a warning look. "I mean, yes, of course. We'd appreciate that so much."

"Good," Dahlia said. "And I hope the two of you are planning to have a similar conversation with Xavier's mother, if you haven't already."

"Absolutely," Xavier said. Only Violet noticed the strain in his smile.

Before Violet even knew what was happening, Dahlia was gathering her and Xavier up into a tight hug.

"Marriage isn't a game," she said. She pulled away, eyeing them sternly. "It requires patience and grace. You hear me?"

They nodded. Violet gulped.

"Good."

Then Dahlia walked away toward the kitchen, yelling for Iris to tell her what she was cooking.

"If you ever need us, we're right here in town. Don't forget that," Benjamin said, before following Dahlia.

Violet and Xavier were left alone, staring at each other.

"Well," she mumbled awkwardly. "I guess I should pack my stuff."

"Yeah," he replied, already moving to help guide her down the hall.

This was decidedly *not* how Violet had expected her day to unfold when she'd woken up this morning. Now she was pretend married. To *Xavier*.

10

XAVIER LASTED IN VIOLET'S TEMPORARY GUEST BEDROOM for all of five minutes before her sisters kicked him out, saying they'd help Violet pack instead, after which Violet filled them in on her and Xavier's new plan.

"This is ridiculous, Vi," Iris was saying as she zipped one of Violet's suitcases closed. "Okay, whatever, you're going through with this absurd, sham marriage plan—that I don't agree with, by the way—but that doesn't mean you have to leave."

"I don't *want* to leave, but do you know of any happily married couples that willingly live apart?" Violet asked.

Iris frowned. "Not off the top of my head, but I'm sure I could find a few."

"I read somewhere that Victoria and David Beckham live in different parts of their house," Lily offered. "They seem pretty happy."

"They're rich," Violet said, sliding on her Hunter snow boot. "Despite what people say, most of the time, money *does* buy happiness." She looked up at her sisters. "I'll be fine. And

I have a few work things to keep me busy. I have a virtual fitting with Angel for the Grammys and I'll finally have time to update my portfolio. Xavier said he lives like ten minutes away from you. If anything happens, I'll come right back."

Iris sighed, still dissatisfied with this new arrangement, but she didn't continue to argue. "I hope that you will," she said.

"For some reason, I have a good feeling about this," Lily said, holding one of Violet's crutches as Violet slipped on her pea coat.

Violet raised an eyebrow. "You have a good feeling about my fake marriage?"

Lily nodded. "Just keep an open mind about things."

Whatever that meant. Violet shook her head at Lily and went to meet Xavier in the hallway. He took her suitcases from Iris, and Violet hugged her sisters and shouted good-bye to her parents and Calla in the kitchen.

"Auntie, where are you going?" Calla asked, suddenly appearing in the hallway.

"Not too far. I'll be staying at my friend's house a few minutes away." Violet held out her arms. "Come on, give me a hug."

Tentatively, Calla approached Violet, but her eyes were on Xavier. He smiled and waved at Calla and she shyly waved back. "You're leaving with him?" she whispered as Violet wrapped her in a tight hug. Violet nodded. "Who is he?"

"His name is Xavier," Violet answered. "I knew him in high school."

Calla's expression turned somewhat thoughtful. She spared Xavier another shy glance. "It's all right if he draws on your cast, just tell him he can't draw over my flower, okay?"

"I will," Violet said. "I promise."

Outside, Xavier walked closely beside Violet down the snowy driveway and helped her into the passenger seat of his black Nissan Altima before placing her crutches and suitcases in the back seat. The inside of his car smelled like his cologne. She couldn't ignore how he was treating her with such care because of her injury.

"Thank you," she said.

"For what?" he asked as he backed out of the driveway and drove down Iris's street.

She swallowed and shrugged. "Carrying my things. And . . . um, helping me with my parents. I appreciate it."

"No problem," Xavier said. "It felt like your mom was about to tell us that we were grounded."

Violet laughed and shook her head. They fell quiet as they left Iris's neighborhood and ventured farther into Willow Ridge, passing the ShopRite, the library and the community center. You could drive from one end of Willow Ridge to the other in about fifteen minutes flat. Violet didn't know where Xavier lived now exactly, but she knew it was somewhere on the opposite side of town. He made a left at the post office and pulled into the parking lot. Confused, Violet glanced over at him.

"Do you have to mail something?" she asked.

"Oh, nah," he said, not looking at her. "I live here."

She blinked. "At the post office?"

That got a small laugh out of him. "The apartment *behind* the post office."

He nodded, and Violet looked toward his apartment, which was attached directly to the back of the post office. She'd never really thought about the space when she was younger. She'd always kind of assumed it was used for extra storage. She certainly hadn't assumed someone lived there.

"You remember the post office manager, Mr. Young? He owns the apartment and rented it to me for cheap a few years ago," Xavier said. He cleared his throat. "It was all I could afford at the time, so I took it."

"That makes sense," she said. He still wasn't looking at her. It was almost like he was too nervous to meet her eye. Why?

He cut the engine and opened his door, and after a slightly complicated yet short trek from the car, during which Violet struggled through the snow on her crutches and Xavier tried not to slip while holding her suitcases, he unlocked his front door, revealing the inside of his apartment.

As Violet stepped over the threshold and looked around, her first thought was that Xavier's apartment was the epitome of cozy. By the door there was a small bookshelf, and from a quick glance, she could see that it was stacked with works about pedagogy, as well as classic novels like *Jazz* by Toni Morrison and *Notes of a Native Son* by James Baldwin. There were knit blankets draped on the arms of the brown couch in front of the television. Some type of large plant was potted in the corner of the room by the window. And past the living room, there was a small kitchen with a circular wooden table and four matching chairs. The walls were painted light blue. Years ago, during her intern days, she'd helped style a holiday photo shoot for a spread in *Elle*, and they'd designed the set to look strikingly similar to Xavier's apartment. She didn't know what she'd expected from his living space. Maybe for it to look like the typical bachelor pad, bare and cold. She had to admit that she was impressed.

"Um, so this is where I live," Xavier said.

Violet realized she was still standing in the doorway.

"Sorry," she said, moving aside so that Xavier could close the door behind her.

"I know what you're thinking—this is almost better than the Plaza Hotel. That's what everyone says."

Violet laughed quietly. "I like your apartment."

His eyes widened. "You do?"

"Yeah, it's nice."

"Thank you." He scratched the back of his neck and looked around. "I can give you a very short tour. Here's the living room and kitchen. And down the hall is the bathroom and bedroom."

As she followed him through the living room and down the short hallway, the awkwardness of their situation began to settle over her again. She would be sharing this space with him for four weeks. And while his apartment was cozy, it was also small. They'd practically be living on top of each other.

Xavier clicked on the light in his bathroom. She spotted collagen supplements on the sink, and he quickly grabbed them and placed them in the medicine cabinet. Her dad took collagen supplements whenever he spent too much time kneeling in the garden. They were supposed to help with joint pain.

"Is everything okay with you?" she asked, then wondered if maybe that was too personal a question.

"Yeah, my lower calf just bothers me sometimes."

"Oh. From your injury in college?"

He nodded. She didn't know the details of his decision to leave Kentucky, but she figured his torn Achilles had something to do with it. She wouldn't pry, though. And anyway, her attention was held by something new when Xavier led her to his bedroom.

It was probably the largest room in his apartment, large enough to fit a king-size bed, a dresser on one side of the room and a full closet on the other. His bed was covered with a dark blue comforter. Her own bed was a full, so his king looked massive. Once again, unwarranted, the image of them sleeping naked side by side in Vegas materialized in her mind. She felt a flutter in her chest, and an ache spread across her limbs. What was wrong with her?

"Nice," she mumbled.

"Huh?" Xavier said, letting out a heavy breath as he placed her suitcases by the bed.

"Um, I said your room is nice."

"Well, by now you know it's definitely *not* the Plaza, but thanks." He shrugged and smiled, slightly self-deprecating. This was the same person who'd once boasted to her about how he was the shit because he had a BlackBerry, even though the screen was cracked. Violet found his new somewhat bashful behavior so endearing, she smiled a little in return. And they stood there like smiling idiots until Violet realized that they were having some sort of moment, and she needed to put an end to it.

She pointedly looked away from him. Xavier cleared his throat and turned to his dresser, where he began to remove the clothes in his top drawer.

"You can, uh, put some of your things there if you want," he said. "And I just washed the sheets this morning, so everything is clean." He took his pile of clothes and dropped them inside a basket in his closet. "I'll leave you to unpack."

"You're sure you don't mind sleeping on the couch?" she asked as he moved past her to the hallway.

"I'm gonna have a crick in my neck tomorrow morning, for sure," he said. He smirked at her. "I hope you're cool with paying for the physical therapy that I'll need, since this is kind of all your fault."

She gasped, crossing her arms over her chest defensively. "Yeah, at first it was my fault, but keeping up with the lie was *your* idea. You know what? I'll sleep on the couch, and that way I'll have a crick in my neck *and* a messed-up ankle, and I'll be in so much pain after four weeks, I'll never be able to leave, and then you'll be stuck with me."

Xavier's brows rose as he continued to smirk, and she immediately regretted even joking about imposing herself on him for eternity.

"I was playing," he said, eyes on her as he backed into the hall. "I've fallen asleep on the couch more times than I can count. I'll be fine." He turned in the direction of the living room, then doubled back. "Actually, I should proba-bly shower now to get out of your way." He grabbed a few items of clothing from the bottom drawer of his dresser. "Let me know if you need anything."

"I will," she said. She glanced at the T-shirt and shorts

in his hands. "I'll be unpacked by the time you finish show-ering. You can get dressed in your room. I don't want to in-convenience you." Then she added, "Thank you."

He shrugged like it wasn't a big deal to him either way and left the room. She didn't sit on his bed until she heard the bathroom door close. Then she sighed and took another moment to look around his room. He'd claimed that, de-spite the time and distance, they still knew each other, but she wasn't so sure. If anything, being in his apartment made it glaringly obvious just how much she didn't know about him. This apartment was a reflection of who he'd become in the years since their breakup. He was a fully fledged adult with plants and books and real furniture, and she'd had no part in any of it. He was foreign to her. Suddenly, she felt incredibly, confusingly sad.

Her confusing feelings delayed her unpacking, so she had only managed to put her underwear in the top drawer of his dresser when she heard the creak of the bathroom door opening. She attempted to quickly leave so that Xavier could get dressed, which was difficult on her crutches. And on her way out of his room, she crashed right into Xavier and his bare, damp chest.

"Oh!" She started.

"Sorry." He reached both arms out to steady her. She glanced down, and the towel around his waist thankfully stayed in place. "I thought you'd be finished unpacking."

She looked back up and at his pecs. His muscular pecs. And, God, he smelled amazing. What *was* that body wash he used? Absurdly, she conjured an image of herself licking his chest. What was wrong with her?! Jesus, she hadn't had sex in . . . Wait, no, the last time she'd had sex was two weeks ago with Xavier and she couldn't remember any of it! No wonder seeing him like this turned her into a hornball.

His hands settled lightly at her upper arms as she backed away. Her eyes were drawn to the tattoo of a violet on the inside of his right bicep again. Her touchstone whenever he was shirtless in her presence, apparently. His bicep flexed, and she looked up at him. A ghost of a smile crossed his lips. Had he done that on purpose?

"You okay?" he asked.

No, she wasn't.

This was too much. Xavier shirtless. The tattoo. Living in his apartment, where she would be for the next month.

"I'm fine." It came out like a squeak. "I'll be out there, um, in the living room."

She swore she heard him softly chuckling as she made her way down the hall.

She was absolutely in over her head with this plan to be Xavier's pretend wife. There was no way she was going to survive four weeks here with him.

11

XAVIER TURNED THE KEY IN THE LOCK AND ENTERED HIS quiet apartment. He placed his keys on the coffee table and glanced down the hallway. His bedroom door was slightly ajar, and he could hear the murmur of Violet's voice as she spoke in a steady, quick rhythm. She was most likely on a video call. It had been three days since she'd temporarily moved in, and despite their agreement to switch beds, Xavier fully planned to let her sleep in his room every night. He wouldn't subject her to his uncomfortable pullout couch. He'd never been more aware of the small size of his apartment, or the nicks in his kitchen table, or the drab green of his shower curtain until he tried to view everything through Violet's eyes.

He couldn't help wondering what she thought of his place. She'd deemed it nice, but he wasn't sure if she was just trying to be polite. His apartment wasn't immaculate and modern like her parents' or Iris's houses. Although he hadn't seen it, he was sure his place wasn't much compared to Violet's apartment in the city. And he was positive that his apartment paled in comparison to her ex's place, her ex who took her on vacation to the Maldives. For all Xavier knew, her ex lived in a mansion. But at least Violet didn't need to climb any stairs to get to Xavier's front door.

He walked into the kitchen to warm up a frozen dinner before he had to head back to the school for tonight's game. They were playing Yardley High, one of Willow Ridge's biggest rivals. Willow Ridge would have to put up a fight to continue their undefeated season, but Xavier had faith that the boys would continue their winning streak, fly through the playoffs, and make it to the championships this year.

He pulled his frozen chicken-and-rice dinner from the freezer and popped it into the microwave. When he opened the fridge to grab a bottle of Gatorade, he saw two cartons of Thai takeout. Yesterday, it had been a Chipotle burrito bowl container. Either Violet was hesitant to use his pots and pans or she wasn't much of a cook. He had no room to judge. He hardly cooked either. Not because he lacked the skill; he just rarely had the energy by the time he got home from work. He and Violet hadn't eaten a meal together yet. So far, their evening routine was that he came home late after practice, scarfed down some food while working on his lesson plans or grading papers before going to the gym, while Violet typed away on her laptop on the living room couch or in his bedroom, and by the time he returned from his workout, she was already in bed. When she heard him arranging the pullout couch, she'd ask if he was sure that he didn't mind sleeping in the living room. He'd say no, he didn't mind, and let her think that the couch was perfectly comfortable, while silently cursing the joints he already knew would ache in the morning, and then they'd both fall asleep in their respective areas of his little apartment.

He hoped she felt comfortable. He hoped she didn't hate being here. He wished he had more to offer. Even though she was the one who'd gotten them into this mess in the first place.

The microwave beeped, snapping Xavier to attention. He was sitting at the table, blowing on his steaming food, when Violet made her way into the kitchen on her crutches. She was wearing a simple black knit sweater and yoga pants. Her hair was pulled away from her face in a low, curly ponytail. Her skin looked shiny and soft, like the women in makeup commercials. His heartbeat sped up as he gazed at her. She'd probably always have that effect on him. On instinct, he stood to help move the chairs out of her way.

"Thank you," she said, "and sorry. I wouldn't have taken my meeting in your room if I knew you were coming home earlier. Your room has the best natural light."

"It's no problem. We have a game tonight instead of practice, so that's why I'm here." He watched as she retrieved her takeout from the fridge and warmed it up in the microwave. "I'm still trying to schedule a dinner date with the head coach at Riley University, by the way. He said he'd get back to me by the end of this week."

"Cool." She took her food out of the microwave and sat across from him, leaning her crutches against the chair beside her.

He nodded at her pad Thai. "Looks good."

"It is." She glanced up at him. "Want to try some?"

"No, thanks." He pointed his fork at his sad frozen dinner. "Michelin-star quality right here."

She laughed softly and gave his meal a doubtful look. "I bet."

A silence expanded between them as they ate their food. Xavier was unsure of what to say or even if he should bother saying anything more at all. It was funny to think that there had once been a time when conversation between them had flowed easier than breathing.

He spared her another glance and saw that she was smirking at him.

"What?" he asked, feeling himself smile in response.

"We're being so awkward. You would think we didn't take each other's virginity."

Xavier snorted, caught off guard. "Damn. That's one way to address the elephant in the room."

She shrugged. "I never claimed to be subtle."

"True." He checked the time on his phone. He still had about thirty minutes before he needed to be back at the school. He relaxed in his chair. "How was your day?"

"It was okay." She sighed and set down her fork. "Actually, it was kind of painful."

He sat up, alert. "You mean your ankle?"

"No, no. That's fine. It's New York Fashion Week, and usually I'd be running around, seeing the best shows and getting the first look at the new fashion of the season, but I can't because of my ankle. My assistant has been going to the shows in my place. I was just on a video call with her, and everything seems to be going smoothly. She'll probably go to London and Milan in my place too, maybe Paris. I just wish I was there to handle it myself. There are setbacks to seeing clothes virtually as opposed to in person."

"Like what?" he asked, genuinely curious.

"Well, if I'm not there in person, it's not as easy to see the end result of an outfit or visualize how a client might look on a red carpet," she explained. "My assistant does a great job at taking photos from several angles so that I have more to work with. It's not the end of the world, of course. But I tend to have this nagging thought in the back of my mind that if I screw up somehow while I'm working remotely, everything will fall apart and my clients will fire me."

"But who else would they even hire?" he asked. "I don't think I've ever met anyone who takes fashion as seriously as you do. Even when we were younger, I don't ever remember you repeating an outfit. You said you wanted to be a celebrity stylist and now that's exactly what you're doing. I know you probably hustled your ass off."

"For sure," she said. "Hustling was the only way. After college I took a job as a styling assistant for a team that mostly worked with rappers on music video shoots, and I did that for a few years while organizing people's closets on the side for extra income. Then on one shoot, I met Gigi Harrison, who was a video model, and we became cool, and when she got her first role in that comedy with Jerrod Carmichael, she asked me to dress her for the premiere. That got the ball rolling, and I've tried my best to keep it rolling ever since."

"Gigi Harrison," he said, nodding. "I know her. She was in that Wonder Woman movie a couple months ago."

"Energy Girl," Violet corrected, smiling.

"Right, right. That's what I meant. That's really impressive, Vi."

"Thanks." She picked up her fork. "Anyway, how was *your* day?"

"It wasn't too bad. My classes finished reading *Lord of the Flies* earlier this week, so I spent most of today watching the movie every period."

"The same black-and-white version that we watched in high school?"

He grinned, shaking his head. "Nah, the 1990 movie. I try my best not to bore them. We're reading *The Things They Carried* next."

"I thought you said you try not to bore them," she said, laughing.

He felt lighter at the sound of her laughter. His grin widened. "Come on, it's a good book."

"I didn't say it wasn't good. But it was confusing. What was real and what was fake? All I know is that I almost bombed my midterm because of that book."

"See, the theme of truth versus reality is what makes it so compelling. It reads like a work of nonfiction, but it's actually *metafiction*."

"Wow," she said, staring at him. "You really are an English teacher. I'm curious to hear how you decided that teaching was what you wanted to do."

He shrugged. "I don't know if it's something I actively decided. I didn't go back to Kentucky after my surgery because . . . I'd lost confidence in myself, I guess. So I transferred to Riley, and after college I struggled to find work. Honestly, I was just really lost. I took a job subbing and then a long-term position opened up when Mr. Rodney was out for surgery. I really liked working with the kids, and I saw that the course material really needed an update, so I started a committee to come up with a new reading list for the English classes. I think the administration must have liked that because when another teacher retired, they offered to hire me once I got my certification." He laughed softly. "It's definitely different from all those NBA dreams I used to share with you."

She titled her head slightly, still smiling. "It's not the NBA. And it's not what I expected from you at all, really, but I'm impressed, Xavier."

If he were a peacock, he would have puffed his chest up and spread his feathers.

"Thanks," he said.

Then an alarm sounded on his phone, ending their moment.

"Shit, I have to go," he said. He stood slowly, reluctantly.

"Who are you playing tonight?"

"Yardley." He walked around the table and dropped the plastic dinner carton in the recycling bin. "They're good this year too."

Violet cupped her hands and began an old dance team chant. "We can strike like lightning. We can roll like thunder, and if you mess with us, we'll put you six feet under!" She barked a laugh. "I can't believe they used to let us say that cheer. Good luck. I hope you win."

"Thanks." Then, like a fool, he blurted, "You should come to the game with me." Violet's eyes widened. It was too late to backtrack now. He forged ahead, hastily adding, "It would probably look good for, you know, our marriage."

"Oh." She glanced down. "I don't know if I really feel up to seeing anyone tonight. I should probably stay home."

He nodded, mentally kicking himself for even making the suggestion. He'd gotten carried away by their simple conversation about work.

"Yeah, I get it. Well, I'll see you later, then."

"Bye," she said quietly.

Accompanying him to high school basketball games wasn't part of their temporary arrangement. He shook off his silly feelings of disappointment as he walked outside to his car. Because there was no need to be disappointed.

Despite their history, despite how she still seemed to send his heart racing, they weren't actually a couple. That was the reality.

WHEN THE SECOND quarter began, Willow Ridge was up, beating Yardley 27–12. Dante Jones, a sophomore and the burgeoning star of Willow Ridge's team, dribbled down the court and let the ball fly from his grasp, effortlessly scoring a three-pointer. The crowd cheered, and Dante grinned from ear to ear, winking at the home bleachers as he ran back up the court. In a town like Willow Ridge where there wasn't much to do, attending high school basketball games was a source of entertainment for everyone. Especially this year with the team's undefeated streak.

Xavier stood on the sidelines beside Mr. Rodney, who'd

been his basketball coach during his tenure at Willow Ridge. While Mr. Rodney was technically the head coach, most of the coaching these days fell to Xavier, because despite Mr. Rodney's love for and commitment to the school, he was a little checked out. Xavier couldn't blame him. Mr. Rodney had been teaching and coaching basketball for decades, and Xavier respected that he didn't want to retire. But that was one of the reasons he felt like he needed to move on from Willow Ridge. He didn't want to be the high school's assistant coach forever.

On the court, Elijah Dawson passed the ball to Dante, who was supposed to pass it back so that Elijah could cut down the middle and score a layup, but at the last minute, Dante kept the ball to himself and attempted another three-pointer. The ball arced through the air and landed in the hoop, only to spin around the rim and fall out. Someone on Yardley's team snatched the ball and raced down the court, hitting a layup. A collective groan of disappointment erupted from the crowd. Elijah and the rest of the team aimed pissed-off glances at Dante. For his part, Dante did appear remorseful. His head dropped, and he let out a deep sigh. When he glanced up and made eye contact with Xavier, Xavier gave him a knowing look.

Play like you're on a team, he mouthed.

Dante nodded. It wasn't the first time Xavier had said this to him.

In a way, Dante reminded Xavier of his younger self. Dante was naturally talented and could be a cocky showman at times. Xavier didn't want to dim any of his players' shine, but he wanted them to stay grounded. That way they wouldn't end up like him. He'd stepped onto the University of Kentucky's campus thinking he was the shit. Colleges from all over the country had scouted him, and after weeks of letting coaches wine and dine him and his mother, Xavier had chosen Kentucky. The cultural differences in his new state were hard to adapt to, and once basketball practice started, Xavier realized just how skilled his teammates were. He'd gone from being a big fish in a small pond to a guppy in an ocean filled with whales.

His teammates were already being handpicked for the NBA, and instead of using that as motivation to become a better player, Xavier got caught up playing the comparison game. He wasn't fast enough, his technique wasn't clean enough. His jealousy affected how he played. He rarely saw eye to eye with the head coach, who didn't give him enough playing time. Instead of listening to the coach's advice about how to improve his skills, Xavier took being benched as a personal slight. He could have gone to any basketball program, and instead he was in Kentucky, wasting his time. Didn't they know who he was? Couldn't they see his potential? But secretly, he wondered if he'd ever had any real potential to begin with. When he tore his Achilles tendon after failing to execute a fancy trick during practice, he'd wounded his body and his pride. He went home to Willow Ridge with his tail between his legs. Instead of grinding harder and returning to Kentucky, he gave up on himself and enrolled at Riley. Now he was reaping the consequences of that decision.

He'd spent the years since feeling unfulfilled, like he let himself and everyone else down. It was why he wanted the new coaching position at Riley so bad. The NBA was no longer in the cards for him, if it ever had been, but he could help build Riley's basketball program to be one of the best in the state, maybe even the country. He needed a way to redeem himself. To prove that he wasn't a failure or a has-been.

The halftime buzzer rang and Xavier, Mr. Rodney and the team went into the locker room. Instantly, the other boys ripped into Dante, admonishing him for his silly, selfish play. Mr. Rodney attempted to gain control of the situation to no avail.

"Ay!" Xavier shouted, and they finally quieted. "I know y'all are upset, but let's not lose focus, all right? Use that energy when you're back on the court." He looked at Dante, who leaned against a locker, staring fixedly at his feet. "You owe your teammates an apology, Dante."

"I'm sorry," Dante mumbled. Then he looked up into their faces. His expression was open and earnest. "Really."

The rest of the boys nodded, and Xavier refocused their attention on plays for the second half. When they reentered the gym, Xavier's steps faltered as he spotted Violet sitting on the bottom row of the home bleachers beside Bianca and Raheem. She was bouncing their one-year-old son, RJ, in her lap and angling her head this way and that to get a look around the gym. Her gaze finally landed on Xavier, and she lifted her hand in a tentative wave. He waved back, wondering what had changed her mind about coming tonight.

During his high school games, he'd always felt better knowing that she was there, cheering him on. Now, as the game resumed, Xavier concentrated on his players, all too conscious of Violet's presence. Each time Willow Ridge scored, he found himself casting a quick glance across the court to where Violet was seated. She was unable to jump to her feet and cheer along with the rest of the crowd, but she did clap and smile. He guessed her normal weeknight activities were usually much more entertaining, but it looked like she was enjoying herself somewhat.

The final buzzer rang, and Willow Ridge beat Yardley 53–36. The undefeated streak continued.

Afterward, as Xavier exchanged greetings with some of the parents, he felt a gentle tap on his shoulder. He turned around and Violet was standing behind him.

"Hey," she said, smiling hesitantly. She nodded at Dante as he walked out of the locker room with his duffel bag slung over his shoulder. "That one boy reminds me of you."

"Dante? Yeah, he's the real deal. Needs some handling every now and then, though." He paused. "What made you decide to come?"

"Honestly? I got bored. I called Bianca and asked if she wanted to hang out and she said she was coming here, so . . ." She trailed off, shrugging. "She and Raheem had to leave early because RJ was getting cranky, but I wanted to stay until the end of the game. Can I ride home with you?"

"Of course," he said. "Just let me get my stuff, and we can go."

"You don't have to rush." She shifted on her crutches, and he noticed something flash on her left hand. The rings from Vegas. Her brown cheeks reddened when she realized what had caught his attention. She began fidgeting with the rings, spinning them around her finger.

"I thought I should wear them," she said. "For appearances and everything."

"Yeah, same." He lifted his hand, showing that he wore his ring as well. He focused on the flushed skin of her cheeks. When they were younger, he used to find Violet's beauty distracting. She was even more captivating now.

"Violet Greene!"

Xavier and Violet startled, and he turned around to see Mrs. Franklin rushing over to them. She hip checked Xavier out of the way and wrapped Violet in a borderline aggressive hug.

"I am so happy to see you, young lady," she said, squeezing Violet's torso.

Violet blinked and her lips slightly parted in surprise. She hadn't exactly been Mrs. Franklin's favorite student. He could understand why Violet was so shocked.

"We're very proud of you," Mrs. Franklin said, pulling away but maintaining a firm grip on Violet's shoulders. "And what a beautiful new bride you are! I always knew the two of you would end up together. Didn't I say that, Xavier?"

"Yeah, you did," Xavier said, watching as Violet attempted to release herself from Mrs. Franklin's hold. Smoothly, he eased behind Violet and placed his arm around her shoulders, causing Mrs. Franklin to finally let go.

"Thank you," Violet whispered low enough for only him to hear. She looked at Mrs. Franklin and smiled in the deceptively sweet way that she'd reserved for authority figures years ago. "It's nice to see you again."

"You are a *gorgeous* couple." Mrs. Franklin beamed. "Just gorgeous!"

"That's nice of you to say." Xavier began to back away, his arm still secured around Violet's shoulders. "We're about to head home, actually."

But then the rest of his colleagues appeared, introducing themselves to Violet and telling her how nice it was to meet the woman who'd stolen Xavier's heart. Violet's eyes darted from face to face. Her lips were frozen in a pleasant smile.

"You're coming to the school fundraiser at the bowling alley Saturday night, right?" asked Nadia Morales.

Violet turned to Xavier for further explanation. "Oh," he said. "You don't—"

"You didn't tell her about the fundraiser?" Mrs. Franklin gasped. You would have thought he'd committed a crime. "You organized it!" To Violet, she said, "We're raising money to get new uniforms for the sports teams. It was Xavier's idea."

"Really?" Violet said. She was looking at him the way she had in the kitchen earlier. With intrigued surprise. It made him want to puff out his chest like a peacock again.

"Yeah, but it's not a big deal," he said. "I know you're busy with work."

"It's your fundraiser, and I'm your wife." She shot him a private look. One that said, *How bad would it look if I wasn't there?* "Of course I'll come."

She had a point. She *should* be there. And it was good that she was going along with appearances.

So then why did the thought of exposing the mundane activities of his day-to-day life make him so nervous?

12

"SO DID Y'ALL HAVE SOBER SEX YET OR WHAT?" KARINA asked.

Violet rushed to lower the volume on her phone, and Karina let out a mischievous cackle.

"Girl, *no*," Violet whispered, throwing a quick glance over her shoulder. She was in Xavier's bedroom, using the mirror above his dresser to flat twist her hair while Xavier was eating a snack in the kitchen. "I told you this is just a temporary arrangement."

Tonight, she and Xavier were going to the bowling alley fundraiser, and for reasons Violet could not explain, she felt nervous. Maybe it was because she was unsure of what to expect. Or more accurately, what was expected of her. Xavier had organized the fundraiser, and as his "wife," she wondered what the extent of her participation would be. Maybe she'd simply have to stand beside him and smile the whole night. She could do that. She loathed the idea of running into people from high school and the questions they'd have about her and Xavier's surprise reunion, but this was the short-term role she'd signed up for, so she'd just have to

suck it up, because running into half of the town's population was inevitable. Fundraisers in Willow Ridge always had
a high turnout. She remembered how many people would
show up to buy cupcakes and snickerdoodles whenever the
dance team held bake sales at the community center. Yesterday, while at the nail salon with Iris and Calla, she'd
spotted a flyer for tonight's fundraiser taped to the wall beside the gel polishes.

"Where's he at now?" Karina asked. She was sitting inside her trailer on the set of *Up Next*, opening a box of
Goobers.

"In the kitchen," Violet said.

Karina smiled in response.

Violet narrowed her eyes. "Stop it."

"What?" Karina shook a handful of chocolate-covered
peanuts into her mouth. While chewing, she said, "It's kind
of *domestic*, though. Don't you think? You're doing your
hair in the bedroom mirror while he's in the kitchen. You
sleep in his bed every night. Don't be mad at me. I'm simply
making an observation."

"You're conveniently ignoring that he sleeps on the pullout bed in the living room."

"For the time being," Karina said, wiggling her eyebrows.
Violet gave her another exasperated look, and Karina sighed,
although she was still smiling. "Okay, okay. I'll stop now."

"Thank you." Violet focused on smoothing down her
edges. She glanced at the reflection of Xavier's king-size
bed in the mirror. She'd slept like a baby in that bed every
day this week. She kept meaning to ask where he'd bought
his mattress, but doing so would call attention to the fact

that she was, indeed, sleeping in his bed every night. And while she'd made a joke the other day about them taking each other's virginity, she didn't want a conversation about his mattress to lead to another conversation about how they'd woken up side by side in a different king-size bed weeks ago.

Their decision to play house had happened so quickly, Violet hadn't really come to terms yet with how she felt about being here. In the evenings, while she uploaded photos of her clients at various events to her Instagram, he graded papers in the living room. And she still couldn't get over him wearing glasses. He used to pass high school eye exams with flying colors. To make matters worse, the glasses made him look sexier. It embarrassed her that she was still so attracted to him.

Also embarrassing was the quick flash of . . . something that flared up inside her more than once when she caught a glimpse of him as he walked from one room to the next, or when he strolled through the front door after practice. She couldn't put a name to the feeling. It was a seizing deep in her gut. Anxiety? Apprehension? A mixture of the two? She'd spent years forcing herself not to think about him and now she was constantly confronted with his presence. It was hard to handle.

Still on FaceTime, Karina's trailer door opened, and Brian and Melody appeared in the camera behind her.

"Vi!" Melody said, her mouth splitting into a wide smile. "How are you doing?"

"I'm okay," she said. Her heart ached looking at them. "I miss y'all."

Brian raised an eyebrow. "Miss us for what? Aren't you shacking up with your new suburban boo? I would be laid up *all day* if I were you."

Violet rolled her eyes and he laughed.

"We miss you too, girl," Karina said. "You'll be back with us soon."

"Not soon enough," Violet mumbled, looking pointedly at her cast.

Melody and Brian needed to touch up Karina's hair and makeup before she went back on set. Reluctantly, Violet bid her friends goodbye and sighed.

She gave herself another once-over in the mirror. She was wearing a loose-fitting cream-colored cashmere turtleneck and dark blue wide-leg jeans. Her cast kept the jeans from giving their full effect, but oh well. She swiped on wine red lipstick and did a quick cat eye. She didn't know if her look gave off Young Wife of Local Teacher, but it would have to do.

She opened the dresser's top drawer, where she kept her underwear and socks, searching for a sock to wear tonight, but the drawer jammed as she pulled. She fidgeted with it until she was able to yank it off its slides, and then a small photograph fluttered to the ground. She crouched down and examined the photo more closely. It was the picture that she and Xavier took at the chapel in Vegas, clasping at each other, kissing like their lives depended on it.

"Violet, you ready?"

She snapped to attention when Xavier called her name from the living room.

"Yeah, coming!" she called back.

She returned the photograph to the bottom of the drawer and placed the drawer back on its slides, wondering why Xavier had kept the photo instead of throwing it away. She didn't want to compare it to the way she'd kept the rings.

WHEN THEY ARRIVED at the bowling alley, some of Xavier's colleagues were already setting up the sign-in table and another table not too far from the door where people could purchase baked goods. Like Xavier, his colleagues wore Willow Ridge sweatshirts and jeans, and Violet wondered if she was too overdressed or looked out of place in her cashmere turtleneck. She turned to him, about to ask his opinion, when they were interrupted by Mrs. Franklin.

"Good, you're here," Mrs. Franklin said, holding up her phone. "I'm taking pictures for the newsletter. I'd love to get a few shots of the newlyweds."

"Oh, sure," Xavier said, glancing down at Violet. He wrapped his arm around her and she easily leaned into him, feeling his warmth. They smiled as Mrs. Franklin snapped several photos.

"Okay, now do something else," she said. "Give Violet a kiss or something, Xavier."

They froze. Violet blinked, and Xavier's arm went slack around her shoulders.

"Oh," he said, "I don't—"

"Come on, don't be shy!"

The volume of Mrs. Franklin's voice caught the attention of Xavier's other colleagues, who also began to encourage their kiss, cheering them on. Someone even whistled.

Violet gulped and looked up at Xavier. He stared back, his expression stricken. It would look bad if they outright refused to kiss, wouldn't it? Married people kissed. This was part of their role. She took a deep breath and angled her face upward. Xavier's eyes widened, and he raised an eyebrow, like he was asking if she was sure. Her heart pounded as she nodded in a small, almost imperceptible motion.

Violet held her breath as Xavier leaned down to her. She kept her gaze on his face, his direct stare and his full lips. She told herself that she had no reason to be nervous. It was going to be a short and sweet peck. But then Xavier cradled the left side of her face with his hand and gently pressed his lips against hers, and she felt the warmth and softness of his mouth. Time slowed for the briefest moment as his lips moved over hers, and Violet found herself closing her eyes. She pressed closer to him, her pulse pounding. Then he pulled away all too soon, and Violet blinked at him, dazed. Xavier stared back at her in equal fascination. Around them, his colleagues burst into applause.

"Beautiful!" Mrs. Franklin declared.

Xavier cleared his throat. Somewhere during their kiss, they'd locked hands.

"All right, Xavier, I need you to speak to the manager and make sure the discount on shoes is still in effect," Mrs. Franklin said. "Violet, can I put you on raffle ticket duty?"

Violet nodded quickly, still in a daze. "Um, yes, sure."

Xavier stepped away from her, dropping her hand, and immediately she felt his absence. His expression was reluctant. "Will you be okay?" he asked.

Violet nodded again, and he smiled at her before walking away.

"Oh, don't look like that!" Mrs. Franklin said, nudging Violet. "He's only going to the other end of the bowling alley. He won't be that far from you." She grinned and sighed. "I remember how I was when my husband and I were first married. I didn't want to let him out of my sight for a second either."

Violet jerked to look at Mrs. Franklin. *What?* No, she definitely was not staring after Xavier because she didn't want him to leave her side. She was looking at him because . . . well . . . because . . . Actually, it didn't matter why! What mattered was that she needed to sit and rest her ankle.

"Where's the raffle ticket station?" she asked, and then she let Mrs. Franklin lead her to the bar, where they'd set up the raffle ticket bucket.

The bowling alley swiftly became packed. A portion of each entry fee went toward the fundraiser. People raved over the baked goods, but the big draw was the raffle prizes: Brooklyn Nets season tickets, dinner for two at the local Italian restaurant, Il Forno, and a toaster oven air fryer.

Perched on a stool at the cash bar, Violet had an open vantage point of the bowling alley, which in turn meant everyone could see her as well. She'd already participated in small talk with three former high school classmates when Shalia McNair, Xavier's senior-year prom date, approached her. Shalia and her mom owned a catering business and had provided the baked goods.

"So the two of you got married, just like that?" Shalia asked, quirking an eyebrow. At first, Violet hadn't recognized Shalia. In high school, Shalia had been short with dark and wild curly hair. Violet and Bianca used to joke that Shalia's hair was so big because it held everyone's secrets. She'd gossiped that much. Now her locks were honey blond and bone straight like she got keratin treatments. She'd also experienced a growth spurt. She towered over Violet in a pair of interesting-looking platform booties.

"Mm-hmm," Violet said, taking another sip of her wine. "How are *you*, though? Hair looks bomb."

"Thank you, but when did y'all reconnect, exactly?" Shalia continued, undeterred. Apparently, she still had a penchant for gossip. "Because I saw Xavier at Applebee's like three weeks ago and he didn't mention anything about you."

Violet frowned slightly, positive that Shalia meant for her words to come across as a barb. Shalia had a crush on Xavier in high school, and after he'd taken her to prom but left with Violet, Shalia had decided that Violet was public enemy number one, and she'd tried her hardest to spread false rumors about Violet, but to no avail, because Violet had been too well-liked. Plus, there had been no reason for Shalia to take Violet and Xavier's actions so personally. They'd had blinders on when it came to everyone but each other back then.

She looked past Shalia's shoulder now, searching for Xavier. She spotted him at one of the lanes, surrounded by a group of his students. He smiled warmly at them as they talked over one another, fighting for his attention. He held up his index finger, telling them he'd be right back, and Violet's gaze followed him as he walked over to one of his colleagues at the bake sale table. People called out to him in greeting as they entered the bowling alley. Years ago, Violet had been drawn to him because he was someone new in a place riddled with boring familiarity. They'd bonded because they had both wanted to escape. But Xavier had decided to stay, and now he was integral to this community in a way she couldn't have expected. And temporarily, she was the one there at his side. Her lips tingled, thinking about their kiss.

"We were keeping things low-key at first," Violet said, turning back to Shalia. "Next time you go to Applebee's, let me know. I haven't been in forever. Maybe the three of us can go together."

Shalia glowered, and Violet smiled sweetly. Was it a petty comment to make? Yes. But she figured she was allowed to stir the pot just a little since Shalia essentially tried to insinuate that Xavier had purposely kept Violet a secret.

"Oh. Well, congratulations, I guess," Shalia said dully. She sent a wistful gaze across the bowling alley to Xavier.

Thankfully, at that moment, Bianca and Raheem arrived with RJ. Violet waved, catching Bianca's attention; she made a beeline for Violet, pushing RJ in a stroller, while Raheem talked with Xavier by the door.

"It was *so* nice to see you, Shalia, but I really need to focus on my duties," Violet said, ready for their interaction to end. She held up the raffle jar. "This fundraiser is *very* important to my husband. Are you going to buy a ticket to support the kids? They're two dollars each."

Shalia grumbled as she tossed money to Violet and stuffed her raffle ticket in her purse. She didn't even bother to say goodbye before she walked away.

"Willow Ridge High thanks you for your donation!" Violet called after her.

Bianca slid onto the stool beside Violet and unbuckled RJ from his stroller, propping him in her lap. "Uh-oh, I haven't seen your evil grin in years. What did Shalia say to you?"

"She hates me for making Xavier unavailable again." Violet could speak freely to Bianca since she and Raheem already knew the truth behind their marriage agreement. Violet held out her hands for RJ. "Gimme gimme."

Bianca gently placed RJ in Violet's arms and he smiled up at her and began babbling earnest baby talk. Violet nodded along like she could understand everything he was trying to say.

"If she hasn't managed to entice Xavier over the last decade, I doubt it's going to happen now," Bianca said, waving down the bartender and ordering a glass of wine. "He was never really available to her in the first place."

Violet shrugged. Who Xavier made himself available to wasn't her business, and it wasn't something she wanted to think about. Instead, she focused on making kissy faces at RJ, who laughed like she was the funniest person in the world. Babies were awesome. Well, other people's babies, who could be returned to their parents once they started to cry.

"Do you think you and Raheem will have another baby?" she asked.

"I'd like to, definitely," Bianca said, smiling at her son. "After the wedding next year."

RJ reached up and grabbed one of Violet's hoop earrings. She slowly removed his hold before he ripped her earlobe, and he laughed again. He resembled Bianca so much with his wide, round eyes and deep brown skin. But his expressive eyebrows and gleeful countenance were all Raheem.

Violet looked at Bianca, the only person she'd made a point of staying in touch with after graduation. While Violet had left for LA, Bianca had stayed behind in Willow Ridge and enrolled in cosmetology school. Now she operated her own glam salon out of her house, and she was a beautiful new mom. Their lives couldn't be more different. Violet didn't covet Bianca's life, but she envied how Bianca seemed so at peace. Violet couldn't remember the last time she'd felt that way. It had probably been years.

"What about you?" Bianca asked.

"What about me?" Violet said, tickling RJ's chubby belly.

"Marriage. Do you think you'll try to do it again? Like for real, I mean."

"Oh," Violet said. "I don't know."

Bianca eyed Violet, taking another sip of her wine. "Because of what happened with Eddy?"

"Yes and no," Violet said. "Honestly, I'm married to my career, and I'm not ashamed to say that. If I give my career everything I have, the chances of things working out in my favor are high. But it doesn't work like that with relationships. Sometimes you give it your all, or the all that you're capable of giving in the moment, and it doesn't really matter in the end if the other person doesn't meet you halfway. Or, like, do the bare minimum and keep his dick in his pants." Violet paused when she took in Bianca's disheartened expression. "What? Don't look at me like that. I'm not saying this because I want you to feel bad for me. I love my job, and right now that's more than enough."

"I know, Vi," Bianca said, sighing softly. "And you're killing it, but work isn't everything. You deserve to fall in love."

"*Blah*." Violet stuck her finger in her mouth and pretended to gag. The sound caused RJ to burst into another fit of giggles.

Bianca was wrong. Falling in love didn't always equal a happy ending. But her words did bring something else to mind.

"What was Xavier's ex-girlfriend like?" Violet asked. "The one who broke up with him and left the country."

"Michelle? She was sweet. Kind." She shrugged easily.

"Were they happy together?" Violet didn't know why she was bothering to ask, but she was overcome with curiosity.

"I think Xavier cared about her a lot, but I'm not sure if he was in love with her. Michelle told me she always felt like Xavier was waiting for his life to change, and that made her feel like she wasn't enough for him. To be fair, I don't think she was in love with him either. But it doesn't matter. Backpacking was always something she wanted to do, so she finally went for it."

"Huh," Violet said, mulling this over. Would they have stayed together if Michelle hadn't left? Would they get back together if she returned? Why did that thought make Violet's skin prickle?

"We should stop talking about this," Bianca whispered.

Violet frowned. "Why?"

"Because Xavier is walking over here."

Violet spun around, and sure enough, Xavier was heading their way. His stride was sure and confident. Her heartbeat sped up as she recalled the feeling of his mouth against hers.

Bianca took RJ from Violet's embrace and stood.

"Wait, where are you going?" Violet asked, grabbing Bianca's hand. "You don't have to leave."

Suddenly, she didn't trust herself to be alone with Xavier.

Bianca smiled, giving Violet's hand a gentle squeeze before letting go. "I'm gonna get some snacks, and I promised Raheem I'd bowl with him." She handed Violet two dollars for the raffle and leaned closer, lowering her voice. "Would it be so bad if the two of you at least became friends again?"

Violet wasn't sure if being friends with Xavier was a good idea, and that was the problem.

"What's up, B?" Xavier said, hugging Bianca and rubbing RJ's head.

He and Bianca talked for a few minutes before she pushed RJ away toward the snack bar, leaving the two of them alone. Xavier looked at Violet, giving her another one of his small smiles. She tamped down her fluttering stomach.

"I thought I'd come over and check on you," he said, taking Bianca's vacated seat. "How's the raffle going?"

"Good, I think." She placed the jar on the bar top and slid it toward him. "John Carson of Carson and Carson Realty bought at least twenty tickets. He really wants that toaster oven air fryer."

"Ah. They're all the rage."

"So I'm told," she said. "Why don't you have one?"

He shrugged. "Never felt like I needed one, I guess. Do you have one?"

"No, but that's because I don't cook."

He smirked. "I've noticed."

"I don't see you cooking either," she pointed out.

"Yeah, but I know how to."

She squinted at him. "Are you implying that *I* don't know how to cook?"

"Your words, not mine," he said, grinning.

"Well, you'd be right, but that's because I've never taken the time to learn. However, I'll have you know that I make a very good grilled cheese."

"Oh, really?" He nodded, like he found this to be impressive. "I doubt it tastes better than mine, though. I use gourmet Gouda from the deli."

Her eyes widened. Gouda? Really? Another detail she would not have expected.

"And I use Kraft brand from the dairy aisle," she said. "The classic way to make a grilled cheese."

He raised an eyebrow and leaned toward her slightly. "Sounds to me like we need to have a cook-off to figure out who makes the best sandwich."

"I guess so," she said. She felt herself leaning toward him too, once again controlled by an invisible string.

She pictured them cooking together side by side in his kitchen, and then Karina's voice popped into her head.

It's kind of domestic, *though. Don't you think?*

Violet leaned away. They needed a subject change. "The fundraiser seems like a success."

"Yeah, I'm pretty pleased with the turnout." Xavier picked up the raffle jar and shook it. "The school budget gets cut more and more every year. It's fucked up that we even have to raise money this way so that the students aren't reading books with broken spines or wearing the same uniforms that we wore in high school."

He breathed a frustrated sigh. Violet was moved by his genuine desire to help.

"Your students are lucky to have someone like you," she said.

"I'm not doing anything special," he said, shrugging. "It's the bare minimum for teachers to care."

She couldn't help smiling at him.

"What?" he said, looking at her.

"Nothing, you're just so . . . humble. It's different."

"I was pretty full of myself before, wasn't I?" He laughed and pushed his glasses farther up his nose. Why did she love it so much when he did that? "But people change. I mean, look at you. I saw you talking with Shalia McNair."

"Oh, we definitely are not friends," Violet said. "She still doesn't like me."

Xavier shook his head, smiling. "Why not?"

Because me being here means she can't have you.

"Holding on to high school drama, I suppose," she said instead.

He returned the raffle jar to the bar counter and yawned, placing both hands flat in front of him. Violet looked at his wedding band again. It was simple and thick, a slightly duller gold than her rings. She held her hand up beside his and tilted her head, examining their rings more closely. When their fingers lightly brushed, a tingle zipped through her veins.

"They make a nice set," she said, swallowing. "Even though they're not real."

"Yeah." His voice seemed quieter.

She could feel him looking at her, but she kept her eyes on their hands as she asked the question she'd been pondering for weeks. "Do you remember a lot from that night in Vegas?"

"Some of it," he said.

"I mean between the two of us," she clarified, finally returning his gaze. She took a deep breath and trudged onward. "When we hooked up. Because I can't remember anything." *And I wish I did.*

His cheeks took on a slightly reddish hue. "Sometimes I get brief flashes of holding you close. But otherwise, it's pretty fuzzy for me too."

"Oh, okay." She imagined him wrapping his arms around her in a tight embrace, and heat crept up her neck. She let her hand fall to her side. "We probably should have talked about boundaries."

"Right," he said, angling on his stool so that he was facing her fully. "Physical contact. When to hold hands or hug. I know that kiss was a surprise."

"We've kissed before," she said, keeping her voice casual. "But we probably should have practiced."

Xavier smirked. "We can practice now. Just to make sure we've still really got it."

Violet blinked. Her gaze fell to his lips. The hot tingle continued its crawl through her veins.

"Really?" she asked.

"Why not?" His eyes were glued to her face. "No one is paying attention, and if they were, what's so weird about a husband and wife kissing? But we don't have to, if you're not comfortable."

The frustrating truth was that she wanted to kiss him again.

She leaned closer once more. "Come here," she said.

Xavier listened, bringing his face closer to hers. He lightly brushed a stray curl behind her ear, and Violet sucked in a breath as their eyes locked. Her heart pounded faster in anticipation. Xavier's lips parted slightly, and when his mouth was less than an inch from hers and she felt his breath against her lips, she realized how excited she felt. How eager. To kiss Xavier a second time. Suddenly, that anxious tightening of her gut flared up. *Retreat*, it screamed. She lost her bravado, and at the last second she pivoted and kissed his cheek, leaving behind a lipstick print.

He chuckled softly, watching her as she pulled away. "That was nice."

She smiled, like a kiss on the cheek was what she'd been planning to do all along. Like she hadn't just experienced a minor freak-out over her desire to kiss him.

Xavier stood and scooped up the raffle ticket jar. "They're probably going to announce the winners soon. We should take these over to Mrs. Franklin."

"Wait," she said, taking a napkin and gently wiping the lipstick from his cheek. He waited patiently as she slid off the stool and grabbed her crutches.

They made their way across the bowling alley, and Violet noticed people watching them. At least they were accomplishing what they'd set out to do: convince the people of Willow Ridge that they were the real deal. It was too bad her parents weren't here tonight to see them in action.

She'd been meaning to ask if Xavier had spoken to his mom about any of this. Tricia had been so kind to Violet when she was younger. There had been times when Violet wished that laid-back and nonjudgmental Tricia was her actual mother. One of the reasons that she and Xavier had agreed to this arrangement was for the benefit of Violet's parents, but for some reason, Violet didn't like the idea of tricking Tricia into believing that she and Xavier were legitimately married. Hopefully she'd stay in Florida until after Violet went back to her real life.

Violet stood beside Xavier as he announced the raffle winners. John Carson's twenty-ticket purchase paid off when he won the toaster oven air fryer, and one of Xavier's students almost passed out when he won the Brooklyn Nets season passes. To Violet's petty satisfaction, Shalia McNair won nothing.

Afterward as she helped Mrs. Franklin count money, Violet watched Xavier say goodbye to his students and everyone else who came out in support. He was so kind and patient with each person. Judging by how he interacted with his students, he'd probably make a great father one day. He might be a great husband too. For the woman he truly married.

But that woman wasn't going to be Violet.

She'd meant what she said to Bianca. She didn't have time for falling in love. Especially not with Xavier, because in reality she couldn't be a supportive partner like she was being tonight. She was only able to be there on a random weeknight because she wasn't working. If she couldn't make things work with Eddy, who had a schedule similar to her own, how could it work with someone like Xavier?

And more importantly, Xavier had been the first person to break her heart. If they gave each other a real shot, in the back of her mind, she would always wonder if he'd wake up one day and change his mind about them again.

She'd been burned one time too many. Falling in love was for the birds.

13

THE FOLLOWING WEEK, XAVIER BURST INTO HIS APART-
ment after work and found Violet kneeling on a chair in
front of his kitchen cabinets, rows and rows of spices lined
up in front of her. A Karamel Kitty song blasted from her
phone speaker, and his mom's old wool quilt lay across the
arm of the couch. The show she liked about the wealthy
Black wives who lived in DC or something was playing on
the television. He had no idea what he'd just walked into,
but the sight of her creating slight chaos in his space caused
an unexpected feeling of warmth to expand in his chest.
He had to remind himself that he shouldn't get used to
coming home and seeing her there. Because in a couple of
short weeks she'd be gone, and they'd both move on with
their separate lives.

"Um, what are you doing?" he asked, tossing his messenger bag onto the couch.

Violet turned toward the sound of his voice. "I'm re-
organizing your spice cabinet by color coordination," she
called over the music. "Almost like how I'd organize a fashion

closet. Did you know that you have three different containers of cayenne pepper? You should probably throw out at least one of them."

He approached the counter and surveyed her work. "Sometimes you gotta mix up the brands. But my question is, why are you organizing my spice cabinet?"

"Because I'm *bored*." She turned down the music and tossed up her hands. "I got a little stir-crazy. You also have two different brands of paprika. What *is* paprika, anyway? I've never heard anyone take a bite of food and say, 'Hmm, you can really taste the paprika in this.'"

Xavier smiled. "It's crushed peppers. But can you pause this? Tim Vogel called, and he wants to get dinner tonight."

"*Tonight?*" Violet cut her music off altogether. "But I just ordered Thai!"

"Again?"

"Don't judge! I really like their sesame chicken. And I got an extra carton of fried rice for you because I know you ate some of mine the other day."

He smiled sheepishly. He was also touched that she'd thought of him.

"I'm sorry, I got hungry in the middle of the night. I didn't think you'd notice." She made a face at him. "I said I was sorry! I'll buy you some more tomorrow, okay? Can you cancel the order? I'll pay you back if they charge you."

"It's fine. I literally placed the order right before you came home." She pulled herself to her feet and grabbed her crutches. "But where are we going for dinner? Like, what's the vibe? What should I wear? Why didn't the coach give you more of a heads-up?"

Xavier had asked himself the same question. Even though he'd followed up with Tim Vogel multiple times since he'd received Tim's congratulatory text, Xavier hadn't heard from him until twenty minutes ago while driving home. Tim had called and asked if Xavier and Violet happened to be free for dinner that evening.

"He's a busy person," Xavier said, following Violet as they walked to his bedroom. "He wants to meet at Bistro 21 in Montclair. I've never heard of it."

"I have," Violet said. She paused in front of the small section of his closet where her clothes hung. "It's hella upscale. Damn, what can I wear? My really cute clothes are at my apartment. And this cast ruins every outfit."

She pulled a dark green mid-length turtleneck dress from a hanger and laid it on his bed. She surveyed the dress with a disappointed frown and sighed.

"This will have to do," she said. Then she glanced at Xavier and paused. "Is that what you're wearing?"

"Yes?" He looked down at his white polo and tan khakis. The "park ranger" outfit. "Why? Is it bad?"

"No, you look fine," she said too quickly.

"Don't lie." He walked over to his mirror and studied his reflection. "Do I look like a square?"

She bit her lip. "Will you be mad if I say yes?"

He turned around to face her, suddenly worried. Too much was riding on this dinner tonight. He gave her an imploring look. "Please help me."

Violet smiled as she returned to his closet and began sorting through his dress shirts. "I'll send you a bill."

An hour later, they arrived at Bistro 21 before Tim Vogel

and his wife. The restaurant *was* hella upscale, like Violet had said. The tables were covered with thick white table-cloths that probably cost more than Xavier's bedsheets, and there was a live violin quartet playing in the far corner of the room. The hostess sat Xavier and Violet at a table in the front of the restaurant by the windows so that Violet could lean her crutches against the wall. Xavier stared at the snow flurries that were beginning to fall outside, and he tried to remember the things he needed to say to Tim. Given Tim's unreliable communication, Xavier worried that to-night would be his only chance to convince Tim that he was the right man for the job.

At least he looked good. In the end, Violet dressed him in a slim-fitting black button-up and black slacks, and the black suede dress shoes that he only wore to weddings. He felt like James Bond, with glasses, sans blazer, and he'd worried the look would be too much, but now that they were here, he saw that he fit right in.

"Hey," Violet said. She briefly rested her hand on his knee, stilling his persistent bouncing. "You okay?"

"Yeah, I—" He turned to her and abruptly forgot what he'd been about to say. In the ambient lighting of the restau-rant, Violet's smooth brown skin looked luminous against her dark lipstick. Her curls were pulled back away from her face with some fancy-looking hairclips, and she'd lined her eyes with a dark green eyeliner that matched the color of her dress. He swallowed thickly as his gaze roamed her face. "You look beautiful. I'm sorry, I should have told you that before we left."

"Thank you." Her lips curved into a soft smile. The lips

he'd been thinking about nonstop since they'd kissed at the bowling alley. She reached up and brushed lint off his shoulder, and he held still as she straightened out his collar. He found that he liked the feeling of being looked after by her. "You don't look so bad yourself. Who's your stylist?"

"My new roommate," he said. "But I have to warn you, she's expensive."

Violet laughed, and he wanted to bottle the sound. She lowered her hands, and he caught her left hand in his. Slowly, he interlaced his fingers through hers, and their bands knocked against each other. Her skin was soft and warm. *What was he doing?*

"We didn't finish our conversation about boundaries," he said. "Is hand-holding okay?"

Hand-holding was innocent, juvenile even. But it felt like a brazen question to ask, and he didn't know why he felt compelled to bring it up or suddenly touch her. She was sitting right beside him, but he had the desire to feel even closer. He didn't have the right to her closeness, and wanting to be closer to her this way probably would only lead to further issues down the line for him. Maybe he was lured by her beauty, just like he'd been the first day of junior year when he'd seen her across the gymnasium.

Violet gazed down at their joined hands and nodded. "This is okay."

Earning a tiny bit of her trust caused a wave of relief to sweep over him.

"Apologies for our tardiness. The snow is really starting to come down out there."

Xavier reluctantly tore his eyes away from Violet and

looked up to see Tim Vogel and his wife, Helen, approaching their table. Xavier stood and helped Violet to her feet as they exchanged greetings. He was thankful again for Violet's fashion expertise when he saw how fancy Tim and Helen were dressed. Tim wore a button-up and blazer, while Helen wore some sort of black velvet blouse-and-skirt combo with heels. Did they usually make last-minute reservations at restaurants like this on a weeknight?

"Congratulations on your nuptials," Tim said, shaking Xavier's hand, then moving on to Violet. "My aunt sent me the article about your stylist career. Very impressive."

"Thank you." Violet's voice was tinged with surprise. "Is your aunt interested in fashion?"

"His aunt is Mrs. Franklin," Xavier said. He wanted to kick himself for forgetting to tell Violet about that connection.

"Oh." Violet looked more closely at Tim, most likely trying to find the physical similarities between him and the school secretary. There weren't many. While Tim was tall and stocky, Mrs. Franklin was lithe and petite, barely five feet tall. The only things they had in common were their brown complexions and hazel eyes.

"If it weren't for my aunt, I wouldn't know Xavier at all," Tim said as everyone sat down.

When Xavier had decided he wasn't going back to Kentucky, he took the following semester off and sat at home every day, wondering what the fuck he was going to do with his life. At the very least, he knew he wanted to finish his degree, so later that fall he enrolled at Riley, which was only a forty-minute drive from Willow Ridge. When Mrs. Franklin found out that Xavier had transferred, she'd called Tim, who had just been hired as the head basketball coach, and told him about Xavier and his basketball history. Tim then convinced Xavier to try out for the team. Xavier had been uncertain. He'd abandoned all far-fetched dreams of making it to the NBA, and Kentucky had left him with only a smidgen of confidence. But the stakes were relatively low playing at Riley. The team was small with a so-so record. And, ultimately, joining the team gave Xavier something to do and a way to stay in shape. His Achilles tendon bothered him sometimes if he went too hard, giving him no choice but to miss a few games. Overall, it had been a pretty humbling experience.

"So tell me your story," Helen said, glancing between Xavier and Violet. "Tim says you met in high school?"

Xavier nodded. "Junior year. I was new, and she was the prettiest girl in school. She took pity on me and let me take her out on a date."

"That's not true," Violet said, laughing a little. "I went out with him because I wanted to."

She rolled her eyes and smiled at him. He smiled back and wiggled his eyebrows, which made her laugh again. He realized he missed having the ability to make her laugh so easily.

"It's wonderful that you found each other back then." Helen rested her chin in the palm of her hand, charmed by the young couple. "It's difficult to sustain a relationship for so many years when you meet at that age."

"Oh, we broke up in college," Violet said, no longer looking at Xavier. For a split second, he feared she'd go into more detail about how their breakup transpired, but instead she added, "Our reunion was very recent."

"Well, love isn't always linear," Helen said.

Violet nodded sagely, like this was the wisest thing she'd ever heard. Xavier, however, wasn't entirely sure what the saying meant, which made him wonder if he lacked the depth necessary to understand.

"I'm sure your parents have probably told you this," Tim said after the server walked away with their drink orders, "but let me also advise that marriage takes a lot of work. It's not just shacking up and getting a dog. Day in and day out, you have to commit to your partner. It's an undertaking."

Xavier's parents, who'd argued almost every single day of his adolescence, were the last people who should tell him about how to conduct a marriage, but he nodded along as if this advice had already been given to him.

"I have to admit, I was quite shocked when my aunt shared your news with me," Tim said. "You didn't seem like the type to settle down. You're young, and quite frankly I thought you came across as somewhat aimless. I wasn't entirely convinced you'd be a good fit for Riley. Don't take that personally; a lot of young people your age still don't know what they're doing with their lives. Some of you are starting companies and saving the planet, and the rest of you are distracted by Intergram and Tic Tac—"

"*Insta*gram and TikTok, honey," Helen interjected, patting Tim's arm.

"—and your phones! You stare at them all day! It's a wonder your eyes don't fall right out of your head."

Tim and Helen chuckled. Xavier forced a laugh too, swallowing his annoyance at Tim's assessment of him. Tim had been a decent basketball coach, but Xavier hadn't always been a fan of Tim's brash personality. Xavier had hoped that Tim had softened a bit over the years, but apparently not. Xavier might not have done anything impressive like found a startup and he wasn't a climate change expert, and he'd needed direction before, but what about him screamed *aimless* now?

"Xavier isn't aimless," Violet said. She was the only one who hadn't laughed. In fact, she stared at Tim, completely straight-faced. "He's very dedicated to his job and his students. And social media isn't as useless as you may think. Having a presence on Instagram actually helps my career by bringing visibility to my work. And to your point about the planet, scientists use their social media accounts to spread awareness about how we can help reverse global warming, and it creates a space for the younger generation, the next change makers. Social media makes knowledge more accessible."

Tim's eyes widened at Violet, as if he was taken aback, unused to someone disagreeing with him. Before he could respond, the server returned to the table with their beverages and bread, ready to take their dinner orders. Violet and Helen chose the special, a black sea bass dish with broccolini, while Xavier and Tim kept it simple and ordered steaks.

After the server walked away, Violet reached for Xavier's hand under the table. She bit her lip lightly and sent him a questioning glance. She looked worried, like the way she'd spoken to Tim might have negatively affected Xavier's standing. He shook his head and gave her hand a reassuring squeeze. He appreciated that she'd stood up for him when he'd felt as though he was in too awkward a position to say anything himself.

"Tim," Xavier said, "I was watching some of the highlights from your team's game against TCNJ—"

"We don't have to discuss basketball tonight," Tim said, waving his hand. He smiled at Helen. "She hates when I talk shop at the table."

Xavier deflated. "Ah, sure."

What, then, was the point of this dinner if not to better present himself as the best candidate for the assistant coach position?

"I'd love to hear more about *your* work, though," Helen said to Violet. "Your job must be quite exciting, being around celebrities so often."

"It can be," Violet answered. She was still holding Xavier's hand under the table. He didn't question why she was doing so, because it was a comfort.

"Who's your favorite celebrity you've met?" Helen asked. "Oh, wait, there's this newer singer that our sixteen-year-old daughter absolutely loves. She wears the cutest little outfits! They play her song on the radio all the time. Something about being single for the summer."

Helen hummed a tune that Xavier didn't recognize. Beside him, Violet stilled.

"Meela Baybee," Violet said. "I've met her."

"Yes, her! What's she like?" Helen asked. "Have you worked with her before?"

"I have." Violet smiled and didn't elaborate. Xavier gently ran his thumb across her palm, and her stiff shoulders relaxed slightly.

"Isn't she the one who barely covers herself up?" Tim asked. "Entertainers today dress so scantily. They leave absolutely nothing to the imagination." He looked at Violet. "You help them appear that way?"

"Yes," she said tightly. "I do. I find it empowering."

Tim scoffed. "*Empowering?* Come on."

"Violet's clients look great," Xavier said. He'd lost his patience with Tim. He wouldn't be able to point Meela Whoever out in a lineup, but he'd have to live under a rock to not know about Karamel Kitty. He'd never really paid close to attention to what Karamel Kitty wore in the pictures he saw, but Violet's work was important to her, so it was important to Xavier. "I'm proud of my wife."

He felt a surge in his chest, being able to claim her as such, even if it wasn't completely true.

"Thanks, babe." Violet shot Tim a quick, annoyed look that he didn't see because he was too busy buttering his bread roll. Then she leaned over and planted a brief yet soft kiss on Xavier's cheek. The sensation of her lips against his skin caused all of his senses to jolt to attention, focusing on that one point of contact.

Babe. She'd said the endearment for show, but it made his pulse spike nonetheless.

By the time their food came, Xavier and Violet were

ready for the night to end. Tim and Helen spent an inordinate amount of time talking about their Christmas vacation to Bora Bora, and Xavier mumbled "mm-hmm" and "oh" whenever appropriate, while Violet kept a pleasant smile glued to her face as she ate.

"Do you like your food?" he asked her when there was a break in the conversation.

"Yeah." She shifted her plate toward him. "Want to try some?"

"Nah, I'm good. Want some steak?"

She shook her head. "I stopped eating red meat a while ago."

"Really?" He thought of how she used to beg him to drive her to Burger King for a late-night Whopper back in the day before he dropped her home after a party. "Why?"

"Messes with my stomach."

"Uh-oh," Tim said. "You don't know your wife's dietary restrictions? You'd better get on that, my friend." He and Helen laughed.

"He knows everything he needs to know. Don't worry," Violet said. She flashed her sugary-sweet smile, which, from his experience, Xavier knew meant that she'd reached the stage of contemplating murder.

He waved down the server for the check. They'd be better off taking the rest of their food to go.

THEY WERE SILENT on the car ride home; there was just the sound of the windshield wipers whipping back and forth, pushing snow out of the way so that Xavier could see the road. He kept replaying the dinner in his mind. It had not gone the way he'd hoped. Tim Vogel was an ass. The previous assistant coach most likely left because he was tired of putting up with Tim's shit. But Xavier wanted the assistant coach job badly. He had no choice but to grin and bear it. As they'd walked to their cars, Tim told Xavier he would call him later that week. If he didn't call by Saturday, Xavier would follow up with him. Again.

"Can I ask you a question?" Violet's voice broke through his gloomy train of thought.

"Sure."

"Why do you want to work for him?"

"Tim?" He glanced at her.

"Yeah, he's kind of an asshole. And he talks down to you. He talks down to everyone."

Xavier sighed and put on his blinker as their exit came up. "He won't be at Riley forever. I don't want to work for him so much as the university."

"But what about your current job?" she asked. "Teaching and coaching at the high school?"

"That's temporary."

"But I thought you liked it." She shifted in her seat, angling to face him.

"That's it right there," he said. "I like it. It's something I'm good at, but I don't know. I think I'm meant for more."

She didn't say anything else, and he wondered what she was thinking. They pulled up to the house, and he walked closely behind her to make sure she didn't slip on her crutches in the snow. When he opened the door and they shrugged out of their winter coats, Violet finally spoke again.

"You're too good to be working under someone like that. You'd be compromising your integrity," she said. "Can't you find a different coaching job at another college?"

Now he was even more frustrated. "With what experience? I graduated from Riley and I played for Tim. He's my in. What other university is going to hire me? I don't have the collegiate experience. Riley is my foot in the door."

"There are plenty of people who are hired these days for jobs where they lack the experience. But that's not even your situation. You *are* a basketball coach. Why are you selling yourself short?"

He kicked off his shoes by the door and walked into the kitchen to store their to-go boxes in the fridge. "You wouldn't understand," he said.

"I can try if you explain it to me." She sat on the arm of the couch and watched him, waiting for an answer.

He sucked in a sharp, agitated breath. "You left, Violet. You had your dream and it worked out for you. Mine didn't, and I'm still trying to find what my new dream is. You hate being back home. Why can't you understand that maybe I don't want to be here either?"

"But your being here actually means something to people," she said. "I just don't know if coaching at Riley will be as significant."

"And how would you know?" he asked. "I could go to Riley and make a difference there too. You've been here with me for, what, less than two weeks? What do you really know about my potential? I don't involve myself in your perfect life and whatever you have going on. So please do me the same courtesy, okay?"

Violet stared at him. He watched her chest rise and fall as she took several deep breaths.

"Despite what you may think, Xavier, my life is not perfect. So don't make any assumptions about me either," she said, glowering. "I didn't mean to offend you. That wasn't my intention, and I'm sure you're capable of making a difference at other places. I just know what you mean to people here. But you're right. I shouldn't involve myself in your business." She pushed up off the couch and leaned on her crutches, shaking her head. "I don't know why I even bothered! I'm not your actual wife! This isn't real!"

"Exactly, it's not!" Now he was breathing heavily too. It annoyed him that she still had the ability to rile him up so easily.

"Whatever!" she grumbled. Without another word, she made her way down the hall to his bedroom and closed the door behind her.

Xavier dragged a hand over his face. *Fuck.* He shouldn't have gotten so pissed with her, but it nagged him that she didn't see why he needed to be at Riley.

He plopped on the couch and let his head drop back.

Maybe they should call this whole marriage thing off. They'd gone to dinner with Tim already to no avail, and they could figure out what to do about her parents and possible town gossip later. His stomach sank as he imagined the emptiness he'd feel to come home and not find her on his couch or at the kitchen table.

He'd give it a few minutes so they both could cool off. Then he'd apologize and ask how she wanted to proceed.

But he ended up falling asleep right there on the couch, fully dressed. Until he heard a loud banging in the middle of the night.

14

XAVIER JERKED AWAKE. THE LIGHT FROM THE BATHROOM
flooded the hallway. Startled, he sat up and rubbed his eyes.
He glanced at the microwave clock: 2:34 a.m.

"Violet?" he called.

No response.

He heard another banging noise, like her crutches had
clattered to the floor, and he stood and hurried down the
hall. The bathroom door was slightly ajar, and Violet's
crutches were lodged in the doorway. He pushed the door
wider and found her on the bathroom floor with her head
in the toilet, gagging.

He turned away as she continued to be sick. Luckily, he
wasn't the type who had a weak stomach. When she finally
flushed the toilet, he cautiously entered the bathroom. She
was leaning back against the wall, wearing only a large
pink T-shirt and underwear. Her silk bonnet was slightly
askew as her head lolled to the side. She froze when she
belatedly noticed Xavier's presence.

"Oh no," she muttered, weakly holding up her hand in
front of her face. "Look away. I'm hideous."

"No, you're not." He crouched down in front of her and kept his voice calm, although seeing her this way caused his pulse to spike in alarm. Her T-shirt was damp with sweat. He placed his hand against her forehead and felt her burning skin.

"Shit," he whispered. He scrambled to his feet and grabbed his thermometer from the cabinet above the sink. Then he hurried to grab a cup of water from the kitchen. He crouched in front of her again and gently took her chin in his hand so that she would look at him. "I need to take your temperature. Can you rinse your mouth out?"

"You're not a doctor," she said. But she allowed him to tip the cup of water to her lips, and she rinsed out her mouth. Then she let him place the thermometer under her tongue. He felt her staring at him, but he kept his gaze focused on the thermometer as the number ticked higher and higher. The thermometer finally beeped, and he removed it from her mouth. Her temperature was 102 degrees.

"You have a fever," he said. Worry spread through his limbs. He placed his hand against her forehead again and she closed her eyes.

"Damn broccolini," she mumbled. "I thought it tasted funny."

"You think you have food poisoning?"

She nodded slowly. "I've had it before. Seafood in Miami. At a video shoot for work. I threw up in the ocean."

He'd never had food poisoning. He didn't know what the hell to do, but he couldn't let her sit here like this. "I need to get you to the hospital."

Violet shook her head. "No. Virtual doctor."

"What?"

"A doctor. Virtual chat." She pointed vaguely in the direction of his bedroom. "My phone. Please?"

Xavier rushed to his room and grabbed her phone off his nightstand. Through her feverish haze, it took Violet a few minutes to direct Xavier to her telehealth app, but they finally were able to connect with an on-call emergency physician. She was a Black woman with clear-framed glasses and braids. She introduced herself as Dr. Williams.

"Hi, Dr. Williams," Violet croaked. "I'm puking." She gestured a floppy hand toward Xavier. "This is Xavier."

Xavier took the phone from Violet's weak grasp. "Her name is Violet Greene," he said. "But you should already have that information from her profile, right?"

Dr. Williams nodded. "What seems to be the problem?"

Xavier explained Violet's symptoms and her assumption that she might have food poisoning. Based on what she'd been told, Dr. Williams agreed with their assessment.

"What can I do to help her?" Xavier asked as Violet's head drooped against his shoulder.

"Her body will slowly work the infection out of her system on its own. Keep her hydrated. Water will do the job, but I'd also suggest liquids with electrolytes, like Gatorade and Pedialyte."

Xavier nodded. "Okay, I have Gatorade."

"Good. If she hasn't improved within forty-eight hours, I'd make an in-person appointment with her primary care physician."

Dr. Williams's gaze suddenly shifted, and she blinked, clearing her throat. Xavier glanced over to see Violet struggling to take off her shirt.

"Hey, hey, wait," he said, gently holding her arm. "Keep that on."

She sent him a miserable glare. "I'm *hot*. It doesn't matter. You've seen my boobs before."

He felt his cheeks heat as he turned his attention back to Dr. Williams. "I think we've got it from here. Thank you."

He ended the call and convinced Violet to keep her shirt on as he ran a washcloth under cold water. He wiped it across her forehead, neck and collarbones, and then he wiped down her arms as well. She was motionless under his delicate ministrations.

"Thank you," she murmured. She closed her eyes again and sighed deeply. It sounded more like a wheeze.

"I'm so sorry, Violet," he said quietly.

"Why? You didn't cook the broccolini." She struggled to peek one eye open. "Did you?"

That got a small smile out of him. "No. I'm sorry because we wouldn't have gone to that restaurant tonight if it weren't for me trying to get in good with Tim Vogel."

She feebly lifted her hand and rested it against his cheek. He didn't dare move.

"Not your fault," she breathed.

Then she got a funny look on her face and lurched forward to the toilet, getting sick again.

Afterward, she grumbled while Xavier instructed her to rinse her mouth, and he wiped her lips. He picked her up and carried her into his room, gently placing her down on his bed. He rummaged through his drawers and produced an old, thin Knicks T-shirt. Hopefully she'd feel cooler in this fabric.

"Here," he said, holding it out to her. "You can wear this."

"The Knicks play at Madison Square Garden," she mumbled, taking the shirt. He wasn't sure if she was actually trying to converse with him by stating that well-known fact or if it was just the fever talking.

Either way, he responded, "Yep, they do."

While she changed, he went to the fridge and grabbed a bottle of Gatorade. When he returned to the room, Violet was lying flat on her back. She'd put the T-shirt on backward. Her face was scrunched up in discomfort, her arm draped across her stomach. He grabbed a pillow and used it to elevate her ankle.

He sat beside her and coaxed her to sit up. "Can you drink some of this?"

She grimaced at the bottle. "Gatorade is nasty."

"You need it to keep from getting dehydrated. Can you try? Please?"

She nodded weakly, but her hands shook as she held the bottle. Xavier eased it from her grasp. "I'll help," he said.

He held the bottle to her lips, using his other hand to cup the base of her neck as she tipped her head back. She took hesitant, tiny sips and wiped her mouth when Xavier set the bottle on the nightstand.

"Thank you," she said quietly. She eased back until she was lying down again. "This is mortifying," she whispered. "I'm sorry."

"You don't need to apologize." He used his thumb to form soothing circles on the inside of her wrist. She closed her eyes, breathing deeply.

"Xavier," she said after a moment.

"Yes?"

"I love your bed."

He felt himself grin. "You do?"

"Mm-hmm. It's huge." She spread her arms out on either side of her. "A bed for a whale."

He laughed. She was delirious. "A whale?"

"*Bluuurrrrp.*"

He snorted. "What was that?"

"Whale noise." She turned her face into his pillow and let out a heavy sigh. "It smells like you."

"Really?" he asked, raising an eyebrow. "What do I smell like?"

She made a soft mumble and closed her eyes again. She finally looked a bit peaceful. He hoped she'd be able to drift off to sleep. He didn't want to leave her in his room alone in case she needed to get to the bathroom again. But he needed to change. He was still in his clothes from last night. He moved to stand and suddenly Violet's arm shot out, gripping him with unexpected force.

"Don't leave," she said, her gaze pleading.

"I'm not leaving." He placed his hand over hers. "I swear. I'm just changing my clothes."

"Okay." She loosened her grip and eyed him suspiciously.

He went to his closet and switched his clothes for a tank and basketball shorts. He removed his glasses and approached the bed again. Violet scooted over to make room for him, which was unnecessary, because as she'd noted, his bed was rather huge. He lay down next to her, putting at least a foot of space between them. She turned onto her side to face him, and he touched her forehead, gauging her temperature. She'd cooled down slightly, but not that much. It worried him, but he'd have to trust that the doctor was right and Violet would heal on her own soon.

"I feel gross," she mumbled. "Do I look gross?"

He shook his head, taking in her pasty complexion and chapped lips. "No. You're beautiful."

She sighed, cracking a slight smile. "You're lying, but that's okay."

"I wouldn't lie to you," he said softly.

They fell quiet as her gaze traveled across his face.

"I'm sorry for getting upset with you like that earlier," he said. "You didn't deserve it. I don't want to fight with you."

"I don't either," she murmured.

Her hand moved lightly up to touch his face again. He remained motionless as she ever so gently let her fingers skim across his nose, down to his mustache, drifting over his lips and landing on his chin. He held his breath, his heart beating loudly.

"You still have a nice face," she declared.

He laughed. "Thank you."

"I'm serious." She frowned slightly. "It made me mad when I first saw you again."

Her frown only made him smile bigger. "You were mad that I had a nice face?"

"Yes." She offered no further explanation, like her simple response made perfect sense. In her current state, it probably did. "Do you still have those gold chains? From senior year?"

He laughed again, surprised by the question. "Yeah. I don't wear them anymore, though."

"Why not?"

"Too flashy."

He reached for her hand and she automatically interlaced her fingers through his. Holding hands was okay. He slowly traced his thumb across her knuckles.

"I like your hands," she said. Her eyelids were drooping closed.

He smiled again. "I like yours too."

"I liked your hands more than anyone's." She let out another sigh. "I liked *you*. I've never liked anyone as much as you." Her eyes opened suddenly. "I missed you."

His clasp on her hand tightened. He felt like his heart was trying to climb out of his chest. "I missed you too. So much, Violet."

She stared at him, her brows furrowed in confusion.

"You said that you regretted breaking up with me," she whispered. "But why did you do it?"

He could tell that it pained her to ask. It pained him even more to answer.

"Because I wanted you to be happy."

She blinked, shaking her head. "But you made me so sad."

He pressed his forehead against hers. "I'm so sorry."

She didn't say anything. The room was quiet; there was just the sound of their breathing.

"I'm so tired," she finally mumbled. "Will you stay?"

"Yes," he said.

She moved closer and he wrapped his arm around her back, drawing her in toward his chest.

He couldn't take back breaking her heart. But he could give her this, his embrace. His care and undivided attention while she was here.

15

VIOLET'S DREAMS WERE LOOPY AND DISJOINTED. IN ONE dream, she was at New York Fashion Week and the season's new must-have accessory was an ankle cast. Tom Ford himself waded into the audience to find Violet and asked her to offer her expertise. In another dream, she was walking in New York City freely without a fractured ankle. She skipped across the street but froze when a driver slammed on their horn. She turned to see the same taxi barreling toward her. But moments before she was flattened, a pigeon landed at her feet.

"Do you want more Gatorade?" the pigeon asked. It was a male pigeon, who strangely sounded a lot like Xavier.

"Yes?" She was about to be run over, but she recognized that she was quite thirsty.

The pigeon offered her the Gatorade, but for some reason, she was too weak to hold the bottle. The pigeon placed its wings on top of her hands and helped angle the bottle toward her mouth. She was able to take a few sips.

"Good," said the pigeon, who'd stolen Xavier's voice.

Violet preened under its praise.

In another dream, she was at dance team practice in high school, but she somehow remained an adult. Bianca was there too with RJ. Behind them, the rest of the squad was assembled in their signature halftime-show pyramid.

"You have to climb to the top," Bianca told Violet. "That's where you'll fall in love and be happy."

"But I don't want to climb the pyramid," Violet said. "I tried before, and I fell."

"You have to try again." Bianca's voice was grave. "It's the only way."

"It's the only way," RJ repeated.

Violet stared in shock. When had RJ learned to speak in full sentences?

Against her better judgment, Violet began to climb over the backs of her teammates. The ascent was wobbly and filled with uncertainty. Violet didn't know if she wanted to be at the top of the pyramid. What if she didn't find what she was looking for once she got there? She finally pulled her way to the top and stood, looking out at the empty bleachers. Bianca and RJ stared up at her.

"Where is the love and happiness?" she called down to Bianca.

Bianca frowned. "You can't see them? They're right there."

Violet glanced around. "I don't see them!"

Bianca shook her head. "You're looking too hard, yet not hard enough."

"What does that mean?!"

The foundation beneath Violet began to shake. Her teammates were tumbling out of position. She wasn't going to find love and happiness. They would remain elusive to her.

She'd climbed up here for no reason. It was all a lie. Suddenly, she slipped backward, falling, falling, falling. Then she landed in a solid pair of arms. She looked up to find Xavier cradling her. He wore a Willow Ridge High basketball sweatshirt with a whistle around his neck.

"Thank you, Coach," she said, gratefully turning her face into his chest.

He gave her a bemused smile and brought his cool fingers to her forehead. "You're not as hot as before."

"But I thought you said I was beautiful." She hung her head, dismayed.

"You are," he said, chuckling softly.

She blinked, widening her eyes. They weren't in their high school gym. They were in Xavier's apartment and he was carrying her from the bathroom again. Her throat felt raw and sore. Her body ached. She was exhausted. Xavier gently set her down on the bed, and she shivered as he pulled the covers over her.

"Did you find the pigeon?" she mumbled.

He paused, looking down at her. "What pigeon?"

"The one who stole your voice."

He was quiet for a moment. "No," he said, smoothing the loose curls away from her face. "But I'll find it soon."

"Okay." She nodded and drifted off once more.

She was unsure how much time had passed when she woke again. She felt groggy but no longer nauseous. Sunlight peeked through the blinds and cast a soft glow around the bedroom. Her thigh was wrapped around Xavier's hip, his hand settled on her waist. Her face was in the crook of his neck, and her lips were at the base of his throat. She could feel the thudding of his pulse. They used to sleep like this so often as teenagers, huddled together in her twin-size bed. She leaned away and looked at his face. He was fast asleep, his lips slightly parted. He looked peaceful. Her fever had broken, thankfully, but a different kind of heat flooded her body, being pressed against him this way.

She recalled images of him carrying her back and forth from his room to the bathroom, wiping down her sweaty limbs. He was probably so tired. How long had he been looking after her?

As if he sensed her movements, he slowly stirred awake. He blinked a few times, and his gaze settled on her. They stared at each other in silence, still tangled together. The corner of his mouth lifted into a soft smile.

"Hey," he said. "How are you feeling?"

"Better." She licked her lips and attempted to smooth her hair back. Her curls felt dry and frazzled. She probably looked like a bed-head creature. But Xavier didn't seem to care. He rubbed his hand up and down her arm, and she eased into the motion, resting her head on her pillow. "How long was I out?"

"Um." He twisted away and grabbed his phone, checking the time. "It's a little after eleven a.m., so almost a day and a half."

"What?" She sat up suddenly and was hit with a brief dizzy spell. "Did you miss work?"

He nodded, and Violet sucked in a breath. "It's okay," he said. "It was only yesterday and today."

"That's two of your sick days, though. You should have left me here."

"I wasn't going to do that," he said, frowning. "I thought about calling your mom and asking her to come by, but when I made the suggestion, you held me in a death grip and begged me not to."

Violet shook her head, annoyed at her own dramatics. It was true that Dahlia's method of caretaking was of the tough-love variety. While rubbing Violet's back as she puked, Dahlia probably would have chastised her for eating the broccolini in the first place. *It's a hybrid vegetable, Violet. What were you thinking?* Being with Dahlia would have been more stressful, and Violet definitely preferred Xavier's company, but she knew that teachers didn't get many sick days, and she didn't like that he'd used two of his days on her behalf.

"Thank you, Xavier," she said. He began to wave her off as if it wasn't a big deal and she stopped him. "I'm serious. I don't know how I can ever repay you for taking care of me."

"It's nothing, really," he said. He grinned. "In sickness and in health, right?"

She gazed at him and felt her chest tighten. The feeling was so strong, she had to look away and gather her bearings.

"Do you think you can eat something?" he asked. "You've mostly been nibbling on crackers."

She had zero memory of eating crackers, but she glanced over at his nightstand and saw an open sleeve of saltines. Her stomach grumbled. She could do with something a little heartier.

"I could eat."

He rolled out of bed and stretched, rubbing his side. She

glanced at his tattoo of a violet, and the hem of his shirt lifted, showing his lower abdomen. She openly stared at him, and the sudden heat she'd experienced at their cuddling returned. She wanted him to come back to bed so that she could touch him again. Xavier, oblivious to her gawking, scratched the back of his head and yawned.

"Damn, sleeping in my bed again feels so much better than sleeping on the couch," he said as he walked into the kitchen.

Once the coast was clear, Violet scrambled to grab her phone and opened her front-facing camera. Dear Lord. She looked like something straight out of a horror movie! Her bonnet had been misplaced at some point, and her curls were a tangled bird's nest. Her usually smooth skin was oily and covered in heat bumps from sweating so much. She hurried to retie her hair into a semblance of a neat bun. There was nothing to be done about her zombielike complexion or resurgence of adult acne.

"Tim Vogel called and said his wife got sick too," Xavier said, reappearing in the doorway. He walked toward her, holding two pieces of toast on a paper plate. She must have looked disappointed because he said, "You need to stick to the BRAT diet. Bananas, rice, applesauce and toast."

"Oh, okay." How did he know something like that? Had he looked it up? "Thank you."

She settled the plate on her lap and took tiny rabbit bites. Her empty stomach gratefully accepted the new sustenance. Xavier stood in front of her, arms akimbo. He seemed satisfied that she was eating.

"I'm gonna head to the grocery store to get bananas and some stuff to cook for dinner," he said. "You think you'll be okay?"

She nodded. "What's your Venmo? We can split it."

"Nah." He shrugged on a pair of sweatpants over his basketball shorts and pulled a sweater from his closet. "Just get some rest. I'll be back in a bit."

Then he bent down, kissed her heat-bump-infested forehead and left the room before she had a chance to react.

She rose to her knees and looked out the window as he started his car and pulled out into the street. The ground was blanketed with a soft layer of snow. She settled back down in his bed and lightly touched the spot on her forehead where his lips had been. Against her will, she smiled.

VIOLET SLEPT ON and off all day. When she woke again in the evening, she heard the sound of laughter coming from the kitchen. She stilled and listened closer, this time hearing the light trill of Calla's voice, paired with Iris's calm, even tone. Violet relaxed again. She checked the time on her phone. It was almost seven p.m.

She climbed out of bed, stripped the sheets off the mattress and put them in the washer. Then she slipped on her cast cover and took a blissful hot shower, where she finally washed her hair, used a three-minute deep conditioner and scrubbed the sweaty grime from her skin. By the time she walked into the kitchen wearing her cream cashmere sweater and Everlane sweatpants, she felt like a new woman.

Iris was standing at the stove, stirring something that smelled both fragrant and spicy. Xavier and Calla sat at the kitchen table with one of Calla's worksheets in front of them. Xavier glanced up, adjusting his glasses, and smiled at Violet. Her stomach somersaulted when she recalled how they'd cuddled that morning.

"Auntie!" Calla shouted, racing to Violet and wrapping her small arms around Violet's torso. "You're awake now. I was worried."

Violet grinned down at her niece, who sported a pinched expression. She gently ran her hand over Calla's hair. "Thanks for coming to see me."

"Feeling better?" Xavier asked, gaze intent.

She swallowed thickly and nodded. "Yes. Much better."

"Welcome back to the land of the living," Iris said over her shoulder. She wore a plain white button-up and black slacks, her usual work attire. "You weren't answering your phone, so we came by to pay a wellness visit, and Xavier told us that you ate poisonous broccolini."

"You should have seen the way she barged in wanting to know where you were," Xavier said with a smirk. "She was acting like I killed you."

"Quite the opposite," Violet said as she hugged Iris from behind, resting her chin on Iris's shoulder. "Xavier saved me. What are you making?"

"Mom's chicken gumbo," Iris said.

"She told me that your mom used to make that for y'all whenever you got sick," Xavier said. "I thought you might prefer that over Gouda grilled cheese and tomato soup."

"The gumbo is pretty good," Violet said, sitting at the

table across from him. "But I still want to try that grilled cheese of yours."

He grinned at her, and her abdomen involuntarily filled with butterflies.

"Xavier, where do you keep your bowls?" Iris asked, interrupting their moment.

"Bottom left cabinet," he answered, eyes still locked on Violet. He finally looked away when Calla pulled on his shirtsleeve and redirected his attention to her worksheet.

"Homework?" Violet asked, just to have a reason to keep talking to him.

Xavier returned his gaze to her and nodded.

"I don't like math," Calla declared. "Xavier said that he doesn't either."

"There's a reason I'm an English teacher," he said wryly.

"Well, baby girl, it's okay if you don't like math now," Iris said, placing bowls of gumbo in front of everyone. She waved her hands in a show of nonchalance when Violet and Xavier thanked her for cooking. "I didn't get good at math until much later."

"Yeah, and your mom was the smartest in every subject," Violet said, nudging Iris as she sat down beside her. "I was a decent student and made good grades, but I didn't push myself as hard as I could have. I didn't care about a lot back then. Especially not in high school."

"You cared about some things," Xavier said, quirking an eyebrow.

"Yeah," she agreed. "Some."

They shared a smile.

What was happening?

"You know what I thought about the other day?" Iris asked, watching them with a curious gaze. "One night, during the summer after my freshman year of college, I met up with some of my old debate-team friends, and one of them dropped me off at around two a.m. I saw someone climbing the sycamore tree on the side of our house. I thought we were being robbed, so my friend and I were about to call the police. Then Violet opened her bedroom window and let the tree climber inside and I realized that he was Xavier." Iris laughed. "I thought to myself that you two were crazy. Absolutely crazy in love."

Violet and Xavier exchanged another smile. She thought of the many times she'd let him sneak into her room in the middle of the night, and how thrilling it had felt to watch him climb up toward her. She'd thought they were being so stealthy.

"Why didn't you ever tell me that you knew?" Violet asked.

"Because I figured the secrecy was what you enjoyed," Iris said. "I would have warned you if I'd felt like Mom and Dad had caught on. Also, speaking of our parents, Mom told me that she's throwing you two a dinner next month since you didn't have a wedding. Are you aware of this?"

Violet groaned. She'd hoped that Dahlia would have been too busy preparing Valentine's Day orders at the shop to remember that she'd decided to plan a dinner.

"She did mention that," Violet said, sighing.

"I wonder if she'll hire Shalia McNair's catering business.

They catered the Juneteenth festival in the park last year," Iris said. "Xavier, you were there too, right? Do you remember those fried macaroni-and-cheese balls they served? They were so good."

Xavier nodded eagerly. "And the potato salad."

Hearing Xavier praise Shalia's cooking made Violet grimace. Then she cringed, realizing that her annoyance was rooted in nonsensical jealousy. Why should she be jealous?

As they ate dinner, Xavier and Iris reminisced about the Juneteenth festival, and Violet watched Xavier as he spoke. She stared at his lips and large hands. The hands that had cradled her and checked her temperature countless times over the last couple of days. She noticed the way laugh lines appeared around his mouth when he smiled. She watched him as he looked over and grinned at Calla, attentively helping her work through another math question.

He glanced up at Violet and caught her looking at him. Then he winked.

She realized that the gut clench of anxiety she'd previously experienced around him was no longer present. What had changed? Since he'd cared for her, she now felt more at ease in his presence. Those pesky butterflies began to swarm in her stomach again.

Oh no. This was bad. Bad bad bad.

After dinner, Xavier hugged Iris and Calla goodbye and stayed behind in the kitchen, while Violet walked with them to the door.

"So how is faux-married life?" Iris asked quietly as Calla slid on her snow boots. "Blissful?"

Violet lifted her shoulders in an awkward shrug. "It's . . .

I don't know. Fine? There's only a couple more weeks until my ankle heals. Then I'll leave, and eventually we'll tell everyone we're getting divorced."

Iris smiled in a way that made Violet feel as though Iris knew something that Violet didn't. "There's enough gumbo left for dinner tomorrow," she said. "Calla, give Auntie a hug."

Violet hugged her niece and watched her and Iris amble through the snow to Iris's car. She waited until they drove away to close the door. Xavier was piling the bowls by the sink.

"I can do the dishes," she said.

He looked over at her. "You sure?"

"Yeah, but not right now." She plopped down on the couch, resting her crutches beside her. "Do you, um, want to watch TV?"

He walked closer and leaned against the kitchen entryway. "Are you gonna put on that show you like with the housewives?"

"*The Real Housewives of Potomac*?" She perked up. "We can watch that, but I'm willing to find common ground."

He smirked. "I'll give it a try. One sec."

He opened the cabinet and retrieved a bag of salt-and-vinegar chips. Her favorite kind. Her lips spread into a grin.

"I saw these at the grocery store," he said, coming over to sit beside her. The couch depressed under his weight. She took the chips from him and eagerly opened the bag, grateful that the pungent smell didn't make her nauseous.

"Thank you," she said.

She was so grateful, she could kiss him.

God, *listen* to her. Over a bag of chips!

"No problem. I figure someone has to keep the salt-and-vinegar-chip people in business."

"Whatever." She laughed as she opened the streaming app. "Just so you know, I'm not caught up on the current season yet, so these are older episodes."

"You out here slacking," he joked, as if her place in the season made any real difference to him. He relaxed and spread his arm out on top of the couch behind her. She had the urge to move closer and remove the distance between them. But she would *not* do that because she wasn't an insatiable thirst bucket over her ex-boyfriend turned fake husband.

She shook away her intrusive thoughts and resumed her place in the season. But truly, she could hardly focus on the show and instead spent most of the episode sneaking glances at Xavier. He squinted at the television, blinking in surprise when arguments suddenly broke out during dinner, or smirking during candid confessionals.

"I don't get it," he said eventually. "Half of these women don't even live in Potomac. Why are they on the show?"

"That's a great question," Violet said, laughing.

As the next episode started, she explained the backstory for each woman, and Xavier sat forward, becoming increasingly interested in their drama. Halfway through, Violet remembered to throw the sheets in the dryer, and then she washed the dishes before she got too sleepy.

When she came back into the living room, Xavier was making up the pullout bed. She remembered his comment earlier that morning about how much more comfortable he'd felt sleeping in his own bed last night. After everything he'd done for her, she couldn't let him sleep on the couch again.

"You can sleep in your bed," she said. "I don't mind."

He glanced up at her. "You mean . . . with you in it?"

"Oh." Her cheeks began to burn. He probably wanted to switch places and finally have his bed to himself. "I can sleep out here. That's fine." She laughed, attempting to hide her embarrassment.

Xavier observed her jittery reaction with a subtle tilt of his head.

"We can sleep in my bed together," he said slowly. "If you're cool with that."

She nodded and mentally tried to quiet her insistent stomach butterflies. "I am."

"Okay."

He turned off the television. Violet's pulse thumped a mile a minute as he followed her to his room. She set her crutches by the bed and swallowed thickly when he pulled off his sweatshirt, leaving on his ribbed tank underneath. While his back was turned, she slipped out of her sweater and sweatpants and put on a fresh T-shirt and pajama shorts. Xavier turned off the light and pulled back the covers. They climbed into bed at the same time.

Even though his bed was wide, they both moved toward the middle as if they had an unspoken agreement to resume the same spots from that morning. He helped her rest her ankle on a pillow, and then a quietness settled over them as they stared at each other. Violet felt braver in the dark. Brave enough to ask the question that had been in the back of her mind all day.

"The other night," she started, "you said you broke up with me because you wanted me to be happy. What did you mean by that?"

Xavier remained silent for a moment. Then he took a weighted breath. "After my time in Kentucky and my injury, my confidence was shot. I felt like shit, and I had no idea who I was or what I was going do to with my life anymore, because I'd realized the original plan wasn't going to work. But you were out in LA, doing the things you'd always wanted to. You were taking off. I thought that if you stayed with me, I'd drag you down, and I didn't want to do that."

Violet turned his words over in her mind. After so many years, she finally had an explanation for his actions. He hadn't left her because he'd fallen out of love or because he'd thought she was an inattentive girlfriend. Finally knowing the truth brought relief, but she was still sad he hadn't communicated his feelings to her all those years ago.

"I wish you would have told me then," she said quietly. "I would have understood, and I would have told you that you were wrong."

"I wish I had told you everything too," he said. "I've thought about the day we broke up so many times, wishing I could go back and change it. I hate that I hurt you. I'm so sorry. All I can say is that I was stupid and young. But it makes me happy to know that you became who you always wanted to be. I'm so proud of you, Violet."

She smiled softly, even though the irony of his words stung her. On paper, yes, she matched what she'd manifested in high school. She was successful. She loved her job. But she felt an emptiness inside her.

"Did you have dreams about dance team while you were sick?" Xavier asked, reaching for her hand. "You kept mumbling in your sleep about a pyramid."

Her dreams had been a fuzzy haze, but there was a key moment that stood out clearly to her. She pressed her palm against Xavier's, and the contact with his warm skin sent a shiver through her.

"I fell off a pyramid," she said, "and you caught me."

He brought her hand up to his lips and kissed her knuckles. "I'm glad I was there."

They fell asleep that way, facing each other, hands interlocked.

In the middle of the night, Violet woke with the urge to pee. But she stilled when she realized she was safely locked in Xavier's embrace. Her back was pressed to his chest, his arms wrapped around her. She felt his chest rise and fall as he breathed. They fit together like Tetris pieces.

She closed her eyes and went back to sleep. She didn't want to think about what it meant that she didn't have the desire to move away.

16

ON VALENTINE'S DAY MORNING, XAVIER QUIETLY EASED out of bed while Violet snuggled deeper underneath the covers. She looked so peaceful, he wished he could climb back into bed with her. They'd been sleeping together every night for a little over a week. They didn't do anything besides cuddle. No kissing, no sex. It meant that he woke up with blue balls every morning, but he didn't care. Waking up with her curled against his chest was his favorite moment of the day, followed closely by the moment when they slipped into bed at night and automatically linked hands.

But their peaceful domesticity would end soon. Violet was getting her cast off next week, and then she'd be gone from his life again. He tried not to think about how gutted he might feel afterward. This was always the plan. He just had to prepare himself for the end.

He shrugged on his puffer jacket and went out to his car, where a bouquet of violets waited for him. He'd ordered the arrangement from her parents' shop, of course, and when he'd picked it up yesterday evening, Dahlia had cornered him and asked a handful of questions about his thoughts on their wedding dinner, because apparently, Violet was being selective about when she wanted to answer Dahlia's calls. Dahlia had asked whether or not Xavier's mom would be back in town for the dinner, and he gave a noncommittal shrug.

Somehow, even all the way in Florida, Tricia had caught wind of Xavier and Violet's alleged marriage. Over FaceTime, Xavier told Tricia he'd explain more in person once she came back in March, which he hoped would be after this situation had blown over.

When Xavier had finally been able to free himself from Dahlia's questioning, Benjamin had nodded in approval on Xavier's way out of the shop.

"Violet will like those," he'd said, pointing to the bouquet, which was filled with dark and light violets.

Xavier could have made the excuse that buying flowers for his "wife" from her parents' floral shop was a good look and helped them appear more believable as a couple. But really, it was Valentine's Day, and he wasn't going to let the holiday go by without giving Violet *something*. He might have been rusty when it came to dating, and he and Violet weren't actually married, but he still had some game.

He reentered his apartment and placed the bouquet, complete with a crystal-clear vase, on the kitchen table. Then he showered and dressed for work. Violet continued to sleep through all of it. Even though she was no longer sick, she slept *a lot*. He figured she must have needed the rest, given how hectic her life usually seemed. But there were still moments when he could tell that she must be feeling restless. Like when he came home to find her randomly re-organizing his closet or when she'd spent an entire afternoon sitting with Mr. Young in the post office, helping him sort through their stamp collection because she needed a project to keep herself busy. Afterward, she'd convinced Mr. Young to take her to the mall so that she could help him pick out new clothes to freshen his wardrobe, which Xavier found hilarious.

He was pouring coffee in his to-go mug when Violet surprised him and walked into the kitchen, supported by her crutches, dressed in pajamas with her hair wrapped in a silk scarf.

"Good morn— Oh my gosh. Are those for me?" she asked, pointing at the flowers.

Her face lit up, and his heart squeezed.

"Yeah," he said, walking to the table. "Happy Valentine's Day."

He stood in front of her. They might have easily embraced each other at night, but what were their rules in the light of day? In the end, he hugged her and breathed deeply when she wrapped her arms around him. Her hair smelled like the citrusy shampoo she used.

She stepped away and bent down to smell the flowers. "These are beautiful, Xavier. Thank you." She smiled up at him. "From my parents' shop?"

"Of course."

"I can tell," she said. Then she produced a card from behind her back and held it out to him. "I got something for you too. It's silly."

"Oh, wow." Surprised, he took the card from her and opened the envelope. On the front of the card, there was an illustration of a heart-shaped basketball. Inside, it read, *You're a slam dunk.* She'd signed it, *From your pretend wife, Vi.*

The force of his grin could power an entire city.

"I didn't know if we were exchanging gifts," she said quickly, biting her lip. "Or if that was even something fake spouses did, but I saw the card when I was at Rite Aid with Iris the other day, and I thought it would be perfect for you, so I bought it."

"It is perfect," he said, and she visibly relaxed. "Thank you."

"You're welcome." She picked up the vase and lifted the flowers to her face for another sniff.

He had the sudden urge to ask her to dinner, but then his phone vibrated in his pocket, interrupting his train of thought. It was a text from Raheem.

> Sorry, cuz, can't make it to the school today. RJ has a cold and I'm staying home with him so that Bianca doesn't have to cancel her appointments. I'll make it up to your students and come another day!

"Damn," Xavier said quietly.

Violet looked up at him. "What?"

"Once a year, I have a guest come in to speak to my sophomore classes for an unofficial career day. Raheem was supposed to speak to them today, but he had to cancel because RJ's sick. It's too late to find a replacement."

He started to think of alternatives. Maybe they could watch YouTube videos about mechanics instead?

"I'll do it!" Violet said.

He blinked. "You'll do what? Career day?"

"Yes, please! Give me something to do. A reason to feel useful." She continued to hold the vase of flowers to her chest, bouncing her shoulders. "I mean, I'm no mechanic, but I think some of the students might find my job interesting, right?"

"That goes without saying," he said, staring at her. "But are you sure? You'd have to talk to three of my classes. Fourth, fifth and seventh period."

"Yes, I'm sure. So sure. It's not like I have anything else going on." She smiled and gestured around his apartment. "I have nothing but time. And I want to help you."

"Okay," he finally said. He didn't want to inconvenience her, but he genuinely appreciated her desire to help. Plus, his students would probably love to meet her.

"Let me go prepare a presentation." She clapped her hands and rubbed her palms together. "This is exciting!"

She muttered to herself about what she'd wear as she left the kitchen, and Xavier laughed as he watched her go.

WHEN FOURTH PERIOD arrived, Xavier explained to his students that there would be a change of plans regarding the guest speaker. Instead of speaking to his cousin, the mechanic, they'd be speaking to his wife. He glanced at the door, wondering if Violet had had any trouble getting to the school. He'd offered to come and pick her up, but she'd told him that her dad would give her a ride.

"Oh my gosh," Jerrica Brown said, smiling. "We'll finally get to meet her! You both looked so cute at the bowling alley fundraiser. We all were like, wow, look at Mr. Wright and his wife. They're so cute!"

In front of Jerrica, Cherise Fisher nodded. "Yeah, super cute."

Xavier smiled, then realized how goofy he probably looked.

"This presentation is about her career as a stylist, okay?" he said. "Please don't ask her any personal questions." *Like about our marriage.*

"My mom said you probably got married so quickly because your wife is pregnant," Jeffrey Colson said. "Is that true?"

"What? No." Xavier frowned. "And that was a personal question. You can't ask her anything like that."

Violet appeared at the door then, and she waved at Xavier, smiling brightly. His heartbeat sped up at the sight of her.

"Okay, she's here," Xavier said. "Everyone, please be on your best behavior."

"Hi," Violet said when he opened the door. She eased by him on her crutches. Underneath her pea coat, she was wearing a black turtleneck and wide-leg black pants, partially covering her cast. Her curls were smoothed into a neat bun on top of her head, and she was wearing her dark lipstick again. "Hello, class," she said, waving at his students.

Intrigued and nosy, the students stared at her and waved back.

Xavier took Violet's coat and helped connect her laptop to the whiteboard so that her presentation would display for the class to see. Then he waited as Violet settled onto the stool he'd set up at the front of the classroom.

"Class," Xavier said, "This is my wife, Ms. Greene. She—" He paused when Dante Jones raised his hand. "Yes, Dante?"

"Why doesn't she have the same last name as you?" Dante asked, completely ignoring Xavier's no-personal-questions rule.

"She doesn't have to take his last name if she doesn't want to," Jerrica cut in, rolling her eyes. She beamed at Violet. "I think it's cool that you kept your own last name."

"Thank you," Violet said, smiling back at Jerrica.

"Please give Ms. Greene your undivided attention *and* utmost respect," Xavier continued. To Violet, he whispered, "Ready?"

She nodded. "Can you get the lights, please?"

"The lights?"

"Yes, hurry. I want to make sure I have enough time for questions at the end."

Sporting a bemused smile, Xavier turned off the lights. Then he returned to his desk and shared Violet's presentation to the whiteboard behind her. The first slide featured a picture collage with several photos of Violet posing beside her various clients. Written across the slide in big, bold letters was *Violet Greene, Stylist to the Stars*. His students sat up in their seats.

Violet produced a tiny speaker from her bag and began to play "Diamonds" by Rihanna.

"Everyone, please close your eyes," she instructed. Xavier smirked, watching as his class listened obediently.

"I'm going to set a scene for you," Violet said. "The year is 2012. Rihanna's hit song 'Diamonds' is climbing up the charts. Beyoncé has given birth to her firstborn child, Blue Ivy. *Twilight: Breaking Dawn* is dominating the box office, and I, Violet Greene, am a high school sophomore just like you, dreaming about one thing and one thing only: fashion. You can open your eyes now." She stopped the music. To Xavier, she said, "Next slide, please."

Xavier clicked to the next slide, which showed a picture of fifteen-year-old Violet wearing a black-and-white polka-dot button-up, red high-waisted shorts and black loafers.

"Retro was in," she said. "My closet was filled with shirts and shorts just like these in various colors. I always paid attention to what was going on in the fashion world. I would sit in the back of the classroom with a copy of *Vogue* in my lap, while my teachers thought I was doing classwork."

Some of the students snickered and Violet shot Xavier an apologetic look. He made a tsk sound, pretending to admonish her.

"My biggest priority was making sure I was constantly up-to-date on whatever new looks were in demand every season," she said. "Next slide, please."

The following slide had more pictures of Violet in high school. In the bottom right corner, there was a photograph of her and Xavier that had been taken their senior year of high school in Raheem's living room. Violet wore a black crop top and a knee-length pencil skirt with Doc Martens.

Xavier wore a navy blue polo, jeans and a pair of white-and-black Jordans. They looked so young, so carefree.

"Is that Mr. Wright?" asked one of his students, Gina Miller.

"Yep." Violet nodded. "Xavier—I mean Mr. Wright—was also pretty fashionable in high school. He was a sneaker-head. One of the first things I noticed about him was how well he was dressed."

"Damn, Mr. Wright, what happened?" Dante asked. "All you do is wear those boat shoes now."

The class laughed, and Xavier couldn't help but laugh too. Being a high school teacher meant that you were subject to the occasional roasting. Violet smiled and directed Xavier to continue to the next slide, which showed photos of herself as a college student at FIDM and interning at fashion magazines, then photos she'd taken on set while assisting stylists on music video shoots. There were several photos of Gigi Harrison and Destiny Diaz. Then they reached a slide of Karamel Kitty at the VMAs wearing a skintight bodysuit with the words *Eat My Kitty or Die* written across her crotch area.

Xavier glanced at the door, praying that his principal didn't decide to suddenly pay his class a visit.

"I've been working with Karamel Kitty for about two years now, and she is just the best person to collaborate with," Violet said, beaming. "This catsuit was actually my idea. I saw it on the runway at the spring 2020 Moschino show, and I thought Karina would look amazing in it. Shortly before the VMAs, there was a lot of talk in the press about Karina not being a good role model for young women, which is not true, by the way, because she's put at least twenty girls through college, but anyway, we wanted to make a statement that would shut people up. And then we got the idea to put her message directly on her clothes. This was a career highlight for me."

Her presentation continued with more photographs of her clients, along with commentary about their specific styles and how she went about curating their wardrobes. She ended her presentation with a photograph of the R and B singer Angel standing on the red carpet, wearing a black leather vest with no shirt underneath, matching black leather pants and the kind of boots that were worn by dudes in motor-cycle clubs.

When Violet finished speaking, Xavier's students stared at her in awe. She gave Xavier a thumbs-up, and he smiled at her as he turned on the lights.

"Does anyone have questions?" Violet asked.

Every student raised their hand.

Most of them wanted to know what it was like to work with Karamel Kitty, and Violet answered each question with a patient smile. She looked so happy to be talking about her career. It was clear to Xavier that she genuinely loved her job.

"Okay, there's time for one more question," Xavier said, glancing at the clock.

Jeffrey Colson raised his hand and Violet pointed to him.

"What happened to your foot?" Jeffrey asked.

"I fell while running in front of a taxi in New York and fractured my ankle," she said.

Jeffrey nodded as if impressed. "Sick."

"Ms. Greene," Cherise Fisher said, "you are the coolest adult I've ever met." The other students quickly voiced their agreement.

"Thank you!" Violet's grin took up her whole face. Xavier smiled proudly.

The bell rang, and his students gathered their things and said goodbye to Violet.

"Wait! Before you leave, I have parting gifts," Violet said, procuring a stack of pamphlets from her bag. "Styling tips and tricks from a fashion expert. A gift from me to you." She beamed as she handed a pamphlet to each student on their way out the door.

"When did you have time to make these?" Xavier asked once they were alone, turning over a pamphlet in his hands. It was printed on thick card stock, with a photograph of Violet on the front cover, hands on her hips, posing in what must have been her studio.

"Oh, it didn't take long at all," she answered. "Maybe ten minutes? My dad drove me to get them printed at Staples."

Xavier's smile broadened. "That presentation was amazing. Thank you for agreeing to do this."

"Of course. I wish someone from the fashion industry would have talked to me in high school."

He was going to ask if she was still okay with presenting to his fifth- and seventh-period classes as well, but as he took in her beautiful face, so electrified and alive from discussing her work, he heard himself asking something else altogether.

"Would you like to go out with me tonight?" he asked. "For Valentine's Day?"

She blinked, and he held his breath, waiting for her answer. Then she smiled at him, somewhat bashful.

"Yes," she said. "I would."

17

AS VIOLET SAT ON THE BLEACHERS, WAITING FOR XAVIER to finish basketball practice, she thought about how different her Valentine's Day had been last year. She'd woken up in Eddy's bed to the faint sound of a violin playing somewhere downstairs in his loft. The bed had been covered in white roses, and a trail of petals led into the hallway and down the steps. She'd discovered dozens of bouquets arranged throughout his living room. An actual violinist had been there, playing a version of John Legend's "All of Me." Eddy had stood in the center of the room, holding a single rose, his hand outstretched to Violet. A week earlier, he'd proposed in Venice, and the ring had still felt foreign and heavy on her finger.

"Eddy," she'd said, walking up to him, taking in the scene. "This is beautiful. My goodness."

She'd placed her hand in his and he'd pulled her into an embrace.

"Happy Valentine's Day," he'd whispered in her ear. "I can't wait to marry you."

At the time, Violet had been enamored, awed even. But with perspective, she could see cracks in the memory. Like how Eddy didn't stay to have breakfast with her because he preferred to go on a run before taking a meeting downtown. And after a day spent running to and from fittings, Violet had made sure to be on time to their dinner date at Nobu, but when Eddy had arrived almost an hour late, his eyes had been glued to his phone the entire night. Even the white roses seemed ominous now, a warning of what was to come.

Xavier blew his whistle, snapping Violet to attention. The boys stopped running a drill and jogged over to Xavier, huddling around him. After spending the afternoon in his classroom, Violet could see why his students easily followed his lead. When she'd finished presenting to his seventh-period class, there'd been enough time to continue discussing *The Things They Carried*. Xavier taught in a way that made the source material accessible, and he was patient with each of their questions. His students joked around with him, but ultimately, he had their respect.

When she'd first offered to sub in for career day, she'd wanted to help while also having a reason to get out of the house. But she'd been surprised by how much she'd enjoyed being in the classroom with Xavier. The rest of the fashion world was currently tuned in to Paris Fashion Week, and Alex and Karina were there now, attending the Off-White and Chloé shows. Violet wished she could be there too, but oddly . . . she found that she wasn't so frustrated by her current situation anymore. She liked getting a full eight hours of sleep and the luxury of afternoon naps. She hadn't felt the bone-weary fatigue in weeks. Was this what it felt like to be fully rested? She hoped she could hold on to this peace once she got back to work.

Yesterday, Jill had emailed with the news that Black Velvet, a popular sister R and B duo, was interested in working with Violet after their team came across her *Look Magazine* feature. Violet had a meeting scheduled with them in LA two weeks from now, and by then, she'd no longer have her cast because she was finally getting it removed next week. Initially, taking a six-week break from work had felt like a jail sentence, but now time was moving so quickly. Part of her wished it would slow down just a little.

What would become of her and Xavier once she left? Would they stay in contact or part as friends? The thought of losing touch with him a second time made her stomach clench.

Xavier blew his whistle again, ending practice. Violet watched as he conversed with Mr. Rodney while the team entered the locker room. Then he turned and mouthed to her that he'd be done soon before he walked into the locker room as well. She smiled, and a flutter spread across her chest as she remembered the thoughtful bouquet he'd given her that morning. Neither of them had addressed their late-night cuddling, as if it might break the spell. Maybe it was muscle memory that brought them together each night. Or maybe it was something else that she was too afraid to think about.

Soon, Xavier reemerged, shrugging his messenger bag over his shoulder. He smiled as he approached her.

"Ready?" he asked.

For their date.

She smiled too. "Ready."

BECAUSE THEIR DECISION to go out for Valentine's Day had been so last-minute, despite his best efforts, Xavier failed to secure a reservation at any of the restaurants around Willow Ridge. The wait times were at least an hour, sometimes two. Violet turned up the radio as they drove around. It was forty degrees outside, a bit warm for February in New Jersey, but still cold enough that she needed her pea coat and a knit hat.

Xavier pulled into the packed parking lot of Il Forno, the popular Italian restaurant in town, and Violet watched as he walked to the door, only to turn back around a few minutes later after he was told that there was a three-hour wait time. She studied his frowning face as he got back into the car and drove out of the parking lot. She smiled to herself because it was sweet that he was trying so hard to make their Valentine's Day as a fake couple meaningful. They stopped at a red light and he glanced at her.

"I'm sorry. I should have planned this better," he said, glowering. "I promise that I'm still smooth."

"Still?" She scoffed. "Were you ever?"

"Don't play. I used to have you in the palm of my hand." He smirked, and Violet rolled her eyes. It was true, though.

"Conceited," she said.

"*Confident*." The light turned green and he stepped on the gas. "I can drive into the city. Probably more options there."

Violet shook her head. As much as she missed New York, she didn't feel like taking a trip into the city tonight.

They continued to drive through town, passing the crowded restaurants and familiar landmarks. Then they passed the mini-golf course.

"Wait," she said, pointing. "Mini golf!"

His brows furrowed. "It's cold outside."

"Not that cold. And the weather is most likely why no one else is there. Hardly any cars are in the parking lot."

Xavier put on his blinker and turned into the mini-golf complex. "What about your ankle?"

"I think I'll figure it out."

He pulled into the nearly empty parking lot and cut the engine.

"You sure this is what you want to do?" he asked.

The mini-golf course had opened in Willow Ridge years after Violet and Xavier had graduated. As sad as it might sound, or surprising, given the life experiences she'd already accumulated, Violet had never played mini golf before. She wanted to do something simple. Something fun.

She opened her door. "I'm sure. Come on."

The cashier at the ticket desk didn't even blink at two people wanting to play outdoor mini golf in February. She barely looked at Violet and Xavier as she handed over their wristbands. Xavier held their golf clubs and cups of hot chocolate as they walked outside onto the jungle-safari-themed course. The floor of the course was bright green, and trees that were clearly inspired by the art in *The Lion King* encircled the area. Violet and Xavier stopped at the first section, which was designed to look like a watering hole with a shallow pond surrounded by small plastic elephants. Up ahead, an elderly couple played on the course, bundled up in their winter coats. They shared a cup of hot chocolate, and Violet smiled, watching them.

"Okay, so how do you wanna do this?" Xavier asked, gesturing to her crutches.

Violet studied the trajectory of the course. "You go first. I'll think about it while I watch you."

"You want to leave it to the professionals. I get that."

She snorted, and he hit the golf ball, easily sending it straight into the hole. He pumped his fist and Violet rolled her eyes. Being naturally good at sports must be so nice.

"Your turn," he said.

Violet pressed her weight down onto her crutches and held her club in her hands. She took a tentative swing, just to test herself, and she wobbled. The club almost slipped from her grasp. She suddenly felt Xavier's hands at her waist, steadying her.

"Try now," he said. His breath tickled her ear and she swallowed thickly, struggling to focus on the golf ball as she lightly knocked it with her club. The ball rolled down the path but stopped a few inches short of the hole.

"Really?!" She sucked her teeth.

Xavier laughed, lips still at her ear. "Better luck next time."

She shivered at the low timbre of his voice. Then she reached backward and pinched him, and he yelped. "Stop gloating," she said.

They continued on through the course. Xavier somehow managed to make a hole in one almost every time. Violet definitely wasn't as successful, but she wasn't going to give up, because every time she swung, Xavier held his hands at her waist to keep her balanced, and she found herself craving his touch more and more, anticipating the moment when he leaned down and lightly teased her right before she swung.

They reached the halfway mark, which was designed to look like the den of a lion pride, with plastic lions propped on either side of them. A younger couple had entered the course a few feet behind them, and the girl kept stealing kisses, distracting the boy each time he tried to swing. They looked like high schoolers.

"Remember when we were like that?" Violet asked, nodding at the teens.

Xavier knocked his ball farther down and then glanced back at the younger couple. "PDA obsessed?"

"No." Violet laughed. "Obsessed with each other."

He smiled, and his gaze lingered on her for a prolonged moment. "I do."

He resumed his spot behind her, hands at her waist. She hit her ball and could not care less where it landed. She was too focused on Xavier's nearness. When he stepped away from her and carried their clubs to the next section, Violet watched his assured stride and graceful movements. He drew her attention in a way that no one else had ever managed to do. Sourly, she wondered if he'd ever had a minigolf date with his ex, Michelle. She thought of how Bianca told her that Michelle had felt like she wasn't enough for Xavier.

"Your ex-girlfriend," she blurted. "Did you love her?"

Xavier was quiet, his head averted as he knocked his golf ball into a lion's mouth. "Michelle?" he said. "Yeah, I did."

His admission settled unpleasantly in Violet's gut.

"But we weren't in love."

She couldn't deny her relief. "Oh."

"I think we got together because it was convenient," he said. "We saw each other every day at school and got along, but I don't know if either of us was that fulfilled in the relationship. We work better as friends."

Violet mulled over his words. After she broke up with Eddy, she realized that she hadn't been in love with him either. Why did people stay in relationships if they weren't in love? Maybe sometimes it was necessary when it came to security and healthcare. But Violet hadn't needed Eddy for either of those things. She'd just wanted to get rid of the question mark in that area of her life. She was ashamed to admit that, at the time, the convenience of their relationship had mattered more than real happiness.

"If Eddy hadn't cheated, you'd be married right now," Xavier said, once again coming to stand behind her. This time, his hold on her waist was less firm, almost questioning.

She nodded. "Yeah," she said quietly. "I guess we would be."

"Is that what you wish happened?"

"No," Violet said immediately. "Of course I wish he didn't cheat on me, because it was painful and embarrassing to be betrayed like that. But I think it was the universe's way of waking me up and sending me down a different path. I had stubbornly ignored the truth, which was that Eddy wasn't the right person for me."

She hit her ball and it landed nowhere near the lion's mouth. She sighed and vowed to return one day and make this golf course her bitch.

"Who do you think that person is?" Xavier asked. His deep voice enveloped her ear. "The right person?"

She angled her face slightly to see him better. His lips were inches from her own. His warm breath fanned across her mouth, and the air between them changed, growing thicker.

"I don't know," she whispered.

You, her stupid, traitorous brain screamed. *You're the right person.*

She'd officially lost her mind.

Her cheeks flushed hot as Xavier's fingers spread on her lower abdomen, sending tingles of heat throughout her body. She thought of their late-night cuddling, his warm skin pressed against hers. She licked her lips and his eyes widened.

"Excuse me, are you done here?"

Violet and Xavier froze. The teenagers had caught up and were looking at them with annoyed expressions.

"Um, yes, sorry," Violet mumbled, heart hammering as she moved away from Xavier.

They finished their game, but the tension between them lasted for the rest of the evening and while Xavier stopped at Burger King on the way home. Violet could barely think straight. Her nerves were on fire. Her thoughts were a tangled web filled with images of Xavier's mouth hovering above hers. She squeezed her thighs together, praying that the ache in her body would magically disappear, yet simultaneously wishing it stayed.

Xavier pulled up to his apartment. He kept the engine running, and a heavy silence bloomed between them as they sat motionless inside his car. Violet took a deep breath and turned to face Xavier, only to find that he was already looking at her. His gaze was on her mouth.

"Violet," he said, his voice low. Just her name. A possibility. An invitation.

She finally allowed herself to stop fighting what she desired. She unbuckled her seat belt and moved closer to Xavier, pushing herself up on the center console, and brushed her lips against his. The familiarity of his lips sent tremors through her. She kissed him again, and he brought his hands up, cupping her face. One hand slid to the nape of her neck, holding her closer. He tilted his face and deepened the kiss. Violet let out a soft moan as he slid his tongue into her mouth, his hand tightening behind her neck as he continued to hold her in place, tonguing her mouth so languidly, she felt boneless and too aroused to function. Xavier's breathing was rough and fast as his hands lowered to her waist, brushing over her breasts. He grasped her thighs and she felt his hand slip in between her legs. She bit his bottom lip as he cupped her heat, and his grip tightened on her. She lost all sense of time and place, struggling to scramble closer to him with her heavy cast as their mouths remained glued together. Her trembling hands roamed over him, pulling at his coat zipper, wanting to feel more of him. She brought her mouth to his neck, licking and sucking on his hot skin. He groaned and gripped her tighter.

Yes! Her thirsty brain screamed. *Finally!*

A loud thumping noise caused them to jump. Startled, Violet looked up to find Dahlia standing at Xavier's driver's-side window.

Oh, dear Lord.

"*Jesus, Mom*," Violet hissed, pulling away from Xavier. She smoothed down her hair and Xavier hurried to zip up his coat, trying to catch his breath. His cheeks flushed.

"Mrs. Greene," Xavier said, rolling down the window. "Hi. Um, do you want to come inside? My apartment, I mean! Not my car . . ."

"No, that's all right." Dahlia frowned at them like they were naughty schoolchildren. "I couldn't get a hold of Violet, so I thought I'd stop by and speak to her in person."

"Right," he said. "Okay."

Xavier glanced at Violet, his expression so filled with longing, it made her think many indecent thoughts that she'd rather not consider while her mother was mere feet away.

She and Xavier got out of the car, and Xavier took their food into the house, leaving Violet outside in the driveway with Dahlia. Violet kept her eyes on Xavier until he closed the door behind him. Then she looked at her mother.

"Where is your decorum, Vi?" Dahlia asked, crossing her arms over her chest. "Kissing in public like that for everyone to see?"

Violet sighed. Was it a crime to kiss your pretend husband outside of his apartment? She thought not! She didn't even need to point out that no one else was outside to see them. Well, no one except her mother.

"Hello to you too, Mom. What's going on?"

"I came to talk about the dinner," she said. "Does March fifteenth work for you?"

Violet held back a groan. Not this dinner business again.

"I have to check my schedule. That's right after the premiere party for *The Kat House*."

"The what now?"

Violet shook her head. She'd definitely mentioned her work on Karina's visual album to her mother before, but she didn't have the energy to explain again. "It's a work thing."

"Well, can you figure out your schedule, please, and get back to me?" Dahlia blew on her hands. "Getting in touch with you is harder than contacting the president. I simply want to plan a nice dinner for my daughter and son-in-law to celebrate their marriage."

"Who are you inviting?" Violet said, skeptical. "I thought this was just going to be a small thing at the house."

Dahlia huffed. "Don't you think your extended family will be upset if they aren't invited too? What about people from the community?"

"Mom, please." Violet fought the urge to roll her eyes, because then Dahlia would only yell at her about her lack of manners. But if this wedding dinner had to happen, Violet had certain stipulations, because the agreement between her and Xavier would be over soon. By the end of March, they were supposed to tell everyone that they'd decided to separate, not have a party celebrating their union. The fewer people involved, the better. "Immediate family only."

Dahlia grumbled. "Fine."

"Okay then," Violet said. "March fifteenth. I'll make it work."

Satisfied, Dahlia left, and Violet walked into Xavier's apartment. She leaned her crutches against the wall. Xavier was standing in the kitchen entryway, like he'd been waiting for her.

"What did your mom say?" he asked.

Talking about the wedding dinner with Dahlia had thrown a bucket of cold water onto Violet. What were she and Xavier thinking kissing in his car like that? She guessed that was the problem. They *hadn't* been thinking. Their arrangement was just that: an arrangement. It didn't matter if she liked Xavier. Because she did like him. Too much. She knew how she got when it came to him. She'd lose all sense of herself, and chances were, one of them would only end up hurt. With her luck, she'd be the recipient. She couldn't handle another broken heart. It might break her for good.

"She wanted to set a date for our wedding dinner," Violet said quietly. "March fifteenth."

"Ah." He walked toward her and helped her take off her coat. He leaned down and pressed a gentle kiss to her throat, obviously ready to pick up where they left off. It took all of Violet's strength to put her hands on his shoulders, lightly easing him away.

"We shouldn't do this," she said, focusing on his collarbone because she was unable to look at his face. "It complicates things."

When she finally raised her gaze, she saw that he was staring down at her with crinkled brows. After a weighted silence, he murmured, "Yeah . . . right. Okay."

A chasm formed in her chest as he walked away from her into the kitchen. She no longer had an appetite for her nuggets and fries. Tense and confused, she went into his room and changed into her pajamas.

That night, they slept together in his bed, close, but not touching.

When she woke in the morning, Xavier had already left for work. Emptiness shrouded her as she looked over at his side of the bed.

But very soon, she'd have to get used to this. A life without Xavier was her reality.

She tried to tell herself that it was a reality she could accept.

18

XAVIER WAS AT RAHEEM AND BIANCA'S HOUSE THAT SUN-
day afternoon, watching the Nets game, when his phone
vibrated with a text from Tim Vogel.

> It was great speaking with you the other day. My
> assistant will email you on Monday to schedule an
> official interview.

Xavier let out a sigh of relief. Once again, Tim had called
Xavier out of the blue, this time without so much as a hello,
and had lobbed question after question at Xavier regarding
his coaching principles. Xavier had quickly realized he'd
been participating in an informal interview of sorts. Even
though he'd been caught off guard, apparently he'd been
impressive enough.

By the way, Tim's follow-up text read, Helen and I would
love to get dinner again with you and Violet. What a fire-
cracker you've got there!

Thanks, Tim, Xavier responded. Looking forward to the
interview.

He wouldn't comment on having another dinner with Violet because it wasn't a possibility. Tomorrow she was getting her cast taken off, and that would be it. The end of Violet and Xavier 2.0, the pretend version. Even though that initial dinner with Tim and Helen Vogel had been slightly disastrous, it painted Xavier in a favorable light. The young, devoted husband. Their plan had worked in Xavier's favor after all.

He and Violet had retreated to their separate areas of his apartment since they'd kissed in his car on Valentine's Day. At night, they no longer cuddled, even though she lay only inches away from him. Tension hovered in the air, and he wished things could go back to how they were before, when he and Violet had finally reached an easy level of comfort. But he couldn't say that he regretted kissing her. He'd felt as though he'd finally come alive after a nine-year slumber.

Being alone with Violet was dangerous. When in her presence, he felt as though he was constantly on the verge of saying something he wouldn't be able to take back. Like that he wanted to see where things could go if they gave each other a real chance. That having her in his life made everything feel right again, and he regretted letting his insecurities push her away at age nineteen, and he should have held on to her with all his might. He wanted to tell her that he wouldn't make the same stupid mistake again. But he couldn't say those things because they weren't what Violet wanted to hear. She wanted to return to her life, and there was nothing he could do but accept her choice.

"Brooklyn is getting their ass handed to them," Raheem

said, walking into the living room. He'd just put RJ down for a nap, and Bianca had driven to Philly for the day for a cosmetology conference.

Raheem settled on the couch beside Xavier. The Hornets were beating the Nets 57–50. Xavier hadn't really been paying attention to the game, too preoccupied with thoughts about Violet.

"Ay, I want your opinion on something," Raheem said, digging in his back pocket. He pulled out a ring box, set it down on the coffee table and opened it to reveal a dazzling rock. "I'm giving B a new engagement ring next month now that I can finally afford something bigger."

Xavier picked up the velvet box and examined the ring more closely. The diamond sparkled, along with a diamond-encrusted silver band. "Damn, cuzzo, this is dope. B is gonna love it."

Raheem grinned proudly. "She's the love of my life, and I can't wait to make her my wife."

"Is that a song lyric?"

Raheem squinted one eye. "Maybe?"

"Are you nervous?"

"To get married? Nah, not really." He clapped Xavier on the shoulder. "You would know."

Xavier blinked. "Me? How would I know?"

"You and Vi," Raheem said, shrugging. "Y'all make married life look simple."

"But we're not—" Xavier shook his head. "You know that our situation isn't real."

"What's not real about it? You live together, you care about each other and from what I can see, you support each other.

That's what B and I have. What's different about you and Violet?"

"She's moving out tomorrow," Xavier said.

"So that's it? It's over that quickly?"

"Yeah." Xavier averted his gaze back to the television.

Raheem sucked his teeth. "Y'all are very annoying."

Xavier shrugged helplessly. "This was always the plan. We'd pretend and then she'd leave. Why are you giving me shit?"

"Because *I* was there back in the day when your mopey ass didn't wanna get up off the couch after y'all broke up. I love you and all, but I don't want to deal with that again. You care about her, don't you?"

"Of course."

"Then you need to stop being stupid and tell her how you feel."

Xavier sighed. If only it were that easy.

"I don't have anything to offer her," he said quietly, more to himself than to Raheem, staring down at his wedding band.

What could he give her that she didn't already have? That she couldn't find a better version of elsewhere? Someone with a real house who could take her on lavish vacations and literally give her the world.

"You have lots to offer, cuzzo," Raheem said. "Come on, now. I'm not entertaining this negativity. Stop selling yourself short."

But Xavier knew that he wasn't selling himself short. He was just being realistic.

Long ago, he'd learned the risks of getting his hopes up

too high, and he was wary of making the same mistake again.

All too soon, the following morning arrived. Xavier was off from work for President's Day, and he drove Violet into the city to her podiatrist's office. Her suitcases were piled in the back seat. The car ride was quiet, agonizingly so. Violet gazed out the window as they drove over the George Washington Bridge, and a faint smile touched her lips. Her smile grew wider once they parked on a street in Midtown Manhattan.

She rolled down the window and closed her eyes, taking a deep inhale. "Do you smell that?"

Xavier sniffed the air and caught a whiff of the hot dog truck a few feet away, mixed with the scent of garbage from the overflowing trash can beside them. "It smells terrible."

"I know," she said, grinning. "It's good to be home."

At the doctor's office, Xavier and Violet watched intently as her podiatrist, a short, kind-faced man named Dr. Pinto, sawed down the middle of her cast.

"I can see my foot again!" Violet sang as he cracked the cast open. She lifted her leg and slowly wiggled her foot in a circle. The skin around her ankle was dry, making her flower tattoo appear wilted. Her ankle looked slight, but Violet obviously did not care. "My beautiful foot! Look, Xavier! Look at it!"

She beamed at him, and he laughed. Dr. Pinto chuckled too and briefly examined her ankle, which had healed nicely. He advised that she might experience brief swelling or stiffness and that she should give her muscles a few days to adjust and it would be best to avoid any activities that could stress the bone or tissue, like playing contact sports. At that, Violet laughed.

"Won't be a problem at all," she said. "Unless you count wearing high heels."

"I do," Dr. Pinto said, very serious. He proceeded to tell her about the physical therapy she would need to continue her recovery.

Afterward, as they rode the elevator down to the lobby, Violet couldn't stop staring at her feet. She'd changed into a comfortable pair of black Nikes, which she said had memory foam material. The brisk air whooshed around them as they stepped outside, and Xavier swallowed, turning to Violet. He hated the words that were about to come out of his mouth.

"Should I take you to your apartment now?" he asked.

"We're right by Central Park," she said, pointing to their left. He saw a horse and carriage trotting down Fifth Avenue. "Can we walk around a little? I know it's kind of cold today, but I just really want to walk." She paused. "Unless you have plans, of course. It is your day off, so I understand if you'd rather go back home."

"Nah, I don't have plans," he said, relieved. "Let's walk."

They strolled at a leisurely pace through Central Park, stopping to buy honey-roasted peanuts and to admire people's dogs. The wind whipped around them, but Xavier didn't mind. And he didn't even mind that he and Violet weren't talking very much. He simply wanted to cherish these last moments with her before their lives split into separate directions again.

When her ankle began to feel stiff, they decided they'd

walked enough and turned back in the direction of his car. His heart was in his throat as they drove to her apartment in Union Square. Once again, he got lucky with street parking, and he cut the engine.

"Do you need help with your suitcases?" he asked.

He prepared himself for the worst, for her to say no, chuck the deuces and hop out of his car.

"Yes, that would be great," she said softly. "Thank you."

They entered the lobby of her high-rise apartment building and Xavier surveyed the open area, impressed by the pristine furniture and the lobby attendant who greeted them.

"Hey, Lucas," Violet said, smiling at the attendant. To Xavier, she whispered, "Don't be so impressed by what you see in the lobby. It once took the management an entire month to send someone to fix my washer and dryer. The elevators were finally fixed after being out of service for almost two months, and they call it luxury living." She shrugged. "But I love the location."

They rode the elevator up to her apartment, and as the doors opened to the fourteenth floor, Xavier was surprised to see Lily standing there beside a tall guy with dark brown skin.

"Lily!" Violet shrieked. She leaped forward and hugged her sister, then lifted her foot. "My ankle is healed!" She turned to the guy standing beside Lily. "Look, Nick! My ankle!"

Lily and Nick laughed. "I hope you're planning to hold off on the heels," Lily said. She glanced at Xavier. "Hey, Xavier. It's nice to see you."

"Oh, sorry," Violet said. "Xavier, this is Nick, Lily's boyfriend. He lives down the hall from me. Nick, this is my—This is Xavier."

"What's up?" Xavier said, dapping Nick up, noticing Violet's hesitation over how to classify his role in her life.

"Nice to finally meet you," Nick said. "I've heard a lot about you." Lily discreetly nudged Nick in the side, which let Xavier know that she'd most likely told Nick all about Xavier and Violet's fake marriage.

"Nice to meet you too," Xavier said.

"So what are you up to?" Lily asked, glancing between him and Violet. Her eyes sparkled with curiosity.

"Xavier helped carry up my suitcases," Violet said. "Where are you going? Let me guess, the bookstore?"

"Bingo," Lily said. She and Nick smiled at each other.

"Ugh, you are just too cute, aren't you?" Violet said, rolling her eyes, but she grinned. "Have fun. I'll text you later."

The sisters hugged goodbye and Xavier and Nick shook hands again before he and Lily got onto the elevator.

"Nick is an author," Violet explained as they continued down the hall to her door. "He writes about, um, dragons, I think? I actually haven't read his book yet, but don't tell him that."

She turned the key and opened the door to her apartment. Xavier carried her suitcases inside, and his eyes immediately were drawn to the blown-up framed magazine covers of various women rappers on her wall. He recognized Karamel Kitty right away, and possibly Megan Thee Stallion.

"I styled those shoots," Violet explained. "Freelance work. Except for the one with Karina."

Then he noticed the wooden coffee table, which was carved into the silhouette of a naked woman. If he didn't know any better, he'd say the table was modeled after Violet's body.

"That's me," she said proudly, following his line of sight. "I had it commissioned in Morocco."

"It looks dope." He walked farther into her apartment, continuing to look around. Her deep red couch was a statement piece in the overall white room. She had floor-to-ceiling windows and spotless white walls. He was right when he assumed her apartment was much nicer than his.

"Do you want anything to drink?" she asked, and he turned around to face her.

She opened her fridge and frowned when she discovered that it was basically empty.

"Looks like you need to go grocery shopping," he said, leaning against the kitchen island.

"Yeah, another day. I'm just gonna order out tonight . . ." She closed the fridge and glanced at him over her shoulder. "Do you want to stay for dinner?"

"Yes." He responded so quickly it was borderline embarrassing.

She smiled. "Thai?"

"Why am I not surprised," he said, smiling too. "Thai is cool."

She went to stand at her large windows as she placed the order using an app on her phone. Then she simply stared outside at the street below. A deep longing pierced his heart while he watched her. She was so close, yet so far.

"Are you happy to be back?" he asked, coming to stand

beside her. He followed her gaze, looking at the cars driving down the street and the people walking to and fro. It was definitely busier than Willow Ridge.

"I am happy," she said. "I missed the city. It's funny, though, because before I left, I felt this sense of dread every morning, like I was immediately overwhelmed by the city and all the things I had to do for work. I wasn't taking care of myself like I should have been. I really did need a break." She turned to him and softly added, "Thanks for letting me stay with you."

"Of course." Then, because he couldn't help himself, "My place is always there for you, whenever you need a break."

"I appreciate that," she said. "I already know I'll miss your comfortable bed." Her cheeks reddened, and she looked away.

He stared at her profile. After years of thinking about her and wondering what could have been, she was right here in front of him. Was he really going to fumble the ball a second time? He heard Raheem's voice in his head. *Stop being stupid and tell her how you feel.* It sounded simple, but in reality, it was so fucking frightening.

"Violet," he murmured, taking a deep breath. "There's something I want to say to you."

Slowly, she turned to look at him, taking in the serious tone of his voice. "Okay."

"In high school, I never would have imagined that our lives would have gone in such different directions, or that we would go almost a decade without speaking. Truthfully, no longer having you in my life ate me up inside, and I just learned to deal with it because I was the one who broke up with you and I didn't think I deserved a place in your life anymore. I don't know why we ran into each other in Vegas. It might have been a weird coincidence or maybe a stroke of fate. All I know is that our paths somehow crossed."

He paused, and she stared at him fixedly. Her chest rose and fell in quick movements.

"Our marriage might be fake and temporary," he continued, "but I hope we can give this thing between us a try for real, because . . ."

He paused once more, fear causing him to hesitate. Violet blinked, waiting for him to finish his sentence. If he wanted a chance with her, he'd have to plainly lay it all on the line.

"Because," he said, finding his courage, "I can't bear the thought of losing you again."

19

VIOLET'S HEART THUMPED WILDLY IN HER CHEST AS SHE absorbed Xavier's words. His arrested gaze was glued to her face. Raw emotion burned intensely in his eyes.

"I . . ." she started, then stopped. She struggled to speak. Her thoughts were a frantic, swarming hive.

"I've never been to LA," he said. "I'm not rich and I might not be able to travel with you that much because of my school schedule, but I hope you might be able to see beyond that—"

"Xavier, I don't care about those things," she said, stopping him. "You're a wonderful teacher, and I admire the career you've built. And of course I don't care that you're not rich. That doesn't matter to me." Her heart continued to thrash around, like it wanted to claw its way up her throat. Nervously, she rubbed small circles on her chest. "That's not why I'm hesitant about being with you."

"Then what is it?" He stepped closer and gently touched her elbow, causing her to cease her fevered rubbing.

She stared at him, too overwhelmed and wholly unprepared to talk about this, about *them*. When she spoke, her voice was barely a whisper. "The truth is that you scare me."

Xavier froze, letting his hand drop away from her. "I scare you?"

She shook her head, seeing that he didn't completely understand her. "What I mean is . . . I'm afraid of who I'll become if I let you in again."

Xavier fell silent, brows crinkled in confusion.

"I think about myself in high school and my first year of college, and how I couldn't see anything other than you," she continued. "Thank God I loved fashion as much as I did, because it kept me motivated. Otherwise, I would have been completely lost after we broke up. I don't regret loving you the way that I did, because very few people get to experience that kind of love. But I don't know if I can go through it again because I'm afraid you'll hurt me just like before." Quietly, she added, "And this time I might not survive it."

Xavier absorbed her words, motionless save for the quick jumping of his pulse at the base of his throat.

"Violet," he said, softly taking her hand. The warmth of his palm startled her. "I will never forgive myself for hurting you the way I did when we were younger. I was nineteen and I was an idiot. I told you that breaking up with you was one of my biggest regrets, but that wasn't the whole truth. It *is* my biggest regret, full stop. Even more than leaving Kentucky."

She blinked at him as his hand curled around hers. He was saying exactly what she'd wanted to hear for years. It was too much.

Her ankle went stiff again.

"I need to sit down," she said weakly, moving to the couch and easing down onto the center cushion.

Xavier stayed by the window, watching her. His expression was open and vulnerable.

"Back then," she said, returning his gaze, "you broke up with me because you said we were too different. Even if that wasn't the real reason, it's definitely true about us now. What if you wake up one day and decide our differences are too much for you?"

He came over and crouched in front of her, taking both of her perspiring hands in his. His head was bent as he ran his thumbs over her knuckles in a soothing rhythm.

"On paper, we don't have a lot in common," he said. "That's true. But I'm twenty-nine. I'm not a kid anymore. I know the importance of what we have, and what we can be. Maybe at first glance we're different." He lifted his hand and lightly pressed it over her heart. "But here, we're the same. I've spent nine years trying to fill the gap that you left behind, but I can't replace you and I don't want to. I wouldn't make the same mistake and risk losing you again."

As Violet stared into his eyes, she realized that she believed him. And that scared her all the more. Because if she placed her faith in him and he betrayed her, she'd never be able to trust her own judgment again.

"I think maybe I should leave and give you time to think," Xavier said, slowly rising to his feet. "I know this is a lot, and I probably should have waited to bring this up at a better time." He rubbed the back of his neck and glanced away, his face stricken with distress. "As soon as you call me, I'll come back. Or if you'd rather just talk on the phone, that's okay too. Whatever you want."

He began to back away and she grasped his hand, stilling him.

She'd proven over the last nine years that she could live without Xavier. Even though she'd often felt like a piece of her was missing and found herself reaching out for something that no longer existed, like a phantom limb, she'd moved on and made new memories. She'd found genuine fulfillment in her job. She had the love of her sisters and friends. Xavier's presence in her life wasn't necessary to her survival. She *could* live without him.

But she realized then that given the choice, she'd rather have him be part of her life.

"No," she said, staring up into his face. "Don't leave."

He lowered himself down onto the couch beside her. Their hands remained entwined.

"I don't know if I'll be any good at this," she whispered.

He smiled softly. "I think you'll be okay."

"No, I mean it. My work schedule is *a lot*. I'll miss out on important things sometimes, and I might not always get to see you when I want to . . . but I want to try with you. I really do."

"Me too." He leaned his forehead against hers. "I'm also gonna try my best. But one thing I know is that I won't break your heart again, Vi. I swear on everything."

She closed her eyes, reveling in his closeness. "Please don't make a promise to me that you can't keep."

He cupped her cheeks in his hands and tilted her face upward to look him in the eye.

"I swear," he repeated with conviction.

She gazed at him, simultaneously seeing the magnetic boy she'd fallen in love with long ago and the grounded man who captivated her now. His hands were still gently pressed to either side of her face. She inched forward, an almost imperceptible movement, drawn by her desire to feel closer to him, like when they were younger and it had felt as though they'd lived in each other's skin. The feeling of his warm, rough palms against her cheeks kindled a flame inside her, and she brought her hands up to his face as well, brushing over the thickness of his goatee. His pulse jumped, and she watched as his gaze dropped to her mouth. Her breath quickened as he licked his lips and lowered his hand to the curve of her waist.

"Vi," he said, voice low, almost like a question.

In answer, she claimed the remaining space between them and pressed her mouth against his. Xavier breathed deeply and pulled closer, bending his head to take her kiss. A soft moan sounded from his throat, sending shivers down her spine. She wanted more of that sound, more of him. She opened her mouth, welcoming his tongue, and their kiss quickly eased from tentative to hungry. Kissing him felt so good, so exhilarating. She wrapped her arms around his neck, and his grip tightened on her hips, clutching her closer and bringing her flush against his chest. He kissed along her jaw and brought his mouth to her exposed throat, sucking and licking her skin. Violet's breath caught, and she reached under his sweatshirt, running her hands along his tight abdomen. Her fingers went lower, brushing against his hardness, and he groaned.

"Violet," he whispered, his eyes glazed over with heat.

She pushed against his shoulders, easing him backward, and she straddled his lap. She kissed him again, her tongue seeking his. He tugged at the hem of her sweater and she fervently tried to take the garment off without breaking the kiss. Xavier laughed, a deep, husky chuckle that made her limbs quiver, and he deftly pulled her sweater over her head. She unhooked her bra and tossed it to the side, and Xavier stared at her, mesmerized. He leaned forward and gently cradled her breasts, rubbing his thumbs across her nipples, causing heat to shoot through her. She rocked her hips against his, and he brought her left breast to his mouth, kissing softly and then sucking before moving on to her right breast. She loved the way he touched her with such reverence, like she was cherished. When his attentive lips on her breasts made her stimulated beyond control, she pulled on his sweatshirt.

"Off, please," she murmured.

He smiled and whipped off his shirt in record time. Eagerly, she ran her hands across the smooth, hard expanse of his chest. As if they had an unspoken agreement, they reached for each other, frantic and hungry, pulling down her tights and unbuckling his belt and sliding off his jeans.

"I don't have a condom," Xavier said as his hands clutched her hips.

"One second," she whispered breathlessly as she dashed to her bedroom as fast as her ankle would allow and retrieved a condom from the bottom drawer of her nightstand.

When she returned to the living room, Xavier's gaze blazed as she approached him. He took her hand and kissed her palm, and she resettled onto his lap. They were chest to chest this time, with no barriers between their skin. He slid on the condom, she felt his thickness brush between her legs and she sucked in a breath. She bent to kiss him again, sliding her tongue across his full bottom lip, and she reached down and took his thickness in her palm. In a slow, torturous rhythm, she moved her hand up and down.

"*Fuck*," Xavier said, lifting his hips, his breaths jagged.

She kissed his neck again and dragged her hot tongue across his collarbone. He grasped her thighs with need.

"I want to be inside of you," he said.

His deep, seductive voice caused heat to pool between her legs. She brought her mouth back to his as she slowly sank down onto him.

"Oh my God," she whispered as he filled her. She dug her fingers into his back, and he cupped her ass, breathing hard as he found a quick rhythm, pumping into her. She wrapped her arms around his neck and held on, rolling her hips against his. The angle and pace enveloped her in pleasure. It was almost too much to handle. She moaned in his ear, and his thrusts grew more erratic.

"You feel so good," he said. "So fucking good."

He slid his hands down to where their sweat-dampened bodies were joined and used his thumb to rub her slowly between her legs as he continued his relentless strokes. She stood no chance when he touched her that way, and she easily came apart at the seams. Seconds later, Xavier followed her, groaning with intensity.

They fell into a quiet stillness, clasping each other, panting hard.

"That," she said, dazed and disoriented, "was *way* better than when we were teenagers."

Xavier laughed and used the rest of his strength to lightly squeeze her ass.

A knock at the door startled them and Violet jerked upward. Xavier tightened his hold at her waist, keeping her in place.

Her phone vibrated on the couch beside them with an alert that their food had been delivered at the door.

"Food's here," she said, smiling at him.

THEY SAT ON the floor around Violet's coffee table and shared pad Thai and basil fried rice, each donning one of her plush robes. The robe that Xavier wore barely reached his knees, and she laughed at how silly yet comfortable he looked sitting beside her. Her legs were crossed over his, and they stared at each other grinning goofy, lovesick grins. Like teenagers. Like themselves.

"I kind of want to shower," Violet said, glancing down at the ashy skin around her ankle.

"Me too." Xavier was looking at her with renewed heat.

She hurried to get her shower cap.

IN THE SHOWER, they explored each other further. This time their movements were patient and unhurried. With a washcloth, Violet spread soapy circles across Xavier's chest and arms, pausing at the violet tattoo on the inside of his bicep, giving it a closer inspection. The purple petals had faded slightly, but otherwise the tattoo looked exactly the same as it had the day he'd gotten it. Xavier leisurely ran his hands up and down her back, settling at her ass and giving it a faint squeeze. He trailed kisses down her body, beginning at her mouth, then moving to her jaw and collarbone, until he was crouched in front of her. The water from the showerhead sprayed his shoulders. He ran his fingers over the X on her hip and glanced up at her. She saw something in his eyes, so warm and soft, it melted her. He kissed her hip and continued his kisses until he'd reached the spot between her legs, using his tongue to kiss her deeper. She moaned as he lifted one of her legs, propping it on his shoulder for better access.

This is what I've been missing for nine years, she thought, moments before his skillful tongue sent her over the edge.

LATER, THEIR LIMBS were tangled together, snuggled under a mountain made of Violet's winter comforter and flannel sheets. They gazed at each other in the dark, blinking and breathing. Not speaking, appreciating the silence. Xavier had just set an alarm for five thirty the next morning in order to beat the George Washington Bridge traffic back into Jersey. Violet wished they could prolong their time together.

She nuzzled closer to him and leaned her head against his chest. Xavier wrapped an arm around her and kissed the top of her head. She listened to his heartbeat and felt the easy rise and fall of his chest.

"I love you," he said quietly. "I never stopped."

Violet looked up at him. He gazed back at her.

She did know that he still loved her. In hindsight, she'd known it the minute they'd run into each other at the hotel lobby in Vegas. His love for her had been clear in his eyes. It had been in his fierce hug. And it had been present in the way he'd cared for her while she was sick, and how he so easily went along with her lie about being married.

"I check your Instagram every now and then to make sure you're doing okay," he continued. "I've been doing that since we broke up."

"So you *do* have social media," she said. She leaned closer and kissed him softly, lingering there. When she pulled away, she said, "I love you too."

Because here and now she could finally admit to herself that she'd never stopped loving him either. It felt so good to voice this truth, like her heart, which had been encased in fear and doubt, was finally allowed to be free. She didn't have to decide whether or not she'd give her heart to Xavier, when it had been in his possession all along.

The smile he gave her made her dizzy with happiness.

"I don't use Instagram often," he said. "I've never even posted a picture."

"I'm going to find your account." Exhaustion weighed down her eyelids. "In the morning."

She heard the faint sound of his laugh.

"We'll be okay," he whispered to her, seconds before she fell asleep. "Whatever happens."

She closed her eyes with trustful ease; she believed him.

20

A FEW DAYS LATER, VIOLET WAS BACK TO WORK, AND SHE hit the ground running. Or briskly walking, if you took her ankle into account and the fact that her new physical therapist strongly advised her to take things easy. She arrived at her office early, just as the sun was rising, armed with a strawberry-banana smoothie and her laptop. By the time Alex arrived a little before eight a.m., Violet was wide awake and energized.

"Good morning, I brought sustenance," Alex said, holding a cup of coffee and a paper bag. "Muffins."

"Good morning." Violet smiled and pointed at her empty smoothie cup. "Believe it or not, I already ate."

Alex blinked as she sat down on the other side of Violet's desk. "Wow, and I didn't even have to remind you first."

"Nope." Violet beamed. She couldn't take all the credit for this small change, though. Last night while on the phone with Xavier, she'd told him that she struggled to eat breakfast while working because she had a hard time pausing to eat on the go when she was in the zone. Xavier had suggested smoothies because they were quick and easy. Then he'd gone into a longer explanation about the benefits of using oat milk in smoothies, and she'd smiled, nodding along to the soothing sound of his voice, even though she hadn't understood a word he'd said about enzymes or bone-strengthening minerals.

"Anyway, I missed you," Violet said, hugging Alex. "Thank you so much for holding everything down while I was away."

Alex grinned and shrugged demurely. "I was just doing my job."

"And you did it beautifully." Violet returned to her seat and rubbed her hands together. "All right. Hit me. Where are we at?"

Alex opened her laptop and pulled up their schedule. "Okay, so we've got the photo shoot with Angel today for *Billboard*, and a fitting with Gigi Harrison on Friday for her feature in *The Cut*." Alex continued scrolling through her meticulously created spreadsheet. "While you're in LA next week, we have a second fitting with Karina for the *Kat House* press tour, and you have a preliminary meeting with Black Velvet."

"Right," Violet said, reaching for a chocolate chip muffin and breaking off a chunk. "The Black Velvet sisters are pretty young. I think the older of the two just turned twenty. I'd be interested to hear what kind of vibe they're looking for, moving forward."

"Maybe they want an image revamp like you did for Destiny Diaz, less teenybopper, more chic and serious," Alex said.

"Yeah, maybe," Violet said. Then her phone vibrated on

her desk, grabbing her attention. She smiled as she read a text from Xavier.

Have a good day. I'll see you later tonight.

She replied that she was looking forward to seeing him, and when she glanced up, Alex was watching her with a smirk.

"Might that be the husband?" Alex asked.

"Well, we're kind of dating now, actually . . ." Violet laughed when Alex blinked in surprise for the second time that morning.

"Wow, Vi," she said. "That's huge. I'm happy for you."

"Thank you." Violet grinned. She found it ironic that people would probably be more shocked to learn that she was dating again than to learn that she was pretending to be married. She stood and brushed the muffin crumbs off her pants. "Let's get going, shall we?"

WHEN THEY ARRIVED at the *Billboard* offices for Angel's photo shoot, the staff had thankfully already unpacked and hung the clothes that Violet had arranged to be delivered to the set. She and Alex were flipping through the racks and pulling the options that they'd offer to Angel first, when someone bear-hugged Violet from behind.

"Big sis!" Angel said. His melodic voice boomed in her ear. "I'm glad you're healed up!"

Angel whirled Violet around so that she could see him, and he hugged her again, folding his tall frame down to meet hers. Violet smiled up at his ridiculously handsome face.

"Hello to you too," she said, laughing.

Violet had met Angel last year through Eddy, who had acted as Angel's manager until Angel fired him. Angel had been discovered at the age of eighteen after a video of him singing a solo in his church choir went viral. Then he had a short stint as a gospel singer before switching over to R and B. Because of his sheltered upbringing, he'd been shell-shocked when he'd left his small town in Georgia to sign a deal with a record label in LA. Now, at twenty-six, he was well on his way to true powerhouse stardom. Last summer, he'd attended Violet's anti-wedding party and had stayed late into the night, entertaining everyone.

"So, what's this I hear about you and a new hubby?" Angel asked, taking Violet's left hand and looking pointedly at her rings.

Violet smiled and waved him away. She and Xavier had been so cozily swaddled in their rediscovered love, neither had thought to address how to make the transition from fake spouses to two people who were simply dating.

"It's a long story," she said. "I'll tell you about it when we're not working."

Angel frowned and crossed his long arms over his chest. "Why can't you let me in on girl talk like you do with Karina?"

Violet laughed. "Stop pouting and look at the clothes Alex and I pulled for you."

They turned their attention to the clothing racks. For his first look, they went with a silver Saint Laurent trench coat and black leather pants, no shirt underneath, because he'd been working out and wanted to show off his sculpted abs.

Violet and Alex stood off to the side and watched Angel work his magic for the photographer. Music blasted as he danced around, brushing his trench coat back and spinning in a circle. He licked his lips and crouched down, gazing at the camera. Then he leaned back and laughed, like he'd heard the funniest joke in the world. It seemed like a lot of effort to the untrained eye, but it was worth it because the shots came out amazing.

For his second look, Angel wore a cable-knit lime green Balmain sweater and white Dior chinos. He observed himself in the mirror and lifted his shirt, displaying his abs again.

"Sheesh, I look good," he said.

Violet and Alex snorted, and Angel laughed.

"What?" he said, flashing them a smile. "I'm just trying to give the people what they want."

Violet shook her head as she rolled the sleeves of his sweater, further displaying his forearms. "You're something else."

Angel smiled at her, then he suddenly blinked, like he'd just had a thought. "By the way, you know they broke up, right?"

Violet tilted her head. "Who?"

"Eddy and Meela."

"Oh." She glanced at Alex, who shrugged. "I didn't know that."

"Eddy reached out a few days ago," Angel continued.

"Apparently, Meela started a fling with one of her backup dancers and fired Eddy, so I guess he's looking for new clients. He wants to work with me again, but I said nah. Not after how he treated you."

Violet waited to feel something at Angel's revelation about Eddy and Meela. Maybe satisfaction or justification. But she felt . . . nothing. She didn't care at all.

"Ay," Angel said, bringing her attention back to him. "You're coming to my show in LA next week, right? Can you bring your sister?"

Violet gave him a look. Last summer, she'd tried to hook Angel up with Lily, but then Lily had met Nick and the rest was history. "Lily has a boyfriend now."

"I know that." He quirked an eyebrow. "I'm not talking about Lily."

"Then . . ." Violet paused, frowning as realization dawned. "You mean Iris?"

Angel nodded. His lips formed a slow, coy smile. "We talked a little at your anti-wedding party last year. I felt a vibe. A real one."

"Um, okay," Violet said. The fact that Iris hadn't bothered to mention her conversation with Angel told Violet all she needed to know about Iris's level of interest. But even on the rare chance that Iris *had* found Angel mildly intriguing, she'd never act on it. Iris didn't date. Not since Terry. Violet honestly had a hard time picturing her sister with someone else. "I don't think that would be a good idea."

"Why not?" Angel asked.

Violet gently patted his arm. "There are thousands of

women throwing themselves at you every day. Focus on one of them."

He laughed as he was escorted back to set.

AFTER THE PHOTO shoot, Violet and Alex returned to her office, where she answered more emails, prepped for Gigi Harrison's fitting, photographed inventory and packed up the clothes that needed to be returned to designers.

"Should I order dinner?" Alex asked at a certain point.

Violet glanced at the time on her phone and gasped. "Oh! I have to go!" She shot up from her desk and went to grab her coat. "I should have left an hour ago! Xavier's coming over tonight and I'm cooking dinner!"

Alex balked. "*You?*"

"Oh, don't look so shocked!" Then Violet paused and acquiesced. "Okay, you can look a little shocked." She hastened to button her pea coat. "Xavier has been teasing me about not knowing how to cook, so I'm going to show him that I can. He's always had a way of bringing out my competitive side."

"But, Violet," Alex said soberly, "you *can't* cook."

"Neither could Julia Child in the beginning, and look at how she turned out." She tossed her laptop in her bag and gave Alex a hug goodbye. "Have faith in me. And, come on, you go home too. Go out with your roommates and have a drink or something."

Alex stared at Violet, slowly shaking her head. "Where is my boss and what have you done with her?"

"She's still here," Violet said, laughing as she hurried out the door.

VIOLET WAS SECONDS away from burning down her apartment and possibly the entire building.

She'd had the brilliant yet overconfident idea to sauté a steak for Xavier, like the one he'd eaten at the restaurant in Montclair that had given her food poisoning. She'd bought lobster tails for herself and premade baked macaroni and cheese and collard greens as sides. She'd been so pleased as she rolled her cart through the aisles at Citarella. Then she'd returned home, started a YouTube cooking tutorial, seasoned the meat, placed the steak in a pan, boiled the water for her lobster tails, dropped the lobster tails in the pot and . . . that was when things turned hairy, because she got distracted with a FaceTime call from Karina, who had a thirty-minute break on the set of *Up Next*, and Violet had gone into her room to try on her brand new Off-White green plaid minidress so that she could show Karina what she planned to wear for dinner. Then the next thing she knew, her smoke detector was going off.

"Oh my God," she screeched, dashing into the kitchen. She gaped at the state of her stove. The steak was charred to a crisp, concealed by a billow of smoke. The water in the lobster pot was boiling over and running across her stovetop. She hurried to turn off the flames and fanned the area with a paper towel.

"Damn, girl," Karina said, still on FaceTime. She was lying on the couch in her trailer, watching Violet like she was on a television show. Today Karina's wig was a soft lavender color, and big and wavy old-Hollywood-style curls framed her face.

"This is a disaster." Violet set her phone down so that Karina could still see her. She waved a towel underneath the smoke until the beeping ceased. Then she cracked open her windows, willing to suffer through the late-evening chill in order to get rid of the remaining smoke.

"This is the type of nutty behavior that people get into when they're dickmatized," Karina calmly explained. "He's got you all up in the kitchen in your heels, even though you know you're the type to burn butter."

Violet sent Karina an exasperated look. "I'm not wearing heels!"

Her apartment phone rang with a call from the front desk, letting her know that Xavier was downstairs in the lobby.

"Please send him up," she said evenly. To Karina, she shrieked, "Xavier is here! He's early!"

"It's eight thirty," Karina pointed out. "He's right on time."

"*Oh God.*"

Violet grimaced, wondering how she could salvage this. Maybe she could simply serve the macaroni and cheese and collard greens? What would Julia Child do?

"Girl, you know he's not coming over there to eat your food," Karina said. "Meet him at the door in nothing but a trench coat and some lingerie, and he'll be so distracted, he won't even smell the smoke."

That was an idea, but Violet didn't have time to change

her clothes, because not even a second later, there was a knock at her door.

"Okay, I have to go. Love you," she said to Karina before hanging up.

She opened her door, and Xavier stood on the other side, smiling at her. The sight of him warmed her heart and made her briefly forget about her culinary failures.

"Hi," she said, taking his hand and pulling him inside.

"Hey." He bent down and kissed her. Violet loved the feeling of his mouth against hers. He wrapped his arms around her waist and held her close. Then he pulled back and sniffed. "Is something burning?"

"So, about that," she said, stepping in front of him to block his view of the kitchen area, which was pointless, given that he was much taller than her and could clearly see right over her head. "There's been a change in dinner plans."

"Oh?" Xavier smirked as he placed his duffel bag on the floor. He walked over to the stove and whistled, taking in the disastrous scene before him. He poked the blackened steak with his index finger. "Did you light it on fire?"

"I accidentally burned dinner," she said, throwing her hands up. "I'm not Julia Child, and Gordon Ramsay would probably have me thrown in prison."

Xavier laughed, lifting the pot lid and peeking at the wasted lobster tails. "Hmm. I'll give you an A for effort."

"You're just saying that to be nice." She stood beside him and frowned at her mess.

"Nah, I grade very fairly. Ask my students," he said. He put his arm around her shoulders and placed an affectionate kiss on top of her head. "I appreciate that you went through so much trouble, Vi. For real."

She leaned her head against his arm and sighed. "It was going to be amazing."

"I believe it," he said, laughing a little. Then his stomach grumbled loudly.

"Let's go out for dinner instead," she suggested.

THEY WENT TO a taqueria around the corner and ordered burritos and lime-flavored Jarritos sodas. They sat huddled side by side at a booth in the back of the restaurant while they ate.

"I have an interview with Tim and the other coaches at Riley next week," Xavier told her as he balled up the foil from his burrito. He'd inhaled his food in about five seconds.

"Wait, that's amazing." Violet beamed at him, but Xavier looked less enthused. "What's wrong? This is what you wanted, right?"

He nodded. "Yeah, I'm just concerned about my students. The staff at Willow Ridge is great, and I know they'll be in good hands, but I feel responsible for them. Especially the boys on the team. It's weird to think this could be my last year with them. Mr. Rodney doesn't have the same energy to coach anymore."

"I get that," Violet said, rubbing his back. She knew Xavier's students would be hard-pressed to find another teacher like him, but coaching at Riley was his goal, and despite her lackluster opinions about Tim Vogel, she was going to support Xavier. "But they'll be fine, and it's not like you can't still keep in touch with them."

"That's true. And Riley is a better opportunity for me. More money, more growth. I have to remind myself of that."

Xavier turned to his side, facing her. She did the same and reached for his hand. She was so happy to have him here with her. That he'd made time to see her on a school night.

"What do you think we should tell people about us now?" she asked. "Originally, we were supposed to let everyone know that we were separating."

He brushed a stray curl behind her ear and tenderly caressed her cheek. "Honestly, I don't care what anyone thinks or has to say anymore. How about we tell our parents the truth at the dinner your mom is planning, and after that, we don't need to explain ourselves. If people find out we aren't really married, whatever. It's not their business."

"That sounds good to me," she murmured, grinning. She loved his sudden screw-the-world attitude. It was kind of a turn-on.

She moved closer to him and licked her lips. Xavier's eyes flashed, and he lowered his mouth to hers and immediately began an ardent campaign to kiss her senseless. His hands went to her waist, and she linked her arms around his neck, pulling him against her. They groped at each other hungrily, releasing their pent-up desire. She was practically climbing onto his lap when the server appeared at their table and cleared her throat. Violet glanced up alertly and noticed that others in the small restaurant were gaping at her and Xavier.

"Would you like any dessert?" the server asked, blushing.

"Um, no, thank you," Violet said, easing away from Xavier. She dabbed at her smeared lipstick with a napkin.

"Just the check, please," Xavier said.

They speed walked through the cold back to her apartment, hand in hand. The minute she opened her door, Xavier had her pinned against the wall, rushing to unbutton her coat and leaving a trail of sensuous kisses along her throat.

"I have an extra ticket to Angel's show next Saturday in LA," she said, breathless and dazed. "I know you have your basketball schedule, but if you can make it, do you want to come to the show with me?"

Xavier paused and lifted his heated gaze to her face. "We have a bye week next Saturday, so I'm free. I'll be there."

"Okay. You may carry on." She smiled as he continued his kissing descent of her body.

21

BEING BACK IN RILEY'S GYMNASIUM MADE XAVIER FEEL
strange. He was sitting on the bleachers, watching Tim Vogel and the other assistant coaches, Justin and Vince, lead
the team through their practice drills. As the students dribbled and ran up and down the court, Xavier couldn't help
but remember when he'd been just like them, wearing a
practice jersey, trying to get his groove back after his injury
and switching schools.

After practice ended, Xavier expected Tim to ask him to
meet him in his office to conduct the interview, but instead
they sat right on the bleachers, along with Vince and Justin,
who looked exhausted and more than ready to get the hell
out of there.

"So, Xavier," Tim said, "what do you think of the team?"

"They're a decent group," Xavier said, trying to be diplo-
matic. He was pretty convinced that his high schoolers
would be able to beat them. He was already thinking about
the many ways in which to help Riley improve.

Tim sucked his teeth and waved his hand. "Ah, you can be straight with me. They're a bunch of bums."

Xavier's eyes widened. Behind Tim, Justin's shoulders sagged in a silent sigh. Vince's chin was propped in his palm. He looked like he was falling asleep.

"Try as we might, something isn't clicking with this crop of kids," Tim continued. "Not like when you were here." To Justin and Vince, Tim explained, "Xavier used to play for Riley, about, what was that, Xavier, ten years ago?"

Xavier nodded. "Almost."

"Those two years were some of the best we had," Tim said. He gazed off, nostalgic. Justin rolled his eyes. Vince was definitely softly snoring. "I heard that your team at Willow Ridge is undefeated this year. That's quite impressive."

"Thank you," Xavier said. "We're hoping to make it to the championships. We're headed to the state semifinals next week."

Tim nodded. "We need some of that energy at Riley. How would you go about bringing it?"

Ah, the real interview questions. "Well, first, I think it might be best to start with simpler drills. Really go back to the basics and make sure each player has a handle on what they're doing. It might help to implement a two-a-day schedule, practice in the morning before classes and at night afterward."

"Hmm," Tim mumbled, rubbing his chin. "Not a bad idea. You know, it's really important for these boys to have mentor figures in their lives. They come to play basketball, but a lot of them don't know their head from their foot. Do you consider yourself to be a mentor to your players?"

Xavier thought of his players at Willow Ridge, how they came to him for advice and looked up to him.

"I would like to think so," he answered. "I try to be a good role model."

Tim was nodding again. "That's what we're lacking." He gave a pointed glance over his shoulder at Justin and Vince. Justin looked wounded at the slight, but Vince was rubbing his eyes, like Justin had just shaken him awake seconds before.

Then Tim stood, and Xavier stood as well, expecting the interview to be moved to Tim's office, but instead Tim stuck out his hand for a shake. "This was good."

"Oh," Xavier said, surprised that the interview was ending so quickly. "Are there any other questions you have for me?"

"My assistant will email you later this week to set up a second interview with myself and the athletic director. Standard protocol, you understand. There are a lot of people vying for this position, Xavier. Even though you're a legacy, we're giving everyone a fair shot."

"Yes, of course. I understand completely."

"Great." Then Tim walked off toward the locker room. Justin and Vince gave half-hearted goodbyes as they followed.

That had gone way easier than expected. Justin and Vince's checked-out behavior was weird, but Xavier still felt hopeful. As he walked to his car, he texted the news of his second interview to Violet. He didn't expect to get a response from her for a while because she was busy with work.

As he drove past the high school on his way home, he pictured his students' smiling faces and felt a pang in his chest. They'd be okay without him. He knew that. If anything, taking a new position at Riley should inspire his students. He just wished that thought brought him more comfort.

THAT SATURDAY, XAVIER flew to LA on a cheap last-minute flight. As the plane began its descent into LAX, Xavier smoothed out his jeans and did a quick fit check, noting that his black sweater and J's looked fresh. The last thing he wanted was to be the eyesore in Violet's dazzling life.

She was still working when his flight landed, so she told him to go to her hotel and that she'd meet him later for an early dinner before Angel's show. When he arrived at Violet's hotel, the front desk had already received instructions to give Violet's extra key card to Xavier. The room was spacious, with a queen-size bed and a small white love seat pushed up against the wall. Sunlight spilled through the window, and Xavier placed his suitcase beside the bed and sat down. It was two p.m., but his body was still on East Coast time. He was supposed to have dinner with Violet in two hours, and he'd wanted to spend his spare time exploring because this was his first time visiting LA, but he was tired from the flight. He yawned and eased back on the bed and turned on the television. He closed his eyes for a moment, letting them rest. Soon he was fast asleep.

Later, he woke to the sensation of someone gently brushing their fingers across his brow. He blinked, and his vision cleared, revealing Violet smiling down at him.

"Hi," she said, planting a soft kiss against his lips.

"Hi." His voice was groggy as he rubbed his eyes. The sun had gone down somewhat. "What time is it?"

"Almost seven."

"Seven?" He sat up in a flash. "Shit, we were supposed to get dinner."

"It's okay. I've only been here for about forty minutes. Karina's fitting this afternoon ran a lot longer than expected. I called you a couple times." With a smirk, she added, "Now I know why you didn't answer."

He ran a hand over his face. "I'm sorry. I was knocked out."

"You don't have to apologize. You probably needed the rest. I was about to lie down next to you, actually."

Now that he was more awake, he was able to fully take Violet in. She looked beautiful as usual. Her hair was blown out and layered softly around her face, and she was wearing a loose-fitting white button-up with dark blue jeans. But something in her expression looked strained, and she had bags under her eyes. He reclined on the bed and opened his arms. "Come here."

She went to him readily and curled up against his chest.

He rubbed her back in slow, wide circles. "Did you have a good day?" he asked.

She took a deep breath, then paused. "I wouldn't say good, but it's much better now that you're here."

"You want to talk about it?"

She shook her head. "Not really. It's not important."

He wished he knew what was bothering her, but he wouldn't push. Instead, he massaged the back of her neck and she sighed deeply, snuggling closer to him. He wanted to hold on to this moment longer. The two of them embracing like this in their quiet bubble.

"I wish we didn't have to leave," she mumbled, as if she'd read his mind. "But I promised Angel."

She sat up and he reached for her in protest. She smiled and bent to him again, this time adjusting her position so that her mouth hovered above his. He cradled her face in his hands and kissed her, cherishing the feel of her soft lips. He ran his hands down the slope of her back to settle on her ass. When she pulled away, he groaned.

"I know, I'm sorry," she said. "We have to go to the show, but then it will be you-and-me time."

She wiggled her eyebrows suggestively, and he laughed, still feeling aroused. She went to the mirror and reapplied the dark plum lipstick that he loved.

"Is what I'm wearing okay?" he asked, sitting up, letting her see his black crewneck sweater and his dark blue jeans.

She glanced at his reflection in the mirror and grinned. "You look perfect."

AT THE VENUE, Xavier and Violet didn't have to wait in line but instead were escorted backstage. They followed a security guard, who easily maneuvered through hordes of Angel's fans, mostly teenage girls waiting in line for T-shirts and other swag. After finishing a trek through what felt like an elaborate maze, they stopped at a door backstage. The security guard knocked twice, and a second security guard opened the door, revealing a room full of people, including Angel, Karamel Kitty and two of Violet's other friends, Brian and Melody, whom Xavier remembered meeting in Vegas.

"Big sis!" Angel said, hopping out of his chair. He was tall and slender, almost as tall as Xavier. "You made it!"

"Hey," Violet said, grinning as Angel wrapped her in a hug. She stepped away and gestured toward Xavier. "This is Xavier, my partner."

Xavier's chest warmed at hearing her say those words.

"What's up? Nice to meet you," Xavier said, dapping Angel up.

"Same, bro." Angel smiled at him, brimming with energy. "I'm glad you could make it tonight." He looked at Violet. "Almost makes up for you not bringing your sister."

Violet frowned. "Yeah, I still don't understand what's going on there." To Xavier, she explained, "Angel has a thing for Iris because he talked to her for two seconds at one of my parties."

"*Iris?*" Xavier's eyes widened. If there was ever a more mismatched pair, it would probably be the high-spirited dude in front of him and Violet's reserved older sister. But hey, to each their own. "That's what's up."

Angel brightened even more, if that was possible. "See, that's what I said. You know how you meet somebody and you feel a spark? That's what happened with us."

Violet laughed and shook her head. "I'm sorry to break it to you, but my sister most likely did not feel that same spark." She looped her arm through Xavier's and steered him toward Karamel Kitty. "You remember my friends Karina, Brian and Melody."

She referred to Karamel Kitty so casually, as if she wasn't one of the most famous people in the country.

"Yeah," Xavier said, trying to sound as chill as Violet. "What's up, everybody?"

"Hi, Xavier," Karina, Brian and Melody said in unison, as if they were Charlie's mischievous Angels. Each sported a Cheshire cat smile and cast furtive glances between Xavier and Violet. He had the distinct feeling that he'd been this friend group's topic of conversation more than once.

Soon, drinks were passed around, and Violet and her friends shared a bottle of expensive-looking champagne. Xavier glanced around the room, noticing how sleek and fashionable everyone looked. He looked down at his relaxed outfit and wondered if he appeared out of place. But Violet had told him that he looked fine. *Perfect* was actually the word she'd used. And she held his hand while she spoke to her friends, relaxed and comfortable. He brushed his thumb across her knuckles, and she turned to him and smiled, giving his hand a squeeze.

When they went and found their seats in the front row on the plush red couches, people held up their phone cameras toward Karamel Kitty, and Xavier had the urge to move out of the way, but Violet seemed totally chill. She was used to this, of course, so he tried to relax too. He felt better once the lights went down and Angel's show started. He hadn't listened to much of Angel's music before, so he was pleasantly surprised to learn that Angel sounded great live and was a good dancer. He was kinda like if they combined Usher and D'Angelo in a lab.

Violet sang along, nodding and dancing. But every now and then, her phone vibrated with an alert and the same perturbed frown that she'd sported earlier in their hotel room crept across her face.

"Everything okay?" Xavier asked, leaning down to her.

"Yeah, just my agent." She stuffed her phone back in her pocket.

The third time she pulled out her phone, Karina, who was standing on the other side of her, sighed. "Girl, fuck him. You know those girls are going to fire him soon. He's trash. Don't even trip."

"Who's trash?" Xavier asked.

"It's nothing," Violet said quickly. She turned to Xavier and shook her head. "Really, it's nothing."

His brows knit together. "It doesn't sound like nothing. What's going on?"

She fell silent for a moment and glanced at the stage, like she was contemplating whether or not she wanted to answer him. Finally, she said, "You remember the sister duo I told you about that wants to work with me, Black Velvet?"

"Yes."

"Eddy is their new manager," she said. "I had a meeting with the girls this morning and he showed up. They hired him recently and I didn't know."

Xavier stared at her. "Eddy, your ex-fiancé?"

Violet nodded.

"Is that why you were upset earlier?" he asked.

"A little, yes." She bit her lip, her expression growing troubled.

Xavier squinted, struggling to understand why she would keep that from him. "Why didn't you tell me earlier when I asked you what was wrong?"

"Because I haven't seen you in over a week and I didn't want to waste time talking about Eddy." She lowered her voice and gave him an imploring look. "Can we talk about this when we're at the hotel, please?"

He quietly studied her face. "Yeah."

She wrapped her fingers through his and squeezed his hand again in an attempt to be reassuring. Xavier appreciated her effort, but his mind began to race nonetheless, imagining a million scenarios in which her rich, successful ex got in between them.

22

VIOLET AND XAVIER DIDN'T SPEAK FOR THE REST OF THE show, although their hands remained intertwined. They opted not to go out with Karina and Angel after the show ended, and instead went back to the hotel. They held hands during the car ride as well, but Violet felt the shift between them. She knew how bad it looked that she'd concealed her run-in with Eddy, but it wasn't because she was trying to be sneaky. She simply hadn't wanted her interaction with him to hold any importance. Even though it troubled her that she and Eddy were bound to have more interactions in the future.

Earlier that morning, she and Alex had gone to the Blu Jam Café to have breakfast with Black Velvet. When the sisters, Willow and Harlow, arrived, they were all smiles as they gushed about how much they loved Violet's work with Karamel Kitty and Destiny Diaz. Even though they were two years apart, the sisters looked almost identical with their medium brown complexions and long burgundy goddess braids. They were branching out into acting and wanted a more grown-up look to match their new direction. They'd also just recorded a track for the upcoming Maya Angelou biopic, and the song was already receiving Oscar nom buzz.

These sorts of preliminary meetings with potential clients were standard. It was a way to check vibes so that a stylist and client could determine if they'd work well together. So far, it seemed as though Violet and Black Velvet had an easy rapport, and Violet was already considering which designers she'd contact for their first fitting. Then Willow, the elder of the two, glanced at her phone and said, "Our new manager is joining us to say hello."

"Oh," Violet said. "That's fine."

It wasn't super common for managers to sit in on these meetings, but some clients needed more hand-holding than others. And if their manager was new, Violet could understand why they might want to make sure the meeting was going smoothly.

But those logical explanations sailed right out the window when Eddy strolled through the restaurant door. Violet's first thought was that it was odd that she'd managed to avoid Eddy since their breakup, and yet she finally spotted him on her first trip back to LA. Then the hostess pointed Eddy in the direction of their table, and Eddy's eyes landed on Violet. Then it clicked. Eddy was Black Velvet's new manager.

Rendered speechless, Violet stared at Eddy as he made his way to their table. He looked sleek as always, having donned a crisp button-up and slim-fitting slacks. His brown skin was dewy thanks to his extensive skincare routine, and his bald head shone under the restaurant lights.

"Ladies," he said smoothly. His lips turned up in the corners, producing a smile. "Good morning."

He hugged his clients, and Alex didn't hide her frown as Eddy went for a hug and she stiffly held out her hand for a shake as if they hadn't met before. Then he came around to Violet's chair, and she blinked up at him, still fighting through her fog of shock.

"It's nice to see you, Vi," he said.

His use of her nickname snapped her to attention.

"Hello, Eddy," she said, letting professionalism take over. She forced a smile and politely accepted his hug. She discreetly cleared her throat when he held on for a beat too long.

"How've you been?" he asked, pulling up a chair between Violet and Harlow.

"I'm well." Violet kept her voice even, conscious that this was a work meeting and she'd have to treat it as such. "You?"

He was staring at her closely, like he was refamiliarizing himself with the details of her face. "I've been all right."

"We hope it's okay that Eddy is joining us," Willow said. "He started managing us last week, and we knew that he worked with you in the past with previous clients . . ."

Willow trailed off and glanced at her sister. The awkwardness of her statement permeated the air around their table. Of course Violet's history with Eddy was no secret. They'd been spotted at various events together throughout the course of their relationship. And if you moved in certain circles, you were well aware of how Violet and Eddy's relationship had crashed and burned when he'd cheated with Meela.

But Violet refused to let that past situation get in the way of her work. Regardless of how uncomfortable she felt in the moment.

"Oh, it's totally fine," she said quickly. She even mustered the ability to smile at Eddy to put the girls at ease. She shifted to look at Harlow and Willow. "Let's talk about some of your favorite designers."

The girls began to tell Violet about how much they loved Fe Noel, and Violet nodded along, inserting commentary when necessary, but all the while, she could feel Eddy staring at her, and her discomfort increased. When the meeting ended, and the girls were whisked away by an assistant to their next meeting, Eddy lingered. Violet and Alex gathered their things, sharing private glances with each other and avoiding eye contact with Eddy. Then he reached out and touched Violet's elbow. She recoiled on instinct.

"Can I speak to you for a moment?" he asked.

If this were a normal run-in with an ex, Violet would have said no and walked away. But Eddy was her newest clients' manager, and if she wanted her working relationship with Black Velvet to be smooth, she had to play nice.

"Sure," she said, placing her purse on the table.

Alex's brows furrowed. She eyed Eddy with a frown. To Violet, she said, "I'll be outside. Our car will be here in five minutes."

Violet nodded, and she turned to Eddy, waiting for him to speak.

"It really is nice to see you," he said. "I've tried calling you a few times."

Violet blinked, confused. Then she remembered she'd

blocked him after they broke up. She'd been so angry then. Deservedly so, but now she regretted that she'd ever wasted so much energy on him.

"You know you didn't have to show up to the meeting today," she said. "What are you doing here? Are you the reason that the girls want me to style them?"

"No, I just started working with them myself. That part is true. Did I use today's meeting as an opportunity to see you? Yes, I did. I won't lie."

She sighed, struggling to fight her annoyance at the earnest look on his face.

"I won't beat around the bush. I'm sorry about what happened with Meela," he said, lowering his voice. "It was a mistake. What I did was wrong, *so* wrong, and I ruined everything we had."

"Eddy, please." Violet held up her hand, stopping him. She didn't care to hear one more word on the subject. "We don't have to talk about it. Let the past stay in the past."

He rubbed the back of his neck with a dejected expression.

"Okay," he mumbled. "Yeah, you're right."

He was probably only speaking to Violet this way because Meela had dumped him. Violet couldn't believe that she used to think he was so straightforward and genuine. Now she saw through his facade. It was a Hollywood act to get exactly what he wanted. Like how he'd cornered her at the Halloween party when they'd first met and talked about his desires to settle down and get married. She'd found his direct attitude refreshing. Now it simply seemed manipulative and fake.

She slung her purse over her shoulder and spotted Alex standing outside the restaurant, waving down a black car that was most likely their Uber.

"I have to go," she said, making her way to the door. To her continued annoyance, Eddy followed closely.

"I hear congratulations are in order," he said.

She glanced over her shoulder at him. "What?"

"I read your interview in *Look Magazine*," he said. "You mentioned that you're married."

He glanced at her rings and she shifted her hand out of his line of sight. She and Xavier had agreed to let people think whatever they wanted, whether they were actually married or not. But Eddy was not one of the people she wanted commenting on their relationship.

"Nice feature, by the way," he continued. "The '30 Under 30' is very impressive."

"Thanks."

She was passing the hostess stand now, feet from the door. Eddy was at her heels, still speaking.

"So, you ended up with the high school sweetheart," he said. "The one whose initial you have tattooed."

She heard the note of jealousy in his voice. She'd never spoken in depth to Eddy about her past with Xavier. She'd only shared that Xavier was her high school boyfriend and they'd gotten tattoos together one night. She'd suspected more than once that her tattoo, and her decision to not get it removed, had irritated Eddy. Now she had proof.

She reached the door and turned to face him. "That's not really any of your business."

"It's not," he said easily. "I'm just commenting on what I

read in your interview. I'm assuming he lives in your hometown. And he's a teacher, right? That must be difficult."

His carefully cool tone made her defensive. "What are you trying to get at, exactly?"

He shrugged. "Nothing. I'm genuinely wondering how you make it work. You said yourself that the reason you liked being with me was because I understood your career and the work ethic that went along with it, because I had a similar lifestyle. Even with that understanding, things between us weren't easy."

"Yes, because you cheated on me," she said flatly.

"I did, and I apologize for that because it was wrong," he said. "Spending so much time with Meela when I couldn't see you messed with my head. I take full responsibility for my mistake. I could have been more present, but you weren't present either, Violet. You put work before everything, so I did the same thing. Maybe your new husband is a very patient man and coming second won't matter to him."

She glared at Eddy, trying not to show how his words wounded her. He stared back, in a standoff with her in the doorway.

"Violet, the car is here," Alex called.

Violet stepped outside, keeping her hard gaze on Eddy's face. "The only thing you need to know about my husband is that he's a good man. And he would never embarrass me the way that you did."

Eddy inclined his head, all false manners and grace. "I hope you're both very happy," he said, keeping his same cool tone.

Violet turned on her heel and walked away from him, wordlessly climbing into the car with Alex.

"You okay?" Alex asked as Violet buckled her seat belt.

Violet nodded and took a deep breath. "I'm fine."

They had to rush to Karina's fitting, so Violet's focus immediately went to the next task at hand, but Eddy's words took up residence in the back of her mind for the rest of the day. She emailed Jill to let her know about Eddy being Black Velvet's new manager and asked how that detail could have bypassed them. She wanted to know what they could do to make sure that she and Eddy had the least amount of interaction possible. She'd been so excited to work with the two sisters, and she might even have an opportunity to dress them for next year's Academy Awards, her dream event. But now everything was tinged with Eddy's involvement. Violet fumed, realizing that he'd thrown a monkey wrench into her career *again*.

By the time her workday ended and she walked into her hotel room, she was so relieved to see Xavier sleeping peacefully, she almost wanted to cry. He was her safe harbor, so far removed from her professional life. She hadn't wanted to taint their reunion by mentioning Eddy.

Xavier was silent as they reentered her hotel room. In easy strides, he crossed the floor and sat on the love seat by the window. His posture was tense as he leaned forward, placing his elbows on his knees, and looked at her.

"Can you tell me what happened now?" he asked.

She went and sat beside him. He turned to face her, and with a deep breath, she told him the entire story of her exchange with Eddy. When she finished speaking, Xavier's eyebrows were drawn together.

"When I asked what was bothering you earlier, why didn't you say anything then?" he asked.

"I wanted to forget that it even happened. It was the last thing I wanted to talk about with you after we hadn't seen each other in days."

"I understand that," he said. "But I want you to feel like you can talk to me whenever something is upsetting you."

"I *do* feel that way. I think I was trying to protect our time together, but it backfired. I'm sorry."

Xavier shook his head. His lips formed into a deep-set frown. "You don't need to apologize. I'm not mad at you. I'm pissed at him. He was disrespectful to you, he was bothering you while you were trying to work, and he high-key insinuated that our relationship won't last. If I wasn't in the picture, he'd probably try to win you back."

"That will *never* happen," Violet said, grossly appalled by the thought. "I can't stress that enough. Even if I wasn't with you, I would not consider dating Eddy again."

Xavier glanced out the window. His expression was unreadable. "I can't give you the things he can," he said quietly. "The gifts and trips. At least, I can't do that right now. With the new job, my money situation would be better, though."

"Xavier." She gently touched his cheek, causing him to look at her face. "I already told you. I don't care about those things. Eddy might have made some very lavish gestures in the past, but he also lied to me. What I want is to be with someone who is trustworthy and genuinely cares about me.

That's you." She lowered her hand from his face and rested it on his thigh. "Do you know what I wanted to do this weekend? Lie in bed with you. That's it. And, like, maybe watch television and eat salt-and-vinegar chips."

He smirked. When he looped his fingers through hers once again, the tension finally lifted from her shoulders.

"I think that we should try our best to be honest with each other moving forward," he said. "If something is bothering one of us, or if something happens that we feel the other person should know, we should just tell each other. I keep thinking about how I wasn't real with you about my feelings after I left Kentucky, and I broke up with you like an asshole, and then we lost nine years. I don't want that to happen again."

"Neither do I. No secrets." She smiled a little. "I think we'll both be relieved after we talk to our parents at this dinner. Your mom will be there, right?"

"Yeah, I was hoping she'd come back after we came clean, but your mom messaged her on Facebook and invited her. She's flying back the day before the dinner."

"Well, look at it this way. After it's over, we'll be free to live our lives as an unmarried couple."

He laughed, and she moved closer, seeking his embrace. He enfolded her in his arms, and she rested her head against his chest, marveling at how they'd both matured. In high school, they used to blow up at each other for the smallest infractions. Now they'd talked through an issue and came out on the other side unscathed.

But something that Eddy had said still bothered Violet. She sat up and looked Xavier in the eye.

"I'm going to try my best to be present," she said. "I promise."

Xavier rested his hands on either side of her face. "I'll do the same."

She gazed at him, and her chest felt warm and fizzy, bubbling over with emotion.

"I love you," she said. It was the first time in this iteration of Violet and Xavier 2.0 that she'd been the one to initiate those words.

His eyes softened. "I love you too."

He pulled her toward him and kissed her deeply. Electricity shot through her veins, and her core began to smolder as his kisses grew slower and heavier. She sighed with pleasure as her hands sought out his skin. She lifted his sweater and spread her fingers along his lower abdomen. His grasp on her tightened, and she moaned when his hands drifted down to cup her ass. In one fluid motion, he was up on his feet, wrapping Violet's legs around his waist and carrying her across the room. She grinned, insanely aroused by his strength as he swiftly settled her down on the bed. He kissed her again, and she reached for his belt buckle, unclasping it.

"I've thought about this all week," he said thickly, pulling down his pants and boxers, then removing his sweater.

"Me too." Her heart raced as she stared at his gorgeously naked body. She unzipped her jeans and shimmied them down her hips, along with her underwear. Xavier helped pull them off and tossed them aside, and she eased out of her white Alexander McQueen mock-neck top, carefully because it was vintage. All that was left was her bra, and when she reached around and unhooked it from the back and tossed it aside too, Xavier sucked in a breath. She loved that he reacted that way, as if he hadn't seen her breasts many times before.

She reached for him, and he lowered himself on top of her. His warm skin heated her body, and she felt the pounding of his heartbeat as they lay chest to chest. Their eyes locked and their lips found each other. They kissed languorously, selfishly, like they had all the time in the world. Xavier hooked his hands under her knees and hitched her legs up to his waist as she kissed his bottom lip, his jaw, then his neck. He reached in between her legs and she moaned as he continued to touch her until she felt like she might shatter into a million stimulated pieces. Smoothly, he reached for his jeans and retrieved a condom from his wallet. She helped him roll it on, loving the feel of him in her hands. Then with exquisite slowness, he sank into her. They found a rhythm led by his deep, unhurried strokes.

"I love you," he whispered roughly, eyes boring into hers.

She was so happy, and he felt so good, she began to tear up. "I love you too." She kissed him again, swirling her tongue around his. His strokes grew harder and faster, and soon they unraveled together, left panting in each other's arms.

Afterward, they climbed under the covers and Xavier spooned her from behind and quickly fell asleep. Violet, however, remained wide awake. She was too giddy to close her eyes, overwhelmed with her happiness and her sudden deep satisfaction with the state of her life. Being with Xavier was so easy.

Almost too easy.

The fact that they'd rediscovered each other felt too good to be true after she'd resigned herself to never falling in love again and focusing on her career instead. What if she was incapable of nurturing both her love life and her professional life? She was suddenly overcome with the fear that she might lose him. That after everything they'd been through, she'd inevitably find a way to screw things up.

She snuggled deeper under the covers and turned over to face Xavier, letting his embrace keep her fears at bay.

23

ANXIETY SWEPT OVER XAVIER AS HIS EYES DARTED FROM the scoreboard to his players on the court. After a season of undefeated domination, they'd driven an hour and a half down to southern New Jersey, and they were going to lose to Saulsboro High School by three points in the last game of the semifinals with fifteen seconds left on the clock.

"Pass the ball, Dante!" Xavier called. "Remember the play!"

Dante, who was six feet one, looked fun-size compared to the hulking boy who guarded him. If Xavier didn't have legitimate proof that they were teenagers, he would have suspected that his students were playing against grown-ass men.

"Come on, Dante," he shouted. "You got this!"

Six seconds left on the clock.

What Dante lacked in bulk, he made up for in speed. He crossed up the Saulsboro boy and drove the ball down the center of the court, passing it to Elijah Dawson, who did a pump fake and then sent the ball back to Dante. With three seconds left, Dante went for a three-pointer. Xavier, and everyone in the gymnasium, held their breath as the basketball soared through the air.

The ball bounced off the rim.

The buzzer sounded.

They'd lost: 62–59.

Xavier blinked, momentarily stunned. Then he felt Mr. Rodney clap him on the shoulder. He slowly snapped back into action and went to shake hands with the Saulsboro coaches, offering them his congratulations. He watched his students' sullen faces as they dutifully shook hands with the winning team.

This was his fault. His head wasn't in the game the way it should have been.

Ever since his trip to LA, Xavier couldn't stop thinking about the things Violet's ex-fiancé had said to her. The insinuation that their relationship would become strained because their careers pulled them in different directions. At first, Xavier had been annoyed, and he'd written it off as a bunch of bullshit. But the more he thought about it, the more he begrudgingly realized there was some truth to what Eddy had said. Xavier and Violet didn't have as much time for each other as he'd like, given their opposing schedules, and he was worried about what it meant for their future.

That nagging feeling was what motivated him days ago during his second interview with Tim Vogel and the athletic director at Riley. Xavier had given it everything he'd had. He expected to wait weeks for their decision. But within two days, he received a call with a job offer. He'd accepted the position and higher salary without needing to think it over. He'd finish out the school year at Willow Ridge and start at Riley during their summer-intensive program.

It was going to be a great move for his career, yes. But it also meant that his schedule would become more flexible. During the off season, he'd be able to take more last-minute trips to see Violet wherever she was working, and if he moved closer to campus, he'd only be thirty minutes away from the city, compared to the hour drive or train ride from Willow Ridge. Maybe in a year or so, if Violet was willing, they could find an apartment together. In every way he could see, taking the job at Riley was the better decision for his personal and professional life.

He just wished he didn't feel a tightening in his stomach every time he thought about walking away from Willow Ridge and leaving his students behind. Mr. Rodney already knew about Xavier's decision to accept the job at Riley, but Xavier had been waiting to tell the team until after their season finished, which he'd hoped would have ended with a championship win. But now, not only had they lost, he'd have to share the news that he was leaving them as well.

A morose silence filled the locker room as they packed up their things. Before they filed out of the room, Mr. Rodney called them to attention.

"This has been a spectacular season," he said. "You put up an amazing fight tonight. We didn't make it to the finals, but that doesn't mean that we don't have many reasons to celebrate all you've accomplished."

The boys nodded. But their eyes were on Xavier. They were waiting for him to speak as well. Xavier stuffed his hands in his pockets. What could he say? He never wanted his students to feel this deep-rooted disappointment. He felt like he'd failed them. But that wasn't what they wanted to hear right now. They needed encouragement.

"When I was your age," he said, "I had a hard time learning from my perceived failures. I would have taken a loss like tonight and stressed about it for weeks, only remembering the bad. I wouldn't have been able to see the good or the growth. And that's what I want y'all to focus on. I want you to remember and take pride in the way this team came together and played beautifully for months on end. Your talent and drive, and your *bond*, have blown me away. I might be your coach, but you've taught me just as much as I've taught you. You inspire me, honestly."

Some of the boys were tearing up and looking away to wipe their eyes. Their attempts at emotional discretion made Xavier smile.

"I know you're disappointed that we didn't make it to the finals," he continued. "I am too. But we still have this bond, and that's something we won't ever lose. This is the furthest Willow Ridge has gotten in years. *Years.* You've made history. That's something to be proud of right there. Regardless of whether or not we have a trophy, you're winners in my eyes. I couldn't be prouder."

Xavier cleared his throat and looked around the room at his team. He opened his arms, gesturing for one last huddle, which turned into more of a group hug. There were sniffles and chuckles, sighs of disappointment and acceptance.

"It's all good, Mr. Wright," Dante said, breaking the silence. "We got it next year."

"Yeah, next year for sure," Elijah Dawson said, and the other boys chimed in to say the same. Elijah looked hopefully at Xavier. "Right?"

Shit. Xavier glanced at Mr. Rodney, who smiled softly and nodded. Xavier took a deep breath.

"That's something I want to talk to you about," he said.

The boys paused, eyeing Xavier with keen interest.

"I've accepted a position as an assistant coach at Riley University," he said slowly. One by one, he watched pure dejection overcome his students. "I won't be back next year."

You could hear a pin drop.

"I'm really, *really* sorry to leave you," Xavier said. His heart was breaking as he spoke. "I wish there was a way that I could stay."

"Then stay," Dante said, speaking up and wiping his eyes. "We need you here, Mr. Wright. More than the clowns at Riley. They a bunch of losers!"

"We're losers too," Elijah mumbled, hanging his head.

"You're *not* losers," Xavier said. "Don't talk about yourselves like that. You lost one game. You had a nearly perfect season."

"Yeah, because of you," Dante said. Some of the other boys mumbled in agreement.

They didn't even look angry, and that was what threw Xavier. He expected them to be pissed and frustrated. But instead, they looked heart-wrenchingly sad. Xavier didn't know what to say, how to make this better.

"I'll still be here for you," he said. "I just won't be your teacher and coach."

The boys were quiet, looking at Xavier with downcast expressions. Watching them, Xavier felt like crying himself.

"We're thankful for everything you've done, Xavier," Mr. Rodney said. "Aren't we, boys?"

The team nodded and murmured their thanks. Several silent moments passed. Then Dante cleared his throat.

"I guess this means we'll all have to hope we get accepted at Riley so that you can coach us again," he said. He flashed a soft smile, and the tension in the room began to ease.

Xavier pulled Dante close in a one-armed hug, and soon the whole team surrounded Xavier in another huddle, thanking him and telling him how much he was appreciated.

By the time Xavier got back home, he was exhausted, emotionally and physically. He couldn't stop seeing his students' disappointed faces. It was almost midnight, and he knew that Violet was in the city, working with Karina during her several press tour appearances. The *Kat House* premiere was that Sunday, and Xavier was going as Violet's date. Because she was so busy, he didn't really expect to see or speak to her much until then. But he was feeling so low, and he needed to talk to her and hear the sound of her voice.

He called, and she answered right before it went to voice mail.

"Hey, babe," she said. Her voice sounded strained.

"Hey, everything okay?"

"Yeah, it's fine." She breathed out a heavy sigh. "One of the straps broke on the shoes that Karina is supposed to wear on *Jimmy Fallon* tomorrow, and it's been hell trying to find a replacement that doesn't totally kill the look. And Angel's clothes for his performance at a festival in LA got lost at the airport, so I was on the phone with the airline for hours trying to figure out what happened. I've been awake since five and we're still doing inventory. I almost missed physical therapy this afternoon. It's just been a lot. But nothing unusual, honestly. How are you?" Then she perked up. "Wait, oh my goodness, how was the big game?"

"We lost," Xavier said. Now it was his time to sigh.

"Oh no, I'm so sorry."

"Yeah, it sucks." He sat down on his bed and glanced over at the empty side that Violet used to occupy. "I told the team that I was taking the job at Riley. They were pretty upset."

"I know that must have been hard," she said softly.

"It was. I want to do something for them. Maybe have a pizza party, or—"

He paused when he heard someone speaking to Violet in the background.

"Xavier, I'm so sorry, I have to go," she said. "I finally have someone from Valentino on the phone to discuss shipping out another dress for Karina's press tour. Can I call you in a little while? Or maybe in the morning? It will be early, like, before five a.m., because of the early call time for Karina's *Good Morning America* appearance."

"I, uh . . . you know what, it's fine," he said, shoving aside his disappointment. "Don't worry about it. I'll see you on Sunday. We can talk more then."

"Are you sure?"

"Yeah," he said, hoping he sounded believable.

"Okay, I love you."

"I love you too," he said. But she'd hung up before he finished his sentence.

He lay back on his bed and closed his eyes. He couldn't be mad at Violet. She was hustling. Her dedication to her job was one of the many things he admired about her. He just wished they had more time for each other.

This was why taking the job at Riley made more sense.

His hope was that there'd be less distance between them.

24

THE DAY OF THE *KAT HOUSE* PREMIERE, VIOLET WAS RUN-
ning on fumes, and she was so behind schedule, it was laugh-
able. While helping Karina get dressed, the zipper pull of
Karina's vintage leopard-print Alexander McQueen gown
had popped clean off, and of course Violet had run out of
replacements in her stylist suitcase. She'd sent Alex to the
nearest arts and crafts store to find a replacement that didn't
look too gaudy. Once Alex returned and the zipper fire issue was extinguished, Violet, Melody and Brian added the
finishing touches to Karina's look. Just as Violet was about
to leave to get dressed herself, Karina looked in the mirror
and was overcome with pre-premiere jitters. Suddenly, she
hated her outfit. Everything from her hair to her shoes was
wrong.

Violet and the team were accustomed to Karina's last-
minute bursts of anxiety before a big event, so they patiently reassured her that she looked amazing, which took
a good thirty minutes to accomplish. Then, finally, with
less than an hour before the premiere, Violet hopped in a

cab downtown to her apartment. She should have booked a room at Karina's hotel and gotten dressed there, but she'd wanted to get dressed at her apartment with Xavier. He was her date tonight, even though he had to be back in Jersey tomorrow for work. And he was waiting for her now.

Lately, she felt like he was in a constant state of waiting. Waiting for her to call him back or answer his text. To show him the same attentiveness that he provided her. Sometimes she was so deep in the zone, texting Xavier back or returning his call floated in the back of her mind like a faded afterthought. And she felt so guilty when she realized hours had gone by before she remembered to respond to him. She was trying her best to be present, but it wasn't always easy. Relationships were such fragile things. She knew that better than anyone. And she was worried she was failing at being a good girlfriend.

Maybe she was letting Eddy's words haunt her. He'd made it seem as though she'd pushed him away right into Meela's arms. Eddy was an asshole, and cheaters should never blame their partners for their poor behavior. But Violet hadn't been the most present in their relationship. Her career had been her true love.

It was different with Xavier, of course. She'd loved him before she'd even stepped foot on the set of a photo shoot or been awed by a magazine's fashion closet. She didn't want to lose him. But by keeping him, was she being unfair, knowing that her lifestyle might not be conducive to what he wanted or needed? She couldn't shake the worry. The dinner at her parents' house was in two days. She had one more quick work trip to Miami tomorrow morning, and then the

following day, they'd go to the dinner and finally come clean
to their families about their little white lie. Some of the
tension would definitely lift, and they could move forward.
At least, that's what she told herself.

When she finally arrived at her apartment, Xavier was
already dressed in a fine black tux that he'd rented for the
occasion.

"Hi," she said, rushing over to give him a quick kiss.

"Hi." His lips lingered against hers for a fraction of a
second, then he pulled away. "You should get dressed."

His small smirk encouraged her to relax somewhat. She
jogged to her room and threw off the athleisure she'd worn
all day in exchange for a strapless black Tom Ford jumpsuit.
She was trying to decide between a pair of black pointed-
toe heels and a gold pair that matched her hoop earrings—
both only three inches high and preapproved by her physical
therapist. She put one shoe on each foot and walked into
the living room to ask which option Xavier liked better, but
she froze when she found him sitting on the couch with his
head in his hands.

"What's wrong?" she asked. Anxiety sprouted in her
stomach.

He startled and looked up at her. He adjusted his posture and shook his head. "Nothing. You look beautiful," he
said. "You might get cold, though. Will you bring a jacket?"

"Thank you," she said slowly. "And I have a blazer."

She eyed him, unwilling to pretend that she didn't just
catch him in such a contemplative mood. She walked closer
until she was standing right in front of him. Her phone vibrated with a call from Alex, but she silenced it.

"Tell me what's wrong," she said.

He paused for a moment. Then sighed. "It's nothing. I'm just thinking about work and my students. The changes I'll be making."

"They'll be okay," she said softly, observing his stressed expression. "But you know, you don't have to leave Willow Ridge if you don't want to. Taking the job at Riley isn't a requirement."

He gave her a funny look. "Of course I do. If I don't, I'll continue to feel stuck."

"What are you talking about? You're not stuck."

"Yes, I am. I think about all the potential I had and the things I could have done with my life, but instead I came back to Willow Ridge and stayed."

"You've done plenty with your life," she said. "And you still have potential. Everyone loves you, Xavier. Who do you have to prove anything to?"

He didn't respond, just shook his head and looked away.

"I didn't know that you had been stressing so much about it," she said.

"Well, we haven't had much time to talk lately."

Violet stilled. Her phone vibrated again. Another call from Alex that she let go to voice mail.

"I know that I've been busy, but I'm not a mind reader either," she said. "You could have brought it up."

"I would have," he said. "But our phone calls are pretty short or they don't happen at all. It wasn't something I wanted to talk about over text."

She wrung her hands together, growing more anxious. "It's a hectic time for me right now."

"No, wait. I'm not blaming you," he said. "I'm only saying that's why you might feel out of the loop with what's going on with me."

Violet didn't say anything. She didn't know what she *could* say. Xavier broke the silence first.

"I miss you," he said quietly. "When we're together, it's like I have you and then you're gone."

"It won't always be like this," she said, even though she knew this was usually the norm. But one day, in the semi-distant future, when she was established enough to slow down, she'd feel more comfortable taking time off.

"You have a lot going on." Xavier stood, taking her hands in his. "It's your job. You *should* be grinding. I understand that. I've just been thinking about ways to make things easier on us, and working at Riley will help. I wanted to talk to you about it."

She studied his serious expression. "What do you mean?"

Her phone vibrated again before he could answer. Alex calling once more.

"We're running late," he said. "Let's talk about this after the premiere and everything, okay?"

She didn't want to leave in the middle of this conversation, but they had to go.

"Yeah, okay," she said. Then she texted Alex to say that she was on her way, and she decided on the gold pumps.

During the entire ride to the premiere at the AMC theater in Lincoln Square, and as she trailed a few paces behind Karina on the red carpet, and while sitting in the auditorium during the showing of the visual album, Violet tried to stay in the moment, but in the back of her mind, she couldn't stop wondering exactly what Xavier had meant when he said that taking the job at Riley would be easier on their relationship. She thought he wanted to work at Riley because of his desire to move his career in a different direction. She didn't know that she had anything to do with his decision.

The knowledge weighed heavily on her. Especially since she was unsure if she was capable of meeting him halfway.

When the hour-and-a-half-long visual ended, the crowd erupted into a standing ovation. Karina beckoned Violet and the rest of the team to the front of the auditorium so that they could take a bow. Violet caught eyes with Xavier and he beamed at her, looking so overwhelmingly proud and supportive. For a moment, Violet forgot the tension between them. Her heart warmed as she smiled back.

At the after-party, Violet spent a long while being interviewed by the journalists in attendance. Everyone complimented her on her work as head stylist, and she was running on an adrenaline high, smiling widely, with bright eyes. This was a major moment, the kind she'd been waiting for. And it meant so much to her that Xavier could share in the moment with her too. He dutifully stood off to the side, watching as she spoke with the press, still looking as proud as he had in the auditorium.

After her interviews ended, Violet and Xavier hung out by the open bar while Karina and the rest of their crew were out on the dance floor. Violet was too tired to dance. Before taking a sip of her whiskey sour, she yawned three times in a row.

"You okay?" Xavier asked.

"Yeah." She yawned again. Xavier smirked, and she shook

her head. "No, really. I should stay until the end." She paused, noticing that Xavier looked tired too. "Do you want to leave?"

"I'm cool to stay if you are."

"You really don't have to," she said, feeling guilty, thinking about how he'd have to drive back to Jersey in the morning. "I'll meet you at home later."

"No, this is your night, and I want to be here with you. I'll stay. It's fine. Don't worry about me."

She bit her lip and nodded, taking another sip of her drink. But then she placed it on the bar top, figuring that it would be better if she were sober later tonight when she and Xavier had a chance to continue their conversation from earlier.

She stood on tiptoe and leaned toward his ear, shouting over the music, "I'm gonna head to the bathroom."

He nodded, and she maneuvered her way through the crowd and sighed once she reached the bathroom alcove and saw the clusters of people taking photographs in front of the mirror that spanned the entire wall. As she squeezed by the influencers and partygoers, she felt someone touch her hand and say her name before she reached the bathroom door. She turned and immediately grimaced.

Eddy.

"Great party, right?" he said, smiling at her.

Violet frowned and tugged her hand from his grasp. "What are you doing here?"

"I was invited?" he said, like it was a silly question. Like it was a given that he'd be here. "Last minute. I was in the city and pulled a few strings. The work you did on that visual album was phenomenal."

She narrowed her eyes at him, unable to even conjure the desire to say thank you.

"Bye," she said, beginning to walk away, but Eddy moved to block her.

"Don't do me like that. Why can't we be cordial? We're sharing a client now, remember?"

"I'm *trying* to be cordial. You're being annoying."

"I really don't want any problems with you." He smirked and nodded at her hand. "I'm glad I can finally get a good look at your ring. It's . . . subtle."

Violet glanced down at her fake wedding rings. The fake diamond was cloudy, and the gold looked garish in this light.

"Leave me alone." She kept her voice to a whisper, unwilling to cause a scene.

Eddy's smile dropped, and he lost all pretense of pleasantry. "You can't be serious with this guy," he said. "With that diamond? What are you doing? Are you just trying to make me jealous?"

She stared at him, aghast. "As if I would go out of my way to do anything for your benefit. *Goodbye*, Eddy."

He held on to her elbow. "Wait, Violet."

She yanked her arm away, glaring at him.

"What's up?" A deep voice cut in.

Violet turned around and Xavier was standing right behind her.

XAVIER STARED DOWN Violet's ex-fiancé. He was shorter than he looked in Violet's since-deleted Instagram photos. His bald head shone under the flashing club lights, and his expensive-looking burgundy suit was cut perfectly to his slender frame. His whole demeanor reeked of insincerity. It was in the way his lips were screwed up into the world's fakest smile as he blinked at Xavier in surprise.

"You must be Violet's husband," he said, sticking out his hand. "Eddy Coltrane."

Xavier had only caught the tail end of Violet and Eddy's conversation, but he'd heard him ask Violet if she was serious about Xavier and if she'd only married him to make Eddy jealous. What a self-centered piece of shit.

Xavier ignored Eddy's outstretched hand. "Is there a problem here?"

"Of course not." Eddy smoothly stuffed his hand in his pocket. He looked to Violet. "Is there?"

Violet narrowed her eyes at Eddy and took Xavier's hand. "Let's just go."

But Xavier was unwilling to let him off that easy. "You think it's cool to harass her like this while she's working?"

Eddy had the nerve to look affronted. "I wasn't *harassing* her." Then, as if Xavier was the biggest idiot in the room, he added, "It's an after-party. She isn't required to work this event."

Xavier glared at him. He wasn't in the mood for this shit. He'd been feeling like hell all week about leaving his job at the high school and how distant he felt from Violet. He didn't know how she would respond to his idea to move closer to the campus and New York, and the possibility of them moving in together in the future. And he also had to deal with the fact that she wasn't so keen on the idea of him working with Tim. He just wished they could have at least twenty minutes alone together to talk more. She wanted to stay until the party ended, which he understood. He was trying to keep his energy up to last through the night. Otherwise, he feared he'd fall asleep on the car ride home and their conversation would have to be postponed until they saw each other again. But now his energy was through the roof, dealing with her trash ex-fiancé.

"Leave Violet alone, like she told you," Xavier said, his voice deathly quiet. "I mean that shit. Don't speak to her. Don't even fucking look at her."

Eddy's eyes hardened, but his mouth curved into a smirk. "That will be hard since we'll have to work together."

"Xavier, let's go," Violet repeated, staring up at him imploringly. She glanced around, and that was when Xavier noticed that others in the bathroom alcove were watching them. Violet squeezed his hand, and Xavier decided to let this shit with Eddy drop. *She* was the most important thing right now. He wouldn't waste their limited time together arguing with her ex, and he didn't want to further upset her. He took a deep breath, then kissed her temple.

"Okay," he said. "Come on."

She sighed in relief, and he began to lead her away. When he glanced back at Eddy, he saw a flare of bitter jealousy peek through his cool demeanor. Eddy had fumbled the bag when it came to Violet, and that was his loss. He would simply have to get over it. Xavier didn't have anything else to say to him.

"Hit me up once he goes back to the schoolroom, Vi," Eddy called out. "I'll be here."

Xavier turned in a flash, advancing on Eddy. "Fuck you just say?" he hissed.

"Security!" Eddy shouted before Xavier had even reached him. "Somebody, please help!"

"Xavier!" Violet said, pulling on him.

It was Violet's voice that stopped him. He let her pull him away back to the heart of the club and through the throbbing crowd. He was swimming through his haze of anger. Distantly, he saw Violet wave to catch Alex's attention and tell her that they were leaving. He and Violet reached the club exit and walked outside onto the street. She hailed a cab and they hopped inside.

"Sixteenth and Fifth," Violet said to the cab driver. Frazzled, she ran her hands through her hair and looked at Xavier. The concern on her face was what finally caused his anger to recede, although adrenaline still pumped wildly through his veins as the weight of his actions came crashing down on him.

"Fuck, I'm sorry, Violet," he said. "I shouldn't have reacted like that. Are you okay?"

"I'm fine. You didn't even touch him." She shook her head, releasing a frustrated breath. "There's no way I can work with Black Velvet as long as he's managing them. I won't be able to stand it. I'm emailing Jill in the morning." She moved closer to him. "Are *you* okay?"

He wasn't. He'd embarrassed himself at her work event. He should have returned Eddy's coolness with a few snide remarks of his own. But he'd been pushed to the limit, seeing Eddy bothering Violet.

Too many thoughts were running through his mind. There was so much he'd been waiting to say to Violet all night, all week. Without really thinking, he blurted the thought that had consumed him for days.

"I think we should move in together."

VIOLET GAWKED AT Xavier, completely thrown.

She'd asked Xavier if he was okay, and his response was that they should move in together. Where was the logic in his line of thinking?

"What?" she mumbled. "Move in together? Where is this coming from?"

"Not right now, I mean. In the future," he said. "I've been thinking about it a lot, and aside from the career advancement opportunity with Riley, if I move closer to campus, I'll be closer to you. And maybe down the line, we can move in together. Somewhere that's in between the city and the campus. Depending on where we moved, there are trains that can get you to New York in like twenty minutes."

So *this* was what he'd wanted to discuss earlier.

Xavier's gaze was searching, waiting for her approval of his plan.

Violet shook her head as her heart hammered in her chest. "I can't let you do that. You can't make a career decision based on me."

"It's not based on you," he said. "I'm pointing out that it's an added plus. We'd see each other more." The crinkle between his eyebrows appeared. "I miss those small moments. Coming home and knowing I'll get to see you. Having dinner together. Sleeping beside you every night. Don't you miss it?"

"Of course I do," she said. "But it wasn't our reality. We were living in a bubble. I wasn't working. I couldn't do anything or go anywhere. That's not what my actual life is like."

"I know, and that's why I think living closer would make things easier. We might not have those moments all the time, but it would be more than what we have now."

"Yes, at night once I finally get home from my office, and when I'm not traveling," she said. "Either way, more often than not, we'll be like two ships passing in the night."

The cab pulled up in front of her building. Xavier's face was set in a distressed frown as he paid the cab driver and they walked into her building toward the elevator.

"It worries me that we aren't on the same page about this," she said, breaking the silence as the elevator doors closed and they were taken up to her floor.

"You're right," he said. "We're not on the same page. We just have to talk it through to find some compromise."

The elevator reached her floor, and their conversation was cut short when a woman and her dog stepped onto the elevator as they exited. As they walked to her door, Violet's brain went into overdrive. Xavier wanted things from her that she was unsure she could provide. She was already messing things up now. Imagine how much worse they would get if she became his live-in girlfriend. It would only give him more opportunity to be disappointed in her. And eventually, he would realize that she could never give him what he really needed in a partner, at least not right now. She saw the impending heartbreak that could await her, and she suddenly felt suffocated with fear. Fear of those long, dark days she'd experienced when they'd broken up before. She couldn't relive that. She *couldn't*.

They entered her apartment and Xavier went to stand by her kitchen island and turned toward her. He was ready to continue their discussion. He was the type to roll up his sleeves and keep talking until they'd reached an understanding. It was what she loved about him.

But she was too afraid of what understanding they'd reach.

It was fear that drove her to say what she said next: "Can we talk more in the morning? I'm so tired."

Xavier stared at her. "You have an early flight to Miami."

"I know, before that. I'll get breakfast and bring it back and we can sit down and talk."

He continued to stare at her, quietly observing her stiff posture. After a long beat, he sighed. "Yeah, okay. I know you're tired. We should both sleep."

She let out an inward sigh of relief. He went to her bedroom to undress and she peeled off her jumpsuit and blazer and draped them on her couch. She shut herself in her bathroom and ran the shower, closing her eyes and leaning against the door. She pictured the sycamore tree outside her childhood bedroom window. Her heart ached as she remembered how Xavier's face used to brighten when she opened her window and let him climb through. They'd felt so unstoppable then. So carefree and devoted.

If only everything could feel as simple as two teenagers falling in love.

In the morning before Xavier woke, Violet didn't buy bagels and orange juice from the bodega across the street. Instead, she quickly and quietly packed her bags and left for JFK. By the time she reached the airport, Xavier was still sleeping.

She was the worst. She knew that. But she was driven by fear. If she could postpone a conversation that could lead to Xavier realizing that she wasn't the one for him, she would put it off for as long as she could.

The selfish and unfair yet simple truth was that she loved him too much to let him go.

25

DURING FOURTH PERIOD, WHILE XAVIER'S STUDENTS DID silent reading, he stared out the window, spinning his ring around his finger, replaying last night's events over and over. He studied his conversation with Violet from every angle, trying to determine how he could have prevented that fearful look in her eyes and the way she'd left her apartment that morning without saying goodbye. When he woke up, he saw a text from her flashing on his screen.

I'm sorry, but I had to go to the airport early.

She was already in the air by the time he got into his car to drive back to Willow Ridge.

He'd screwed up the whole conversation. He shouldn't have brought up the prospect of moving in together so soon. It had obviously spooked her. He felt like someone had placed his heart in the washing machine on high speed and then haphazardly tossed it back to him, soggy and misshapen.

And the timing couldn't be worse. They had to have dinner with their parents tomorrow and admit that they weren't actually married.

"Mr. Wright?"

Xavier was startled out of his despondent spiral and glanced over at Cherise. "Yes?"

"Brandon's hand has been raised for, like, five minutes. He's gonna pee himself."

Xavier looked at Brandon Givens, seated in the back of the room. He was biting his lip with his hand held high in the hair.

"Shoot, go ahead, Brandon," Xavier said quickly. "I'm sorry."

Brandon scrambled to his feet and rushed from the room. Some of the class snickered and Xavier quieted them down.

"Mr. Wright," Cherise said, "don't take this the wrong way, okay? But you look like you need a spa day *bad*."

The rest of the class nodded in agreement.

"A spa day," Xavier repeated, giving himself a once-over.

"Yeah, your energy is giving stressed-out," Jerrica said. She dug around in her bag. "Matter of fact, I have some crystals for you."

"Is it because you'll miss us next year?" Dante asked.

His students looked at him with longing, hopeful expressions.

"Of course I'm going to miss you," he said, so full of heartfelt honesty, it pained him. "*Of course* I will."

"You don't have to be sad about leaving, Mr. Wright," Cherise said. "We'll still be here. You can always visit."

"And you can bring Ms. Greene too," Jerrica added. "She's our new fave."

Xavier smiled, pretending that their words didn't shake him. Who knew where he and Violet would be next year?

Soon the lunch bell rang, and his students scattered for the cafeteria. Xavier walked to the teachers' lounge to grab his lunch from the fridge. He'd planned to eat in his car. He didn't know if he could handle the constant chatter of his colleagues today. When he'd been offered the job at Riley, he'd expected them to be happy that he was moving on, in a new direction, like he'd always wanted. But instead, they'd offered their congratulations while also expressing their genuine sadness at losing him. Their reaction had thrown Xavier. He'd assumed that they'd thought that his time at Willow Ridge would be temporary.

He reached the teachers' lounge and took a deep inhale before turning the doorknob. Inside the room, he found his colleagues crowded around the table as Mrs. Franklin and Mr. Rodney opened several packages, revealing brand-new green-and-yellow jerseys for the basketball teams. Another box contained new uniforms for field hockey and softball. The fruits of their fundraiser labor.

Mrs. Franklin glanced up and saw Xavier standing in the doorway. She smiled at him. "Come and see, Xavier," she said.

Everyone else looked up and beckoned him over. Xavier went to stand beside Mr. Rodney, who held up one of the basketball jerseys for Xavier to see. Xavier ran his fingers over the shiny material, realizing that the jerseys looked great. Like something his students would be proud to wear.

"No more decade-old uniforms," Mr. Rodney said, patting Xavier on the shoulder. "Thanks to you."

"Me?" Xavier repeated. "We all pitched in."

"No," Mrs. Franklin said. "The fundraiser was your idea. Take the credit."

"You're leaving your students with a gift," Mr. Rodney said. "In more ways than one."

"We wish you were staying," Mrs. Franklin added sullenly, and Mr. Rodney nudged her with a pointed look. "*But* we are very proud of you nonetheless."

His other colleagues said the same. Xavier always knew that he would miss his students once he left, but for the first time he realized he would miss his colleagues too.

"Thank you," he said softly.

He decided to stay and eat his lunch in the teachers' lounge. Xavier used to find it frustrating that people in Willow Ridge were so involved in everyone else's business, and he'd itched to escape. But now he realized that being around people who cared about your well-being and the well-being of your mother and everyone else you knew was quite special. These were people who would support you even though you were planning to leave. He wouldn't find this community anywhere else, and he'd taken it for granted.

Somehow, he strongly doubted he'd feel the same at Riley with Tim Vogel. He was having dinner with Tim and the other coaches later that night. A celebratory welcome to the team. But Xavier had a feeling that the meal wouldn't feel celebratory, just like his previous dinner with Tim, which had been tense and stressful.

After school, while he drove to meet Tim and the other

coaches, Xavier felt increasingly weighed down, and when he pulled into the parking lot, he didn't want to get out of the car.

Last night, Violet had asked Xavier who he felt he needed to prove himself to, and he hadn't answered because he'd been too embarrassed to admit that *she* was who he needed to prove himself to. But now he realized it wasn't only Violet.

He'd been so caught up in his previous failures in college and his desire to do something more "impressive" with his life, he'd lost sight of what really mattered. He'd been trying to prove to himself that he was worthy, and along the way he'd become insecure. It was why he'd let Eddy get him so riled up, and why he'd so eagerly gunned for Riley and jumped at the offer without really considering his place at Willow Ridge. His feelings of inadequacy had driven him to put pressure on his relationship with Violet, thinking that moving in together would fix his fear that he wasn't enough for her.

Originally, he hadn't wanted to be a teacher. That was true. It was a role he'd fallen into. He hadn't stayed in Kentucky. He wasn't a multimillion-dollar athlete. But sometimes things didn't go to plan and life turned out okay anyway.

What Violet had said to Xavier all those weeks ago had been true. He *did* mean something to the people at Willow Ridge. He'd been so consumed with his own shit that he hadn't looked around and realized he'd struck gold years ago.

He made himself get out of the car and walk into the

restaurant. He spotted Tim, Justin and Vince seated at a table in the back of the room. Tim lorded over the conversation with his booming voice, gesturing with his hands, almost hitting Vince in the nose without even noticing. Justin and Vince sported weary expressions as Tim spoke. That would be Xavier's fate. Listening to Tim and his bullshit every day. *Truly* stuck.

"There he is," Tim said as Xavier approached the table. "Late by three minutes. Not a good look, Xavier. We'll have to work on that."

Yeah, no. He couldn't do this. He would go where he was needed. *Really* needed.

"Thank you so much for the opportunity, Tim," Xavier said. He didn't even bother to sit down. "But I don't think I'll be able to take the job after all."

Justin and Vince stared wide-eyed. An angry flush crept up Tim's throat and spread across his face.

"I *knew* it," Tim spat, pointing a shaky finger at Xavier. "Aimless. Careless. Undedicated!"

"He's the only one who wanted the job," Justin mumbled. "Everyone else was warned away from working with you."

Tim sent Justin a withering glare. "Untrue!" he cried.

"I'm really sorry," Xavier said. He was sorry that he'd wasted anyone's time during the interview process. He was sorry that *he'd* wasted time trying to bend over backward to impress Tim. But he wasn't sorry about walking away. "You deserve to hire someone who will stick around, just like you wanted."

Tim was still sputtering one-word insults at Xavier as

he left the restaurant, but his words easily bounced off Xavier's shoulders. He was hardly listening.

He climbed back into his car and instinctively started to call Violet to tell her the news, but with a sinking feeling, he remembered how she'd left that morning, and how she'd hardly responded to his texts.

Instead of calling Violet, he drafted an email to the school principal, asking if he could keep his job after all, in response to which he received an exuberant yes.

That night, he picked his mom up from the airport. She was a breath of fresh air, still glowing from her months spent under the Florida sun. Xavier embraced his mom and held her close.

"Missed you, Ma," he said.

Tricia kissed him on the cheek. "I missed you too, baby. I also missed my coffee maker because Harry's is terrible." She smiled at Xavier and wrapped her light jacket tighter around her. "It's freezing here, but I'm happy to be back."

Xavier carried her suitcases to the trunk, and when they got on the road, Tricia wasted no time bringing up Violet.

"So are you going to explain to me why you and Violet decided to elope in Las Vegas and not tell anyone?" she asked, leveling him with a direct stare.

He took a breath and let it out quickly. Might as well get it over with. "Violet and I aren't really married."

Tricia blinked. "Say what now?"

Then he explained everything. From their fake wedding in Vegas to Violet's magazine interview, to Xavier's idea to keep the lie going to get the job at Riley. While he spoke,

Tricia's eyes grew wider and wider. She shook her head once he finished catching her up.

"Only you and Violet would get yourselves involved in something like this, I swear," she said. "What are the two of you going to do?"

"We were going to tell you and her parents the truth tomorrow night," he said. "I'm sorry for not telling you from the beginning, but we had this plan, and I don't know, I think for a moment we stopped thinking about the lie and were only focusing on each other."

Tricia shook her head again, placing her hand on his arm. "No, I mean what are your intentions with Violet?"

"Oh." Her line of questioning caught him off guard. "We're together. We're just not married."

"So you fell in love again while pretending to be husband and wife." Tricia laughed then. "You and Violet always knew how to keep things exciting. I'll give you that."

Xavier glanced at his mother and her joyful ease. She'd just left her boyfriend and wouldn't see him again at least until the summer. Months away from now, and she seemed totally content.

"How do you and Harry do it?" he asked.

"Do what?"

"The distance. Not seeing each other. It must be hard."

"It is because I miss him often," she said. "But I think we're both confident that our love is strong enough to carry us through. Our lives are in separate places, and we both like our own space. When the time is right we'll settle down in the same place."

"Huh." He was struck by the simplicity of her answer.

"Violet and I . . . we kind of struggle to find time for each other. Our lives are not very similar."

Tricia tilted her head, looking at him more closely. "I always felt like every girl you dated after Violet was living in her shadow," she said. "Like no matter how well you got along or how happy you were, Violet was the one you were really waiting for. Would you say that's the truth?"

He nodded slowly. "Yeah, that's true."

"Sometimes you fall in love with a person, and regardless of where life takes you, your heart refuses to let go," she said. "That's what it's like with Harry and me. It's why the distance doesn't get in the way of what really matters. And I think that's why you found Violet again. You'll both figure it out. Just don't lose faith in each other, and make sure you show up every day."

"Yeah," he said softly. "You're right."

He wasn't going to give up on them. And he was going to show up. Even if Violet needed a little more time to meet him there.

They didn't need to live together, and they didn't need to have similar lifestyles, at least not right now. What mattered was if they wanted to do life together, side by side. They'd get through this rough patch because they loved each other. Yes, her career made it so that she was on the go, and since he was staying at Willow Ridge now, he wouldn't be able to meet her across the country as often, but that just meant they needed to cherish their time together even more.

Their love was enough to stand the test of time through almost a decade spent apart. Their love was more than enough.

Their relationship wasn't perfect, but it was real. And

that was exactly what he'd tell her when he saw her tomorrow. He was eager to speak to her now, but he wanted to give her the space she needed.

He'd waited nine years to find her again. He could wait a little longer.

26

THAT NIGHT, VIOLET WAS SEATED AT THE OUTDOOR CHA-
nel Cruise Collection show in Miami. Her heavy fatigue
had made a triumphant return, and she fought to keep her
energy up as she watched models strut down the beach on
a lit runway. This special Chanel line drew inspiration from
Monte Carlo and the Riviera. Donning crisp tennis whites,
checkered-flag jackets and risqué swimsuits in various red
hues, the models stared straight ahead as the Miami breeze
whipped through the humid night air. Violet usually loved
attending the itinerant fashion shows that took place outside of fashion month, and this show should have felt even
more special since she'd missed the most recent fashion
month altogether. But she was distracted. She couldn't stop
glancing at her fake wedding rings. Or thinking about
Xavier and the way she'd practically run away from him this
morning.

He'd texted her a few times, first to make sure she'd
landed safely; she confirmed she had. And then he'd asked
if she was okay, wanting to know if she was upset with him.

She wasn't. She wanted nothing more than to call him. But she still doubted her ability to be a fair and giving partner. And she feared that he had since come to the same conclusion, given her behavior. It was best to speak in person tomorrow when they were reunited at her parents' house for dinner and when they told their parents the truth about their sham marriage.

So instead of texting Xavier back, she threw herself into work. Like always.

Sighing deeply, she spun her rings around her finger, and she jumped when the audience broke into applause. Down in the front row, Karina and Angel sat side by side, smiling as they were photographed. Several rows back, Violet sat among a handful of other stylists and fashion journalists. She wished Alex were there with her, but she was in Charleston for her brother's wedding. Violet wasn't going to allow Alex to miss such an important family event. Why was it so easy for Violet to make sure that her assistant maintained a work-life balance, but she couldn't do the same for herself?

The fashion show was only halfway over, and Violet let out a deep breath. God, she was *tired*. And there was still the after-party to attend. She soldiered through the rest of the show, and afterward, she stood and clapped along with the audience. Then she made her way down to Karina and Angel and waited off to the side as they posed for picture after picture. Angel was dressed in a men's racer jacket, while Karina wore one of the white tennis outfits. Once the photographers moved on to the next set of celebrities, Violet finally made her approach.

"You ready to hit up this party?" Angel asked her, grinning from ear to ear.

Violet mustered a smile. "You definitely are."

"You okay?" Karina peered at Violet, brows furrowing in concern.

"I'm fine." Violet waved her off. As long as she was in bed by at least three a.m., she'd have about four hours to sleep before her flight back to New York, and then she could sleep on the plane.

"You sure?" Karina asked. "Because you can take a car back to my house."

"If she wants to party, let her party," Angel said. Karina shot him a look and he mimicked zipping his lips.

"I'm fine," Violet assured her. "Really."

"Okay," Karina said slowly.

Going to the after-party was basically expected of anyone who'd been invited to the show. It was borderline rude to not make an appearance. Plus, the after-party was being held in the outdoor space of the Rubell Museum, so at least she'd be in the fresh air and not crammed like a sardine inside a hot club.

However, as it turned out, Violet could only bear the loud bass at the after-party for a good twenty minutes before she felt like her brain was going to seep right out of her ears. While Karina and Angel danced and took photos with admirers and other celebrities, Violet slipped inside. Thankfully, the bass of the music was less pronounced in the bathroom, and Violet leaned her hip against one of the sinks and rubbed her temples. She looked up at her reflection in the mirror. Her makeup and hair looked flawless. Not one curl out of place in the Miami heat. That was one saving grace.

As people buzzed in and out of the bathroom, Violet tried to make herself look busy, like she was checking emails on her phone instead of avoiding the party altogether. She froze when a high-pitched voice suddenly said, "*Violet?*"

Violet glanced up and blinked as her old client Meela Baybee walked toward her. Meela still sported her short, silver pixie cut. But her outfit was all wrong. She was wearing one of the line's new bright red tennis tops with low-rise skintight checkered black-and-green leather racer pants and a pair of pointed-toe sling-back heels. She looked like an early aughts nightmare. Even more of a mess than when Violet had first met her. Who in the world was her stylist now?

"What's up?" Meela asked as Violet gawked at her.

What's up? Those were the first words out of her mouth? This was the woman who'd knowingly contributed to the dissolution of Violet's relationship two weeks before her wedding, and all she had to say was, *What's up?*

Despite her agitation, Violet kept her voice even and professional. "Hello."

"You've been on my mind a lot," Meela said. "I've been feeling, like, mad guilty, and I started seeing a new meditation coach, who said I really need to work through the things that contribute to my deep feelings of guilt. What I did with Eddy was so shady. You have all the right to beat my ass."

Violet's cheeks heated. Two of the women washing their hands glanced over at them. Meela was probably speaking loud enough to be heard in the men's bathroom too.

"Don't worry," Violet said, smiling lightly as if she and Meela were sharing an inside joke. "I don't have the energy to fight right now."

"Eddy is a dickhead," Meela continued, still loud, still unaware. "I mean, for real. He had me going for a while. He love bombed the shit out of me. I guess you know what I mean because you dated him too. Once you take a step back, though, you realize he's kind of annoying, and he always wanted everything to be his way."

Involuntarily, Violet smirked. "That's true."

"He was so mad that you called off the wedding. He brought it up all the time," she said. "As if I wasn't his new girlfriend. So damn rude!" She trailed off when she realized Violet's lips had set into a thin line. "Anyway, I heard that he got into an argument with you and your husband at Karina's party last night and it made me so mad. Like, Eddy needs to get over you. Congratulations, by the way."

She glanced at Violet's left hand, and Violet's impulse was to hide her rings because they weren't real gold or fancy. But . . . while these cheap, admittedly ugly rings might have been procured through a drunken mistake, they meant something to Violet. Karina had been right. Of all the things she and Xavier could have done in Vegas, they'd decided to take a phony trip down the aisle when they could have gone to the casino or the strip club or literally anywhere else.

Violet loved her tacky rings and the man who'd placed them on her finger.

"Is it true that your husband threatened Eddy to never speak to you again?" Meela asked.

Violet's knee-jerk reaction was to manipulate the truth and present her life in a better light. To say that what Meela had heard about last night's party wasn't true. But Violet's urge to tailor her image was what had landed her in trouble in the first place. It had pushed her to stay in a relationship with Eddy and accept his proposal when she hadn't loved him and he hadn't really loved her. And it was why she'd lied to Olivia Hutch about being married during her interview. Violet was so exhausted with keeping up appearances. Accepting reality was so much easier.

"Yes, my husband did tell Eddy not to speak to me again, because Eddy was being disrespectful," she said. "Big surprise there. And, Meela, what you and Eddy did to me *was* shady as hell. I was pissed at both of you for a long time. But, honestly, you did me a favor. Marrying Eddy would have been the biggest mistake of my life." She gave her reflection one final check in the mirror and noticed that several women were now observing her and Meela's conversation with rapt attention. "And I'm not actually married, but Xavier is my boyfriend."

Meela and the other eavesdropping women gasped. Violet turned on her heel and walked to the door, and Meela followed closely behind.

"What do you mean you're not married?" she asked.

"It's a long story." And Violet didn't have the energy to explain the details, least of all to Meela. She turned and looked at her. "Good luck with everything."

And she found that she sincerely meant it.

Meela gripped Violet's hand before she could walk away.

"Wait, do you think, I mean, would you consider maybe being my stylist again? I parted ways with my last stylist because she didn't get my vibe, and I've been struggling."

"I've noticed," she said, looking at Meela's outfit again. "I don't think it would be a good idea for us to work together. But Alex is brilliant. She might be willing to take you on."

Meela nodded eagerly. "Yeah, of course. I love Alex."

"I'll talk to her," Violet said as she extricated herself from Meela's grasp.

Alex was fiercely loyal, and Violet doubted she'd agree to work with Meela. But Violet figured as long as Alex kept any future boyfriends away from Meela, they'd be fine. And it was time for Alex to experience what it was like to have a client of her own.

Violet found Karina and Angel dancing in the center of the crowd, sharing the life-of-the-party limelight. Violet smiled as she watched them. They were at the top of their game, and so was she. Right now wasn't the right time for her career to slow down, but she could do better at prioritizing what was important and make a real effort to maintain a more balanced life.

And she'd start right now by leaving an event early for once, because she was dead tired.

"I'm heading out," she shouted to Karina after she squeezed her way through the crowd.

"Now?" Angel yelled back. He tossed back a shot and his voice was slurred as he said, "We just got started."

Karina swatted his arm and gave Violet a tight hug. "Get some rest, boo. I'll see you in a couple weeks."

Violet hugged Karina, and then she hugged a very drunk Angel, who gave her a sloppy kiss on the cheek.

"Tell Iris I said hi," he mumbled, winking.

Violet laughed. And then she left the party and took a car back to Karina's huge mansion, with no guilt or FOMO. It was that easy. Go figure.

She had to wonder what she'd been so afraid of. In her professional life *and* her personal life. She'd run away from Xavier out of fear that he'd discover he didn't want to be with her. While she'd embraced her reconnection with Xavier and how they'd both grown over the last decade, she realized that a part of her had been holding on to the past, fearing that he'd break up with her out of the blue again. She'd been so happy with him over the last couple of months, she didn't notice that she'd been waiting for the other shoe to drop, and out of anxiety, she'd orchestrated the drop herself.

Xavier had told her he wouldn't hurt her again, and he'd proven that. She'd have to trust him wholeheartedly, which was scary. Even scarier was deciding to trust herself and know that while there was always room for her to grow, she was a good partner as she was. She was just as loyal to him as he was to her. And she was trying her best.

She wanted a life with Xavier, however it looked. Be it living together in the future or hopping on last-minute flights to make his basketball games or bringing him along with her to Europe during fashion month. Or even deciding to get married for real one day.

She was going to do whatever it took to salvage things between them tomorrow night. But she'd start right now.

Hey, she texted.

She bit her lip as she watched his response bubbles appear.

Hey

She let out a grateful sigh that he'd responded.

I'm really sorry about the radio silence today, she texted. Do you think you can pick me up from the train station tomorrow before dinner?

His reply came right away. I'll be there.

27

UNFORTUNATELY, THE HEARTFELT REUNION WITH XAVIER that Violet had pictured did not go to plan. That following night, Lily ended up catching the train with Violet from the city, so the two of them stood on the platform waiting for Xavier to pick them up.

"I'm so hungry," Lily said. "What do you think Mom cooked for dinner?"

"I don't know." Violet was distracted, eyeing the cars as they pulled into the train station, looking for Xavier's black Altima.

"I bet she got it catered," Lily said. Then she nodded to herself. "Yeah, I bet that's what happened. I wonder if she hired Shalia McNair to do it. Too bad Nick couldn't come. He would have loved Shalia's fried mac-and-cheese balls."

Violet frowned at Lily. If Shalia McNair had any hand in her fake wedding dinner, Violet would take it as a bad omen. She was about to say just that, but then she paused when she saw Xavier's car turn into the parking lot. Her stomach tightened in anticipation. When he pulled up in front of them, she was surprised to see Tricia sitting in the passenger seat.

"Violet, honey, it's so good to see you," Tricia said, hurrying to climb out of the car and wrap Violet in a tight hug. She leaned away and raised an eyebrow with a sly smile. "You and my son have been quite busy, huh?"

Violet locked eyes with Xavier, who was walking around the front of the car toward her.

"She already knows the truth," he explained. "I told her last night."

"Oh," Violet said. She turned back to Tricia and gulped. "Are you mad?"

"Mad?" Tricia shook her head. "No. More confused, but why would I be mad? It's your lives, not mine. Oh, Lily! Hi, sweetheart!"

Tricia moved her attention to Lily, and as they slid into the back seat, Violet and Xavier stood outside the car, staring at each other. There was so much she wanted to say to him on the drive to her parents' house, but now his mom and Lily were here with them.

"Hi," she said weakly.

"Hey," he said. And then he smiled softly at her.

Like magnets, they were drawn to each other. She stepped into his embrace and he squeezed her close to his chest. She inhaled his familiar cologne and turned her face upward to look at him. She reached down and grabbed his hand, intertwining their fingers with a fierce hold.

"I wanted to talk to you about the other night, but—" She gestured toward Tricia and Lily, who were waiting in the back seat.

"I know, it's fine." He placed a soft kiss on the top of her head. "We can talk later. After dinner."

She nodded eagerly. "Okay."

During the short ride to her parents' house, Tricia entertained them with a story about how her boyfriend taught her to fly-fish down in Florida, but Violet and Xavier hardly listened as they kept sneaking glances at each other. She wanted to get this dinner over with so that they could finally be alone and talk.

They turned onto her parents' block, and cars were lined up and down the street on both sides.

"Someone else must be having a party tonight," Lily said.

"Looks like it," Violet mumbled.

But as they neared their parents' house and saw the white-and-gold balloon arch in front of their door, the hairs rose on the back of Violet's neck. Through the living room and kitchen windows, they could see clusters of people mingling inside the house.

"Oh no," Violet whispered.

Xavier pulled up and cut the engine. They stared open-mouthed at the bright gold sign on the door. *Congratulations, Violet and Xavier!*

Violet rolled down her window. "What . . . ?"

Then the front door swung open, revealing Dahlia.

"It's about time you got here!" she called, hurrying down to the car. She opened Violet's door. "Come, come. People are waiting for you. Hi, Tricia! Look at you! That Florida sun got you nice and sun-kissed, lady!"

"Mom, I said immediate family *only*," Violet hissed as Dahlia helped her out of the car. "This is a party!"

"Just a small party," Dahlia amended, taking Violet's hand and guiding her up the driveway. She turned and gestured for Xavier to join them. Robotically, he blinked at Dahlia as he followed. "Everyone wanted the chance to celebrate you, and I knew if I told you the full details, you wouldn't let me invite them." She glanced back at Lily, who trailed after them, equally confused. "I didn't tell you or Iris either, because I knew you'd tell Violet."

Violet gaped at her mother as she pulled her and Xavier inside. The house was filled with people from town. Xavier's coworkers and her parents' friends. Her aunts, uncles and cousins who lived nearby. The living room and dining room were decorated with gold and white streamers hanging from the ceiling. The smell of soul food dishes wafted from the kitchen. How did Dahlia plan all of this right under Violet's nose? She'd been so consumed with work and Xavier, she hadn't thought to check. Their plan to reveal the truth about their little white lie at a small family dinner went right down the drain.

"Look who finally arrived," Dahlia announced to the room.

Everyone turned their attention to the front door and cheered. Violet reached for Xavier's hand and they exchanged a frantic look as they were bombarded by the party guests, who took the opportunity to formally congratulate them on their marriage. Through it all, Xavier didn't let go of Violet's hand, even as her palm grew impossibly clammy.

"Xavier, can I talk to you for a moment?" Mr. Rodney said, appearing at Xavier's side.

Xavier raised an eyebrow. "*Right now?*"

"It'll only take a few minutes, I promise."

Xavier glanced at Violet. "Will you be okay?"

"I'm fine," she said. "Go, I'll find you later."

At least one of them could momentarily escape this disaster.

"You sure?" he asked.

She nodded and then her aunt Doreen came forward and squeezed her in a bear hug, interrupting them. Out the corner of her eye, she watched Xavier follow Mr. Rodney through the living room, pausing every few feet as someone else wished him congratulations.

Why couldn't Dahlia just have been chill and had a small dinner at her house like they'd agreed to? Now she'd spent money on this extravagant party, giving Violet even *more* reason to feel guilty!

Once Aunt Doreen released her, Violet made a beeline for her sisters and pulled them into the kitchen. In the process she bumped into Shalia McNair, who was wearing an apron that said *Meals by McNair* in orange script. *Of course* Shalia was catering this party.

"Hey, Violet," Shalia said. She held out a tray of fried mac-and-cheese balls. "Anybody want to try one of these before I take them into the living room?"

Violet and Iris shook their heads. Lily, however, grabbed two mac-and-cheese balls and placed them on a napkin in her palm.

"I'm taking some back for Nick," she explained.

"You should take one for Xavier," Shalia said sweetly to

Violet. "He loved when I made these at the basketball banquet last year. He told me they were the best mac-and-cheese balls he'd ever had."

If Violet had X-ray vision, she would have fried Shalia to a crisp.

Instead, she smiled tightly. "I'm sure he'll find you if he wants them."

The sisters moved to the side to let Shalia and the rest of the catering staff pass by. Once the kitchen was completely empty, Violet glanced around cautiously before lowering her voice to a whisper.

"Help me," she begged. "We have to find a way to end this party."

"How are we supposed to do that?" Iris asked.

"I don't know," Violet said. "Let's blame it on Shalia. We can tell everyone that she used expired ingredients in the food. It's a health hazard and everyone should go home in case they get sick."

Lily paused while chewing her mac-and-cheese ball. "Um."

"You probably shouldn't have agreed to a dinner in the first place," Iris said, as if that would help anything. "You know how Mom gets."

"Obviously, I didn't want to agree," Violet said. "But I thought it would help! She was so upset about the idea of us eloping in Vegas, and she still hates me because of the anti-wedding party."

Lily frowned. "She doesn't hate you."

"She hates almost everything that I do," Violet said. "This was supposed to be a small, intimate dinner with immediate family. Now it's like a family reunion and community center event rolled into one. We were supposed to tell Mom and Dad the truth tonight."

"You should still tell them tonight anyway," Iris said.

"How, Iris?" Violet threw her hands up. "What do you want me to do? Admit in front of everyone that our marriage is fake?"

Suddenly, Lily sucked in a breath and Iris's eyes widened, fixed on something beyond Violet's shoulder. Violet whipped around to see Shalia standing at the kitchen entrance, holding her empty appetizer tray, staring at Violet, slack-jawed.

Oh, God.

"I'm joking, of course," Violet hastened to say. She forced a laugh.

Shalia blinked, then hustled over to the oven and pulled out a pan of sizzling meatballs. "It's okay," she mumbled. "I won't say anything, I swear." At record pace, she began stabbing toothpicks into the meatballs and arranging them on her serving tray. "Your secret is safe with me."

Then, without looking at Violet, she hurried back into the living room.

Violet and her sisters stared after Shalia in silence.

"In about five minutes," Iris said, "everyone at this party will know your business."

"*Shit,*" Violet hissed.

28

"WHAT'S GOING ON?" XAVIER ASKED MR. RODNEY AS THEY stood on the patio.

A few guests lingered in the backyard as well, but otherwise the area was mostly deserted, and for that Xavier was grateful. Dahlia had invited damn near half of Willow Ridge to her home. It was a whole-ass shindig! Xavier had forced himself to smile so much in the last twenty minutes, he felt like his cheeks were going to bruise. He glanced inside, scanning the packed living room for Violet, but he couldn't find her.

"I've met someone," Mr. Rodney said. Xavier turned back to him, and Mr. Rodney's face broke open into a euphoric smile. "Her name's Misty. She lives in Tulsa. We met on a dating website for seniors."

"Oh, wow. That's great, congratulations." Xavier clapped Mr. Rodney on the shoulder, happy for his friend and mentor, but slightly bemused that Mr. Rodney felt this information was so important that he had to pull Xavier away in the middle of the party.

"I wanted you to be the first to know because I'm moving to Tulsa to be with Misty," Mr. Rodney said. "I'm retiring at the end of the school year."

Shock rendered Xavier speechless. Then he sputtered, "Wh-what?"

"It's about time," he said. "I love the job, but I've been teaching a long while. I'm not the same as I used to be. I can't keep up with the kids. And we both know you did the heavy lifting with the team this year."

Xavier could only stare, stupefied, in a state of disbelief. Mr. Rodney was *retiring*? He was supposed to stay at Willow Ridge forever.

"But the students love you," Xavier said.

Mr. Rodney patted Xavier's shoulder. "And they love you too. I'm recommending that you be promoted to head coach. It comes with a pay raise."

Suddenly, Xavier felt like he needed to sit down. There was too much happening tonight.

Before he could fully wrap his head around Mr. Rodney's news, the patio door slid open and Violet stepped outside, heading straight for Xavier.

"Hey," he said, relieved to be reunited with her amid the chaos, but then he took in her distraught expression. "What's wrong?"

She waited for Mr. Rodney to excuse himself to give them privacy. Then she looked at Xavier and bit her lip.

"I'm pretty sure everyone knows the truth about us," she whispered.

He hesitated. Slowly, he asked, "What do you mean?"

Violet told him about Shalia overhearing her conversation

with her sisters, and how the truth was most likely spreading throughout the party. Xavier's whole body tensed. But Violet looked so stressed, his first instinct was to comfort her.

"It's okay," he said, wrapping his arms around her, although his heart began to race as the weight of their predicament set in. He'd told Violet before that if people found out that they weren't actually married, it didn't matter. It wasn't their business. But . . . he hadn't thought half the town's population would discover the truth while gathered together at her parents' house before he and Violet even had a chance to tell said parents.

"I don't care what anyone else thinks," she said. "I just don't want to embarrass my mom."

"Then we should tell them now," he said.

Violet took a deep breath and nodded. When they reentered the living room, it seemed that the partygoers had assembled in one place. One by one, all heads whipped in their direction. They gawked at Xavier and Violet, whispering among themselves. Xavier spotted Raheem and Bianca near the foyer entrance, and Raheem looked at him with wide-eyed apprehension, discreetly shaking his head. Okay. So that was enough proof of what they were walking into. Out the corner of his eye, he saw Mrs. Franklin hustling over to them, her face set in a deep frown. Thankfully, Tricia intercepted her before she could reach Xavier or Violet.

The only people who seemed oblivious to the gossip were Dahlia and Benjamin. They stood at the front of the party by the fireplace, laughing with a couple of Violet's aunts. Dahlia glanced in Xavier and Violet's direction and, noticing that they'd entered the room, she held up her champagne glass and clinked it with a plastic knife.

"Everyone, everyone," she sang, refocusing the crowd's attention on the front of the room. "I'd like to make a toast to my daughter and son-in-law. Violet and Xavier, please come here."

With a look of focus, Violet linked her hand through Xavier's and they slowly navigated through the murmuring crowd. He felt like they were about to walk the plank. From the kitchen archway, Shalia McNair shot him the stink eye. And that was what made him say *fuck it*. So what if people knew that he and Violet weren't married? They loved each other. Did he feel bad that he'd lied? Of course. But everyone had their own dirty laundry. Who were they to judge him and Violet? He only wanted to be sensitive where Violet's parents were concerned.

"Mom," Violet whispered gently yet urgently. "There's something Xavier and I need to talk to you about."

"Of course. Just allow me to give my toast first." Dahlia grinned. Her cheeks were slightly flushed from the heat of the room and her half-finished glass of champagne.

"Mom, no, wait—"

"I have to be honest with you all," Dahlia said to the party guests, ignoring Violet's pleas. "Violet and Xavier didn't know that tonight was going to be an event to this scale. They thought I was planning a small dinner. But so many of you in this room watched their love blossom as young people, and even though their high school shenanigans definitely gave me a few premature gray hairs, I think it's infinitely precious that they found each other again, and I wanted to celebrate them and their love properly." Dahlia lifted her glass. "To the beautiful couple. I wish you many, many years of happiness."

Benjamin and Violet's aunts, who stood beside her mom, clapped. By the kitchen, Iris and Lily winced and raised their glasses. From their spot by the foyer, Raheem and Bianca did the same. But otherwise, an awkward silence expanded throughout the room. Xavier felt Violet's palm grow damp in his hand again.

"Excuse me," Mrs. Franklin suddenly said, soldiering her way to the front of the room. "I have something that I'd like to say."

"Oh, please do." Dahlia smiled, delighted. "We welcome all well-wishes for the happy couple."

"That's not really necessary," Xavier said quickly, trying to steer Mrs. Franklin away, but she waved him off and made room for herself between Dahlia and Violet. She glowered at the crowd.

"Someone here has spread a malicious rumor that Violet and Xavier aren't truly married," she said. Her voice dripped in disapproval. "It's childish and I don't like it. Have some respect."

Oh, fuck. Xavier resisted the urge to drag a hand over his face.

Benjamin frowned. Beside him, Dahlia blinked. "What? Who said this?"

Mrs. Franklin sent a pointed look to Shalia McNair, and everyone turned in Shalia's direction.

"I—I . . ." Shalia stammered. "Don't look at me! *Violet* is the one who said it first. I'm not making it up! This isn't my drama!"

The room fell silent again as everyone redirected their attention to Violet.

"Violet?" Dahlia sent a questioning look to her daughter.

"Um," Violet mumbled. Her grip on Xavier's hand tightened. "We . . ."

"We're married," Xavier said, angling himself in front of Violet to block everyone's inquiring gazes. His desire to protect her overtook his decision to no longer care about what anyone thought.

Then Violet dropped his hand and shocked him when she said, "No, the rumor is true."

VIOLET HEARD XAVIER'S swift intake of breath.

He turned sharply and looked down at her, lowering his voice so that only she could hear. "What are you doing?"

"What I should have done when the article first published," she said.

Violet could leave town tonight, and what people said wouldn't matter to her. She'd return to Willow Ridge for the occasional holiday or family party and be off again. But Xavier lived here. He taught here, at least for now. This rumor, and the questionable nature of their relationship, would affect him. They'd been too enamored with each other before to see the reality of their situation. Xavier deserved better than this. Her parents deserved better than this too.

"This is my fault," she said, addressing the party guests. "Months ago, I gave an interview where I lied and said that I was married. I didn't mention anyone by name, but it was obvious that I was talking about Xavier. I lied to salvage my reputation in my industry, and Xavier went along with it to help me. He doesn't deserve any judgment or mistreatment. And neither do my parents. They had nothing to do with this." She turned to Dahlia and Benjamin. "Mom, Dad, I'm so sorry. We were planning to tell you tonight when we thought it would be a small dinner with family. I'm sorry that you had to find out this way."

Dahlia gaped at her, blinking rapidly. Benjamin, usually so stoic and silent, balked, equally shocked.

"We're both sorry," Xavier clarified, retaking her hand. "Violet lied first, but I was the one who said we should keep the lie going because I thought being married would give me a better chance at getting a new job, which I ended up turning down in the end."

Now it was Violet's turn to look at him in startled confusion. "What? You're not taking the job at Riley?"

He shook his head, and she had so many questions, but now wasn't the right time to ask them.

"It wasn't entirely a hoax, though," Lily called out, attempting to be helpful. "You're actually dating! You're in love!"

That sent the crowd into a new flutter of murmurs. A loud chatter filled the air, and Violet looked up at Xavier, who returned her gaze with a reassuring nod. She was relieved that they were on the same team. But she felt guilty about her parents, who were still shocked into silence.

"Well," Mrs. Franklin said, "I'll have to think of a way to include *this* in the monthly newsletter."

Some people laughed and the tension in the room eased as people's voices grew louder, talking over one another, trying to determine what to make of this new piece of town gossip.

"I think it's best if everyone goes home now," Tricia said, appearing beside Dahlia and Benjamin, rubbing Dahlia's shoulder to comfort her.

Slowly, the partygoers left, casting newly intrigued glances at Violet and Xavier.

"People lie for worse reasons when it comes to work," Mrs. Franklin said to them. "Principal Maroney was fired from his last position as vice principal down in Burlington County, and he didn't even mention it in his interview. And think of those billionaires we hear about in the news who commit fraud with their companies." She hugged Xavier, then hugged Violet as well. "This will blow over soon, don't worry. There's always a new story to capture everyone's attention."

Violet nodded, and then she caught eyes with Shalia, who sent her an apologetic, abashed look as she and her team carried their supplies outside. Then the house emptied until only Violet, Xavier, Tricia, Violet's parents and her sisters were left.

"Help me make sense of this, Violet," Dahlia said, shaking her head. "Why lie? *Why?*"

Before, Violet might have hung her head in shame. But she wouldn't do that now. She just had to own it. People made mistakes. Sometimes very silly, ill-conceived mistakes. This wasn't the first mistake Violet had made and it wouldn't be the last. But she was trying to learn from them and that was what mattered.

"I thought the truth would be more disappointing to you," she admitted.

"But by lying, you made the situation worse," Dahlia said. "I invited these people into our home to celebrate you."

"I didn't ask you to do that," Violet said fiercely, ignoring her father's reproving glance. "I'm sorry that you went to all this trouble. I really am, Mom. But I told you we didn't want a party, and you went behind our backs and planned one anyway."

"Forgive me for wanting to do something nice for my daughter," Dahlia said, offended. "You treat your father and me as if we're an afterthought. A tiny blip in your important life. If you didn't feel an obligation to come home for holidays, we'd never see you. You were staying with Xavier less than ten minutes away for an entire month and you didn't stop by the house even once. It's no wonder we believed that you eloped in Las Vegas without telling us. When do you tell us anything?"

"I tell you things all the time," Violet said quietly. "I just don't think you care enough to remember."

Violet winced at Dahlia's wounded expression, but she didn't want to lie anymore.

"Of course we care about you and everything going on in your life," Benjamin said.

Violet lifted her shoulders in a small shrug. "I don't always feel that way. I think we've struggled to find common ground for a long time."

The room fell silent. Xavier gently placed his hand on Violet's shoulder and she was grateful for his comforting presence beside her.

"I've always tried to understand you, Violet," Dahlia said. "Even though it may not seem like it." She glanced at Benjamin and bit her lip before looking at Violet again. "I'll admit that I shouldn't have planned the party. I wanted to feel involved in your life, and I went a little over the top. I do apologize for that." She sighed. "It wouldn't be the first time I overstepped. Lily had to set me right last year too."

Violet glanced at her younger sister, who smiled softly at their mother. Last year, Lily had to tell Dahlia to stop trying to push her into a new career, and that conversation had helped their relationship get to a better place. Violet wanted to be in a good place with her mom too. She was realistic enough to know it wouldn't happen overnight, but they had to start somewhere.

"Maybe we can try a little harder to meet each other halfway," Violet said.

Dahlia nodded. "I would like that."

Violet, along with everyone else in the room, heaved a sigh of relief.

"On that note, I think it's time for me to get on home," Tricia said, hugging Dahlia and Benjamin. "Let's plan another night, with just us." Then she hugged Violet and whispered in her ear, "I'm so happy the two of you got back together."

Violet's heart expanded as Xavier's mother enfolded her in a tight embrace. She winked at Violet as she pulled away.

"I have to take her home," Xavier said as his mom went to get her coat. Violet's parents and sisters had left the room.

In the kitchen, she overheard Iris say something about cleaning up before they left. Violet hadn't wanted the party to happen, but her mom had planned it for her.

"I should probably stay and help them clean," she said to him reluctantly. "Can you call me when you get home? Maybe I can come by later?"

"Definitely." He leaned down and kissed her on the forehead.

She closed her eyes briefly. They still had so much to talk about, but that small gesture gave her hope that they'd be okay.

XAVIER WALKED WITH his mom outside to his car.

"Never a dull moment in Willow Ridge," Tricia said, chuckling and shaking her head.

Xavier managed a small laugh and unlocked the doors. An immense weight had been lifted from his shoulders now that everyone knew the truth. He'd have to deal with gossip from his coworkers and students on Monday, and that would be annoying, but at least they could all move on.

He still needed to talk to Violet, though. To tell her that he didn't care how busy she was or where her job took her. He'd still be with her, even if her job required her to be halfway across the world for a year. He loved her that much. They'd barely had a chance to talk to each other tonight without people around them.

He started his car and turned up the heat for his mom, then glanced at Violet's house. He watched as the light in her bedroom clicked on. Suddenly, he had an idea.

"Are you okay with driving yourself home?" he asked Tricia. "I'm gonna walk."

Tricia raised an eyebrow. "What —" Then she paused and shook her head. "Never mind. I'm not even going to ask. You can pick your car up from my house in the morning."

"Thanks," he said. "See you tomorrow."

Xavier smiled at her before he got out of the car and appraised the sturdy sycamore tree.

29

VIOLET HADN'T EVEN THROWN ONE PARTY DECORATION into the trash before she realized she'd made a mistake letting Xavier leave. She could come back to her parents' house and clean all day tomorrow. She needed to see Xavier *now*. But first, she had to change out of her Stuart Weitzman boots because they'd been pinching the crap out of her toes all night, and she'd rather not continue to deal with the pain.

Holding Iris's car keys in her palm, she dashed up to her childhood bedroom and dropped down to the floor, searching for a discarded pair of old sneakers under her bed. She spotted her pair of white low-top Converse from high school, and as she pulled them toward her, something else caught her eye: the shoebox that contained the photographs from her and Xavier's past. The photographs that she hadn't been able to bring herself to get rid of all those years ago.

She pulled the box from underneath her bed and opened it, staring down at the pictures of her and Xavier dancing together at prom. Splashing in the ocean at the beach the day that seagull stole her chips. The day before he left for

Kentucky, folded up together on the couch at his mom's house. She'd loved him deeply. That much was clear in these photos. She didn't know how long she sat gazing at the photographs before she realized she was wasting precious time and needed to drive to Xavier's house.

She hopped up and slid on her sneakers. Then she heard something knock against her window, someone calling her name. She whirled around to see Xavier at her window, perched on the outstretched limb of the sycamore tree.

She blinked for an astonished moment. Then she jumped into action and slid her window open. Ungracefully, Xavier tumbled through, knocking into her dresser lamp with his long limbs and landing in a heap on the floor.

"Oh my goodness," Violet whispered, picking up his glasses, which had been thrown from his face in the process.

"I used to be *so* much better at that," he said, slowly sitting up. He winced and rubbed the back of his head.

"Violet!" Benjamin called from somewhere downstairs. She and Xavier froze, eyes locked. "Everything okay up there?"

"Yes! Everything's fine!"

She hurried to close her bedroom door and then returned to Xavier, crouching in front of him. She slid his glasses back onto his face and tenderly touched the back of his head.

"Are you okay?" she asked.

He nodded. "I'm okay."

When she pulled away, he caught her hand and held it to his chest. He smiled, and she couldn't help it as laughter bubbled up inside her. Xavier laughed too, and she grinned, feeling airless.

"I swear that tree got bigger," he said. "I don't remember it being nearly as hard to climb before."

She shook her head at him, still laughing. "You could have used the front door this time, you know."

"I was trying to be romantic." He tilted his head. "Did it work?"

"A for effort," she said. "And I grade very fairly."

He laughed again and glanced at the car keys in her hand. "Where were you going?"

"To see you."

The look that he gave her was so warm and soft, it melted her heart right there on the spot. She shifted from her crouch and sat on her knees in front of him.

"The other night, when you asked if we could move in together down the road, I panicked," she said. "I had been worried that I wasn't capable of being a good partner to you, and there were things you needed from me that I wouldn't be able to give, mainly my time. And I was afraid that you'd realize one day that I wasn't enough for you and you'd leave me. I was afraid of experiencing that heartbreak again. That was why I left in the morning without saying goodbye. You deserved so much better than that, and I'm so, so sorry. I'm sorry for pushing you away when I should have been honest with you about how I was feeling. I realized that I just needed to trust you, and I *do*."

"Vi, I don't think you're a bad partner," he said, still pressing her hand against his chest. "I never thought that. Not now and not then. *I'm* sorry. I was tripping, thinking *I* wasn't enough for *you*, and that I had nothing to offer you."

"That couldn't be further from the truth," she said, leaning closer to him. "You offer me your love and support. That is exactly what I need."

"I know that now." He leaned closer too, wrapping his arms around her waist. "I let my insecurities get in the way of seeing what really matters with us, and I'm sorry for that. I love you more than anything. You could work in Antarctica for a year and we'd figure it out. I have that much faith in us."

"I would never take a job that had me in Antarctica for a year," she said, and he smiled. "No, really. I mean it. I love my job, but it isn't my whole world, and I don't want it to be. What we have is important to me." Then with a smirk, she added, "And I do want to move in together one day, but not yet because I love my apartment and I just renewed my lease."

"That's okay," he said. "I know you love your apartment. And as shitty as my apartment is, I love my space too."

"Your apartment isn't shitty," she said, frowning. "I love your apartment too."

"Good thing you do, because I'm keeping it. I'm staying at Willow Ridge."

"Oh yeah!" she said. "What happened with Riley?"

"It wasn't the right fit," he said. "I was trying to prove myself for the wrong reasons. You were right when you said I'd be more fulfilled here. And tonight I found out that Mr. Rodney is retiring, so there's a good chance I'll be head coach next year for the basketball team."

"Xavier, that's amazing!" She leaped forward and hugged him.

"It has to get approved," he said, laughing. "But we'll see."

"Of course it will be approved. There's no way it won't be." She leaned back so that she could see his face. "I'm proud of you."

"And I'm proud of you," he said. "I always have been."

They smiled at each other, still embracing. He lifted his hand and cradled Violet's cheek, gazing at her. She closed her eyes, cherishing his touch. Then she remembered the photographs.

"Look at what I found," she said, crawling to retrieve the box. She came to sit beside him again and leaned her back against her dresser as Xavier took the box from her.

He sorted through the photographs, laughing at some, eyes shining with deep emotion at others. A soft smile spread on his face, and he looked up at her. He reached into his back pocket for his wallet and pulled out the folded photograph of them kissing at the chapel in Las Vegas.

"I started carrying this around in my wallet after you moved back to your apartment," he said.

Violet beamed at him. She felt like her heart would burst.

"When we were seniors, I asked you if you'd marry me when the time was right," he said. "I never forgot our plan."

"Neither did I," she said softly.

"I've never loved anyone the way that I love you," he said. "There's nobody else out there for me, Vi. I know we have a lot going on right now and the timing isn't the best, but one day in the future, I still want to marry you."

"I want that too," she said, hugging him. "I love you so much."

She was so overcome with happiness, she could cry. And that was exactly what she started to do. At first, Xavier was startled, but then he understood. He knew her like no other. With the pads of his thumbs, he wiped her tears away.

"This is embarrassing," she said, smiling and sniffling.

He smiled back at her. "I love you like people in this town love to gossip."

She laughed, and her heart warmed as she remembered their game from long ago. "I love you like Mrs. Franklin loves her newsletter."

"I love you like that older couple loved mini golf."

"And *I* love *you* like your basketball team loves winning."

His smirked and his gaze lowered to her mouth. "You'll have to prove it," he said.

She angled her body toward him and leaned in, pressing her lips to his.

He held her close, and with the whole of her being she knew that right there in his arms was exactly where she belonged.

EPILOGUE

One and a half years later

SOMETIMES OLD HABITS DIE HARD.

That would explain why Violet and Xavier were sneaking into Mr. Bishop's pool after midnight.

Quietly, they climbed the gate, sweating in the late August heat. Mr. Bishop was much older now and couldn't hear as well as he used to, but his daughter lived with him, so Violet and Xavier had to move with caution as they tiptoed across the grass, grinning at each other.

Earlier that evening, they'd had dinner next door with Tricia and Harry, who was visiting for a few weeks. And during the afternoon, Xavier had coached the last game of Willow Ridge's summer league. Violet had come to watch him. Seeing him on the court still thrilled her just as much as it had when she was a teen.

Tomorrow, they were having breakfast with her parents. Dahlia was still opinionated and often overbearing, but Violet had gotten better at letting Dahlia know when she was overstepping, and she was trying not to let herself get too annoyed when Dahlia was just trying to show that she cared. Their relationship wasn't perfect, but they were trying. That was what mattered. And even though the true backstory of how she and Xavier had rekindled their relationship had confused Dahlia and Benjamin, they were very supportive of them. Violet and Xavier's wedding party had been the main topic of town gossip for a good two weeks. And then inevitably, a new, more interesting story stole everyone's attention: Mr. Rodney retiring and moving to Tulsa with his new wife, Misty. And after that, the town moved on to another story. That was the way things worked. Violet and Xavier didn't pay it any mind.

They were having a staycation this week. It was going to be Violet's first weeklong vacation, by choice, in over five years. But over the last year, she'd learned a trick to help balance her work and personal life. Whenever she had a work trip, she'd tack on a few days afterward for herself. Sometimes, Xavier joined her, when his school schedule allowed. Like over the summer, when he wasn't teaching, he joined her in Paris after she attended a Mugler exhibit, and they'd taken the train to Barcelona and then on to Lisbon. And when they were home, they both spent a good deal of time riding the NJ Transit back and forth to each other, and they'd finally determined who made the better grilled cheese sandwich: Xavier. But Violet decided that not being able to cook wasn't something to be ashamed of. She was simply living her truth. They'd talked about moving in together and finding an apartment that suited both of their needs.

Maybe somewhere like Jersey City or Hoboken, close enough to the city and to Willow Ridge. They were going to look at apartments once Violet's lease ended the following spring.

Soon, the school year would begin, and Xavier would be back in the classroom. This fall he was teaching a new crop of sophomores, and he didn't regret not taking the job at Riley. In fact, he never mentioned it again, except when he noted that another one of Tim Vogel's assistant coaches had quit as well.

And while Xavier would soon be busy with teaching, Violet would dive into the fall fashion month marathon. She was excited for the shows and the travel, but she had a rule now to establish boundaries. She needed at least seven hours of sleep a night. If that meant leaving an after-party early or skipping it altogether, so be it. She had to eat breakfast before she left her apartment or hotel room. And she'd take a bath to unwind every night.

She'd earned the ability to relax a little more. The *Kat House* visual album was so celebrated, it had opened more doors for Violet, which meant she could turn down certain projects or clients if she didn't feel as though they'd be a good fit. Like when she'd turned down working with Black Velvet, which had been the best choice in the end. They were still being managed by Eddy, and Violet didn't need that drama in her life.

But her elevated status from her work on the visual album also meant that she had the opportunity to do freelance wardrobe styling for television shows. In the long run, she hoped she might be able to style a feature film.

When she and Xavier were sure that the coast was clear,

they approached the pool, and while Xavier paused by the deck chairs, Violet easily slipped out of her Nap Dress and jumped into the water.

"Why did you jump in so fast?" Xavier whispered.

She wiped her eyes and looked at up him. He was still fully dressed in a T-shirt and jeans, standing at the edge of the pool. He was the one who used to cannonball into this pool like nobody's business.

That was when she noticed the bouquet of violets lying on one of the pool chairs, and the small candles he hadn't yet lit.

Slowly, she asked, "Aren't you coming in?"

He shook his head. "I mean, yes. But I wasn't planning to just yet."

He patted his right pocket. He'd been doing that all evening throughout dinner, touching his pocket like he was reassuring himself that something was still there, secured safely in place.

She squinted at him, trying to make sense of his odd behavior and the slightly nervous look on his face. Then it clicked.

"Oh my God," she said. "Are you about to propose?"

His eyes widened, and she watched his Adam's apple bob up and down as he swallowed.

"*Yes*," he finally said. "That was the plan."

"Why didn't you say anything?" she asked as she swam toward him. "You could have told me to wait!"

"I didn't think you'd dive headfirst into the pool! You've literally never done that! You used to take your time getting undressed!"

Her heart thudded in her chest. She quickly glanced at her nails, confirming that her light pink manicure was still intact. She didn't want her hand to look gross as he slid the ring on her finger. The *ring* on her *finger*. Holy shit, he was going to propose!

"Should I get out?" she asked, beginning to lift herself from the pool.

"No, wait there," he said. "I'll come in."

He stripped off his clothes, leaving on just his boxers, and she admired his beautiful body as her heart continued to pound and butterflies swarmed her stomach. He slipped into the pool and carefully held a black ring box above the water. He stopped in front of her and gazed into her eyes.

"Violet Greene, I love you more than life itself," he said. "Will you marry me for real this time?"

"Yes!"

She didn't even have to think about it.

He opened the box and set it on the side of the pool. Then he slid the ring onto her left finger. She laughed when she realized it looked similar to the fake ring from Vegas. Except this diamond was real and dazzling, and the gold glowed. It was beautiful. He was beautiful.

"I love you," she said, putting her arms around his neck and pulling him toward her.

"I love you too." He rested his forehead against hers. "Always will."

So much of their reconnection had been unexpected. But that was the surprise of life. In the end, the plan they'd whispered to each other on prom night had come to fruition. Because sometimes you just knew when you met your person. It was an awareness, a precious feeling. Violet had known when she was sixteen years old and she'd laid her eyes on Xavier for the first time.

There were multiple iterations of their love.

Violet and Xavier then.

Violet and Xavier now.

And when they kissed, they began the version of them that was yet to come.

Acknowledgments

Each book is a labor of love, and *The Partner Plot* was no exception. I'm very grateful for everyone who had a hand in this book's journey.

Thank you to my editors, Angela Kim and Cindy Hwang, for loving this story and for providing guidance to help make it better with each draft. I'm so glad that we get to bring the Greene sisters to life together.

Thank you to my agent, Sara Crowe, for everything, as always.

Thank you to the rest of the team at Berkley who help usher my books into the world: Dache' Rogers, Anika Bates, Megan Elmore, Eileen Chetti, Dorothy Janick, Hannah Black, Christine Legon, Sammy Rice, Heather Haas, Catherine Degenaro, Tawanna Sullivan and Emilie Mills. Thank you to the UK team at Penguin Michael Joseph. And thank you to Lila Selle for another gorgeous cover!

Thank you to my critique partner and friend Alison, who gives the best notes and is endlessly supportive and encouraging.

Thank you to my family and friends who share so much

excitement for each book. Especially my mom, who has reminded me multiple times over the last year that she can't wait to read Violet's book.

Thank you to Jason for always being my inspiration. This one is for you.

And last but definitely not least, my biggest thanks to every reader who has picked up one of my books and talked about them with friends or online. Thank you for your support and for engaging with my work.

The Partner Plot

Kristina Forest

READERS GUIDE

Questions for Discussion

1. Violet is a successful stylist, but her personal life suffers due to the demands of her job. Have you ever struggled with work-life balance? What are some ways to maintain it?

2. Have you ever felt out of place in some way when it came to your partner, the way Xavier does in Violet's celebrity/fashion world?

3. How do you think you'd react if you saw your ex from years ago out of the blue? Would you want to reconnect?

4. Xavier and Violet lead very different lives. What are some things they did that worked and what do you think they can do to continue to improve their relationship?

5. In what ways is Xavier and Violet's present-day relationship similar to their relationship in high school? What are some differences?

6. Xavier changed his dream of becoming a professional basketball player to focus on his career as a teacher. Have you ever had a career pivot?

7. Violet's dream job in high school was to be a stylist. What was your dream job in high school and do you have that career now? If not, can you see yourself having that career at this stage in your life?

8. Violet and her mother have a difficult relationship due to miscommunication and misunderstanding. Have you ever had to overcome differences with family members?

9. Xavier puts pressure on himself to find a new job because he thinks he has to prove himself to overcome his perceived failures. How important do you think it is to change our perspective on failure versus success?

10. Violet and Xavier created many memories together while they dated in high school. What's your favorite high school memory?

KEEP READING FOR AN EXCERPT FROM

The Love Lyric

KRISTINA FOREST'S NEXT NOVEL,
ABOUT VIOLET'S SISTER IRIS!

IRIS DOUBTED THAT ANGEL REMEMBERED HER. THEIR brief conversation at her sister Violet's party three years ago had predated his mega rise to fame, and from the looks of things, his life had drastically changed since then. Before, Iris hadn't heard much about Angel outside of the few times Violet had mentioned him, and Iris had certainly never heard any of his music. He'd also looked slightly different— no burgundy hair or nose ring, and no expensive clothes, as Violet hadn't yet worked her stylist magic on him. Now Iris couldn't turn on the radio without hearing at least one of Angel's songs. He was on television, starring in Adidas and Peloton commercials. He was on the cover of magazines, flexing his muscles, gazing at the camera. She'd once even seen an ad for his recent album on the side of a New York City bus.

His sound was like upbeat R and B . . . maybe pop? Iris couldn't really put her finger on how to describe it, but people liked it, obviously, because he'd won a Grammy earlier this year and was topping the Billboard charts.

Over the last few months, Iris had gotten to know the

details of Angel's face intimately as she pored over images from his photo shoots. He was the new ambassador for Save Face Beauty, and as the director of partnerships, Iris had worked with the PR team to orchestrate a weeklong meet-and-greet tour at several partnering department stores and makeup stores across the country, where Angel would promote their new skincare line. Their intention had been to appeal to a wider audience with the message that skincare should be a universal topic, regardless of gender. And because Angel was the current man of the moment, he'd been the perfect choice. The tour was set to take place in a couple weeks.

Iris peered around the tree trunk as Angel angled his face closer to his phone camera and grinned. Iris was still thrown by the "Woof, woof" he had spoken into his phone a moment ago. Was he talking to a girlfriend? A woman with a kink who liked when he used canine speak?

"Woof, woof, pretty girl," he sang.

Iris couldn't help it. She laughed.

Angel's head jerked up. He glanced over and caught eyes with Iris. A deep pink hue spread across his brown cheeks, and Iris backed away, embarrassed to have been caught.

"I'm sorry," she said quickly. "I didn't mean to eavesdrop." Although she clearly had meant to do just that.

Angel blinked at her, then glanced at his phone. "Bye, girl," he whispered, waving at his phone's camera. He slipped his phone into his pants pocket. He turned to look at Iris again, leaning his shoulder against the tree. The corner of his mouth hitched up, the beginnings of a smile.

"So," he said, "that is what I sound like when I talk to my dog."

"Your dog?" Oh, she had been so wrong. "That makes *a lot* of sense."

"Yeah, she has separation anxiety, so I put one of those doggy cameras in my apartment to check in on her when I'm gone."

"I see." Iris didn't know what else to say. She'd never had a pet growing up and therefore didn't understand Angel's dedication. Lately she'd considered getting an easy pet for Calla, though. A hamster or gerbil. Maybe a goldfish. "Again, I apologize. Please call your dog back and continue your conversation." She waved politely and set off through the vineyard back toward the venue.

"Hey, wait," Angel said, jogging to catch up with her. He easily maneuvered his body, managing not to be sideswiped by an overgrown grape bush. "You're Violet's sister, right? Iris?"

Now it was her turn to blink in surprise. He remembered her.

She slowed her walk, angling herself toward him. "Yes. Hi."

"Hi." He smiled, and it was as though Iris watched the act in slow motion. His full lips lifted then curved. His straight white teeth revealed themselves. His eyes crinkled in the corners. A picture of warmth.

Gorgeous, her brain said.

Well, obviously he was gorgeous. His voice wasn't the only reason that a good portion of the country was currently obsessed with him. Saying that he was gorgeous was simply a fact.

"I'm Angel." He held out his hand. "We met a couple years ago. You probably don't remember."

Iris almost laughed to herself again. To think that he thought that *she* didn't remember *him*.

"I remember," she said. She placed her hand in his, and she felt a zing shoot straight up her arm, from her fingers to her shoulder, as his hand engulfed hers. He didn't break eye contact as their palms pressed together. She took a deep breath and cleared her throat.

"Do you always introduce yourself that way?" she asked after a moment.

Angel lifted his chin, tilting his head slightly. "What do you mean?"

"Angel is your stage name, right?"

"Oh, nah." He laughed softly. It had a melodic quality. "I was intentionally named Angel at birth. My mom is very religious. *Super* devout. My whole family is that way, actually."

"Really?" Iris thought of the images her team had displayed during their many ambassador strategy meetings over the last few months. Photos of Angel shirtless, his abs and muscles lathered in baby oil. Clips from his music videos as he grinded with his backup dancers. She wondered how his mom felt about that.

"Yeah, they're hardcore," he said. "Some kids got beat with a belt when they were in trouble. I got beat with a thick-ass Bible. Why are you out here and not inside?"

His thumb brushed against the knuckle of her pointer

finger and that was when Iris realized that their hands were still clasped together. Blinking, she let her hand drop and she pivoted forward, continuing to walk.

"I just wanted some fresh air," she said, glancing at him sidelong as he walked beside her. He was very tall. And he smelled nice. Like cinnamon.

It was a simple observation. For research purposes. She could now confirm that cinnamon-scented cologne smelled nice on a man. Maybe Save Face Beauty could incorporate cinnamon scents into their products. She'd float the idea at a meeting. That was all.

"I feel you," Angel said. He spread his arms wide. "It's beautiful out here. I thought I'd give my lady a call and let her see some nature."

Iris quirked an eyebrow. "You mean your dog?"

"Yeah, Maxine. She's the only lady in my life at the moment."

"Maxine?" Iris repeated, smiling a little. "That's an elegant name for a dog."

"Maxine is an elegant lady." He pulled out his phone and showed Iris a photo of a brown boxer puppy with a black satin bow tied around her neck. Her tongue lolled out the side of her mouth as she chewed on a bone.

Iris's smile broadened. "Elegant indeed."

"Thank you." Angel's eyes twinkled as he looked at her. "I won't lie, though. I also came out here to escape your younger cousins. They kept taking pictures of me while I was trying to eat. Tomorrow photos of me covering my steak in mashed potatoes will probably be reshared all over Instagram."

Iris laughed, thinking of her teen cousins, who mostly wanted to come to the wedding so that they could get a glimpse of Violet's famous clients. Somewhere back inside the venue, Karamel Kitty, one of today's most popular rappers, was probably being bombarded for photos as well.

"Wait a minute," Iris said. "You cover your steak in mashed potatoes? Is that like a southern thing?"

Angel shrugged. "More like a me thing, I think. How did you know that I'm from the South?"

There was the slight twang in his accent for one, less prominent now than it had been three years ago. From her team's research, she knew that Angel had been born and raised in a small town in Georgia. But she didn't feel like bringing up her role at Save Face Beauty. It was the weekend, she was at her sister's wedding and she didn't want to talk about work. Given the way that Angel disappeared from the party to FaceTime his dog, she would hazard a guess that he didn't want to talk about work either. Plus, her role was more behind the scenes. Client care was a job for the PR team.

"Oh, there's this thing called the internet," she said. "If you use a tool called a search engine, you can find the answer to almost any question."

His brows lifted. "Really? *Any* question? Sounds fake."

"It also lies, so sometimes it is fake."

"See, now that's confusing," he said. Then, "But . . . what you're trying to say is that you googled me?"

She brought her index finger and thumb together. "Only a little."

"Oh, just a little, huh?" he said, laughing. And Iris laughed too. It felt nice to laugh so easily this way. Dusk was beginning to settle, and fireflies swirled in and out of the vine rows, passing in front of her and Angel.

"So, what were you escaping from?" he asked.

Iris looked at him, taken by surprise at his question. She hadn't been escaping, had she? She'd just needed a moment of quiet. Escaping made it sound as though she was trying to outrun her feelings, which, from experience, she knew was impossible.

Angel watched her closely, waiting for her reply. The only thing he knew about her was that she was Violet's older sister. He didn't know about Terry or her tragic backstory. He didn't see "widow" written across her forehead. To him, she could have been anyone.

"I guess you can say I've had a long day," she supplied.

"Me too."

Up ahead, she could see the twinkle lights hung on the back patio. Silhouettes of servers taking smoke breaks moved in and out of her view.

"You know this is the first wedding I've been to in my twenties?" Angel said. "People aren't getting married like that anymore."

"Half of marriages do end in divorce." She lifted her shoulder in a shrug. "But this is the first one of your twenties? How old are you?"

She'd looked up his age at work, but as she'd already noted, sometimes the internet lied.

"I'll be twenty-eight next month," he said. "You?"

"Thirty-two."

He was younger than her, but not by that much.

"The last wedding I went to was back home in Georgia," he said. "I was sixteen and they asked me to sing 'Amazing Love' by Fred Hammond. You know it? It's a gospel song."

Iris shook her head. Her parents had taken her and her sisters to church every Easter and Christmas Eve growing up, but that was as far as her experience with religion went.

"It's a good one, but not my favorite. Anyway, it was the middle of August, and the church was blazing inside. I mean, *blazing*. My button-up was so covered in sweat, you could see right through the cotton. The bride passed out on her way up the altar."

Iris burst into laughter. "Stop. You're messing with me."

"I'm being so serious," Angel said, smile widening as he looked at her. "And while they fanned the bride, they made me stand up and sing way before I was supposed to. I was so dehydrated, I almost passed out myself! My voice was trash that day."

Iris was still laughing. "Did you at least get paid to sing?"

"Of course not. My mom was friends with the bride and she told them I'd do it as a favor."

"Child labor exploitation. Terrible."

"Right? My real jobs were worse than that, though. Cleaning toilets at Cook Out, getting chased by dogs on my paper route." He smirked at her. "What about you? You look like you had a nice, proper job. Like selling perfume at the mall or something."

She shook her head. "Not exactly. I worked at my parents' plant nursey. I was elbow- and knee-deep in soil every weekend."

"Ah," he said, nodding. "Makes sense now. Daughters named after flowers."

"And a church boy named after a spiritual being."

He grinned, inclining his head toward her. "Sometimes I wish my mom named me something more common. Like Jim."

"Or two common names together," she said. "Jim Bob."

"Bobby Tom."

"Tom Wyatt."

"Tom Wyatt," he repeated. "That's got a ring to it. Maybe I should make that my stage name."

"Don't forget to give me credit," she said, and Angel laughed.

"What about you?" he asked. "What's the last wedding you went to?"

It had been her boss's vow renewal two years ago. And before that, it had been her own ceremony.

"It was a while back," she said.

They were close enough to the venue now that she could hear the faint sound of music playing. It was a slow song. "Spend My Life with You" by Eric Benét and Tamia.

She stopped abruptly. Her heart seized. This song had always reminded her of Terry.

"You okay?" Angel asked.

Iris blinked quickly, glancing at him. There was that question again.

She remembered that he didn't really know her. Maybe that was why she answered truthfully. "Not really," she said quietly. "Today has been . . . off."

He nodded slowly, expression devoid of judgment. "It be like that sometimes."

"Yeah." She stared down at the straps of her gold open-toe heels.

"Too much maid of honor pressure?" he asked.

Iris managed a small laugh. She brought her gaze back up to his face and found that he was smiling at her.

"Definitely," she joked. "Try to avoid being a maid of honor if you can."

"I'll take that advice to heart."

She glanced toward the open doors of the venue again. Inside she spotted her parents swaying together. Somewhere Lily and Nick were probably holding hands with Calla, slow dancing too, or maybe the three of them were eating cake. Iris wanted to go back inside and join them. But this *song*.

"Hey," Angel said. "You wanna dance?"

She squinted. "Out here you mean?"

"Sure." At her skeptical expression, he smiled innocently. "Once I step inside, your cousins will go back to recording my every move. This might be my only chance to slow dance all night in peace."

Iris was unable to hold in her chuckle. The song changed then. "I Want to Be Your Man" by Roger filtered outside. The DJ was really throwing it back with that one.

"What do you say?" Angel asked, holding out his hand.

Iris stared at his long, outstretched fingers. His nails were buffed shiny and clean.

It had been so long since she'd danced with someone. She looked up at Angel, who waited patiently for her answer. His mouth curled into a soft smile, dimples deepening. She couldn't say exactly what she saw there in his expression, but whatever it was made her step forward and take his hand. He pulled her close and brought her arms up to loop around his neck. He gently rested his hands at her waist. Slowly, they began to sway from side to side.

"This is nice," he said quietly.

Iris nodded, watching his pulse jump at the base of his throat. She rarely found herself feeling nervous or flustered in the presence of a man these days, but for some reason, being this close to Angel, a literal superstar, she was suddenly tongue-tied.

He began to hum lowly, tapping his fingers against her waist in time to the music. "You're a good dancer," he said, keeping his voice at that deep, low tone. She swallowed thickly as goosebumps spread across her arms.

"I bet you say that to all the girls," she managed.

"No," he said simply.

He gazed down at her, and Iris, who was usually made of much stronger stuff, could only gaze back. The song was winding down. Their moment in time was coming to a close. At the end of this song lay real life, back inside the venue.

Angel's eyes slowly lowered to her mouth. Iris felt her heartbeat pick up its pace.

"Do you . . ." he started, then stopped. "Would you maybe be interested in taking another walk on a different day?"

Iris was shocked by how quickly the word "yes" almost tumbled off her tongue.

What was she *doing*? She'd forgotten herself.

"I'm sorry, I can't do that." She stepped out of his embrace, a quick, jerky movement.

Angel blinked, his empty hands grasping at air. "Wait—"

"Have a good night," she mumbled.

Before he could say anything else, she hurried back into the ballroom, forcing herself to keep her gaze forward. She saw both of her sisters holding hands with Calla, dancing and laughing in the center of the dance floor. They waved when they saw Iris approaching. She didn't slow down until she reached Calla, wrapping her arms around her daughter and squeezing her close, reminding herself of who she was.

Iris was capable. Reliable. She was a problem-solver. Ambitious and motivated. She was often tired. Often lonely. And she didn't live a life where a dance with a famous singer at dusk might lead to a magical love affair. That wasn't her story.

She'd already met the love of her life and he'd died. She didn't need to fall in love again, or even really expect it to happen. Most people didn't end up with their soulmates. They settled for whoever was there at the right time. Or they ended up alone. Iris was lucky to have experienced the years she had with Terry, luckier than most. She told herself that would be enough to get her through the rest of her life.

"You having fun, baby girl?" she asked Calla.

Calla grinned, hugging Iris tightly. "Yes! I've had *so* much cake, Mom."

Iris laughed and pretended as though she couldn't still feel the sensation of Angel's fingers pressed gently at her waist.

Steven Forest

Kristina Forest is the author of romance books for both teens and adults. She earned her MFA in creative writing at the New School and she can often be found rearranging her bookshelf.

VISIT KRISTINA FOREST ONLINE

KristinaForest.com

Ready to find
your next great read?

Let us help.

Visit prh.com/nextread